W9-BNT-438

Navy SEAL turned Secret Service agent
Scot Harvath faces down America's enemies in
these acclaimed bestsellers from

BRAD THOR

TAKEDOWN
New York Times bestseller

"If you're the type who enjoys the TV show *24* and other
high-octane thrillers, *Takedown* is the summer book for
you. . . . Crisp and cinematic, with the focus on gun-blazing,
gut-busting action."

—*The Tennessean*

"Brad Thor is the master of thrillers. . . . [His] descriptions are
gritty, realistic, and true-to-life. . . . Enthralling. . . . *Takedown*
should head the syllabus for anyone taking a class in Thrillers
101. A smart, explosive work that details events about to
happen outside your front door. Highly recommended."

—Bookreporter.com

"An exciting yet frightening thriller. . . . Fans of Dan
Brown and Thomas Harris will want to read Brad Thor's
latest masterpiece."

—*Midwest Book Review*

BLOWBACK

"Haunting, high-voltage stuff. . . . One of the best thriller writers in the business."

—*Ottawa Citizen*

"An incredible international thriller that is worth reading over and over again. The hot issue to spin into bestsellers is terrorism and Thor makes it work brilliantly. [*Blowback*] is an inspired spy-thriller adventure that gripped my attention from the get-go and engaged it until the very last. It has elements of mystery portrayed in *The Da Vinci Code* without being too religious, and the ancient Roman history, scientific discovery, real-life drama, and international political issues make the novel riveting and superior."

—Brunei Press Syndicate

STATE OF THE UNION

"Frighteningly real."

—*Ottawa Citizen*

"[A] blistering, testosterone-fueled espionage thriller."

—*Publishers Weekly*

PATH OF THE ASSASSIN

"Brad Thor will kidnap even the most demanding readers, deprive them of sleep, and convert them into instant devotees."

—Dan Brown

"The action is relentless, the pacing sublime."

—*Ottawa Citizen*

"An explosive novel."

—Newt Gingrich

THE LIONS OF LUCERNE

"Fast-paced, scarily authentic—I just couldn't put it down."
—Vince Flynn

"A hot read for a winter night. . . . Bottom line: *Lions* roars."
—*People*

"For cliff-hanging escapism, this is it."
—*The Sunday Oklahoman*

"Unforgettable. . . . Scot Harvath is the perfect all-American hero for the post-September 11th world; we've always loved guys like this, and now we love them even more."
—Nelson DeMille

"Thor's debut thriller rockets along. . . . A fast-paced and exciting novel."
—*Minneapolis Star-Tribune*

"[Harvath] definitely will take a place beside Cussler's Dirk Pitt® and Clancy's Jack Ryan."
—*Tacoma Reporter* (WA)

BOOKS BY BRAD THOR

Takedown
Blowback
State of the Union
Path of the Assassin
The Lions of Lucerne

BRAD THOR

PATH
OF THE
ASSASSIN

POCKET **STAR** BOOKS
New York   London   Toronto   Sydney

The sale of this book without its cover is unauthorized. If you purchased
this book without a cover, you should be aware that it was reported to
the publisher as "unsold and destroyed." Neither the author nor the
publisher has received payment for the sale of this "stripped book."

A Pocket Star Book published by
POCKET BOOKS, a division of Simon & Schuster, Inc.
1230 Avenue of the Americas, New York, NY 10020

This book is a work of fiction. Names, characters, places and incidents are products of the author's imagination or are used fictitiously.
Any resemblance to actual events or locales or persons living or dead
is entirely coincidental.

Copyright © 2003 by Brad Thor

Originally published in hardcover in 2003 by Atria Books

All rights reserved, including the right to reproduce
this book or portions thereof in any form whatsoever.
For information address Pocket Books, 1230 Avenue
of the Americas, New York, NY 10020

ISBN-13: 978-1-4165-4366-4
ISBN-10:   1-4165-4366-X

This Pocket Star Books paperback edition March 2007

10 9 8 7 6 5 4 3 2 1

POCKET STAR BOOKS and colophon are registered
trademarks of Simon & Schuster, Inc.

Cover design by Jae Song

Manufactured in the United States of America

For information regarding special discounts for bulk purchases,
please contact Simon & Schuster Special Sales at 1-800-456-6798 or
business@simonandschuster.com.

For my father, Brad Thor, Sr.,
my mother, Judy Thor,
and my uncle, Joseph P. Fawcett,
who have shared with me great wisdom,
which I draw upon every day.

Si vis pacem, para bellum.

If you wish peace, prepare for war.

PATH

OF THE

ASSASSIN

1

Dressed in the traditional robes of a Muslim pilgrim, a lone figure tore back the carpeting from beneath a window of the sumptuously appointed room and fastened the feet of a tripod firmly into the concrete floor with a commercial-grade bolt gun.

The equipment had been smuggled into Saudi Arabia's Dar Al Taqwa Inter-Continental Hotel via several large suitcases and a hard-shell golf club case. Arabs, even in Medina, loved their golf, after all, and no one had given any of the cases a second look.

Finally assembled and secured to its launching platform, the second-generation TOW 2 Short missile was something to behold. Though it retained the same three-foot ten-inch profile of the ones Israel had used during the 1973 Yom Kippur War, the effective range of the weapon had increased by almost a thousand yards, and was now the length of forty-one football fields—more than enough to deliver today's deadly payload.

The missile's optical sighting unit was securely positioned in the adjoining hotel room, and its crosshairs were fixed upon its target. An infrared sensor would track the weapon's trajectory and progress, relaying any last-minute adjustments. At such close range though, there'd be no need for adjustments. It would be like shooting fish in a barrel.

The digital fuse was set for ten minutes into the night

prayer session of the Prophet's Mosque, the second-holiest shrine in Islam. Friday was the most important day of worship in the Muslim faith, and the evening prayer sessions were always the most heavily attended. The timing of the attack insured maximum carnage. With a Do Not Disturb sign hung on the doors of both rooms, the terrorist would be resting comfortably on a first-class flight to Cairo by the time the missile launched. From Cairo, a clandestine transport network would round out the journey home just as today's events were being broadcast on the evening news.

As the digital fuse began its devastating countdown, the terrorist spray-painted a large hand cradling the Star of David on the wall.

For a moment, scenes of a happier time flashed through the terrorist's mind. A time before the hatred was so deeply entrenched. Two young lovers from different walks of life, two different sides of the struggle, walked together along a river in fall. Bells rang in the distance and they cherished the good fortune that had brought them together. Though each had been raised to hate the other, love had blossomed between them. But, there were influences at work greater than their love. It was those influences that would change their lives, and the world, forever.

The terrorist's eyes, normally silver in color, now flashed coal black with hate as the final letters were painted beneath the hand. It was a simple, yet chilling three-word message, "Terror For Terror."

Two hours later, a stream of worshippers hurried themselves along, late for the sunset prayer. As they entered the Prophet's Mosque, right leg first as custom dictated, each supplicated, saying, "I seek refuge with the Mighty Allah. I seek protection in His Generous Countenance and His Everlasting Authority. . . . O Allah! Forgive my sins, and open the gates of Your mercy to me."

They fanned out deeper into the mosque, searching for empty spaces to kneel among the other thousands of worshippers. As was the custom, the women were directed into a separate area closed off by large panels of fabric, so as not to distract the men from their prayers. The younger children stayed with their mothers, while older sons, well behaved enough not to disrupt the service, were allowed to sit among the rows of adult men. Most of the families in the Prophet's Mosque were divided this way when a great rumbling erupted overhead and a massive double-detonating warhead crashed through the roof, exploding in a fiery hail of instant death.

By noon the next day, rescue workers were giving up any hope of finding victims alive beneath the wreckage of the Prophet's Mosque. As throngs of Medina's citizens gathered behind emergency-services barricades asking *why*, a broadcast fax went simultaneously to newspapers and news agencies around the globe. It read:

For decades, the Arab world has supported and encouraged terrorism against Israel. Publicly, terrorists are denounced, while privately they continue to be trained and financed by Arab nations. The nation of Israel will no longer tolerate acts of violence upon our soil, or against our people. Henceforward we will speak to the Arab world in the language they have given birth to, the language they have spat bitterly into our mouths, the only language they understand—the language of terrorism.

As it says in Job—"They that plow iniquity and sow mischief shall reap the same."

The fax was signed on behalf of an organization calling itself the *Hand of God*. Beneath the group's name was the same pictogram the Medina police found on the wall of room 611 of the Dar Al Taqwa Inter-Continental, a large hand holding the Star of David in its palm.

The operation had begun.

2

Sixty kilometers across the water west of Hong Kong, the rain beat like sheets of nails against the floating Macau Palace Casino, affectionately known by locals as the Boat of Thieves. The seedy casino was really just an old double-decker ferry, straining now against its moorings in the ever-increasing turbulence of the waters off the South China Sea.

The Macanese waitress smiled as she handed a bottle of beer to her handsome customer. At a trim but muscular five foot ten, with brown hair and blue eyes, Scot Harvath was used to attention. As the waitress moved on to the next customer, the casino's public address system crackled to life. First in Chinese, then Portuguese, and finally in English a voice announced that the Macau Observatory had elevated *Tropical Depression* Anita to *Tropical Storm* Anita. The nearby Guia Lighthouse was flying the "Number 8" signal, indicating that gale-force winds were expected. Patrons were advised that local authorities might close the islands' bridges, as well as the connecting arteries with mainland China, without further notice.

We'd better wrap this up soon, Harvath thought to himself. The last report he had received from the U.S. Naval Pacific Meteorology and Oceanography Center had forecasted the depression would advance to the tropical storm stage, with winds blowing upward of seventy-two miles per hour. Anything stronger than that would amount to a full-blown typhoon, and he knew that at that point the mission would be scrapped. Scrapping, though, was unacceptable to Harvath. He had come too far to let his target go now.

Harvath pulled fifty more Hong Kong dollars from his pocket and placed another bet as he pretended to sip at his cold beer. He was sitting at a table with a mixed group of Anglos and Asians, all hard-core gamblers, none of whom had the good sense to make tracks before the storm got any worse. Next to him was Sammy Cheng of the SDU, the Hong Kong Police Force's secretive counterterrorism unit. Harvath and Cheng had met several years prior, when Harvath's SEAL team had been sent to Hong Kong to help the then-British counterterrorism unit improve upon their water skills.

Though both men appeared to be engrossed in the game, their attention was glued to a Chinese man three tables away.

The man's name was William Lee, and he was one of the SDU's top undercover operatives. Tonight he was posing as an intermediary for an outlawed Chinese extremist organization that was looking to acquire weapons and explosives. The target of the operation was an arms dealer named Philip Jamek.

Extremist groups were Jamek's best customers. He was credited with sales throughout the Philippines, Indonesia, and Japan, and was now making his services, which also included training in the arts of terrorism and assassination, available in China. The Chinese government wanted Jamek taken out of circulation once and for all, and so did Scot Harvath.

Harvath had spent months tracking down this last

member of the Swiss mercenary team known as the Lions of Lucerne, who had kidnapped the American president the year before and left a trail of dead Americans in their wake. The American government believed that all of the deadly Lions had been eliminated or taken into custody, but Harvath had discovered one who had slipped through the cracks—Philip Jamek. Not only was Jamek a proven danger to the world, but Harvath had made a vow to his fallen comrades that he wouldn't rest until every last person responsible for their deaths was brought to justice.

Harvath and Sammy Cheng watched as a waitress approached Lee and set a drink on the table in front of him. She said a few words, and he reached into his pocket to retrieve a tip. When the waitress left, Lee played with his chips for a few moments and then pretended to cough into his hand as he relayed instructions over the tiny microphone sewn into his sleeve.

"Jamek just made contact," Sammy Cheng whispered to Harvath as he picked up the information over his earpiece.

Scot kept his eyes on the table. "The waitress who brought him the drink," he said. "He must be close."

"Close, or he gave the waitress the message and told her to wait ten minutes before delivering it."

"No, he's definitely nearby. He's going to watch to make sure Lee's alone."

"He won't be standing outside in this weather. Either he's got a car waiting or he's already caught one of the last taxis to the Hotel Lisboa."

"The Hotel Lisboa? He's moving the meet again?" asked Harvath.

Cheng nodded his head. Jamek had already switched

the agreed-to meeting place several times that day, making it nearly impossible for a trap to be set. Harvath felt as if he were on a whirlwind tour of the region. They had already ridden the Star Ferry from Hong Kong to Kowloon and back, had suffered two hours of rain in Hong Kong's Wanchai District, had gone up and down the Peak Tram, and had arrived at Hong Kong's Jetfoil terminal just in time to catch the last high-speed boat to Macau.

Moving the game over to Macau was an additionally ingenious twist, as it took Hong Kong law-enforcement officers, which members of the SDU were, out of their jurisdiction. As crafty as this move was, Cheng had seen it coming and had gotten permission for his team to pursue Jamek into Macau. The only problem had been that the rest of the team, following behind in two nondescript vans, had been dressed in full tactical gear. They had had no time to change into plain clothes before the last Jetfoil departed and had to be left behind.

As Lee got up from his table and made his way toward the cashier's cage with his chips, Harvath reflected on how masterfully Jamek had managed to whittle their team of over fifteen operatives down to only three. In addition to the storm, something else was brewing, and Harvath had a bad feeling about how it was going to play out.

3

President Jack Rutledge's National Security Council was waiting for him with a mixture of cautious apprehension and professional unease when he entered the secure conference room beneath the White House known as the situation room. Being called in at such an ungodly hour and on a weekend had everyone on edge.

"Please be seated," said the president as he took his place at the head of the long cherry-wood table. "Thank you for coming in so early and on a Saturday.

"As you all know, the fallout from the terrorist attack on the Prophet's Mosque in Medina has been every bit as bad as we feared it would be. The Israelis are experiencing a surge in homicide bombings, and imams and mullahs throughout the Islamic world are encouraging additional retaliation. And, just as we had anticipated, the rhetoric has been ratcheted up by Muslim extremists who are now calling for attacks on the United States because of our support for Israel.

"To make matters worse, the Israelis are reacting to the latest attacks on their people by going after the Palestinians with a tremendous amount of force. That force is making life extremely difficult for the chief Palestinian negotiator, Ali Hasan, whom we all have seen is quickly becoming one of the key players in the peace process and somebody who will be very involved in the future of Palestine. While Hasan's people, and much of the Arab world, are yelling for blood, he is one of the few voices calling for a peaceful resolution.

"As for the Hand of God organization, Israel claims to be investigating, but says it has no knowledge of any such group and, contrary to reports in the Arab press, is in no way supporting it. We have some reservations as to how forthcoming the Israelis are being with us, and with that said, I'd like to invite CIA director Vaile, to present his report."

"Thank you, Mr. President," said Vaile as his assistant passed folders to each attendee around the long table. "As you all know, the CIA has been actively investigating the terrorist attack in Medina over the last week. In particular, we have been interested in uncovering the identity of a heretofore unknown terrorist group calling itself the Hand of God. We have confirmed that the missile used in the attack was, indeed, an Israeli-manufactured TOW 2 Short. In addition to the president's report of the growing unrest in the Islamic world since the attack, the CIA feels it is important to point out the surging popularity of the Hand of God throughout Israel. There appears to be an increased vigilante fervor among the Israeli public that their government is doing very little to put down. In fact, while most Israeli officials have half-heartedly condemned the attack in public, privately they're praising it, which has caught the interest of our analysts over the last week."

"Are you suggesting the Israeli government was actually involved in the attack on Medina?" asked the Homeland Security director, Alan Driehaus.

"We have no concrete proof of that, but—"

"Well, what do you have?" asked Jennifer Staley, the

secretary of state, as she leafed through the folder that had been handed her.

"After the 1972 massacre of Israeli athletes at the Munich Olympics, Israeli prime minister Golda Meir, along with several high-ranking Israeli officials, intended to send a message, not only to those involved in the Munich massacre, but also to anyone contemplating future attacks on Israel, that such behavior would be met with deadly reprisals.

"To send the message, a covert action team from the Mossad's assassination unit was assembled. There were to be no arrests, no trials, no appeals. Their goal was simple—kill every single person they could get to, whether their involvement in Munich was direct or indirect, and let the rest live in fear, never knowing when their time would come. And it didn't matter where the terrorists were hiding. The team was authorized to hunt them down anywhere in the world."

"I remember that," said the secretary of state. "What did the Israelis name their group?"

"The Wrath of God," said Vaile. All of the attendees who had been perusing the folders in front of them now raised their eyes and locked them on the CIA director.

Homeland Security director Driehaus moved uncomfortably in his chair for a moment before speaking. "Are you telling us you believe the Israelis have reactivated this unit to terrorize the Arab world?"

"We don't know yet, but we're putting a lot of resources into getting to the bottom of it. When it comes to covert operations, the Israelis are one of the best. If they don't want anybody to know they're behind something, most of the time they can make that happen."

"What diplomatic channels have we tried?" asked the secretary of state.

Vaile glanced at President Rutledge before responding. "The president has put the question point-blank to the Israeli prime minister, and he has denied that his country has any involvement with the Hand of God."

"So what, in fact, do we know?" asked the chairman of the Joint Chiefs.

"What we know is that the timing of this couldn't be worse. If you'll permit me, I'd like to explain why the president has called this meeting," said Vaile, who then asked for the lights to be lowered as he activated his laptop. Two, large flat-panel screens at the front of the situation room came to life with the seal of the Central Intelligence Agency as the director began his presentation.

"Before Osama bin Laden appeared on the world stage, the spotlight rested largely upon Abu Nidal, a man who not only wrote the book on international terrorism, but published it as well.

"The Abu Nidal Organization, also known as the Fatah Revolutionary Council, or FRC, has carried out over ninety terrorist attacks across twenty countries, resulting in the death and injury of more than a thousand people. At one point, the State Department classified Nidal and his people as the most dangerous terrorist organization in the world. His targets have included the United States, the United Kingdom, France, Israel, moderate Palestinians, the PLO, and various Arab nations. The organization's number-one priority after the creation of a Palestinian State is the destruction of Israel and then America—"

"Wait a second. These people have been off the radar

screen for years," said the secretary of state. "I thought we were operating under the assumption that Abu Nidal had been assassinated in Baghdad."

"The CIA is inclined to agree with you," responded Vaile.

"Then what are we talking about?"

"This," said Vaile as he advanced to the next slide of his presentation. The long list of Abu Nidal's terrorist activities, including masterminding the Rome and Vienna airport massacres, as well as the Pan Am 103 bombing over Lockerbie, Scotland, disappeared and was replaced by an empty silhouette. "Ladies and gentlemen, meet Hashim Nidal. Abu Nidal's son."

"But there's nothing there," replied the chairman of the Joint Chiefs.

"And therein lies the greatest threat facing our country at this moment," replied Vaile.

"Director Vaile," began the Homeland Security director, "are you telling us that despite the vast resources of the CIA, you don't even have a picture of this man?"

"Unfortunately, that's correct. Abu Nidal went to great lengths to keep the fact that he even had a son hidden. All we've been able to ascertain thus far is his name. Roughly translated from Arabic, *Hashim* means, 'crusher of evil.' "

"Well, that's lovely," said the secretary of state as she closed her folder and pushed it away from her. "Are you suggesting, Mr. Vaile, that Abu Nidal turned the reins of the organization over to his son?"

"Based on the intelligence we have received, that's exactly what we're suggesting."

"And what is this intelligence?"

"According to our sources, Hashim Nidal has united an international network of Islamic terrorist organizations including Hamas, Hezbollah, the al-Aqsa Martyrs Brigades, the remnants of Al Qaeda, the Muslim Brotherhood, Abu Sayyaf in the Philippines . . . The list goes on and on. He has been able to convince them that their service to Allah can best be carried out by joining forces. He knows their strengths, as well as their weaknesses. They have been sharing strategies, intelligence, and even training. There's a deep religious underpinning within all the groups, which Hashim Nidal is using to supercede their political beliefs. For all intents and purposes, he has united them behind a common cause—the destruction of Israel.

"And the threat to the United States is . . . ?" asked Driehaus.

"Extremely serious. According to their doctrine, the destruction of Israel will be immediately followed by the destruction of the United States."

"What's pushed this all to center stage?" asked the secretary of state.

"There's been a conflux of events—increased telephone chatter picked up by the NSA, FBI probes into suspected sleeper cells here in the U.S., and a significant breakthrough by the CIA," said Vaile, with full knowledge that his agency needed to appear two steps ahead of terrorism for once instead of two steps behind.

"And what exactly was this *significant* CIA breakthrough?" asked Driehaus.

"With the help of the NSA, we've been monitoring communications among several of the most serious Islamic terrorist groups. Someone code-named, *Ghazi*, which is

Arabic for "the conqueror," has been repeatedly referenced as the great father of the organizations. Ghazi has also been discussed as masterminding an upcoming event that will begin the shift of world power to the true believers of Islam.

"Now, last night, a senior member of the Islamic Jihad was picked up in Beirut. Under interrogation, he identified Hashim Nidal as the person referred to as Ghazi, but said he'd never met him in person and couldn't provide a description of him. He indicated that Nidal's upcoming event was imminent and would unite the Arab world, once and for all, in decimating Israel, followed by the United States."

Even the most seasoned poker faces around the situation room table couldn't mask their shock and disbelief.

"Does the CIA actually believe this Hashim Nidal has the wherewithal to pull something like this off?" asked the chairman of the Joint Chiefs.

"We can't afford not to believe," answered the president. "We're going to need everyone working together on this. Hashim Nidal has to be stopped and his organization dismantled before he can launch any attacks within or against the United States. We also want to prevent anything that could start a war between Israel and the rest of the Arab world."

"Without knowing what this guy looks like or where he is, how do we even start?" asked Director Sorce of the FBI.

"The CIA has already put the wheels in motion, and we're tracking down several leads. We'll find Hashim Nidal, and we will stop him," replied Vaile.

Most of the people around the table, including the

president, wished they could be as confident in the CIA as its director was. He was flying completely blind and they all knew it. Only a miracle would allow his agency to pull this operation off. The question was, where would they find one?

4

Scot Harvath made it outside just in time to see Lee's cab pull away from the curb. The fierce wind was driving the rain horizontally as he and Sammy Cheng ran for the car they had picked up at the Macau Jetfoil Terminal.

Cheng threw him the keys and indicated he wanted him to drive so he could use his cell phone. Harvath maneuvered himself behind the wheel of the tiny tourist rental known as a Moke, and slid the seat back as far as he could, but was still cramped. *Cell phone my ass*, thought Scot. There wasn't a person in Hong Kong he had met yet who couldn't drive, talk on his cell phone, read the paper, change CDs, and eat lunch all at the same time. Cheng had just wanted the roomier passenger seat.

As they drove, Harvath pulled hard on the wheel to avoid a piece of debris in the road. A strong burst of wind caught the car and raised it up on two wheels before roughly dropping it back onto the street. Scot shot Sammy a look.

Sammy cupped his hand over his cell phone and said to Harvath, "*Dai feng*—Cantonese for 'great wind.'"

"*Blow me*," replied Harvath, "American for 'shitty car.'"

Sammy went back to his phone conversation while Harvath hunched over the steering wheel and tried to peer through the foggy windshield. There was no air-conditioning in the car, as it was meant to be driven with its top down, and opening the window even a crack would allow gallons of water to pour inside. Harvath used the sleeve of his jacket to clean a patch of glass to see through. Though the car had wipers, they weren't strong enough to keep up with the driving rain.

Streetlamps swung violently in the wind, and Scot worried one might topple over and crash through the car's soft convertible top. Cheng punched the *end* button on his cell phone and turned to Harvath.

"They're not releasing any more Jetfoils from Hong Kong. It took some doing, but the rest of the team has scrambled one of the Cougarteks from the Marine Division. That boat's fast, but they're at least forty-five minutes behind us."

As a former SEAL and aficionado of go-fast boats, Harvath knew the craft well, but even with its radar, thermal imaging, and advanced navigation equipment, if the weather got any nastier, the rest of the SDU team could be delayed for hours or worse, forced to turn back for good.

It was best to assume that he and Cheng would not be getting any backup.

"Let's stay as close as we can to our man," said Cheng, "and hope we get lucky. No weapons unless absolutely necessary. The Lisboa is going to be filled with civilians."

Harvath nodded his understanding and swung the car into the driveway of the majestically lit building. Through the windshield, they could just see Lee get out of his taxi and enter the hotel. When they pulled up under the awning, the rain finally abated and the absence of its pounding on the canvas roof of the car was almost deafening. A valet decked out in foul-weather gear opened Harvath's door and welcomed him to the Hotel Lisboa.

Harvath handed him the key and took one last look at the storm before entering the building.

The casino was a four-storied enormity. The gargantuan rotunda was filled with smoke and noise. Gamblers at the tables shouted and competed to be heard over the ringing of slot machines and the clanging of coins into stainless-steel payout trays. Cocktail waitresses floated by, carried on the winds of greed and human avarice, as mountains of chips were won and lost. People didn't come here for a good time—they came to gamble.

And so, too, had Scott Harvath, Sammy Cheng, and William Lee. They were hoping against the odds that they would be able to finally capture Philip Jamek. Harvath had always marveled that these kinds of law-enforcement operations happened around the world on a daily basis and that most people had no idea. So many took civilization for granted without realizing that it was birthed and maintained at the point of a sword. Someone needed to hold that sword and even, on occasion, swing it in order to help stave off chaos.

Around the rotunda were a series of ornate, semiprivate gaming rooms with required minimum bets of a thousand Hong Kong dollars. Thankfully, William Lee had taken a seat at one of the cheaper Pai Kao tables on the main floor. Harvath and Cheng hung back as far as they dared. Several times, they had lost sight of Lee as he made his way through the crowded casino. The Hotel Lisboa billed itself as a city within a city, and there were certainly enough people here to back up that claim. No one seemed to care that there was a major typhoon developing outside. All that mattered was the gambling.

Harvath and Cheng took up positions a few tables away from Lee and continued their surveillance. Harvath was beginning to wonder where their merry little chase would lead next when Cheng broke the silence.

"Contact," he said quietly.

A middle-aged man in a well-tailored linen suit had taken the chair next to Lee. The man's blond head was bowed as he played his cards, but to the trained eye, it was obvious that he and Lee were talking. After a few moments, the man reached inside his suit coat. Harvath tensed and reflexively reached for his pistol, but then relaxed when the man withdrew an oversized gold lighter and placed it on the table in front of him. Their target never withdrew a cigarette.

The conversation between Lee and the stranger continued until Lee twisted the ring on his left hand and then pulled twice at his shirt cuff. *The signal!* He was talking with Jamek himself.

Scot and Sammy collected their chips and prepared to get up from the table. At the same moment, Jamek reached out, placed a ringed hand on Lee's shoulder, and then stood. Lee's body tensed as Jamek quickly moved away from the table. A few moments later, Lee began convulsing. Harvath and Cheng no longer cared if they were spotted, and ran toward the table as Lee fell forward into violent spasms.

Cheng had slightly longer legs, but Harvath was better at pushing people out of his way and made it to William Lee first. When he flipped him over, he saw that his eyes had rolled up into his head. His hands were clenched in tight fists and his rigid back was arched so high you could have driven a truck underneath him. A small group of horrified onlookers had begun to gather.

"What the hell's going on?" Sammy said as he reached them.

"He's been drugged or poisoned," replied Harvath.

"With what?"

"I don't know. We need to get him help. You grab his arms, and I'll get his legs."

Cheng did as Harvath instructed, but when they were only a few feet away from the table, he stopped.

"What are you doing?" yelled Harvath.

"The lighter. That son of a bitch left that big gold lighter on the table. We might be able to get prints off it."

Harvath looked over at the abnormally large lighter sitting on the table, and in a flash, his instincts took over.

"Leave it. We've got to get away from here."

"What?"

"He left it there on purpose. Move!" yelled Harvath.

With Lee between them, the two men began to run for the exit. Seconds later, an explosion rocked the table behind them and sent an enormous fireball rolling through the casino, knocking the trio to the ground. The back of Harvath's jacket was on fire, and he quickly tore it off, revealing the tactical holster tucked at the small of his back. The newly visible pistol only added to the panic of the already screaming casino patrons.

Harvath ignored them and bent over to take Lee's pulse as the sprinkler system kicked in. The convulsions had stopped and Lee's eyes were no longer rolled up into his head. His muscles relaxed, his pulse was normalizing, and his breathing was beginning to steady. Whatever he'd been injected with had had an extremely violent, but short-lived effect, creating the perfect diversion.

When Cheng was convinced that Lee would make it, he pulled a nine-millimeter Beretta pistol from beneath his coat and instructed a nearby security guard to watch over his partner and radio for medical attention right away. Then Cheng turned angrily to Harvath, "First we find him, and then we kill him."

"We've got to take him alive, Sammy," said Harvath as they stood up and began searching for Jamek. He knew Cheng understood why. Harvath had filled him in before the mission began. He'd explained that when President Rutledge had first been kidnapped, the operation launched to recover him. It turned out to be a trap. The entire team the U.S. had sent in was killed. Harvath knew the Lions had contracted it out, but he didn't know to whom. The Lions' former leader, Gerhard Miner, was awaiting trial in Switzerland, but refused to answer any questions. The only other surviving member of the organization was Gerhard Miner's moneyman, Philip Jamek, who had just tried to kill them. Harvath was certain the man knew something. Even the smallest detail might help illuminate the dark abyss in which the American intelligence community was working. Without Jamek, no one would ever know who had been behind the ambush of the Special Operations team and Harvath couldn't let that happen. He had made those fallen men a promise.

He looked directly at Cheng, and awaited his response. He hadn't noticed it before, but apparently Cheng's arm had been injured in the explosion.

"What happened to your arm?"

"It's not my arm, it's my shoulder, and don't worry about it. If there's a chance to bring Jamek down without killing him, I'll try that first, but if I have to go for the kill, I won't hesitate."

"Can you even shoot?" asked Harvath.

"I said don't worry about it. Now, where the hell do we start?" asked Cheng as they moved cautiously forward. "This place is enormous. He could be anywhere by now."

Cheng's question was immediately answered by the sound of gunfire from the front of the casino.

As the pair reached the entrance, they noticed bullet holes everywhere. *What, or who, the hell was this guy shooting at?* The casino's ornate glass doors were completely shattered, and a carpet of broken glass lay across the threshold. Wind and rain whipped inside from the ferocious storm. Harvath had to hold up his arm to shield his face from the weather.

He could barely make out the sky outside. It was an eerie purplish black. Though the hotel had not made any announcements, he knew the storm must now be up to a signal 9, meaning it would be passing close, or possibly even a signal 10, which indicated the typhoon would make a direct hit.

As he continued to peer outside, the movement of a figure under the awning caught his eye. It was Jamek and he had his back to them. Harvath signaled Cheng and tightened his grip around his SDU-issued Glock. They hugged the side of the building and fought against the wind as they crept closer.

Ten meters away, Cheng yelled for Jamek to drop his weapon. Thinking maybe he couldn't hear him above the roar of the wind, Cheng yelled again. There was some-thing that sounded like thunder, but the two claps came too close together. Jamek spun, and both Harvath and Cheng readied to fire. Jamek was holding an MP5K sub-machine gun. In the violence of his spin, his arm careened strangely above his head, and he emptied the weapon's magazine into the awning above. Before either Scot or Sammy could return fire, the man fell facedown onto the pavement.

Confused, they moved cautiously over to Jamek, their weapons ready. When they were close enough, Cheng kicked the man's submachine gun away and Scot turned him over. Blood poured from large bullet wounds to his chest and forehead. Harvath's examination was cut short by the sound of heavy tires spinning on the wet pave-ment as a large, silver Mercedes sedan headed right for them.

The driver was dressed completely in black and wore some sort of ski mask over his face. In the instant that he had, Scot saw only the driver's eyes. Their color, even through the glass of the Mercedes, was like nothing he had ever seen. They were a shade of silver, almost like mercury, that bordered on being black. Harvath was convinced it was a trick of the light, yet he was instantly drawn to them, into them. He shook the feeling off just in time to spin away from the speeding car as Sammy Cheng opened fire. His bullets went wide. Only two managed to reach their target, and even then, all they hit was the trunk of the Mercedes as it sped away.

"Who the hell was that?" yelled Cheng against the wind as he painfully lowered his weapon.

"Looks like we're not the only people hunting lions today," Scot yelled back.

"Let's grab our car and go after him."

"I've got a better idea," said Scot as he motioned Sammy to follow.

Under the awning and off to the side was the valet's padlocked key box. With the butt of his pistol, Harvath hammered the padlock and broke it off with one blow. He quickly looked inside and grabbed the key he wanted. Fifteen feet away was a black Audi TT Roadster.

Harvath unlocked the doors with the remote, and he and Cheng jumped in.

"Good choice," said Sam.

"No kidding."

Harvath tore after the Mercedes and its mysterious assassin. He was on the street and in fifth gear before Cheng even had his seat belt on. There were absolutely no cars on the roads. People were already home with their storm shutters drawn or were camped out in one of Macau's typhoon shelters.

The wind was incredibly strong and it was all Harvath could do to keep them from spinning out of control. Finally, by San Francisco Hill, they caught sight of the Mercedes. Harvath downshifted into fourth and stepped on the pedal, sending the tachometer into the red. Cheng replaced his spent magazine with a fresh one.

Harvath was gaining on the Mercedes when a series of tight turns made him fall behind.

"He's playing with us," said Cheng.

"What do you mean?"

"I mean, our grand tour continues. Only now, you're getting to see the route the Macau Grand Prix takes."

Harvath had been getting the runaround all day and was now officially pissed off. It was time for it to stop.

"Any good straightaways in this race, Sammy?" he asked.

"Right after the Fisherman's Bend. It'll be coming up soon."

"Fine, when we hit it, I want you to grab the wheel."

"Why?"

"Because with your shoulder you can't shoot worth shit and I've got an idea."

"Whatever you're going to do, I hope it works."

Harvath pulled a pair of Cyclone glasses from the pocket of his cargo pants. The wraparound glasses had padded eyecups, which like goggles, protected eyes from wind, debris, and even water at full throttle.

"We're coming up to the straightaway now," said Cheng.

Harvath downshifted and redlined the tachometer once again. He set the cruise control and hit the automatic window button as he popped on the Cyclone glasses and tightened the foam safety band around his head. He let go of the wheel and crawled out the window until he was sitting on the sill.

He kept his face turned into the wind, which helped keep the glasses plastered to his face and the rain out of his eyes. The Glock pistol felt as light as a feather as the wind threatened to tear it from his hands. Summoning all of his strength, he managed to rest it on the roadster's canvas top and point it at the speeding Mercedes. He took aim and let loose a thunderous volley of fire. The Mercedes's rear window shattered, and the left rear tire exploded in a maelstrom of screaming black rubber. For a moment, Harvath thought he could make out the driver's silver-black eyes in the rearview mirror before the Mercedes swerved out of control.

Totally drenched, Harvath quickly slid back inside the Audi.

The driver of the Mercedes had regained some control and was now speeding ahead of them on only three tires and a rim. When they neared the Mandarin Oriental hotel, the Mercedes fishtailed wildly in a hard right, and Scot realized he had come full circle.

"We've got him now," said Harvath as he pressed down on the accelerator.

At that exact moment, the driver of the Mercedes began firing through the open space where the rear window of the Mercedes used to be. Harvath jerked the wheel of the Audi hard to the left as enormous bullets tore holes straight up its hood. The car spun through a slick puddle and Scot saw everything happen in slow motion. Neither vehicle could escape its fate. As the Audi swerved in its inescapable trajectory toward a pile of scaffolding and construction equipment, the Mercedes barreled down on a row of parked cars.

The Audi hit hard on Cheng's side and all the air bags deployed.

Upon slamming into the row of parked cars, the Mercedes was thrust high into the air and came down with a loud crash.

Once he had shaken off the shock of the impact, Harvath's eye caught the bullet hole in the Audi's windshield. Even before he turned to look at Sammy Cheng, he knew his friend had been hit. Harvath could hear the sound of gurgling blood coming from the hole the bullet had carved through Cheng's throat. He tried to stanch the flow, but it was no use. Within seconds, Cheng stopped breathing and was dead.

Enraged, Harvath climbed from the Audi and stumbled down the block to where the Mercedes lay upturned and burning. He approached the car from the rear, trying to steady his Glock. He began applying pressure to the trigger as he neared the driver's side door. In one fluid motion that belied the battered state of his body, he swung the pistol through the window, searching for the car's driver. The Mercedes was empty. Harvath searched the street, thinking that maybe the driver had been thrown clear. There was nothing. Absolutely no sign. The deadly, silver-eyed assassin had vanished into the storm.

5

It was a week since the debacle in Macau and Harvath still couldn't shake his feelings of failure. He had come to Switzerland after Cheng's death to lick his wounds and be with Claudia, but things weren't turning out as he had hoped.

Harvath rolled over and felt the empty space next to him. It was cold. Claudia had long since left for her office. Although he wasn't the sentimental type, it bothered him that she had stopped doing so many things lately. She had stopped kissing him good-bye in the morning, had stopped leaving a coffee cup out for him, had stopped leaving notes in her bathroom, and worst of all, she had stopped trusting him.

When Harvath returned from Hong Kong and Macau, he had expected to be spending a few days with Claudia at her parents' farm in Grindelwald before Gerhard Miner's trial started. Instead, Claudia had "decided" that she needed to spend more time preparing the case and Scot was left in Bern to his own devices.

He knew why she was doing this. No matter how many times he answered her questions, which began the minute she picked him up at the airport in Zurich, she just refused to believe him. Claudia didn't like being stonewalled, nor did Harvath for that matter, but matters of national security couldn't be shared, even if two people were sharing other things, like the same bed.

Though Harvath couldn't say where he had been and refused to let Claudia look at his passport, she knew he had been in Asia. She also knew that he was somehow involved in the killing of Philip Jamek. Jamek would have been useful in her pending prosecution of Miner, but now he was of no use to anyone.

It pained Harvath to see a rift developing between him and Claudia, but he couldn't tell her the truth, not the full truth. He had tried to assure her that he'd had nothing to do with the killing of Jamek. That much was true. Someone else had wanted Jamek dead, but why? The Chinese wouldn't have put a hit out on him. That wouldn't have made any sense. Maybe Jamek had double-crossed somebody in one of his arms deals and the hit was payback. Or maybe it was something else entirely. All Harvath really knew was that the eyes of the assassin still haunted him.

Whether he had been in Asia, Macau specifically, during Jamek's killing was classified and something he couldn't discuss. Claudia would just have to deal with that. And she did.

She dealt with it by burying herself in her work. After helping Scot rescue the president and arrest Gerhard Miner, she had been promoted. She was now a full-fledged prosecutor, her dream come true, and was part of the team that was going to make sure Gerhard Miner never again walked the streets as a free man.

In a move that stunned the rest of the world, Switzerland had steadfastly refused to extradite Miner to stand trial in the United States. The Swiss assured the Americans that they would see to it that justice was done, but that Miner would not be put to death for his crimes. If found guilty, which the Swiss government assured the United States was going to happen, he would spend the rest of his life behind bars.

With the increased demands placed upon Claudia by her promotion, it had become obvious to Scot that their hopes for a workable relationship were fading. Harvath was on a special leave of absence granted by the president, but at some point he would be expected to return home and take up his new position as director of Secret Service Operations for the White House. Once that happened, it would be next to impossible for them to see each other. In both of their occupations, the demands of career came first and personal lives second. Each had worked too hard to get where they were to give it all up and move to another country simply for love.

Though Harvath refused to answer many of Claudia's questions, not a day went by that he didn't ask for access to Gerhard Miner. The Swiss felt they had cooperated fully and had provided unprecedented access to Miner already. Teams of interrogators from both the FBI and CIA, as well as a host of American diplomats had already paraded through the high security facility fifteen kilometers northeast of Bern where Miner was kept. One Secret Service agent, even one as bright as the Swiss realized Scot Harvath to be, was not going to make any difference, in their opinion. Miner had said everything to the Americans he was going to say. What's more, Miner had told the Swiss that he would become extremely uncooperative if his government let Agent Harvath anywhere near him. He even threatened a lawsuit of his own. During the rescue of the president, Harvath had beaten Miner almost to death. Miner still bore much of the trauma, including not only one of the most severe cases of arthritis the Swiss prison doctors had ever seen, but also extensive nerve damage throughout his face from Harvath's having shattered his jaw in seven places. No, the Swiss were not going to let Scot Harvath anywhere near Gerhard Miner. Even a direct appeal from the U.S. president, Jack Rutledge himself, had failed to move the Swiss.

Had Claudia wanted, she could have gotten Scot access, but since he wasn't cooperating with her, she wasn't going to cooperate with him. Plain and simple.

The thought was still lingering in his mind when the phone rang.

"Mueller residence," he said as he answered Claudia's cordless.

"Scot, it's me," replied Claudia.

"Hi."

"Hi."

An awkward silence followed.

"Listen, I want to tell you I'm sorry."

"Sorry for what?" he asked.

"Things haven't been good for us."

"I'm sorry too."

"You know I care for you very much."

"I know."

"It's just . . . I don't know that this is going to work out."

Even though he knew what she was talking about, he still had to ask, "You don't know that *what* is going to work out?"

"Us. A relationship. We went through something very

difficult and very dangerous. It brought us together very fast, probably too fast, but our lives are very different. You have yours back in Washington, and I have mine here in Bern." Then came the dreaded, "We can still be friends, though, right?"

Scot ignored the question and said, "Claudia, why are you telling me this now, over the phone?"

She was silent.

"Claudia? Are you still there?"

"Yes, I'm sorry, I was distracted. Things are very busy here now."

"You still haven't answered my question."

"It's been moved up."

" 'Moved up'? What are you talking about?"

"Miner's case. His attorneys made a motion to the judge that we thought we could knock down. We failed. There's a preliminary hearing this morning and Miner will be present. With the trial moved up, I am going to have a lot of work to do. I'm going to be keeping late hours and I just think maybe we should stop things between us now."

Harvath, usually never at a loss for words or a snappy comeback, for once in his life was silent.

"Scot, are you okay?" asked Claudia.

"How long have you known about this?"

"About the hearing? I have known for a couple of days."

"What's your security like? What do you have in place?"

"Don't worry, Agent Harvath, the Americans aren't the only ones who know how to transport a prisoner and secure a courtroom."

"Claudia, from what you have told me about this Jamek character in Macau—"

"Scot, I don't have time for this, and I don't want to lis-ten to you lie to me about what happened in Macau. I know you were there. When you couldn't get what you wanted out of Miner, you went looking for Jamek, hoping he could tell you something."

"Claudia, I told you. I had nothing to do with Jamek being killed."

"Yes, you did say that, but you have not denied knowing about it, and you also haven't denied being in Macau when it happened."

"You know I can't tell you where I was or what I was doing."

"I know, but it still hurts. You are important to me. You know that."

"Then get me in to see Miner. I need to talk to him. I promise you I won't lay a hand on him."

"I wish I could help you. More than that, I wish I could believe you, but I can't, not about Macau, not about Miner, not about anything. It's just better that we end things, okay? Please don't make this harder than it has to be."

"Okay, Claudia, you're right. You have your life here and I have mine back in D.C. As much as we might have wanted it to, it won't work. But will you do one last thing for me?"

"Scot, I told you I cannot grant you access to Miner."

"No, forget that. How are you transporting Miner?"

"I can't tell you that. Not over the phone."

"Tell me this, then. Will you be part of the team that transports him to the courthouse?"

"Of course."

"Then I want to ride along with you."

"You want to what? That's ridiculous. Besides, I told you I don't trust you to be anywhere near Miner."

"Claudia, this isn't about him. I don't care who you have doing security; they can't possibly know half the things that I do. Call me arrogant, but when it comes to this stuff, no one does it better than the U.S. Secret Service. Think about it as a free security consultation. There's plenty of countries that pay big money for this kind of review."

"I don't think it's a good idea."

"I just want to know your route and the courtroom are safe. That's all. You have my word. I promise. Miner won't even know I'm there. I am doing this out of concern for you."

"For me? Why?"

"Because someone wanted Philip Jamek dead. I'm convinced it wasn't the Chinese. They were going to kill him, all right, but he would have been given at least some semblance of a trial beforehand. Somebody else wanted Jamek dead, and it may or it may not have to do with Miner, but at least I can go home knowing you're safe."

"Okay, Scot, you win. I'll call a cab to bring you to the office. I just hope this is not a mistake."

6

An hour and forty-five minutes later, Harvath was seated in the passenger seat of Claudia's VW as they headed out of Bern on the short trip to the prison. The convoy consisted of eight vehicles. Two police motorcycles led the way, followed by two police cars, the transport van, two more marked police cars, and finally Claudia's car, bringing up the rear.

Even in a country like Switzerland, where the inhabitants prided themselves on their obsession with organization, things could go amiss. Bern was constantly plagued with traffic jams, and today was no exception. Harvath didn't enjoy being in the last vehicle of the convoy, and repeatedly asked Claudia to translate the dialogue with the lead vehicles that was going back and forth over her radio. Claudia assured him it was nothing more than normal Bernese traffic and that the motorcycle police were complaining that people weren't responding quickly enough to their sirens. In all fairness to the people of Bern, it wasn't easy to "hop to" when you heard a police siren, especially when you were stuck in traffic on a narrow, one-way medieval street with cars parked on both sides.

"We're close now," said Claudia, who then spoke rapid-fire Swiss German into her walkie-talkie before peeling off from the convoy.

"What are you doing?" asked Harvath, who immediately sat up straighter in his seat as Claudia broke formation.

"The courthouse is just down a little further. The press has gotten wind that Miner is appearing today, and they are out in full force. I don't want anyone to see you going in the front, so I will take you in another way. You still want to check out the courtroom, don't you?"

"Of course I do, but how did the press get wind of the proceeding being changed to today?"

"How do they find things out in America? People talk."

"Doesn't that bother you?"

"Of course it does, but that's the way the press is. They pay everybody and have sources everywhere, but what can I do about it? Listen, including the personnel in that van, Gerhard Miner is being guarded by over twenty-five of some of the meanest and most heavily armed members of the police and Swiss military. Whether you have noticed it or not, there has been a military helicopter shadowing us the entire time Miner has been outside the prison's walls."

Scot had noticed the helicopter. He was impressed that Claudia had thought so far ahead, but he was still concerned.

"There are additional men posted within the courtroom itself, throughout the building, and even in plain clothes outside among members of the press. Now, Agent Harvath, how would you rate my security?"

"So far I'd have to say you've been pretty thorough—"

"It would take an army to get to Miner."

Scot knew she was wrong. It was dangerous to believe that you were fully prepared. If one person was determined to do harm at any cost, there really was nothing any organization could do to stop him or her. This was the fear the Secret Service lived with twenty-four hours a day, seven days a week. Scot was about to share this with Claudia when her radio crackled to life with frantic shouts from one of the lead vehicles.

"What's going on?" Scot asked.

"Some sort of accident," she replied.

"Accident? What kind of accident?"

Claudia had already slammed on her brakes and was reversing full speed back toward where she had pulled off from the convoy. "I don't know. Both motorcycle drivers are down. I can't work the radio and drive backward at the same time."

Harvath was about to suggest they trade places when an enormous explosion tore through the warm morning air. The roiling thunderball of fire could be seen above the buildings to their right. The radio calls grew in intensity and added to the sounds of chaos throughout the neighborhood. Harvath could distinctly make out the *whoomp whoomp whoomp* of a heavy chopper coming in from above.

Harvath grabbed hold of the wheel from Claudia and turned it hard to the left as he pulled up on the VW's emergency brake. The car spun 180 degrees, gashing the sides of three parked cars. Claudia was too startled by Harvath's move to speak. At least now they were headed forward and could make better time. Scot could apologize later. "Step on it," he said.

When they rounded the corner and came back down the street where they had left the convoy, it looked as if they had driven into a war zone. At least fifteen cars were burning out of control. Glass and flaming wreckage were scattered everywhere, and several shops and nearby buildings were also engulfed in flames.

Claudia drove in as close as she could, and then she and Harvath jumped out of the car and began running. It was immediately evident that this had been no accident. A very large explosive device had been detonated right when the motorcade passed. Harvath saw Claudia draw her weapon.

"How about me?" he asked.

Without breaking stride, Claudia reached underneath her blazer, withdrew a short Walther P38K and tossed it to Harvath. She pressed her walkie-talkie against her mouth and began shouting orders.

When she finally came up for air, she turned to Harvath and said, "One of the plainclothes men said he thinks the motorcycles were taken out by a sniper. When they went down, the convoy stopped and that's when the explosion happened. I have the helicopter searching the area, and the city police are setting up roadblocks."

The fire eventually stopped them from getting any closer, and Scot stood by while Claudia tried to coordinate the collective efforts of the police and military personnel via walkie-talkie. When emergency crews arrived on the scene, it took them over three hours to get the fires under control. It was another four hours before the techs had accumulated any evidence.

The explosive device had been a car bomb. Based on the make and model of the car, residents said they thought it had been parked on the street for at least two days, but nobody was certain, nor could they come up with a description of who had been driving it. The police had only one witness, but they immediately discounted her. She was an old gypsy who roamed the neighborhood poking through garbage cans with a stick, and was thought to be quite mad. She said she had seen the driver and, when asked to describe him, replied simply that it was none other than Satan. The Devil had looked at her with eyes that could change colors—from silver to black, like the moon turning into slate.

Standing nearby, Harvath could make out enough of the woman's heavily accented German, along with her gestures, to pick up on what she was talking about. His suspicions had been right on the mark. The same person who had killed Philip Jamek wanted Gerhard Miner dead. The Lions had known something, and someone had wanted to make sure they were kept quiet—permanently.

Harvath was trying to connect the loose array of dots in his mind when Claudia came over and spoke to him. "There's something up the street I'd like you to take a look at."

"What?" he asked.

She didn't answer. She began walking and Scot followed.

Harvath did not believe in coincidences. As a matter of fact, swearing off coincidences was how you stayed alive in his line of work. They just simply didn't exist. That was what made the attack on the convoy all the more disturbing. His two best leads were now dead. What were the odds that Jamek and Miner had intentionally been killed before they could tell Harvath, or anyone else for that matter, what they knew about that fateful night the Spec Ops team was taken out?

Claudia led him into a narrow apartment building and up several flights of stairs. In typical European fashion, there was no elevator, and they had to hoof it all the way up.

On the top landing, she motioned toward an open apartment door, where inside a team of crime-scene technicians was busy at work. Claudia spoke briefly with the lead investigator and then translated for Scot.

"According to the landlady, the occupant of this flat has been out of town on vacation for the last week. The door shows signs of forced entry, but nothing appears to have been taken."

"And?"

"And wait till you see what's in the bedroom."

Claudia led Harvath past the photographers and men dusting for fingerprints. In the bedroom lying on the bed, next to a pane of glass that had been surgically removed from the window, was a long, black rifle.

"Do you recognize that?" asked Claudia.

"It looks like a fifty-caliber Barrett sniper rifle. One of the best money can buy."

"Very good. Ever seen one of these before?" asked Claudia as she ejected a round from the five-round detachable magazine. "They've already been dusted for prints. There's nothing on them."

Harvath accepted the almost six-inch-long projectile and held it up to the light coming in through the window. "This is a Barnes bullet."

"You can tell the manufacturer just by looking at it?"

"There's nothing else like it. It has a very distinct shape. The U.S. Navy had it developed for use by their SEAL snipers in the Gulf War. This bullet holds the world record at one thousand meters, and SEALs have even reported confirmed kills with it at over two thousand."

"So taking out the motorcycle escorts with head shots at four hundred meters would have been easy."

"I wouldn't say easy. My guess is the shooter used the attached bipod for added stability and was obviously careful with his ammunition selection. If you look here, you can see that he also used a top-of-the-line Leupold scope with an optical filter to reduce sun glare."

"What about a laser range finder?"

"Did your people find one in the apartment?"

"No, it just seems like it would have been helpful for a shot like this."

"Probably, but to tell you the truth, range finder or not, whoever we're dealing with is one incredibly skilled marksman who really knows his equipment."

"Who would want to kill Miner?" Claudia asked as she took back the fifty-caliber bullet from Harvath.

"Where do you want me to start, and how much time do you have? His group did a lot of murder for hire before kidnapping President Rutledge."

"I know, but it was common knowledge that we were going to lock him up and throw away the key. His trial was nothing more than a formality. He was essentially finished for life. Why go to all this trouble?"

"Maybe somebody thought jail was too good for him," Scot offered.

"Maybe. But someone also went to a lot of trouble in Macau to kill Jamek as well. Someone wanted to make sure both Miner and Jamek were definitely dead. Why? It doesn't make sense."

Maybe it didn't make sense to Claudia, but a picture was beginning to form in Harvath's mind.

While Claudia returned to conducting her investigation, Harvath made plans to leave Switzerland. Where he was headed next was one of the last places he thought he would ever see again.

7

Three days later, as his Lufthansa flight turned to make its final approach into Israel's Ben Gurion Airport, Harvath closed his eyes and tried to stop thinking about Claudia. He told himself he had been crazy for believing a solid relationship was within his grasp.

In his line of work, he couldn't become too attached to anything or anyone. It was the axiom he had lived by for more years than he cared to remember. He should have known from the start he couldn't have a future with her. Claudia knew better too, yet they allowed themselves to fall for each other deeply and quickly. It had been as if they had known right at the beginning that the end was in sight and therefore tried to squeeze in as much passion as possible. Harvath thought that the experience should have left him feeling good, somehow satiated, but it hadn't.

When Harvath stepped onto the pavement outside the arrivals hall of Ben Gurion, the hot evening wind on his face felt like the blast from a blow dryer. The normally high airport security presence of Israeli soldiers and police was exponentially higher now as Israel continued to deal with waves of reprisals for the Hand of God attack at Medina. The tension in the air was palpable.

Back in the sandbox, Harvath said to himself. The *sandbox* was the affectionate term American intelligence operatives and Special Operations personnel had for the Mideast. During his tenure with SEAL Six, now known as

Dev Group, Harvath had been involved in many white and black ops in the sandbox. Though he had enjoyed the adrenaline rush that his assignments had provided, he didn't miss the Mideast one bit. It was always too hot or too cold, and the sand got everywhere, no matter what precautions you took. Still, though, Scot longed for his action days. Not that being assigned to protect the president of the United States didn't have its moments. It did, but once you'd played offense, it was almost impossible to move over to defense. Either you took it to them, or you sat back and waited until they brought it to you. Harvath was not made for sitting back and waiting.

Though he didn't particularly like the sandbox, part of him felt it would be worth the heat, the cold, and even the sand just to get back on the offensive. He had to laugh at himself. What was he doing right now? He *was* on the offensive. This was what he loved doing. He was made for this—the hunt, and when necessary, even the kill.

In an odd, roundabout way, Harvath had found his dream job, though he didn't know how long it would last. Even the president would have a limit to his largesse. But for now, Harvath was receiving a healthy Secret Service paycheck to utilize his Special Operations skills. And on top of it all, there was a twist. For once, he was in charge of himself. There was no command structure telling him where to be and what to do. Sure, he was expected to report in and had done so from the U.S. embassies in Hong Kong and Bern, but other than that, he was on his own. He had been given carte blanche, and for good reason. The president and those closest to him knew that Agent Scot Harvath completed his missions no matter what the cost. For him, there was no option other than total success.

He climbed into one of the shared taxis, known by Israelis as a *sherut*, which were always lined up outside the airport. When it was full, it pulled away from the curb and began the twenty-eight-mile drive to Jerusalem. The vans operated on a fixed route. There were no set stops; passengers simply indicated to the driver when they wanted to get out. Though the van would take longer to get to his hotel than would a regular taxi, Harvath preferred the anonymity of the *sherut* and the opportunity it provided to quietly reimmerse himself in Israeli culture.

An hour-and-a-half later, Harvath descended from the *sherut* on Nablus Road in the heart of the ancient city of Jerusalem. The smells and sounds had steadily been drifting through the van's open windows, but it wasn't until he stepped outside that the many memories came flooding back. There was a special aura about Jerusalem, a certain magic, tinged with the perfume of ever-present danger. The Jerusalem from his past that he had known during his SEAL days, had now drawn him back to become part of its present. He suddenly felt haunted by a feeling of foreboding. It was the same feeling he had experienced one night many months ago in the White House situation room as he watched Operation Rapid Return unfold on the flat-panel monitors throughout the room. The feeling had grown in its intensity as he watched the soldiers approach their target. Moments later, he saw the ambush and murder of the entire team and all but one of the support operatives, who were Israeli intelligence agents. The sole survivor of the doomed mission had dropped out of sight immediately afterward. There were even rumors that he had died, but Harvath's intelligence led him to believe otherwise. It was this man that he was here in Israel to meet, and hopefully use to his advantage.

Harvath picked up his bag and stared at the façade of the old Jerusalem Hotel. Conventional wisdom would have one believe that in a war-torn country like Israel the bigger, Western-style hotels were the safest, but Harvath knew differently. If there were any local acts of terrorism, they would be carried out by Palestinians against major Israeli or western targets. No one would waste time on a small hotel like this, especially one with such strong Arab ties. Those were Harvath's tactical reasons; his personal reasons were different.

The Jerusalem Hotel was perfectly situated less than one hundred meters from the Damascus Gate and the Old City. It lay within an old Arab mansion of thick-cut creamy limestone accented with Arabic plasterwork. The fourteen rooms were fitted out with arabesque furnishings, and the traditional architecture included arched windows, high ceilings, flagstone floors, and even a secluded vine garden. The only thing better than the price, at less than one hundred dollars a night, was that the same family had been running the hotel since the 1960s, and neither better nor friendlier service could be found anywhere else in Jerusalem.

After unpacking his bags, Harvath walked back downstairs and hailed a cab, giving the driver the address of one of his favorite restaurants, Le Tsriff, at number 5 Horkanos Street. The driver was a chatty man who immediately asked Harvath where he was from. Harvath gave his standard, nonthreatening answer of "Canada" and made small talk with the man until they reached the restaurant.

The place was just as he had remembered it. Though the decor left a little to be desired, he was here to eat, not to shoot a photo spread for *Architectural Digest*. He was shown to a table in the quaint outdoor dining area, where he enjoyed an excellent meal.

After dinner, Harvath decided to take a stroll. He had long ago learned to take his peaceful moments where he could find them. Who knew what tomorrow would bring?

He tried to ignore Jerusalem's intense security and instead focused on the history of the city as he followed the Jaffa Road and entered the Old City through the Jaffa Gate. He wandered through the Armenian Quarter, past the Christian Cathedral of St. James and into the Jewish Quarter until he found himself standing in the plaza along the Western Wall. Though it was late at night, people were still placing their pieces of paper with their wishes for God into spaces in the wall. Scot thought about Claudia and tried to remind himself that everything had happened for the best. Even so, he still wrote something on a small scrap of paper and placed it between two of the ancient weathered stones.

At the Ecce Homo Arch, he turned around to admire the brilliantly lit Dome of the Rock. The entire Temple Mount, with its Dome of the Rock, Dome of the Chain, al-Aqsa Mosque, and Museum of Islamic Art, was the focus of the Muslim faith in Jerusalem. It had also become the most hotly contested piece of real estate in the Arab-Israeli conflict—recognized as sacred ground by both sides.

The fact that three of the world's greatest religions

could have three of their holiest sites shouldered together within the tiny space of Jerusalem's Old City and yet their followers have such an immensely difficult time getting along had always confounded Harvath. Religions were supposed to represent tolerance. But just like everything else in life, Harvath had learned, it wasn't necessarily the philosophy that was flawed, but rather the human beings who were trying to interpret it.

From the Damascus Gate, it was a short walk back to the Jerusalem Hotel. A student of history and a warrior himself, Harvath reflected upon all of the destruction and death that had been wreaked in the name of religion. He doubted God supported any of it. A Delta Force guy Scot had once known put it best. The man had been brought up Protestant and was marrying an Irish Catholic girl. In the mandated Pre-Cana marriage counseling, the priest asked the hopeful groom how he thought their marriage would fare, considering their different religious backgrounds. The Delta Force operative was quick to respond, "To tell you the truth, Father, I don't think God has a favorite football team, or a favorite religion."

His friend had summed it up pretty well, Harvath believed, and with a little dash of humor thrown in to boot. The priest, though, wasn't amused. He was from Notre Dame.

Reflecting on that story normally made Scot smile, but not tonight. There was an ominous air hanging over the city, as if something evil was about to make itself known.

8

While the Dome of the Rock might have been the crown jewel of Jerusalem, the adjacent al-Aqsa Mosque was the city's main place of Islamic worship. It was from this point that the Prophet Muhammad was said to have ascended into heaven. It was also from here that the al-Aqsa Martyrs Brigades, the infamous Palestinian faction that had long plagued Israel with countless suicide bombings and other deadly terrorist attacks, had taken their name. Friday's noon prayer service at the al-Aqsa always drew enormous crowds of devout Muslims.

Most of the mosque's façade, as well as the façades of several other buildings on the Temple Mount, were undergoing much needed renovations and were covered with scaffolding. The scaffolding was covered with life-size fabric depictions of what each building would look like when completed. As the cracked and dusty earth of the Temple Mount baked in the scorching summer sun, the only hint of a breeze was the occasional flutter of one of the intricate architectural renderings.

When prayers were finished, the worshippers dutifully proceeded down the al-Aqsa's long corridor toward the exit. Though many would have enjoyed lingering in the cool of the mosque's interior, it was only midday on a Friday, and there were important errands and jobs to be gotten to.

Thousands filed outside and began making their way

toward the many ancient gates that led from the Temple Mount back into Jerusalem's Old City. Those without pressing engagements stopped at the holy Al-Kas Fountain and chatted.

As the last of the worshippers filed into the sparsely treed area outside, a spray of machine gun fire leapt out from behind the fabric façade of the mosque's scaffolding. In an instant, the square was engulfed in a storm of panic as bodies were sawn in half from large-caliber rounds. The once parched, pale ground quickly ran crimson with rivers of blood. As the frenzied mob ran from the front of the mosque toward what they hoped would be safety, another course of leaded fire erupted from the scaffolding of the nearby Dome of Learning. Muslim worshippers, as well as crowds of tourists, were running for their lives. The religious protocol dictating that non-Muslims be restricted to using only two of the many gates that led from the Temple Mount was all but forgotten. The only thing that Jews, Christians, and Muslim's alike were thinking about was getting out alive.

Though security forces were on the scene, nothing could be done to stop the carnage. The machine guns chewed through the crowds and the surrounding buildings in less than two minutes. Once their supply of ammunition was exhausted, the guns fell silent.

Suddenly, from the top of the scaffolding covering the Grammar College, came the deadly *thump . . . thump . . . thump* of three mortar rounds being loosed. The projectiles hung in the air like perfect NFL punts, and then came screaming back down toward earth. The first two hit their target with devastating accuracy, and the explosions ripped gaping holes into the gilded Dome of the Rock, ending the lives of thirty-two people inside. The third projectile landed in a heavily populated section of the Muslim Quarter, just north of the Temple Mount, killing scores more. It was the worst terrorist attack in Jerusalem's history.

9

Back at the Jerusalem Hotel, Scot Harvath was sitting outside at the hotel's sunny garden patio restaurant reading *The International Herald Tribune* when the machine gun fire started. Even at this distance, he could tell it was from a heavy-caliber weapon and it was lasting far longer than most such incidents. Jerusalem was not normally the site of prolonged firefights. Those were reserved for the occupied territories, but even they were carried out in bursts, not a continuous stream of fire.

Then came the explosions from the mortar fire—the third and final explosion sounding too close to the hotel for Harvath's liking. So much for his theory of being safe at a minority-owned-and-operated hotel. All at once, the air was filled with the desperate sound of sirens rushing to the scene. Harvath was tempted to investigate, but then thought better of it. He needed to stay put and wait for the man he was hoping would make contact with him.

Before leaving Switzerland, Harvath had spent days making phone calls and had sent countless e-mails trying to track down a man named Ari Schoen. He had been one of the Mossad's top agents and part of the Israeli contingent assigned to Operation Rapid Return. Shortly after the mission, the Israelis claimed that he had died, but Harvath believed otherwise. Through his extensive network of contacts, Harvath had been able to locate the elusive man, who appeared to be very much alive. It was Harvath's hope that Schoen might be able to tell him something, anything, about what had happened that night and who had coordinated the ambush.

After the incident at the Temple Mount, Harvath passed the rest of the day and most of the night inside the hotel glued to either the television set that had been placed in the garden restaurant, or the one in his room.

The next afternoon, halfway through his lunch, a bellboy brought a package to his table. Harvath tipped him a few shekels and, once the boy had walked back inside, carefully opened it. Inside was a digital phone. No note and no number, just the phone. As it was already turned on, Harvath placed it on the table next to him and waited.

Within minutes, the phone rang.

"Shalom," said Harvath as he opened the phone and raised it to his ear.

"Mr. Harvath, how nice that you speak our language," replied the man on the other end. He had a deep voice accentuated by a thick lisp.

"I know enough to get by."

"And enough to choose an inconspicuous, yet excellent hotel."

"I'm starting to have my doubts about its location."

"No doubt you are referring to the attack at the Temple Mount," said the voice.

"No doubt."

"An unfortunate incident and one that I am afraid kept me from contacting you earlier; but, in the face of Arab terror and aggression against the Israeli people, it was inevitable that the Israelis would eventually employ the same tactics."

"So, this was an Israeli attack against Arabs?" asked Harvath.

"Indeed. Two remote-controlled machine guns on the Temple Mount opened fire on a large crowd of Muslims leaving the noon service at the al-Aqsa Mosque."

"Opening fire on a group of innocent people doesn't sound very civilized to me. Is this what Israel has come to?"

"For some, yes."

"Who? The Hand of God?"

"I am confident that sometime today the newspapers and TV stations will break the news that the Hand of God is taking credit for this recent attack. Though many Israelis abhor violence, this group is reaching almost a cultlike status among the young and old alike."

"You seem very well informed, Mr. Schoen."

"You'll find I am extremely well informed, but please refrain from speaking my name in public. I know the phone is digital, but we must still be careful. Now, I trust you had a good lunch?"

"Good enough."

"Excellent. There will be a white taxi waiting for you outside the Damascus Gate to the Old City. The driver is wearing a brown sport coat. Tell him you wish to be taken to a reputable antiques shop, and he will bring you to me."

"And where, exactly, are you?"

"I'd rather not say, Mr. Harvath. My security precautions may seem a bit extreme, but believe me, they are in my own best interest. Please, let's not waste any time. The driver has been instructed to wait no more than five minutes. I will explain everything once you are here."

Harvath didn't like the cloak-and-dagger routine, but he had little choice but to comply.

The driver never said a word as he headed northwest along the Jaffa Road away from the Old City. Harvath noticed the bulge of a rather large weapon beneath his sport coat and guessed that this was no ordinary taxi driver.

Finally, the cab pulled up in front of an old four-story building in the popular Ben Yehuda district. The storefront consisted chiefly of two large windows crammed full of antique furniture, paintings, and fixtures. The gilded sign above the entryway read, "Thames & Cherwell Antiques," followed by translations in Hebrew and Arabic.

With an utter lack of ceremony, the driver popped the power locks and jerked his head toward the left, indicating that Scot should get out of his cab and enter the shop.

"I guess you're not going to get the door for me, so this is probably good-bye. It was a pleasure chatting with you," said Harvath as he climbed out of the taxi. Once his passenger was on the pavement, the driver flipped a switch beneath the dash and the door automatically slammed shut.

Neat trick, thought Harvath as the cab sped away down the street.

When he entered the store, a small brass bell above the door announced Harvath's arrival. He waited a beat, and when no one appeared, began to look around the dimly lit room. It was packed with tapestries, furniture, and no end of faded bric-a-brac.

When he neared a narrow mahogany door, a series of

small bulbs in a brass plaque changed from red to green and the door clicked open.

Another neat trick, Harvath thought as he pulled the door toward him to reveal a small, wood-paneled elevator. Once inside, he waited for the door to close on its own, which it did, and then the elevator slowly started to rise. He waited a second for elevator music to kick in and when it didn't, he started humming "The Girl from Ipanema" to himself.

He was still humming when the elevator stopped and the door opened onto a long hallway, its floor covered by an intricately patterned oriental runner. The walls were painted a deep forest green and were lined with framed prints of foxhunting, fly-fishing, and crumbling abbeys. As Scot walked forward, he noticed infrared sensors placed every few feet and guessed that there were probably pressure sensitive plates beneath the runner. This was one man who took his security precautions very seriously.

At the end of the hall, Scot found himself in a very large room, more dimly lit than the shop downstairs. It was paneled from floor to ceiling, like the elevator, with a rich, deeply colored wood. With its fireplace, billiards table, overstuffed leather chairs and couches, it felt more like a British gentleman's club than the upper-floor office of a shop in West Jerusalem.

"I apologize for the subterfuge, Mr. Harvath," came Schoen's voice from the far corner of the room.

Harvath peered through the semidarkness and could barely make him out. He was sitting near a pair of heavy silk draperies, which had been drawn tight against the windows.

"There are certain people who, if they knew I was still alive, would very much want me dead. So, I do what I have to do," he continued. "I would be happy to bring the lights up a little, but I want to warn you that you may find my appearance a bit difficult."

"I think I can handle it," replied Harvath.

"Lights!" commanded Schoen, and the light level in the room slowly began to increase until he said, "Enough."

Harvath's eyes were now able to see that the man was sitting in a wheelchair. As Schoen rolled himself closer, Scot could see that the man's hands, face, and neck had been terribly burned. Even though Harvath was slightly taken aback by his appearance, he did not allow his face to show what he was feeling.

Schoen's suit was navy blue, and he wore a white shirt with a British regimental tie. A blue-and-green tartan blanket lay across his legs. Now that he saw the man in person, Harvath realized that his lisp sprang from the fact that a good part of his lips had been burned away from his face.

"Please, Mr. Harvath. Take a seat." *Pleeth, Mr. Harvath . . .*

"Thank you," Scot replied as he sat down in one of the oxblood leather club chairs and glanced at the silver-framed photographs the man had positioned on an adjacent console table.

"Are you a whiskey man, Mr. Harvath?"

"Scotch whiskey, yes."

"A man after my own heart."

Schoen wheeled himself over to an antique globe and lifted the hinged northern hemisphere. He retrieved two glasses and a bottle, placed them on a tray across the arms of his wheelchair, and wheeled himself back over next to the chair Harvath was sitting in.

"Nineteen sixty-three Black Bowmore," he said as he placed the tray on the small end table between them. "Look at that color, Mr. Harvath. Black as pitch, as my British friends would say."

"Very nice," replied Harvath as the man began to pour.

"The whiskey was heavily sherried and aged for a very long time. That's where this magnificent color comes from."

"*L'chaim,*" said Harvath, raising his glass in toast.

"God bless America and may he also save the queen," said Schoen with a deformed smile.

They savored the rare scotch in silence for a moment. Such was the nature of doing business in the Middle East. First a refreshment was offered and then polite conversation was made until finally the participants arrived at the point. Negotiations over even the smallest of items could take days. But, as the man who sat next to him was a former intelligence agent, Harvath hoped things would move a bit faster.

"You're quite the anglophile, I notice," said Scot.

"I was based in London for a very long time."

"It's a beautiful city."

"Indeed. And the countryside is amazing. Especially the Cotswolds."

"Did you spend a lot of time in the countryside while in England?"

"Yes, I visited my son quite often."

"Really? What does he do?"

"He rowed at university there, but now he's deceased."

"I'm sorry."

"I am too. All in good time are called to God. Some, though, are called too soon and for the wrong reasons. My son's loss is the hardest thing I have ever had to bear, but that's not why you are here. It's a funny characteristic of the infirm; we learn to live within our memories, the past often being the most pleasant part of our lives, and often forget ourselves in the presence of guests. My day will eventually come, but while I am waiting, let's talk about why you are here."

"I'm here because I need information."

"You want to know what happened that night in Sidon?"

"Yes."

"To save us both some time, why don't you tell me what you already know."

"The night Operation Rapid Return was ambushed, I was in the situation room at the White House. I saw everything up to and including our Special Operations team entering the building where it was thought the president was being held. Then there was the explosion. You were part of the Israeli team on the ground lending logistical support and were the only survivor. Shortly thereafter, the Mossad declared you dead. Why?"

"After the explosion, I tried to ascertain whether there were any other survivors. I didn't see any, but I did see something else."

"What?"

"Someone who didn't belong there."

"What do you mean?"

"He wasn't part of the mission team and was acting far too calm, considering what had just taken place. I remember thinking he was somehow involved with the explosion and had probably remained behind to make sure the job was done."

"What did you do?"

"There wasn't much I could do. I was too badly injured. I raised my pistol and tried to shoot at him, but he got away."

"What did he look like?" asked Harvath.

"I couldn't see him very well, but he obviously got a good look at me."

"Why do you say that?"

"After that night, I was subjected to many long and painful surgeries. To make a long story short, while I was convalescing, the man reappeared and tried to kill me."

"How can you be sure it was the same person?"

"Because of the eyes."

Harvath's body tensed.

"Never in my life have I seen eyes like those," continued Schoen in a slow, deliberate voice. "They were silver, like the color of cold, polished knife blades."

Silence filled the room for several moments. Schoen had struck a nerve. Harvath's silence was an admission that he knew those silver eyes all too well himself.

"But why would he want to kill you?" asked Harvath, trying to sort through the implications of Schoen's account.

"I think he believes I saw his face and could identify him. Terrorists' anonymity is often their best weapon, especially these days. The last thing they need is someone who can identify them in an international court or, worse still, mount a campaign to track them down and take them out. I was a loose end that needed to be tied up."

"So what happened?"

"Two colleagues of mine happened to come to visit quite unexpectedly that evening. They arrived just in time. I was in no condition to defend myself. They surprised the killer, and he leapt from the second-story window of my hospital room. One of my colleagues chased him, but the man managed to escape. Shortly thereafter, I was moved to a secret facility to complete my rehabilitation."

"And you've been in hiding ever since?"

"I don't look at it as hiding, Mr. Harvath. I look at it as a sort of early retirement. I get to keep my hand in the game and sleep at night. Not a lot of people can do that."

"That's true, but if I found you, what's to stop someone else?"

"You found me because I wanted you to find me. We have a common interest, you and I."

"Which is?"

"We both want to get our hands on whoever was responsible for the explosion that killed your Special Operations team and turned me into the shell of a man you see before you."

"Do you have any leads?"

"Yes."

"Have you acted on them?"

"In my own way, I have."

"What about your government? You lost good agents on that assignment as well."

"That is a *sticky* situation as you Americans say. My government seems either unable or unwilling to bring this matter to a close, even though I have been able to gather what I feel is considerable evidence."

"I can't understand why, but I can guarantee you that my government has every intention of bringing to justice whoever was involved in the murder of our operatives."

"I was counting on that."

"Well, keep on counting. I am going to personally see to it that each and every one of them pays. I made a promise, and I have the full backing of the United States."

"Excellent. Why don't you take your drink and follow me. I want to show you what I have been able to compile so far."

Schoen took his time laying out the evidence he had gathered and his theory. When he was finished, Scot could understand why the Israeli government was skeptical. Any single piece of evidence examined by itself was nothing more than circumstantial. Even lumping it all together, there were still huge holes, but in Schoen's defense, there was somewhat of a pattern, especially when he filled in the blanks and explained what he felt the real story was.

"Interesting," said Harvath as he drained the last of his Bowmore.

"It's more than interesting, Mr. Harvath; it's conclusive."

Scot knew it was a good hunch, but it was far from conclusive. Schoen wanted vengeance so badly he could taste it, like bile in his throat. Harvath felt sorry for him. His life was ruined. His only son was dead, and he wanted to hold somebody accountable for what had gone wrong with the world, his world. Somebody needed to pay. Harvath knew the feeling. There were some things in life that could never be forgiven or forgotten. The ambush that wiped out the Rapid Return team and burned Ari Schoen so terribly was one of those things.

"Ari, I give you my word. Whoever is behind this thing, I am going to take them down."

"I want to be there when it happens," said Schoen.

"That's a promise I can't make."

"Then at least keep me in the loop. I have access to a lot of sources and a lot of information. I could be quite valuable to you. Think of me as kind of your man behind the curtain."

"I'll tell you what. I am going to look into this further and maybe I'd be willing to share information with you, but it's a two-way street. I'd expect you to update me with anything you come across."

"Deal."

They traded secure phone numbers, and Scot thanked him again for the scotch. Schoen showed him to the elevator and they shook hands. Harvath wasn't humming on the way down. He felt terrible for the man. That said, everyone knew there was an inherent risk in the job. It was one of those things operatives always thought about—"getting killed, or worse." Schoen was a prime example of what "or worse" could be. Scot wondered if maybe Schoen would have been better off dying that night.

10

Harvath exited Thames & Cherwell Antiques, turned left, and was making his way back toward the Jaffa Road when he heard the squeal of tires.

Just as he turned to look for the source of the noise, three men jumped out of a parked car right in front of him. They were solid, with muscles bulging beneath their suit coats. Their fashionable clothing seemed oddly out of place. Each pair of eyes was set in a cold, hard stare as they closed in on him.

"What is this all about?" Harvath asked, but the men didn't respond.

At that moment, Harvath heard the squeal of tires again, this time as a white baker's van pulled into the street next to them and stopped. When the side door began to slide open, he knew their little party was about to get bigger. Harvath didn't wait for additional men to climb out of the van.

With a swift chop, he popped the man opposite him in the windpipe and watched him crumple to the pavement like a flimsy paper doll. The other two men were on him in an instant. The first man made the mistake of lunging for Harvath's collar. Harvath grabbed his hand and bent it back over his forearm in a move known in the Japanese art of aikido as *kotegaeshi*. The man landed smack on his back on the pavement. When the second man came for him, Harvath reversed the energy of his attack and threw him with a move known as *irimi nage*. The man's head hit the fender of a nearby car, tearing a large, bleeding gash above his right eye.

The first attacker Harvath had put down had righted himself and now sprang from the pavement. Harvath met him halfway with a well swung elbow, catching the man full force in the mouth. He howled in pain as he spat blood and teeth into the street.

Before Harvath could make another move, a second group of men jumped from the van and pinned him down. Someone produced a hypo-gun and jabbed the sharp tip into his shoulder. The drug worked immediately. Harvath's vision started to dim, but not before he saw a face that he thought he recognized.

11

As Harvath came to, he could make out the sound of jet engines and knew he was in some kind of airplane. He tried to move his arms, but as his eyes began to focus, he saw that he was cuffed to his seat. The man whose head he had bounced off the car fender earlier was taking his blood pressure.

"It looks like he's coming around," said the man, sporting two butterfly bandages above his eye.

As a figure appeared from the cockpit, Harvath looked around and realized the small private jet was filled with several other passengers, all more or less of the same build and *don't fuck with me* look. Before Harvath could say anything, the man who had emerged from the cockpit drew alongside him and said, "It looks like sleeping beauty is finally awake."

Harvath had been right. He had indeed recognized one of the men who had jumped him in Jerusalem. "Well, well. If it isn't Rick, the Prick, Morrell. It's been a long time," he said.

"Not long enough," replied the man.

"Let's see here," continued Harvath: "substandard help, a private jet, ability to get me out of the country, and someone foolish enough to bankroll all of this and put you in charge. Still working for the CIA, Ricky?"

"Aren't you clever. You still don't know how to keep your ass out of a sling, though, do you? You've ruffled some pretty serious feathers, Harvath."

"I know. It was very un-Christian of me not to give you that loan for your sex change operation. I still believe you'll regret it, but if you've thought it through and it's what you really want, then I'm behind you one hundred percent. Untie me and I'll write you a check."

Three seats back, someone snickered.

"Zip it!" snapped Morrell, who then turned back to Harvath. "You know, I never thought much of your sense of humor."

"Actually, Ricky, you never thought much of anything—not honor, not integrity, not character . . . and that's why you washed out as a SEAL. But until places like the CIA raise their hiring standards, I guess guys like you will always have a job."

Morrell moved in and smiled at Harvath, but it wasn't with goodwill. "I had full license to bring you in by any means necessary; alive or otherwise. I could have easily overlooked an air bubble in the hypo and left you for dead on the street back in Jerusalem, so don't talk to me about integrity and character. We are exactly alike, you and me."

"That's where you're wrong, Morrell. You and I are nothing alike. We never were. I don't like your politics, and I don't like the way you do business."

"I'll remember that next time I'm asked to use my discretion in bringing you in. Now, it's a long flight back to Virginia. Can I get you anything?"

"Sure. First, I want a cocktail and then I want some answers. Who the fuck authorized you to pick me up, and what's this all about? And while we're at it, take these cuffs off me."

"No, I don't think so. I think I'd prefer to have you stay

right where you are. As far as your answers are concerned, you'll have plenty of time to ask questions when we get home. In the meantime, as I am still within the purview of my discretion, I think I may be able to accommodate you on that cocktail. It won't be exactly what you had in mind, but I think it will make for a very peaceful flight for the rest of us."

Morrell snapped his fingers, and the man with the butterfly bandages handed over a syringe, as well as a moist cotton ball.

Morrell rolled up Harvath's sleeve and swabbed his muscular forearm with antiseptic as he readied the needle.

"You're already looking at a very serious ass-kicking as it is, Ricky," said Scot. "Knock me out again and I'm going to pack a lunch and make it an all-day affair."

"I'll be looking forward to it," said Morrell as he plunged the needle into Harvath's arm and watched his eyes roll back up into his head.

12

In the cozy Hemingway Bar of the Paris Ritz, the assassin sat eating one of the hotel's famous club sandwiches, delighted by the lead story in the paper. The attacks on the mosques in Medina and Jerusalem were officially being called the worst ever against Muslims and two of the worst terrorist attacks in history. Combined, they were projected to exceed the death toll of September 11.

The article also included the full letter sent to *The Jerusalem Post* by the Hand of God Organization claiming credit.

Arab and Muslim countries around the world were calling for sanctions against Israel, while many Israeli citizens supported the organization and claimed that the Muslim world had brought this suffering upon itself. The Israeli government emphatically denied any knowledge of or support for the Hand of God Organization. They also stated that they had no idea how the terrorists got their hands on the Israeli weaponry used in the Medina attack, how equipment for the second attack was smuggled onto the Temple Mount, or how the terrorists knew restoration workers would not be in that area on the day in question.

The assassin smiled. With enough money, anything was possible.

The article went on to detail the bitter outrage felt throughout the Arab world. Legions of Islamic voices called for the blood of the Jews and a true holy war to decimate the nation of Israel and her American supporters once and for all. *Let them come*, the terrorist thought. *Let them come.*

At midnight, the assassin sat in the shadow of the Notre Dame at the Petit Pont Café reading another newspaper and drinking a coffee. A small duffel bag sat beneath the table. Ten minutes later, a blue Renault truck pulled up and double-parked outside. A man in a cap and tan coveralls with the name of his company, Premiere Piscine & Spa, embroidered across the back, entered and ordered a drink at the bar. The assassin watched him. He was right on time.

The man smoked a cigarette and made small talk with the bartender. Ten minutes later, he paid his bill and went downstairs to use the toilet. He had more than enough time to get to his job at the Ritz and they never let him use their toilet. The Ritz demanded that all deliveries, repairs to common areas, and the cleaning of the pool happen in the dead of night, as if by magic, so that guests would never be troubled by the appearance of any stray workmen.

The man stood on the dirty footrests of the Turkish toilet and began to relieve himself. When his steady stream of relief could be heard outside, the assassin emerged from the adjacent *cabine*, jerked open the pool cleaner's door, and put two bullets into the back of his head with a silenced French nine-millimeter MAS pistol. The assassin dragged the lifeless body out, careful not to get any blood on the floor, and crammed it into an adjoining storage closet, where it wouldn't be found until, at the earliest, the next afternoon.

Quickly, the assassin pulled on an identical cap and pair of tan coveralls with Premiere Piscine & Spa embroidered across the back and then threw the duffel into the storage closet and closed the door. With the dangling cigarette and lowered head, no one suspected the figure leaving the café was anyone other than the pool man.

The assassin drove to a narrow, dimly lit street in Paris's thirteenth arrondissement. A large key was fitted into a rusting lock, which opened a set of aging double doors, and the truck was backed into a filthy rented garage. It took the assassin only a matter of moments to load the required materials and be back on the road.

At the service entrance of the Ritz, the assassin parked the blue Renault and off-loaded a host of pool-cleaning supplies onto a handcart, including three large plastic barrels labeled "Chlorine."

The security at the hotel was the absolute best in Paris. With the wide array of celebrities and dignitaries the hotel hosted, it had to be. The guard at the service entrance was paid to be vigilant, and he knew all of the regular service providers, including the pool cleaner.

"Where is Jacques tonight?" he asked, trying to get a good look beneath the cap at the pool cleaner's unusual eyes.

"Migraine," responded the assassin with a disinterested, blue-collar Parisian accent.

"I've never seen you before."

"Jacques keeps all the important jobs for himself. I get the shitty pools out in the suburbs. But, at least I don't have to do them in the middle of the night. Do you have a copy of the fax?"

The man looked through the stack of paperwork he had been handed at the beginning of his shift, and sure enough, it included a fax from Premiere Piscine & Spa, which stated that Jacques would not be able to make it tonight and that his coworker would be doing the pool cleaning. Faking it had been easy. The assassin had contacted Premiere weeks before and had asked to be sent a quote for pool cleaning. With that in hand, all that needed to be done was to copy their cover sheet and program a new fax machine with the correct number, so that when it arrived at the Ritz, everything would appear to be in order.

The guard recognized the blue Renault, the fax was in keeping with hotel service policy, the replacement was wearing the company uniform, and the entire pool area— the entire hotel, for that matter—was monitored with video cameras, so he could see no reason not to let the worker pass. He did, though, have one more question.

"Why all the supplies?"

"Bacteria."

"Bacteria?"

"The last time Jacques was here, he noticed a slight buildup. He didn't have enough chemicals with him to do a proper shock treatment, so it was on the schedule for tonight. If you don't want the pool cleaned . . ."

That was all the guard needed to hear. He buzzed the door and explained where the freight elevator was and how to find the pool. The assassin made sure to use the baseball-style cap as a shield from the surveillance cameras while pushing the handcart deep into the bowels of the hotel.

It was not the first time the assassin had been in the Ritz pool area, nonetheless it was still awe-inspiring. It was the largest pool in Paris and looked like a Roman bath. The walls and ceilings were painted with beautiful frescoes. An elevated, dome-covered bar and dining area looked out over the pool, where guests could swim above the mosaics of mermaids with golden hair playing golden harps. As an added extravagance, the Ritz had installed underwater speakers, which funneled soothing music beneath the water.

Ever mindful of the cameras, the assassin put on a pair of rubber gloves and set to work. First it was necessary to go through the motions of actually cleaning the pool—taking levels, skimming, scrubbing the sides and the bottom, then disabling the filters. Next came the chemical science.

The assassin opened the barrels marked "Chlorine" and, with a large plastic measuring cup, started pouring the powder into different areas around the pool. It was a chlorine hybrid that would continue to allow the water to smell chlorinated, but would create the perfect passive host for what was to come next.

Contained within the final barrel was a deadly toxic chemical named Sadim. The toxin took its name, in reverse, from the famous king whose touch turned everything to gold. In the case of Sadim, everything it touched turned to death. Victims experienced an agonizing and rapid demise. All that was necessary was that the toxin come into contact with bare skin. It was colorless, odorless, and extremely difficult to detect postmortem unless a pathologist or forensic toxicologist knew exactly what he or she was looking for.

After carefully removing the lid, the assassin scooped out the tiny time-release gel caps and began dropping them in the pool, focusing heavily on the deep end. The assassin looked at the wall clock. It was 2:30 A.M. Within three hours the toxin would be dissolved and have circulated throughout the entire pool.

The assassin left the building via the service entrance with the tan baseball cap still pulled down tight. Three blocks away from the Ritz, the truck and coveralls were exchanged for racing leathers and a black Triumph motorcycle. The assassin rode back to the Place Vendôme and waited for the service-entry security guard to finish his shift and make his way home.

When the man left the hotel in his gray, two-door Peugeot, the motorcycle was right behind. Ten minutes later at a stoplight in Pigalle, the assassin pulled alongside the car, withdrew the silenced nine-millimeter MAS, and delivered two perfect shots—one just between the eyes and another clean through the heart. The security guard had been the only one who could have positively identified the assassin, and now he lay slumped over his steering wheel, bathed in the neon lights of the Moulin Rouge. Satisfied with the evening's work, the assassin gunned the motorcycle and disappeared into the night.

13

At precisely 5:29 A.M. Prince Khalil of the Saudi royal family climbed into the small elevator with his two bodyguards and descended to the spa. He enjoyed his visits to Paris and especially the Ritz, where his every whim was catered to. Like many wealthy Arabs from the desert, he had developed an obsession with swimming. It was the one thing he did religiously every morning. He loved the Ritz's swimming pool with its underwater speakers. In fact, he had been toying with the idea of having some installed in his pool at home.

When the elevator opened onto the spa level, the manager was already waiting for the royal party. The spa would not open for regular guests for another hour. Having the pool all to himself was a Ritz perk that the prince distinctly enjoyed. One of the bodyguards handed the manager a Moby CD and the tuxedoed man quickly rushed off to prep the underwater sound system. The royal party proceeded on through the men's changing area and trod through the cold-water footbath before arriving poolside.

The prince was helped out of his plush Ritz bathrobe while he removed his matching slippers. Everything was neatly folded and placed on a nearby chaise lounge. The prince wore a blue Speedo bathing suit, and tinted goggles dangled from around his neck. He swung his arms back and forth to get the blood flowing and then raised the goggles and placed them over his eyes. After several squat thrusts, he moved to the edge of the pool. The manager reappeared and gave the bodyguards a discreet nod, indicating that the prince's music was playing, before disappearing back upstairs to his office.

Track number one on the Moby CD was "Honey," although the "Bodyrock" track might have been more appropriate for what happened when Prince Khalil hit the water. Within seconds he began bleeding from his eyes, his nose, ears, and rectum. At first his bodyguards thought that the prince had cut himself diving into the pool, but they quickly realized it was much more serious. The Prince's blood fanned out through the water like hundreds of crimson ribbons as he began to violently writhe beneath the surface.

Immediately, the royal bodyguards jumped into the pool to save their charge. Though they were fully clothed, the toxin worked its evil magic just as quickly, and soon the largest swimming pool in Paris was tinted bloodred, with three dead bodies floating in it.

Later that morning, the hotel's general manager received a letter containing an explanation of how to properly disinfect the pool and an apology for any inconvenience loss of the pool facilities may have caused hotel guests. It was signed, "The Hand of God."

14

When Scot awoke to sunlight streaming through a nearby window, the first thing he noticed was that he was no longer flexi-cuffed. There was an IV in his left arm, but other than that, he could move freely. He was lying down and had been covered with a blanket. A figure hovered at the foot of his bed.

"What the hell is going on? Where am I?" he asked as the figure began to take the shape of a middle-aged man in a dark, pin-striped suit.

"You were oversedated and have been out for quite some time," said the man. "I believe we owe you an apology, Agent Harvath."

"This has gone far beyond an apology. You can get in line behind Morrell and I'll deal with you next. I want some answers, now. Who are you and where am I?" Scot said groggily as he struggled to sit upright. His head was pounding and he was none too happy about it.

Someone had been standing in a corner of the room and that person now approached. Harvath recognized the voice immediately. It was his friend, the deputy director of the FBI, Gary Lawlor. "You're outside Williamsburg, Virginia, at Camp Peary."

"Gary? What the hell are you doing here? Better yet, what the hell am I doing here, and what have they done to me? My head feels like it's been split open with a sledgehammer," Scot said.

"I'm afraid we may have gotten our signals crossed," answered the man in the pin-striped suit.

"I can guarantee you did," said Scot. He noticed a pitcher on the bedside table. "Is that just plain water, or have you CIA guys put something funny in it?"

"No, it's plain water," said the man, who poured some into a plastic cup and handed it to Scot.

After draining the cup, he handed it back to the man for a refill and took another long swallow before he spoke. "There'd better be a damn good reason why your Harvey Point guys jumped me and brought me here to the farm."

"I can't fully address that issue. There are certain classified operations of the Central Intelligence Agency which I am not permitted to speak about."

"What, that Camp Peary is the CIA's spy school, better known as the Farm, or that Harvey Point, North Carolina, is where your hard-core paramilitary training goes on? Don't bullshit me. My head hurts too much. I know Rick Morrell. I also know what goes on at Harvey Point."

"Agent Harvath, I can't talk about—"

"Fine, let's back up. First, who are you?"

"My name is Frank Mraz. I'm deputy director of the CIA's Directorate of Operations."

"The DO, wonderful. Also known as the Clandestine Service."

"We don't really call it that anymore."

"Different name, same game. Just like Delta Force is now called Combat Applications Group and SEAL Six is Dev Group. Like I said, different name, same game. Morrell and his boys are part of your paramilitary SAS branch—the Special Activities Staff, aren't they?"

"Once again, I can't comment on any ongoing—"

"Jesus Christ, Frank," Lawlor piped in. "We all know about Harvey Point. Agent Harvath is a former SEAL and an active Secret Service agent. Both the SEALs and Secret Service undergo training at Harvey Point. If we're going to work together on this, let's actually *work* together. Okay?"

"I am happy to be as cooperative as my position allows," said Mraz.

"I'll make it easy on you," said Harvath. "Your SAS squad—"

"I have not confirmed that Mr. Morrell and his colleagues are Special Activities Staff, or that such a group even exists."

Gary Lawlor rolled his eyes.

Harvath continued, "Hey, SAS, NFL, NBA . . . you can call them the fuckin' Beach Boys for all I care, but they are under your command, and I'm sure they've each got a parking space at Harvey Point. You don't have to confirm or deny. I know the score. I'm going to also bet that plane Morrell and company brought me back over the pond on is part of your Air Branch fleet, formerly known as Air America. Once again, different name, same game. I want to know why I got jumped in Jerusalem."

"Would you believe it was a case of being in the wrong place at the wrong time?" asked Mraz.

"I wouldn't patronize him, if I were you, Frank," said Lawlor.

"I'm not trying to be patronizing."

"Then cut to the chase," snapped Scot.

"Our sources indicate that Schoen has been trying to penetrate the Abu Nidal Organization."

"Of course he has. He believes they're behind the ambush of our Rapid Return operation."

"He admitted that to you?"

"Sure, but I wasn't too prepared to believe it. His theory, as well as his evidence has too many holes in it. If you really *want* to believe it, it makes sense, but if you look at it piece by piece, it just doesn't hold together."

"Well, we think it does. We've had him under surveillance and knew that he had been trying to hire some outside talent for a covert operation he's working on. When we received word that he had possibly recruited a key Western intelligence operative and then you appeared out of the blue and spent several hours in his private offices, it was thought you might be in bed with him, and so you were picked up."

"That's it? That's your justification for snatching me and pumping me full of God knows what? Why didn't you just ask me what I was doing there?"

"Would you have told us?"

"Probably not, but it would have been the polite thing to do."

"Polite or not, we did what we had to. In all fairness, it wasn't until CIA director Vaile made some phone calls that we finally realized you were operating under direct orders from the president. And it wasn't until Mr. Morrell had you on the plane that he recognized who you were."

"Bullshit, he knew the minute he saw me in Jerusalem."

"Be that as it may, he had his orders and he followed them."

"Orders or not, he made this personal," said Harvath, as even more anger crept into his voice.

"Whether or not that's the case, is not germane to the ongoing crisis."

"What are you talking about?"

"What do you know about an Israeli terrorist group calling itself the Hand of God?"

"Nothing much more than they have been behind two very high profile attacks against Arab targets recently," answered Harvath.

"Three attacks."

"*Three?* Since when?"

"It hasn't been released to the press yet, but we got word early this morning from Paris that Prince Khalil of the Saudi royal family was killed while swimming at the Ritz hotel."

"Killed how?"

"Somebody spiked the pool with a very deadly toxic chemical," said Lawlor. "Soon after, the hotel manager received a note from the Hand of God claiming responsibility. We're convinced they're behind it."

"What does this have to do with Schoen and what happened in Jerusalem?" asked Harvath.

"You're aware that he had a son, correct?" offered Mraz.

"Yeah. He told me he was dead."

"Well, what he probably didn't tell you was that his son had followed in his footsteps. Against his father's wishes, he joined the Mossad. A year later, he died entering an apartment rigged with explosives where a supposed terrorist was holed up. When his son was killed, Schoen's hatred for the Arabs exploded. He began taking missions no one else wanted and was one of the Mossad's most brutal interrogators.

"Fast-forward to our Rapid Return operation in Lebanon. Schoen is terribly disfigured, even more embittered, and decides to go underground. Shortly thereafter, the Hand of God attacks begin."

"Wait a second," said Harvath. "Are you telling me you think there is a connection between Schoen and the Hand of God? That's one hell of a leap in logic."

"Is it? Have you ever heard of a group called the Wrath of God, Agent Harvath?"

"Of course. They were a hit squad of Israeli assassins formed to avenge the killings at the Munich Olympics."

"We prefer to call them an independent covert-action team, but you're essentially correct. To carry out the mission," continued Mraz, "the Mossad activated its thirty-six-person assassination unit know as the 'kidon.' Funds were deposited into Swiss bank accounts for operatives to collect upon successful completion of their assignments. The unit was broken down into teams, which were highly compartmentalized. None of the teams knew about the existence of the others. The only thing they had in common was a shared point of contact, who was a senior Mossad agent."

"Let me guess," said Harvath. "Schoen?"

"The one and only. He was quite ingenious, eliminating the rank structure and encouraging his men to be creative in their assassinations. He gave his operatives anything they needed to get the job done. And he didn't just want to kill his targets; he wanted the terrorists to experience the same terror that the Israeli athletes and their families had faced. He wanted terrorists everywhere to know that if they even thought about committing attacks on Israel, there was no place in the world where they would be safe from reprisals.

"We know that the Wrath of God operation was covertly controlled by the Mossad, but that Schoen operated with total autonomy, completely outside the Israeli government. We think this might be what they're doing again."

"If ever called on the carpet, Schoen could claim sole responsibility and provide them with plausible deniability," said Harvath.

"Exactly. Though the Israeli government denies any connection with the Hand of God, because of Schoen's history, we decided to take a closer look at him. Our sources think that he might be in this more for himself than for Israel, and that's dangerous."

"So Schoen's got several reasons to hate the Arabs. What's this have to do with us?"

"Everything. First of all, if the Israeli government is behind the Hand of God attacks, which we believe they are, they are throwing the Mideast into serious peril. Terrorism on any level is inexcusable, but Israel appears to be taking it to new heights and we cannot have that, especially not now. Not with the resurgence of the FRC."

"I find it hard to believe that Abu Nidal has magically come back to life. I thought we had independent confirmation of his death," said Harvath.

"As far as our intelligence is concerned, he is very much dead."

"So who's running the show, then? He's not giving orders from beyond the grave."

"You'd be surprised. Apparently, Abu Nidal had a son."

"A son? How the hell did we miss that?"

"I don't know, but believe me, we're looking into it."

"So, the old man passed the baton to his son," said Harvath as he reached for his cup to take another sip of water. "What's the connection with the men who kidnapped the president?"

"From what I have seen in the recent reports you filed, you figured it out yourself. Gerhard Miner only had so many men working with him that he could trust. There was no way he could spare any of them to facilitate the explosion in Lebanon that killed the Rapid Return team. So, he contracted it out."

"And you're saying he contracted it out to Abu Nidal's son, who is now the new leader of the old man's Fatah Revolutionary Council?"

"Yes. His name is Hashim. It means—"

" 'Crusher of evil,' I know. I've studied Arabic," said Harvath as he fought to process all the information he was getting. "So, Hashim Nidal is rebuilding his father's organization?"

"Unfortunately, that's the way it looks. And, he appears to be committed to the same objectives as his father—"

"Destroying any peace negotiations or settlements between the Israelis and the Palestinians and wiping out the State of Israel."

"Bingo," said Mraz.

"Then put him on your most-likely-to-bleed list and let Morrell or somebody take him out. The father was bad enough; who knows how much worse the son will be."

"We couldn't agree more, but there's a slight hiccup in this case."

"There's always something. What is it?"

"We have no idea what Hashim Nidal looks like. No one that we know of has ever seen him and lived to tell about it."

"Surely there's got to be somebody?"

"Zip. Not even a good description."

"You can't locate some of his own people and turn them?" asked Harvath.

"The old man had money stashed everywhere, and as far as we know, it's all being watched. The son, though, has apparently been able to get his hands on money from somewhere, whether it's his father's or someone else's. It's been enough to fire the organization back up. And apparently he pays very well. No one's risking their necks or their salaries to talk to us."

Harvath leaned back on his pillow and had a faraway look in his eyes as he rubbed his stubbled chin. "Schoen and I have both come across Nidal's son," he said.

"You've seen his face? Both of you?"

"No, not really. What we each saw were eyes. Silver eyes. The assassin in Macau who got to Jamek before we could, the one who took out Gerhard Miner in Switzerland, and the man who attacked Schoen in Israel, the same one he saw after the ambush in Lebanon, were all the same guy. It has to be Hashim Nidal."

"Or someone working for him," said Mraz.

"Regardless, I'll bet our last two Lions either had met with Nidal's son face-to-face or had enough sensitive information on him that they had to be silenced permanently," replied Harvath.

"That would make sense, as would the boldness of those assassinations. We've already tied the son to a string of deadly terrorist attacks on different continents over the last year and a half. They've all been very bloody, very high risk operations. They make what the father did look like child's play. And what's worse, we've discovered that he's managed to align several different Islamic terrorist organizations under his umbrella. Our people are projecting that left unchecked, his group will grow to become the largest and best organized we've ever encountered. After they light up Israel, who do you think their next target will be?"

"Us," said Harvath, his tone grave.

"Just like dominoes," replied Mraz.

"But that's ridiculous. They've got to know that as Israel's biggest ally we'd come to their aid."

"I'm sure they do know that. And I'm sure they're counting on it. The minute we step into Israel, we're going to see unprecedented acts of terrorism against the United States."

"Do we have any leads at all?"

"We know that the FRC has made several recent attempts to retrieve funds that Abu Nidal thought he had hidden beyond anyone's detection. Each of those attempts has been thwarted. The organization is desperately trying to raise cash, and our intelligence indicates that whatever they're planning, it's coming up fast."

"So what's the operation?" asked Scot.

Mraz spoke up. "The goal of Operation Phantom is to identify and eliminate Hashim Nidal before he can carry out his next attack, and hopefully dismantle his organization once and for all."

"Operation Phantom?" asked Harvath.

"Yes, Abu Nidal's son is, for all intents and purposes, a ghost. We don't know his date of birth, how tall he is . . . not even what he looks like."

"Do you guys actually pay someone to sit around and think these names up?"

"Often, it's the mission directors who develop the code names. In this case, the mission director is Mr. Morrell."

"Well, that explains a lot."

"Regardless of your feelings about Mr. Morrell, I can guarantee you we chose the best man for the job."

"That's highly debatable," replied Scot. "But as long as you have me along, at least I can keep an eye on him and try to keep him from screwing things up too badly."

"And what makes you think you will have anything to do with this operation, Agent Harvath?"

"Because you wouldn't have spent all this time spilling what you know if you didn't plan on bringing me in. Let's also not forget that I am operating under direct orders from the president of the United States, who has the utmost confidence in my abilities, and who with one phone call would have me put on this team, whether you like it or not."

"You are an arrogant man, Agent Harvath," said Mraz.

"No, it's not arrogance, Mr. Mraz, I'm just very good at what I do," replied Harvath evenly.

"Well, I want you to know that I don't think you belong on this team and neither does Director Vaile. But, as you mentioned, the president does have every confidence in your ability, and therefore we have grudgingly decided to put you under Mr. Morrell's command."

"Under *his* command? No way. I command myself, and that's final."

"Agent Harvath, I'm not asking you, I'm telling you. If you wish to be a part of this operation, these are the conditions under which it will happen. You're a former SEAL. You, of all people, should appreciate the need for a clear and definite command."

"You left out 'capable,' " said Harvath.

"It will please you to hear that Mr. Morrell is not at all happy about you being added to the team and that he tried very hard to stop it from happening."

"Thanks. That does make me feel better."

"Per Director Vaile's agreement with the president, you will be on Mr. Morrell's team for the ID and termination of Hashim Nidal, after which you will return to your duties at the White House. Is this understood?"

"There's no plan to try and grab him?" asked Harvath.

"No. Our projection is that if we're lucky, we'll only get one opportunity to put him out of business. If we fail, which is far more likely in a snatch operation than with a sniper team, he'll go so far underground we won't see him again until the dust has settled from whatever major event he has brewing. This is precisely why we cannot afford any interference from Mr. Schoen and the Israelis, especially if Schoen's involvement is more personal than professional. That's how mistakes happen. Now, we're going to need to keep you overnight for observation, and then—"

"No you're not. I feel fine. I'm going home now," said Harvath as he began to raise himself up from the bed.

"Agent Harvath, please don't—"

Now it was Lawlor who interrupted. "Do me a favor and just cooperate, would you, Scot? Okay? I'll come pick you up tomorrow and drive you home."

"And then what am I supposed to do? Sit around and watch *Oprah*?"

"You're free to do whatever you want, Agent Harvath," said Mraz. "You'll be provided with a beeper. As soon as Mr. Morrell's team is ready to move out, you'll be contacted and told where to meet them."

"How can I get ahold of Morrell if I need to?" asked Scot.

"You won't need to. Besides, I don't think it's such a good idea. I'd rather you two stay away from each other. Just wait until he contacts you. Be ready to go at a moment's notice."

"What about gear?"

"Mr. Morrell will handle all of that from here."

"They're not going back to the embassy in Jerusalem?"

"No, we've got another team there now. Mr. Morrell and his team will wait here until we have gathered further intel as to the whereabouts of Hashim Nidal."

"Do you have any idea where he might be?"

"We believe his base of operations is somewhere in Indonesia."

"That would figure, wouldn't it? The Muslims love that warm weather."

Mraz ignored him. "We have assets on the ground in Indonesia who are actively seeking his training camp and base of operations. Once we have located it, if time permits, we'll build a mock-up and practice the assault."

"And if time doesn't permit?"

"We roll and we'll just have to wing it."

Mraz's final comment scared Harvath more than anything else he had heard in the last forty-five minutes.

15

The next day Scot felt well enough to check himself out, and Gary Lawlor drove him home. On the way, they stopped at his favorite burger joint in Alexandria—Five Guys, on King Street. As much as Scot enjoyed traveling, he was always glad to come back home. There was something about seeing the United States from abroad that reaffirmed for him how proud and fortunate he felt to be an American. The other thing foreign travel did was give him an overwhelming craving for a good cheeseburger and fries.

They made one more stop at the deli-market around the corner from Scot's apartment, where he bought a six-pack of Sam Adams, and then Lawlor dropped him in front of his building.

"Morrell is going to want to send a courier over with the file for you to look at. There's not much in it, but it'll put you on the same page as everybody else," said Lawlor.

"Okay," said Harvath as he closed the passenger side door behind him. "Have him send it over this afternoon."

"Do you have a shredder?"

"Yup."

"Good. He'll want you to shred and then burn it when you're through."

"You don't have to worry about my tradecraft," said Harvath. "Let's just hope Special Assholes Staff doesn't botch things up."

"Scot, you've got to give that a rest. There's too much at stake. I know you don't like Morrell, but you're part of their team now, so start acting like it," admonished Lawlor, who then rolled up the window and pulled out into the street.

Harvath didn't like that Lawlor had the final word, but the aroma of his cheeseburger and fries, as it wafted up through the grease-stained bag, quickly made him forget about it.

He held the cold six-pack and burger bag in one hand as he fished in his pockets for his house keys. The few possessions he had on him when he was jumped by Morrell and his colleagues in Jerusalem had been returned. Just to make trouble for Morrell, Harvath had claimed his wallet was about two hundred bucks short. The CIA duty officer signing him out had almost believed him until Lawlor told him to stop screwing around. Harvath was told that his bags had already been retrieved from the Jerusalem Hotel and would be delivered to his apartment in Alexandria. When asked if there was anything else the CIA could do for him, Scot asked who really killed Kennedy, but then Lawlor jabbed him in the ribs and told him to get moving.

He stopped by the building manager's apartment and picked up the shopping bag full of mail she had been collecting for him and then headed up the stairs to his third-floor apartment. He checked to see that the hair he'd wedged into the upper right corner of the doorframe was still there, indicating that the door to his apartment had not been opened in the weeks he had been gone. *Still there.*

Inside, the apartment was hot and muggy. Summers in D.C. could be unbearable. He walked over to his air-conditioning unit and switched it on full blast. He removed two bottles of beer from the carton, and put the rest of the beer in the fridge. He walked into his living room, sat down on the couch, and flipped on the TV while he began his meal.

It was the top of the hour and Fox News was running their top news stories. Scot recognized the façade of the Hotel Ritz in Paris immediately. It was surrounded by police cars and emergency vehicles. Apparently, the Prince Khalil assassination story had broken.

The reporter on the scene talked about a little-known toxic poison called Sadim, what dermal exposure was, and how death must have been for the Saudi prince and his two bodyguards. The Ritz was surely horrified by the publicity. The public still talked about how Princess Diana and her boyfriend, Dodi Al Fayed, had spent their last evening there and had died when their limousine crashed, a drunken Ritz chauffeur at the wheel.

Somehow, the reporter had obtained a copy of the letter in which the Hand of God organization claimed responsibility for the murders. After she had read it verbatim, the screen changed to a feed from Jerusalem and Fox's Jerusalem bureau chief. The dark-haired man spoke for several minutes about escalating tensions and violence in Israel, then segued to a video package edited and narrated earlier that day. It showed footage of the carnage at Medina in Saudi Arabia, as well as the Temple Mount in Jerusalem. There was heavy troop and tank placement throughout villages along the West Bank and Gaza Strip. Israel had closed all of its border crossings in response to sixteen suicide bombings by Palestinians at crowded restaurants, shopping areas, and resorts popular with

Israeli citizens. Hezbollah, Hamas, and the al-Aqsa Martyrs Brigades were all taking credit for the attacks and stated that they were in retaliation for the Hand of God attacks. And so it went, with each subsequent attack ratcheting up the rhetoric and the violence. It was a vicious circle and it was spiraling out of control.

The video then cut to street scenes in Jerusalem in the aftermath of the attack on the Temple Mount. Palestinian youths threw stones at Israeli Defense Forces who returned fire with tear gas and rubber bullets. Jewish shopkeepers pushed and assaulted Palestinian customers and vice versa. It was sheer pandemonium.

Man-on-the-street interviews were volatile, with each side calling for war and the extermination of the other. Not only did the citizens of Palestine and Israel seem to overwhelmingly agree that they should go to war and settle things once and for all, but they were all sure their "God" would lead them to victory.

Just when Harvath could barely stand it any longer and was about to turn the TV off, the piece turned to a man walking through a rubble-strewn Palestinian village. People lined the streets to greet him. When the camera pulled back to reveal the Fox reporter, Scot recognized her right away. It was Jody Burnis, the former CNN reporter who had broken the story of the president's kidnapping and had implicated him as her inside source. He turned up the sound on the remote as a montage of images filled the screen.

". . . Ali Hasan, chief Palestinian negotiator and a rising star on the Palestine political landscape. He grew up on these same mean Ramallah streets, only a stone's throw away from PLO headquarters. He has been a vigorous proponent for an independent Palestinian homeland and establishing a lasting peace with neighboring Israel—a difficult and, some would say, impossible dream.

"As violence worsens here in the wake of the Hand of God terrorist attacks, Hasan's voice is one of the few still calling for calm. It has been his steadfast refusal to condemn terrorism that his detractors most often cite. But by the same token, observers far and wide agree that in the tumultuous arena of Palestinian politics, if he hopes to lead his people, he could not come down on what is seen by most Palestinians as the only tool which allows them to be taken seriously on the world stage.

"Hasan has been a frequent guest speaker at the League of Arab Nations and is on very good terms with most of the region's leaders, both secular and religious alike. He has been compared to a coin flipped high into the desert air. On one side of the coin is the barbed specter of war, the other, the white dove of peace. On which side will the coin fall? Only time will tell, though many here believe that with the European-sponsored peace summit only weeks away, *time* is quickly running out.

"Reporting from Ramallah in the West Bank, this has been Jody Burnis for Fox News."

Scot clicked off the television and walked into his bedroom to change into some workout clothes. After he found a clean pair of white socks and his Nikes, he grabbed a cold bottle of water from the fridge and clipped the CIA beeper to his waist. He locked the apartment door behind him, placed a hair in the upper-right-hand corner of the doorframe, and made his way down to the basement, where the landlady had let him set up his work-out gear in an unused corner.

If there was one thing Harvath couldn't stand, it was sitting on his ass. While he couldn't control how long he would have to wait until Morrell paged him, he could control what he did with his time. Workouts always helped Harvath relax and clear his mind. As he slapped the forty-five-pound plates onto the bar and got ready to do a warm-up set of bench presses, the rest of the world and everything in it began to fade away.

An hour later, Scot had a good sweat going and was on his last set of hammer curls. He felt the satisfying fatigue and burn in his muscles. It was good to get back to the weights. Though he had been relegated to push-ups, dips, and crunches in hotel rooms and Claudia's apartment over the last several weeks, he was still in excellent shape. In fact, he was in just as good shape, if not better, as when he had been in the SEALs. There were few who would dare mess with him, and those that did found him to be extremely lethal.

After putting the dumbbells back where they belonged, Scot did a few exercises to work his obliques and then stretched out his legs. Though he had a treadmill in the basement, when the weather was nice, he preferred to run outside.

Despite the humidity in the summertime, Harvath enjoyed living in Alexandria. Its architecture and layout still retained its historic port city charm. It was the hometown of George Washington, and oftentimes Harvath wondered what the former president would think of Alexandria if he came back and saw how well preserved it was today.

Harvath jogged to the Chinquapin Park Recreation Center, where he was greeted by Tera, one of the front-desk staffers, who knew him on sight. She checked him in and agreed to hold on to his pager and come find him if it went off.

The center had a fully equipped locker room, where Scot kept a swimsuit, a pair of goggles, and some assorted toiletry items. After a quick shower, he jumped into his suit and hit the twenty-five-meter indoor pool.

Having already performed a full weight workout, Harvath felt himself, understandably, growing tired much quicker than he normally would, but he simply adjusted his pace and kept going. Scot liked to push himself. Both in the SEALs and then later when he was recruited into the Secret Service, Harvath was known by his code name, Norseman. It referred to a string of Scandinavian flight attendants he had dated while going through his SEAL training, but seeing him in action suggested another meaning. Whenever he thought he couldn't go any further, he reminded himself of the SEAL motto, "The only easy day was yesterday," and would push himself some more.

After an hour in the pool, Harvath's body was beyond fatigued and his mind was numb. He didn't have the energy to compose a thought any more complicated than grabbing a shower. He stood under the needlelike spray and let the water bounce off his body as he leaned against the wall for support. After twenty minutes of *hot*, he turned the faucet all the way to *cold* and forced himself to stand beneath the spray until his blood was racing through his body and every nerve ending was tingling.

Harvath toweled off and put on his running clothes again. He picked up his pager from Tera, stopped by the snack bar, and chugged down a large bottle of Gatorade before leaving the complex. Morrell hadn't called, and it didn't surprise Harvath. It could easily be weeks before he heard from him.

When he returned to his apartment, he checked the hair before opening the door and letting himself in. He needed to get out of his running clothes and take another shower. Just walking home, he had broken a sweat in the lovely July humidity. As Harvath made his way past the kitchen toward his bathroom, something in the kitchen caught his eye. The refrigerator door was standing wide open. *That was odd.* He wouldn't have left it that way. *Maybe the seal was going,* he thought to himself. As he went to close the fridge, he noticed something else—his remaining four bottles of Sam Adams were gone. He knew he didn't do that. Someone had been in his house, but whoever they were, they'd been clever enough to replace the hair in his doorframe. Coming through a window was out of the question. Entry could have been gained only through the front door.

Because his sidearm was in his bedroom, the best he could do for a weapon was the Louisville Slugger he kept in the hall closet. Quietly he retrieved the baseball bat and crept toward the rear of the apartment. The living room was clear, as was his bathroom. His bedroom door was closed, something he never did, and as he approached it, he tightened his grip around the bat. He took a deep breath and freed his left hand to turn the knob. When the door gave way, he put all of his weight behind it, charged into the bedroom, and fell flat on his face. He had tripped over something.

Harvath quickly spun into a sitting position and raised the bat above his head with both hands, ready to come down hard on the intruder. Then he saw what he had tripped over. He set the bat down and hopped up onto his feet. Sitting on the floor in front of him was his bag from the Jerusalem Hotel. He quickly glanced around his room and noticed that his bed had been turned down. On his pillow was a smiley face with two Hershey's chocolate Kisses for the eyes and four Sam Adams bottle caps for the smile.

"Asshole," Harvath said out loud.

He knew it had to have been Morrell who had gotten into his apartment and placed his bag in the bedroom. Out of all the many distasteful things he remembered about the former Navy SEAL turned CIA assassin, was that he was a fiend for candy. The smiley face was his calling card, all right. On top of getting his ass kicked, Rick Morrell now owed Harvath a six-pack of Sam Adams.

Harvath was just about to unpack his bag when he heard a knock at the front door. He pulled his SIG Sauer from underneath his nightstand and held it behind his back as he approached the front door.

"Who is it?" he asked as he stood to the right of the doorframe.

"Special courier. I have a delivery for Mr. Scot Harvath," said a man's voice.

Harvath stepped in front of the peephole and peered out. Standing in the hall was a tall, blond kid about twenty-five years old. Harvath was only in his early thirties, but any young CIA hard-ons, which this one obviously was, were referred to by guys in the Special Operations community as snot-nosed CIA *kids*. Harvath opened the door.

"Do you have any ID?" Harvath asked the kid, who, now that he could see him full on, looked more like a muscle-bound southern California surfer than a CIA operative.

"Yes, sir," replied the young man, who was wearing a briefcase chained to his right wrist. With his free left hand, he reached inside his suit coat for his wallet. That's when Harvath swung his gun around and pointed it at the kid's forehead.

"Dumb move, dude," said Harvath. "You should never let your guard down like that. Those are very important documents in there. What if I was here to steal them from you?"

At that precise moment, the CIA kid swung hard with the titanium briefcase at Harvath's head, but missed him by a mile. Harvath was much too fast for him and had moved out of the way when the kid telegraphed his intent with his eyes. Harvath answered the assault with a quick blow to the kid's solar plexus. He fell to the floor with the wind knocked out of him.

"That was an even dumber move," said Harvath, offering his hand to help the kid off the floor, but he waved it away, still trying to catch his breath.

Harvath helped himself to the kid's breast pocket and removed his identification.

"Gordon Avigliano," he said, reading the name off the driver's license. "Well, Gordy, what do you have for me?"

Harvath offered the kid his hand again and was once

again waved off. The young man struggled to his feet and, with his wind back again, asked, "Can we do this inside, please?"

"Sure thing, Gordo; just no funny business. I've already seen you do dumb and dumber, but if you go for stupid, you're gonna leave through the window. Understand me?"

The young man nodded his head. Harvath showed him inside and pointed toward one of the two chairs next to the small table in the kitchen. The CIA courier put his briefcase on the table and looked up.

"Can I see some ID please, sir?" he asked.

Harvath, who was rummaging around inside the refrigerator, blindly pointed his pistol over his shoulder at the courier and said, "Tell your boss that Agent Harvath wasn't home, but his buddy Samuel Adams signed for the papers."

"But, sir, I really do need—"

The courier stopped mid sentence when Harvath cocked the hammer of the SIG Sauer.

"They told me this might be difficult, and I said, 'Difficult? Naw, it's just a routine delivery.' Why do I get all the bad jobs?" the courier said to himself.

"Unless you have a nice cold six-pack in that little case of yours, I suggest you give me what you've got and clear out. I am not in the best of moods."

"I can see that."

"What was that, Gordo?" said Harvath, who withdrew his head from the fridge and shot the kid a look.

"Nothing, sir. Nothing at all."

"I didn't think so. Let's get on with it. I've only got ten minutes until *Oprah*."

"Until *Oprah*?" the courier asked, confused.

"Yeah, you heard me. *Oprah*."

"Okay, then, I just need to ask if you've had your domicile swept for bugs recently."

"Bugs? Here do it yourself," said Harvath as he reached next to the fridge for a fly swatter and threw it at the kid. "I don't talk in my sleep, nor do my lips move when I read. I plan on digesting what you have in your lunch box there, and then I will shred and burn all of it." Harvath had no fear of bugs as he had his apartment swept regularly by a friend who was a former FBI agent and now one of the East Coast's top security consultants.

The courier began to reach into his breast pocket, and Harvath pointed the gun back between the young man's eyes. "Ah. Ah. Ah. Remember what I said about leaving by the window."

"It's just a release form, honest. Jesus, this has been hard enough already. Besides, if I was going to pull a gun on you, I would have done it while your head was in the refrigerator."

"Good point," said Harvath as he slowly released the hammer and put his pistol on the kitchen counter. He accepted the form and signed it as he said he would, "*Samuel Adams*."

"Wait a second," said the courier. "I was told I could only release these documents to Mr. Scot Harvath."

"And you have."

"But the name here—"

"Will be perfectly clear to your superior when you report back. Now pop the top and give me what you got."

The courier deactivated the locking system and withdrew a thin manila envelope, which he handed to him. It was sealed and stamped, "Top Secret. Agent Scot Harvath U.S. Secret Service Eyes Only."

Harvath walked the young man into the hall.

"So, are you going to be graduating to *real* fieldwork soon, Gordo?"

"I already have."

"Well, just try not to get any of the wrong people killed, okay? You have a good day now," replied Harvath as he turned back into his apartment and kicked the door shut behind him.

He sat down on his couch and spread the contents of the file on the coffee table. There was a brief history of Abu Nidal followed by a series of photos from scenes of terrorist attacks attributed to his son. Theories and possible strategies occupied the space of a two-page "brainstorming" memo that was long on speculation and short on actual facts.

Lawlor had been right; there wasn't much in this file that Harvath hadn't already been told. At least, though, he was now truly operating off the same page as everyone else. After reviewing the material for a fifth time in as many hours, he ran it through his shredder and then burned the remains in a metal garbage can he had placed in his bathtub.

As Harvath got ready for bed, he thought about Ari Schoen. What role did he *really* play in all of this? Could he be useful? Was he involved with the Hand of God? Was Schoen telling everything he knew? Was the CIA? That was the trouble with this business. You never could tell who was telling the truth and you never knew whom to trust. Everyone was suspect.

Harvath gathered the bottle caps off his pillow and threw them into the garbage can beneath his desk. He unwrapped and ate one of the chocolates before climbing into bed. He was dead tired and looked forward to a good night's sleep. As he crawled beneath the covers, his feet came to an abrupt halt.

Morrell had short-sheeted his bed.

16

Meg Cassidy was never much for following the crowd, but when United Airlines's flight 7755 touched down at Cairo's new Mubarak International Airport, she found herself caught up in the emotion of the moment and joined right in with the wave of applause that swept through the sleek new 747-400 jetliner.

She then leaned her head back against the stylish leather business-class sleeper seat and offered up a prayer of thanks. It was easily the greatest PR coup of the year. Somebody up there liked her. At twenty-seven, the attractive, blond public relations whiz kid was already being called a PR maven, and owned one of Chicago's fastest growing and most successful agencies. Her offices were located in the swanky Beckwith Realty loft building on Hubbard Street, not far from the best seafood restaurant in town, Shaw's Crab House. She had just purchased a new summer home on Wisconsin's famed Lake Geneva, and *Today's Chicago Woman* and *Crain's Chicago Business* were planning cover stories on her within the next month. The editors had sought her out for her street smarts and business acumen, though the fact that she was a dead ringer for Meg Ryan hadn't hurt either.

What she had accomplished was truly amazing. Competing against agencies three times their size, Meg and Cassidy Public Relations had beat out every comer to win the United Airlines local account. The first assignment they were handed was the opening of United's new service to Cairo—the first nonstop route from Chicago to Cairo. Meg had worked tirelessly with United's ad agency and helped to develop a fabulous campaign that included a tag line seen on billboards and buses all over town, "From the heart of America to the heart of the Middle East. No One Unites the World Like United." But she didn't stop there. If this was going to be a Meg Cassidy event, it had to be bigger than big.

Meg was aware of Chicago's numerous sister cities across the globe and was able to convince the new mayor, Jim Fellinger, that Chicago needed a Middle Eastern sister city and that Cairo was the perfect choice. Once those wheels were put in motion, Meg worked tirelessly along with United's CEO, Bob Lawrence, to make sure that United's inaugural Chicago-to-Cairo flight would be the first plane to touch down at Cairo's new Mubarak International Airport. And it was. In a matter of minutes, when the doors of the 747 opened, Chicago mayor Jim Fellinger would be the first to deplane, followed by United CEO Bob Lawrence to shake hands with the host of waiting Egyptian dignitaries.

Meg took a moment and let the relief flow through her. It had been seriously touch and go for a while. With the increased violence in the Middle East, United had thought about scrapping the route altogether, but Meg had hung in there. She convinced all of the players that the new route was a symbolic connection between the people of America and of the Middle East. United knew the demand was there and that the route would be profitable, but the shadow of international terrorism always hung low over the horizon and was an unspoken fact at almost every meeting. Meg had assured her clients that when they had hired her, they had hired the best and that she would make sure their PR was nothing short of exquisite—and it was.

Tickets for the flight sold well, but just to make sure it went out full, Cassidy Public Relations had developed a series of brilliant, high-profile contests for vacations to Cairo. The media exposure United had gained was far beyond anything they could have hoped for. The airline's publicly steadfast refusal to pull out of their new route to Cairo in the face of escalating Mideast violence was hailed by peacemakers everywhere as the type of determination and commitment necessary for the world to not only live, but to thrive in peace. There was no doubt that Meg Cassidy had done an extraordinary job. Her crowning achievement was helping to coordinate a cultural exchange of Egyptian exhibits between Chicago's Field Museum and the Egyptian Museum in Cairo. Flight 7755 was carrying several large crates of artifacts, returning to Egypt for the first time in over one hundred years.

Meg had spent a good portion of the trip in the upper-deck lounge with members of the press, including two of her favorite travel journalists, Bernard Walsh and Georgia Bormann. She had answered all of their questions, which covered everything from United's newest routes and aircraft, to the possibility of additional cultural exchanges between the U.S. and Egypt. By the time the plane touched down, she was exhausted. She had been burning the midnight oil for two weeks straight before the kickoff flight and was looking forward to getting to her hotel, opening a bottle of wine, taking a long hot bath, and crawling into a nice, soft bed for a much deserved rest.

Her reverie was broken by the sound of a sudden commotion. *What could possibly be going on? We're almost at the gate*, Meg thought to herself.

A group of men came running up both aisles from the plane's economy section and stopped not far from Meg's seat. One of the flight attendants had unbuckled himself and approached the men to see what was the matter.

In a flash, the mood in the plane turned from celebration to terror as one of the men attacked the flight attendant, and several of the passengers began screaming.

Two figures clad in black jumpsuits and wearing ski masks appeared on the stairwell that led from the lower-deck fitness area and began handing up a wide array of automatic weapons to the men who had run up from economy class. From the first-class section of the plane, Meg saw one of Mayor Fellinger's Chicago police bodyguards approach. She tried to warn him with a tilt of her head toward the stairwell, but it was too late. One of the masked hijackers saw the bodyguard first, withdrew a silenced pistol and fired two shots into his head, killing him instantly.

Meg couldn't see it, but behind her, a plainclothes air marshal rushed up one of the aisles from the rear of the plane with his gun drawn, yelling for the men to put down their weapons. Another air marshal drew his weapon and ran up the opposite aisle. They were subdued by two "sleeper" hijackers who had remained in their aisle seats until the air marshals had made themselves known. The hijackers had short, black plastic-composite knives, known as CIA letter openers, which they had easily smuggled through security. With a well-rehearsed up, in, and twist motion of the knives, each air marshal was quickly dispatched.

Now the entire plane was in bedlam. Screams of terror could be heard coming from all directions. Several of the hijackers made their way through the cabin and confiscated the onboard stun guns.

The masked hijacker who had killed the mayor's bodyguard motioned to one of his men with his weapon. The man understood the command, pushed past the handful of flight attendants who were seeing to their fallen comrade, and activated the 747's public address system.

In near perfect English he addressed the plane's passengers, "Ladies and gentlemen, if you wish to make it off of this plane alive, you will cooperate fully with our instructions. We have already demonstrated how far we are prepared to go. Out of respect for the women and children, we hoped to spare you this spectacle, but no doubt you now know we are in control of the plane and are fully armed. We guarantee you that we are prepared to use our weapons. As Allah is merciful, so are we. Obey our instructions and no one else will be killed. We ask that you remain in your seats and that those of you sitting near a window lower your window shades completely."

Though many of the terrified passengers only began to sob harder at the confirmation that the plane had been hijacked, they all complied with the instructions and those by the windows lowered their shades.

The hijackers, who were all now heavily armed, took up strategic positions throughout the cabins. Mayor Fellinger's second bodyguard was identified, handcuffed, and led upstairs, where he was knocked unconscious and unceremoniously left in one of the lavatories in the upper-deck lounge.

Knowing that the pilots would stay barricaded behind their reinforced and bulletproof cockpit door, the hijackers contacted them on the intercom system and told them that if they didn't open the door within three seconds, it would be blown off with C4. The pilots had little choice but to surrender. It was the right move. The hijackers had enough explosives to not only knock down the door, but create such a blast that it would likely kill everyone inside the cockpit. Before opening their door, though, they had managed to get a message out that the plane was under siege.

Knowing that many of the passengers, especially the Americans, would be emboldened by the resistance of the September 11 passengers who had helped prevent the fourth pirated plane from reaching its target, the hijackers wasted no time in demonstrating to everyone on board who was in control.

The lead flight attendant, who had been attacked and badly beaten in the initial takeover, was dragged up and down the aisles as a visual deterrent to any passengers thinking about trying any heroics. The message was sent loud and clear, *We are in control here.*

It was all making Meg sick to her stomach. She had been the victim of an attempted rape several years before and had never been able to escape the memory of it. The only child of a Chicago Police Academy training officer, she had felt that the attack had somehow been her fault—that she should have seen it coming and been better able to fight it off. The experience had shaken her to the core.

Afterward, she took self-defense classes at the academy as well as extensive firearms training. Her father had given her a nine-millimeter handgun, which she always kept loaded beside her bed. Though many women might have caved in and lived in fear for the rest of their lives, Meg had used the experience to make her stronger.

A hijacker in the cockpit relayed orders to the tower. The Jetway was to remain retracted, and neither the external air-conditioning nor the external power source were to be attached. The plane was to be immediately refueled, and if anyone other than the refueling crew approached the aircraft, hostages would be killed.

In order to demonstrate their seriousness, the hijacker exited the cockpit and shouted down the stairs from the upper deck. His colleague waiting below motioned to two other hijackers and together they deactivated the water slide and opened the 747's large side door. With contemptuous kicks, they shoved the bloody, lifeless bodies of the mayor's bodyguard and the two air marshals out the door and watched them tumble through the air before landing in a sickening heap of snapping bone on the tarmac below. Their message delivered, they retreated inside and closed the door.

The hijackers next used sheets of aluminum foil and duct tape to cover the cockpit windows and those of any exit doors that didn't have shades. Throughout the cabins, passengers were watched at gunpoint as other hijackers shoved their way into rows and temporarily raised window shades only long enough to place dark, flat, suction-cup-like devices with long yellow tails against the Plexiglas.

The passengers were in shock and were sure the hijackers were wiring the plane with explosives. Meg's seatmate, Bernard Walsh, was positive that was what was happening and, under his breath so as not to attract the attention of the hijackers, said as much to her.

"Relax," Meg whispered back to him. "As long as we do what they say, we'll be okay."

"No we won't. If we stay calm, it just makes it easier for them. Remember nine-eleven? I don't care how brutal these people are. We have to do something, or we're all going to die."

Meg was gripped by fear and had no idea if her seatmate was right. There was no telling if the hijackers were suicidal, or had an agenda. She prayed to God that they did have an agenda because that seemed the only way that they would make it out of this mess alive. Not only was the CEO of United Airlines a passenger on the flight, but so was the mayor of Chicago. Certainly whatever the hijackers wanted, they would get.

At the moment she completed that thought, Meg looked up to see one of the masked hijackers staring at her. His eyes seemed to bore right through her. At first she thought he had noticed her talking and was going to make an example of her. Then she noticed something else in his eyes, something she had seen only once before in her life and hoped never to see again. Getting out of this situation alive might not be as easy as she had thought.

17

Scot Harvath had a lot of enviable talents, but the ability to kill time was not one of them. Patience in battle, he could handle; patience getting to battle was another thing entirely. This morning he had awakened early and gone for a run. When he returned to his apartment he scrambled some eggs for breakfast and then set about some of the "to do" list of chores he had been putting off.

While organizing his desk, he came across a photo of Sam Harper, his mentor at the Secret Service, who had been killed during the president's kidnapping that winter. There were also photos of Agents Maxwell, Ahern, and Houchins—all killed along with Harper trying to protect the president and his daughter. Not a day went by that Harvath didn't remember the promise he had made to avenge the deaths of each and every American who had lost their lives protecting or trying to recover the president. Seeing the photos only reminded him more acutely of his promise.

During his extended leave of absence, tracking down the men responsible for those killings, something inside Scot had changed. He kept telling himself that soon it would all be over. He would go back to his new job at the White House, and things would eventually settle down and return to normal. He knew, though, that he was lying to himself. He couldn't go back to that life. In fact, he was amazed that he had stayed in it as long as he had. Claudia had been the final straw. If it had worked out between them and she had wanted to settle down in D.C., maybe he would have felt differently. Maybe he could have ignored what had been chewing at the edge of his conscience for so long. He knew he was an excellent Secret Service agent, but he also knew that his talents were better suited to a different arena. His mind was made up. Actually, it had been made up for some time, but now he could finally see the decision for what it was. He was avoiding the White House, and the president, because he knew that after he completed this last assignment, it would be time for him to move on. He had no idea where; he just knew he couldn't go back to doing what he had been doing for the Secret Service.

Old habits died hard, and Scot found himself trying to relax his mind and pass the time the way he and his SEAL teammates had in their mission ready room while they waited to be deployed. Though it seemed like a lifetime ago, in reality it had only been a few years, and Scot found the old routine comforting. From the footlocker in his closet, he removed a stack of videocassettes with his name handwritten across each sleeve. He had watched *Cool Hand Luke* and was halfway through *The Good, the Bad, and the Ugly* when his pager went off.

He grabbed the phone and dialed the number from the pager's display.

Morrell answered on the first ring, "Name?"

"Harvath."

"It looks like Hashim Nidal has come up for air."

"Where?"

"Cairo."

"What's the scenario?"

"Hijacking. Lots of passengers."

"When do we move?"

"In forty-five minutes out of Dulles. The rest of the team is already here."

"Thanks for the short notice. I'll be lucky if I can grab my toothbrush and still get there on time."

"Don't grab anything. Not even your passport. Everything will be provided en route. United Airlines is flying us in on identical equipment so we can know it inside out by the time we touch down. Come around through 'general aviation.' Tell them you're with the Wright brothers party, and an agent will bring you to the maintenance hangar where the plane is."

The Wright brothers? Classic, thought Harvath. "Fine. I am on my way, but, Ricky?"

"What?" snapped Morrell, obviously eager to get off the phone.

"Don't even think about leaving without me."

"I wouldn't dream of it."

Scot was ready to say, "Bullshit," but Morrell hung up before he could.

Forty-five minutes to get to Dulles? It *was* bullshit. Obviously Morrell had timed it so it would be impossible for Scot to get there before they took off. It was also obvious that Morrell and the rest of his group had no intention of fully cooperating with him. They were going to do the bare minimum to cover their asses and to hell with Scot Harvath. Well, they had another thing coming.

Harvath dialed Gary Lawlor's office at the J. Edgar Hoover Building in D.C. and crossed his fingers that the man was at his desk. He was and answered on the first ring, "Lawlor."

"Gary, it's Scot Harvath."

"What's up?"

"It looks like we've got a lead on Abu, Jr."

"So, I heard. Where are you?"

"At my apartment."

"Your apartment? Why the hell aren't you scrambled and out at Dulles already?"

"I just got the call."

"You what?"

"Morrell just called me."

"You're not serious."

"I am very serious. Listen, I need your help. It's obvious these guys are not playing ball with us. Morrell called me at the very last minute, knowing I wouldn't be able to make it to Dulles before they took off. He'll say he called me as soon as he could, but you and I both know that's BS. I need to be on that flight, Gary. If they're going to take this guy down, I have to be there."

"Hold on a second," said Lawlor, who withdrew a chart from the credenza behind him. "Do you know Inova Hospital in Alexandria?"

"Yeah, it's on Seminary about four blocks west of I-395. Why?"

"How long would it take you to get there?"

"I could probably be there within fifteen minutes."

"Hold the line again," said Lawlor as he put Scot on hold and made another call. When he came back on just over a minute later, he had good news. "I called Mitch Norberg at Quantico. They're going to fly in a Sikorsky S-76 to the hospital helipad. It's made up to look like a Life Flight bird. It'll be waiting for you."

"Thanks, Gary. I don't know what to say."

"Don't say anything, just nail that bastard. And remember what I said before about getting along with Morrell? Forget it. We might all be on the same team, but that doesn't seem to mean much to these people. Keep your eye on them. I wouldn't trust Morrell or his boss further than I could bowl them."

The look on Rick Morrell's face when Harvath walked into the United Airlines maintenance hangar with ten minutes to spare was priceless.

"What the hell's he doing here?" said one of the SAS men. "I thought he wasn't supposed to make it."

Harvath looked around at the assembled crew. "Well, the gang sure seems to be all here. Sleazy, Slimy, Drippy, Dopey, and even . . . hey, what's up, Doc?"

The man who had been taking Harvath's blood pressure on the plane back from Jerusalem and whose eye Scot had dotted was still sporting two butterfly bandages. Now, he simply gave Harvath the finger and walked away.

"Now that we're all reacquainted," Morrell broke in, "let's get on with it."

The United Airlines security, maintenance, and engineering staff, as well as several representatives from Boeing, finished touring the group, explaining everything they could about the specially modified 747-400. The aircraft was identical to the one that had been hijacked.

In an attempt to keep up with the growing competition from Richard Branson's Virgin Atlantic Airways, United had decided to outfit their planes with numerous perks for business and first-class travelers. Besides the standards of video-on-demand, high-speed Internet access, massages, facials and manicures, there was an upper-deck lounge complete with a fully stocked bar and short-order kitchen, as well as a workout facility with showers on the lower-deck level. It seemed the hotter the competition, the more passenger friendly the "Friendly Skies" became.

When the tour was complete, Harvath, Morrell, and the rest of the team buckled into the overstuffed leather seats inside the lounge behind the flight deck, and the 747-400 was towed out of the hangar and onto the tarmac.

The engines growled to life, and minutes later the enormous craft was cleared and roaring down the runway. Harvath glanced at the 747-400 fact sheet he had been given when he arrived late on the tour and was awed by the statistics. The tail height of the 747-400 was six stories, each wing weighed 28,000 pounds and measured 5,600 square feet—an area large enough to park forty-five medium-sized cars. The "flexible" cabin layout allowed for changes in class and seating configuration in only eight hours and changes of lavatory and galley locations in forty-eight. The Wright brothers' first flight at Kitty Hawk could have been performed within the 150-foot economy-class section.

After the aircraft had leveled off at its cruising altitude of 35,000 feet and the captain had turned off the Fasten Seat Belt sign, Rick Morrell called his twelve-man team to order.

"We've got a long way to go and we'll be getting there in a short amount of time, so listen up. According to our flight plan, we should be touching down in Cairo at approximately oh three-thirty. We'll be landing at the old airport and will be choppered to Mubarak International. Sunrise on site occurs at oh six-twelve. The U.S. has a Combat Applications Group team in country working with the Egyptians, and they are already on-site—"

"'Combat Applications Group'?" broke in Harvath. "What is it with you and all the fancy terminology? Why don't you just call them Delta Force like everybody else?"

"Gentlemen," responded Morrell as he gestured toward Harvath, "I'm sure you all remember our docile charge from Jerusalem, Agent Scot Harvath of the U.S. Secret Service. As I mentioned to you before, by order of the president, he is now officially part of our operation. Let's give him a warm welcome to the team, shall we?"

The upper-deck lounge of the 747-400 was completely silent.

"Good," said Morrell. "Now that we have that out of the way, we can continue. As I was saying, there's already a Combat Applications Group team in country and on-site. As far as the Egyptians are concerned, we are CAG members also and will be there to assist the current CAG team. There are duffels with your names on them in the overhead compartments. You'll find your uniforms in there.

"Here's the scenario. As United Airlines flight 7755 was taxiing to its gate at Mubarak International Airport at approximately fourteen hundred hours local Cairo time, an armed group of hijackers took control of the plane. This was United's first nonstop flight from Chicago to Cairo and carried a host of dignitaries and VIPs including United's CEO and the mayor of Chicago."

"The mayor? You mean James Fellinger?" asked Harvath.

"You know him?" queried Morrell.

"I met him once with the president when we passed through Chicago for a fund-raiser. He's a decent guy. They say he's a shoo-in for Illinois governor in the next race and will probably make a serious bid for the White House eventually."

"In other words, this guy could one day be your boss. Better not fuck up, Harvath," said one of the operatives.

"I don't know who you think you work for," replied Scot, "but we all work for the president. That includes the CIA, though you guys think you're above everything."

"All right, all right," said Morrell. "That's enough. Let's get back to business. Now, three male passengers have already been killed. Their bodies were dumped from a forward exit door onto the tarmac. We believe two of the men were the air marshals working the flight. Preliminary reports seem to indicate that the third man was a guy named Lund, one of Mayor Fellinger's bodyguards. No one has been able to get close enough to the plane to retrieve the bodies, but from what the CAG team can tell, all three were probably dead before they hit the ground.

"The flight manifest indicates that it took off full with three hundred twenty passengers and twenty-three crew members, including the pilots. Upon landing, the captain was able to get off a message that the plane was undergoing a hijacking and that the hijackers had threatened to blow the cockpit door with C4 if it wasn't opened. That was the last that was heard of the captain. He had no idea how many hijackers there were. From that moment on, one of the hijackers took over communication with the tower. He threatened to begin killing passengers if anyone came near. There was some chatter in the cockpit and someone named Ghazi was addressed before a second man took over the radio and relayed the major demands. We know 'Ghazi' to be the code name for Hashim Nidal and believe it was him speaking. First, he demanded the unfreezing of all Abu Nidal assets being held by Egypt, and then demanded ten million dollars in cash, apiece, for Mayor Fellinger and United's CEO, Bob Lawrence."

"What makes you so sure it was Hashim?" asked Harvath.

"With twenty plus million dollars in cash on the line, I don't care how loyal Nidal might think his men are, even the pope wouldn't trust Mother Teresa with that much money. This is the kind of job you suit up for yourself. Now, there was also an additional instruction relayed to the Egyptians that they were not to connect any external power sources or the air-conditioning."

"It's got to be over a hundred degrees on the tarmac. How are they going to survive without AC?" asked one of Morrell's operatives.

"Simple," answered Harvath. "There's an auxiliary power unit mounted in the rear fuselage that allows the aircraft to remain self-sufficient in both the power and air-conditioning arenas."

"How the hell would you know?" asked the operative.

"Your mother told me," said Harvath. "Where do you think I learned it?" He picked up the blue Boeing folder and tapped it with his index finger. "Regardless of what you may think, reading really is fundamental."

The operative fumed and Morrell stepped back in to avoid further confrontation. "We're wasting time here."

"So, is the ransom going to be paid?" asked Harvath.

"Not if we can help it," answered Morrell, who walked over to the lounge's audiovisual cabinet, pressed a button to lower the flat-panel monitors, and inserted a DVD into the player. "This footage was taken at O'Hare International Airport yesterday as United Airlines flight 7755 was boarding. Somewhere in here we believe we have Hashim Nidal himself, as well as all of his men. With an aircraft of this size and almost three hundred fifty passengers and crew, he's going to need a lot of help to keep things under control."

Morrell then powered up his laptop computer, which was attached to a portable projector, and beamed a schematic of the 747-400 against the bulkhead. He gestured with a laser pointer as he spoke. "With a full passenger load, at the very least we figure he would need to post a man at the head and tail of each passenger section. That would make ten men, plus one or two extra to help take shifts and watch the crew.

"As is standard in airline hijackings, all of the window shades have been drawn, and in addition, the hijackers have covered the other windows, such as the cockpit glass, with what looks like aluminum foil," said Morrell as he punched a key on his laptop and another image was projected onto the wall. "This picture was sent to us by the CAG team. You'll notice it's of one of the passenger windows, and there in the middle, there seems to be some sort of suction-cup-like device. Apparently these have been placed on windows throughout the plane. We believe these to be motion detectors of some sort—"

"Those aren't motion detectors," interrupted Harvath.

"What do you mean?" asked Morrell.

"Motion detectors make no sense. Too many things can set one off, and when it goes off, how are the hijackers going to be able to verify what caused the alarm? Are they going to peek out a window and risk being shot? No. These guys are smarter than that."

"Apparently you are too. What do you think we're looking at, Agent Harvath?"

"Cameras."

"Cameras?"

"Yeah, they're called 'flat-lens' cameras. Silicon Valley is developing something like these for consumer use. Instead of the cameras that sit on top of your computer monitor like we have now, flat-lens cameras will be built into the actual monitor frame. It would be simple to rig some of those up as remotes. All you would need is a power source of some sort, maybe something as small as a watch battery. From what I can see, that cord hanging down is most likely an antenna. Hashim's probably got a man somewhere in the plane monitoring the feeds."

"Have you ever seen one of these flat-lens cameras in action?"

"The Secret Service was playing around with them a little bit, but the quality left a lot to be desired. It was hard to distinguish depth of field, but for a single airplane alone on the tarmac, even one close to the gate, having these all over would be like having a thousand eyes."

"If they are remote cameras, couldn't we block their signal?"

"You could try, but not knowing exactly what frequency

they're on, you'd never be absolutely sure you had them blocked."

"There's got to be some way around them."

Harvath thought a moment before responding. "There might be."

"What is it?"

"Nighttime. The cameras are not very good in low light. If you extinguished all of the airport lighting, the hijackers would be blind."

"And we'd have all of our guys using night-vision goggles. Good, we're making progress."

"What do you mean by *'all of our guys'?*" asked Harvath. "Will it be us and the Delta team, or are the Egyptians going to want in on this one too?"

"As a courtesy, President Mubarak has mobilized Egypt's counterterrorism unit."

"Which unit exactly?" asked Harvath, leaning forward in his seat, deep concern etched across his face.

"Unit 777."

"Unit 777? Thunderbolt Force? You've got to be kidding me."

"I am not kidding you, Harvath. Like I said, President Mubarak did it out of courtesy to the U.S."

"*Courtesy* to the U.S.? Morrell, do you conduct all of your operations with your thumb up your ass, or is this one just special?"

"What the hell are you talking about?"

"I'm talking about the Egyptians and their 777 unit. Do you really think they're going to sit idly by and let us run the show? What, if anything, do you know about this group?"

"They're Egypt's crack unit, formed by a presidential directive to conduct counterterrorism and hostage-rescue operations."

"*Crack*, my ass. They've had heavy training from the German GSG9, the French GIGN, and even our very own *Delta Force*, but they're far from being a crack unit. They can't even hold a candle to Delta."

"Which is why they are simply *standing* by."

"You really don't know what you're talking about, do you?"

"Harvath, if you've got a point, then get to it, or else shut your trap."

"November twenty-third, 1985? Egypt Air flight 648? Ring any bells?"

"Not really."

"On the evening of November twenty-third, 1985, one Omar Ali Rezaq and two other men, all card-carrying members of Abu Nidal's Fatah Revolutionary Council, boarded an Egypt Air flight out of Athens. Shortly after the plane took off, these three charmers produced weapons and demanded that the captain fly the plane to Malta. There was an Egyptian plainclothes sky marshal stationed on board, and a gunfight broke out. One of Rezaq's men was killed and the sky marshal was wounded.

"When the plane arrived in Malta, Rezaq demanded that it be refueled; and when the authorities refused, he announced that he would start shooting a passenger every fifteen minutes until the tanks were topped off. The authorities thought he was bluffing, but he wasn't. He shot two Israelis and then three Americans, dumping all of their bodies out the front door onto the tarmac.

"The next day, Unit 777, stormed the plane. It was one of the worst fuckups in counterterrorism history. These guys went in with guns blazing, and fired indiscriminately in every direction. They set off some sort of an explosive device, which sent the plane up in flames. When all was said and done, fifty-seven passengers were dead.

"Fifty-five of those deaths were attributed to the Egyptian 777 unit. When you take all of this into consideration, throw in Egypt's brand-new airport, add a ton of media attention, and the fact that this hijacking is very likely being carried out by the son of the guy who ordered the November '85 job—do you really believe the Egyptians are going to sit back and let us run the show?"

"As far as I'm concerned, our mission is the identification and neutralization of Hashim Nidal. Period. What the Egyptians do is their business. As long as they don't get in our way."

"Well, that's commendable, but what about the passengers?"

"Not our priority."

"'Not our priority'? How the hell can you say that? That plane is packed with hostages, most of whom are Americans. We have a duty to try to rescue them."

"We have a greater duty to make sure Hashim Nidal is eliminated. America does not want another World Trade Center."

"I don't want one either, but we have to at least try to rescue the passengers."

"I'm not saying they're not a consideration, but we're at war and war means casualties . . . sometimes even civilian casualties. It's just the way the game is played."

"Jesus. So this is what happens when a wet work team gets sent into a hostage-rescue situation."

"Harvath, I am not going to argue with you anymore. Our mission is our mission. If you want out, that's fine with me. As a matter of fact, I'm sure it's fine with all of us. But, if you're going to stay aboard, you do it with your mouth shut and you follow my orders. Got it?"

"Yeah, I got it. But I've also got one request."

"*Only* one?" said Morrell, playing to his men, who began to chuckle with him. "If it'll get you to shut up, then by all means, let's hear it."

"I can already see the way this thing is shaping up, so when we do the takedown on that plane, I want to be the first one in."

"You got it."

"And one more thing."

"See," said Morrell, "I knew you didn't want just *one* thing. What is it?"

"When we go in, I want *you* right there next to me."

"I wouldn't have it any other way."

"Neither would I," said Harvath. "Neither would I."

18

By ten P.M. Cairo time, Meg Cassidy knew there was no possible way she was going to be able to sleep. It was a luxury she couldn't afford, no matter how badly she needed it. Twice, she had fallen into short catnaps only to awaken and find the masked hijacker with the brown eyes staring at her. During the one and only bathroom break the hijackers had allowed, the man accosted her when she came out of the lavatory and had run his hands over the fabric of her black Armani pants suit, appraising her body beneath.

Luckily, it seemed to Meg, a second hijacker had appeared out of nowhere, and immediately saw what was happening. Harsh whispers were exchanged, and finally, the first man backed down. Though of the same height, this other hijacker was of a slighter build, with the most hypnotic eyes Meg had ever seen. She was immediately drawn to them. As Meg stared into the two orbs of brilliant silver, her mind went numb and the fear drained from her body. The hijacker gently touched her cheek with the back of a gloved hand and then indicated that she should return to her seat. Meg obeyed, filled with a strange sense of awe and gratitude. This feeling was soon replaced by visceral fear as the brown-eyed hijacker once again maneuvered himself into a position to catch Meg's eye. Only this time, his look registered pure hate.

19

After Morrell finished his briefing, he ran his men through a series of what were known as "exercises on the objective." The team practiced taking down the inside of the aircraft from every entry point, as well as some that they hoped the terrorists wouldn't see coming. They ran through the drills of coming down the aisles with the lights on and then with the lights completely extinguished, assisted by their night-vision goggles. When Morrell was satisfied the men had it completely covered, he dismissed them and they all returned to the upper-deck lounge.

Harvath chose to wander the enormous 747-400 alone, memorizing every detail of its layout. By the time he was done, he knew where every exit, lavatory, galley, and storage compartment was located and how much distance lay between each.

When he was confident that he had taken in as much as he could, Harvath made his way along the main deck into the nose of the aircraft and the first-class section. Much to his delight, he found that the United staff had completely stocked the galley, but someone had failed to inform the SAS team, who were gathered upstairs playing cards, eating bland military MREs, or Meals Ready to Eat, and popping Halcion tablets in preparation for sleep.

While the goat cheese for his salad and his double portion of prime rib were warming up, Harvath checked the AV cabinet, and sure enough, it had been stocked with the latest releases. *Well, this beats the hell out of playing old maid with the guys upstairs*, he thought to himself. Harvath fired up a movie and set a place for himself, complete with linen tablecloth, at one of the elegant first-class sleeper seats. He seriously considered building a huge hot fudge sundae—all the fixings were there—but decided against it. He was, after all, on duty.

His timing was perfect as he kicked off his shoes, covered himself with one of the cashmere first-class blankets, raised his personal video monitor and settled in for his meal. The movie was just starting. All things considered, this really was the only way to fly.

He had selected what looked like a promising film, a sappy love story, and it had the desired effect. Halfway through, he felt his mind relax and his eyelids grow heavy. As Harvath donned an eye mask and inserted earplugs into his ears, he pressed the button on his armrest and the seat automatically reclined to a completely horizontal bed. His colleagues had always remarked at his gift for being able to quiet his thoughts enough to nod off before any type of mission. It wasn't so much sleep as it was a Zen-like state of deep relaxation. Harvath always awoke refreshed and extremely focused, his thoughts and emotions perfectly calm.

When he did awaken and peek at his stainless-steel Rolex Explorer II, a quiet gift from the Swiss government for his role with Claudia in nailing the Lions of Lucerne, Scot calculated there were about two more hours before the plane would touch down. He made his way downstairs to the fitness center and closed the door behind him.

After some quick stretching, Harvath did two fast sets

of bench presses, followed by curls, then dips and finally some pull-ups. He grabbed a quick shower and shaved with the razor he had found in one of the amenity kits in first class. He headed back upstairs to the galley, where he popped an eggs Benedict breakfast into the oven and poured himself a couple of glasses of fresh orange juice. While he ate his breakfast, he brewed a pot of coffee and threw together a platter of lox, bagels, and cream cheese. Some might have called it a peace offering, but those who knew Scot Harvath would have called it what it really was—a rub-it-in-your-face display of what the unimaginative SAS Team had missed by huddling together in the upper-deck lounge for the entire flight.

Harvath changed into the black Nomex Delta Force fatigues, grabbed the coffee and bagels, and made his way to the upper-deck lounge. Several of the SAS team were wide awake and eating tasteless MRE breakfasts when Harvath came up the stairs. Those that weren't awake quickly came to when he set the tray down on the bar and the smell of fresh roasted coffee filled the cabin.

"Where'd you get that?" one of the men asked.

"We passed a Starbucks a little while ago and I thought it was the least I could do, seeing how well you treated me last time we all flew together."

One of the other men, who had already picked up a coffee cup and had the pitcher in his hand, stopped and said, "Wait a second; you didn't piss in this, did you?"

"Only in Morrell's," Scot responded.

The man just stared at Harvath for a moment and then, realizing it was a joke, went back to pouring his coffee.

"There's juice and pastries down in the first-class galley.

I also think I left a little hot water in the fitness-room shower, if anybody wants one."

Several men looked ready to do just that until Morrell piped up, "This isn't a fucking day spa. I've been informed by the pilot that we'll be landing early. We're going to do an equipment check, go over last-minute details, and, if time permits, run through the exercises on the objective again."

Morrell threw his MRE into the trash can behind the bar, grabbed a bagel and a cup of coffee, then brushed past Harvath on the way back to his seat.

"What? No *thank-you?*" said Harvath. "After I slaved over a hot stove all morning? Well, I'm sure glad I didn't serve any of my prime rib up here last night."

"You had prime rib last night?" asked another operative.

"He's pulling your leg. He got lucky and found some bagels and coffee," said Morrell. "Quit causing trouble, Harvath, and sit the fuck down."

A few of the men were obviously torn as to who was telling the truth, but Harvath quickly set them straight. "You bet your ass I had prime rib. And then I had eggs Benedict for breakfast. There's even an ice cream sundae bar down there."

"Ice cream sundaes?" said one of the younger operatives, who had obviously never flown first or business class before. "Now I know you're bullshitting."

"Ah, ya got me," said Harvath as two other men, who could tell he was telling the truth, slipped quietly out of the cabin toward the first-class galley downstairs.

Morrell called the rest of his men to order and began relaying the latest situation report, or *sit rep,* for short.

"The CAG guys are inclined to agree with Agent Harvath on the flat-lens cameras."

"You're welcome," said Harvath.

Morrell ignored him and kept going. "The Egyptians have been using microwave sound amplifiers on the aircraft, but the intelligence gathered thus far has not been helpful. An offer to board maintenance crews to service the plane, restock it with food and water, and unclog any problem toilets was flatly denied. We had hoped that some of the CAG members could pose as maintenance crew and gather intelligence while planting listening devices and our own miniature cameras, but the hijackers repeated their threat to start killing passengers if anyone came near the plane.

"As a show of good faith, the Egyptians have freed up two million dollars, part of Abu Nidal's frozen assets, and per the hijackers' instructions, are pulling the money together in cash. They hope it might gain the release of some of the women and children, but I doubt it. The hijackers say that they're not releasing any passengers until their demands have been met in full."

"Did they set a deadline?" asked Harvath.

"Noon."

"If they don't get their money and assets by noon?"

"I think that's obvious, Harvath. They're going to start blowing the passengers away one by one until their demands are met. They've killed three people already. I don't think there's any doubt in anyone's mind as to whether or not they're serious. The mayor and United's CEO are the big-ticket items, so they're safe for the time being, although it's possible the hijackers might sacrifice one of them, just to make a point."

"Blow away a ten-million-dollar hostage? That's a pretty expensive sacrifice."

"You never know with these people. This is a very sticky situation—especially for the Egyptians."

"How is the good-faith money supposed to be delivered?"

"The hijackers want the full two million in twenties and hundreds placed in clear plastic bags and driven out to the plane in an open-air airport service cart driven by a lone woman."

"A woman?"

"Yeah. I guess the hijackers figure a girl is less threatening."

"Then what?"

"Then the hijackers will select a couple of passengers to lower a net of some sort, the money will be placed into it, and that's that."

"Any chance we can get a listening device or anything like that into the money?"

"If we were using suitcases or briefcases, maybe, but there's no chance of smuggling anything inside clear plastic bags."

"What's the situation at the airport?"

"The CAG guys say it's an absolute circus. It's jammed with media people. Every move President Mubarak makes is being analyzed from a thousand different angles."

"Which means he's going to be pretty jumpy, and so will his 777 guys. What's the plan?" asked Harvath.

"The plan," said Morrell, "is that when we land we'll be met by one of the CAG guys and updated as we chopper to the rendezvous with the rest of the team at the new airport.

There, we'll do a quick collective briefing, and when everything is in order, we take down that plane."

Morrell was winging it, and Harvath knew that in a situation like this, the man didn't have much of a choice, but
his short-term priorities were not in the right order.
Nobody, especially Harvath, wanted another crazed group
of terrorists on the loose, but there were civilians on that
plane and any plan that fell short of providing for their safe
extraction was not a plan worth pursuing—at least not yet.

Harvath's feelings of unease only deepened when Morrell projected a picture of the airport's layout on the bulkhead and said, as he indicated where the aircraft was
parked, "If all else fails, we have been authorized to destroy
the plane."

20

A million things passed through Meg Cassidy's mind as she pondered what the hijackers had in store for her and the several hundred other passengers. There was no question that if provoked, these men would kill any or all of them. They had already proven that. They had also proven that they would act even when not provoked. The flight attendant who had been so badly beaten at the beginning of the hijacking now lay on the floor of the galley not far from where Meg sat. Over the past few hours his breathing had grown more shallow and rapid. Though she was no doctor, Meg suspected that the hijackers had broken at least one of his ribs, which had punctured his lung. The man might very well be dying right before her eyes.

Concentrating on someone else's plight temporarily took her mind off of her own incredible fear. Meg knew that she was an attractive woman. Today though, her good looks were working against her. Though she tried to lean away from the aisle whenever he passed, the masked hijacker who had accosted her earlier found ways to brush up against her. Usually, he would do it by coming up the aisle from behind her, so that she couldn't see him approach. All of the passengers had been told to sit facing forward, or else. No one had to guess at what the *or else* meant.

She had always wondered what the people on the hijacked planes on September 11 must have felt. She had heard recordings of the desperate cell phone calls made to loved ones from passengers who knew they were going to die. There was also the valiant struggle of the passengers on the fourth plane, which was brought down in a field in Pennsylvania. After the well-publicized heroism of those passengers, surely these hijackers would be alert to a passenger uprising. Of course they were. That's why the men worked in shifts and never took their eyes off them, not even for a second.

Meg looked at her watch. Before taking off, she had set it ahead to local Cairo time. It read four A.M. She computed the time difference and realized it was nine o'clock in the evening back in Chicago. She tried to relax, but she couldn't help wondering if she would ever see her home again.

Meg thought about her small band of employees back in Chicago. No matter how many magazine or newspaper interviews she did, Meg never forgot to mention the people who had really made Cassidy Public Relations a success. "Family" was the best way Meg could describe them. In particular, Meg thought about her assistant, Judy, who not only was the most efficient person she had ever met and helped keep Meg's frantic life in order, but doted on her as if she were her own daughter. Judy arrived at the office every morning before any of the other staff to make coffee and often set out her own home-baked cookies or brownies. Though her baking was fabulous, her coffee was terrible, and Meg made it a point to stop in at a local coffee shop on her way each day to fill her stainless steel thermos.

Thinking of her morning routine drew Meg's mind back to her apartment and the nine-millimeter pistol she kept beside her bed. Never once since her father had given it to her had she had reason to use it, but now she wished she had it with her.

Fearing that the hijackers could somehow read her thoughts, Meg self-consciously looked up, but no one was watching her. She closed her eyes again and saw the smiling face of Judy floating in front of her. She wanted to believe that it was a sign that somehow, thousands of miles away in Chicago, Judy was her guardian angel watching over her. Meg's seatmate, Bernard Walsh, stirred from his restless sleep and reached across the armrest to place a reassuring hand atop hers. Meg wanted to appear strong and began to smile at the gesture, but the smile was short-lived. From behind her in the aisle a strong hand reached out and jerked her roughly to her feet. She tried to turn to see who it was, but was punched in the back of her head. She saw stars, and her knees almost buckled as she was pushed forward. Meg didn't really need to see the face to know who the person was. It could only be the masked hijacker who had accosted her earlier. Her worst fears were coming true. She had known he was going to come back for her sooner or later. The specter that had haunted Meg's dreams for several years had taken on a new incarnation, and he was shoving her toward the stairway for the upper deck.

Part of her wanted to die right then and there. Silently she implored God to take her, to not make her relive what no human being should have had to experience, even once in a lifetime.

At that same moment, Bernard leapt from his seat and made a run at the masked hijacker. With the fingers of both hands interlaced, he swung and came down hard upon the man's back. The hijacker grunted in pain, then spun full force and caught Meg's protector in the mouth with his elbow. Bernard was knocked unconscious from the powerful blow and fell down hard across his seat as blood trickled from his split lip. The hijacker removed his silenced pistol and shot him twice in the chest.

The killer then turned to face the rest of the nearby passengers, daring anyone else to try something. Not a single passenger moved. Meg, whose blood now ran as cold as ice, was paralyzed with fear. The masked hijacker once again pushed her toward the stairs. She could tell by the intensity of the man's shoving that he had no intention of being interrupted again. This time, he expected to get what he wanted.

Meg refused to move until the man put his gun back in his jumpsuit and produced a long, razor-sharp blade. He reached over her shoulder and placed it across her throat. What inner force propelled Meg forward, she did not know. When she prayed to God again to bring her death, a voice resonated from deep within her body with but one word, *No.*

Meg Cassidy's will to live was proving even stronger than her fear of reliving her worst nightmare. Without consciously knowing why, she placed one foot in front of the other as she and the hijacker climbed the stairs and finally found themselves alone in the upper-deck lounge.

The man sheathed his blade, but not before warning Meg in his thickly accented English what he would do with it if she cried out or made any trouble. He then wrenched her arm in a quick and painful twist to further make his point. A slight cry, more out of fear than pain, escaped her lips even though she fought to hold it back. She didn't want to give this bastard the satisfaction.

The man ran his hands over her body once again, appraising it, before pushing her down onto the floor. He hesitated a moment, then reached up and removed the ski mask from his head.

My God, Meg thought to herself as she looked at his face. She knew that the man had remained disguised so that no one would be able to identify him. Removing his mask in front of her left no room to doubt that once he had had his way with her, he was going to kill her.

As the man tore off her jacket and ran his hands over her breasts, Meg tried to struggle, but the man struck her again. Blood began to pour from her mouth. He had her outweighed and pinned to the floor of the lounge. Her eyes frantically scanned the area around her for anything that might help. All she saw were drink stirs, peanuts, and crumpled United cocktail napkins scattered across the floor. There was nothing she saw that could help her.

Again she struggled, this time trying to bite her attacker's wrist. The attempt was met with the loud slap and numbing sting of the man's hand once more striking her face. In a flash, he had his long blade unsheathed and placed under her chin with the tip resting behind her ear.

"If you resist me further, I will cut your throat. Do you understand me?" he said.

Meg responded by spitting in his face.

The man lifted the blade ever so slightly away from Meg's throat and swung his other hand, which he'd balled into a heavy fist, in a swift arc. He delivered a searing blow to Meg's abdomen, knocking the wind out of her. She heaved and gasped for air. She could tell he enjoyed watching her writhe beneath him. As he moved the tip of his knife blade toward the button on Meg's pants, there was a sudden shattering noise from the other end of the lounge.

The hijacker spun just in time to see Mayor Fellinger's second bodyguard, who had been handcuffed and locked in one of the upper-deck lavatories, barreling down on top of him. With his wrists secured behind him, the best weapon the guard had was his massive square shoulders. Tucking his chin in to the left, he led with his right shoulder and rammed it into the hijacker. As he did, the cold steel of the man's blade sliced deep into the guard's stomach and flayed him open to the sternum.

Meg, whose breath had just barely returned, knew this was her only chance. While the hijacker struggled to get out from underneath the dying weight of the bodyguard, she frantically looked around again for some sort of a weapon. There was nothing. The only thing she had were her bare hands. Primal instinct took over. Her long nailed fingers immediately curled into talons and she leapt for the hijacker. Just as she was about to close in on his throat, the butt of his pistol, protruding from his jumpsuit, caught her eye.

The hijacker must have sensed what Meg had seen because he stopped trying to get out from under the dead bodyguard long enough to grab her wrist as she lunged for the gun. She managed to slip the man's grasp and grabbed his gun. She pointed it at him and felt her hand tighten around the weapon's grip. She found herself shaking with rage and fought to get control of herself. Though she tried to ease up on the trigger, her finger tightened upon it still further. There was a loud burst of fire followed immediately by another.

It amazed her that a silenced pistol would make so much noise. Just downstairs, when the hijacker had shot Bernard Walsh, the weapon had made nothing more than the sound of two muffled spits. It was then that Meg realized her pistol hadn't even so much as twitched and that the shots she heard hadn't come from the weapon she was holding.

Meg spun just in time to see two hijackers who had mounted the stairs to the upper-deck lounge quickly closing the gap with her. She hit the deck and, remembering what she had been taught by her father, aimed and fired at each man. She watched as they fell to the floor and came to a sliding stop only feet away.

Meg knew that she needed to make sure that they were not just playing dead. As she rose to her feet and was about to make her way over to the fallen hijackers, she felt a searing pain across her ankle. Looking down, she saw her would-be rapist was still alive and moved back before he could swing at her again with his deadly blade.

The man had almost freed himself from beneath the enormous bodyguard. He was going to kill her. She was certain of it. Without a moment's hesitation, she raised the pistol and shot him in the head. As he slumped back to the floor, the blade tumbled from his hand.

Meg examined the wound on her on ankle. The cut was bad, but could have been much worse. She needed to stem the flow of blood, and though she was loath to do it, she reached for the hijacker's ski mask and used his knife to rip part of it into a makeshift bandage, which she tied tightly around her ankle. She knew there was no time to rest. She could hear the dead hijackers' radios crackling with calls in what she assumed was Arabic, probably instructing the men to report on the cause of the gunshots. Though the weapon Meg carried was silenced, the weapons carried by the men shooting at her were not.

She stole a glance behind where she had been standing and saw that the hijackers' shots had not been as wildly placed as she had thought. They had blown out two of the windows on the left-hand side of the aircraft, and from what Meg could see, the remaining shots had just narrowly missed hitting her. Maybe Judy was somehow watching out for her, after all, or maybe, just maybe, her father really had taught her "everything" he knew about shooting.

"We're not done yet," Meg said half to herself as the smell of gunpowder hung in the quiet air of the upper deck. She knew that the decisions she made in the next seconds would undoubtedly mean the difference between life and death not only for her, but for the entire crew and passengers as well.

Carefully, Meg removed two Italian-made, nine-millimeter Beretta model 12S submachine guns from the dead hijackers.

She slung both over her shoulder and, with the silenced pistol carefully gripped in both hands, crept toward the stairwell. Before she could get there, another hijacker emerged from it halfway up. Meg crouched in the ready position, and when he made it to the top of the stairs, she hit him with two shots to the chest. Despite the adrenaline, or maybe because of it, she was dead-on accurate.

As the hijacker fell to the floor, he came dangerously close to sliding backward and falling down the stairs. Meg ran to him and caught him by his collar just in time. The last thing she wanted to do was tip off his friends that she was coming, and bringing hell with her.

Slinging the third hijacker's weapon over her shoulder, she now felt as if she weighed a thousand pounds. Stepping around the dead man's body, she slowly made her way down the stairs. Meg swept her pistol from side to side, just as she had been taught, alert for any movement. *It's only a matter of time*, she told herself. *Be ready*.

By the time she hit the bottom step, Meg knew what her next move would be. Both Mayor Fellinger and United CEO Bob Lawrence were ex-military. If anyone could make a difference here, it was them. Based on the men she had killed upstairs and what she had observed during the hijacking, Meg figured there were *at least* two hijackers left in business class and two more in first.

With her pistol at the ready, she swung out from the stairway into the aisle on the port side of the aircraft. No more than five feet away was one of the hijackers guarding the business-class passengers. He saw Meg and was quick in raising his weapon, but not quick enough. Meg hit the man with a shot in the throat, and he fell in a heap on top of the body of Bernard Walsh. In a flash, a nearby passenger, whom Meg recognized as Dan LeHay from United's ad agency, stripped the newly departed hijacker of his weapon. Meg instructed him to proceed parallel with her up the opposite aisle toward first class. She told him not to shoot unless absolutely necessary. If there was any shooting to be done, she wanted to do it with the silenced pistol.

Another passenger quickly offered his services, and Meg instructed him to watch their backs as she unslung one of the submachine guns and handed it to him. There was no way for her to know how many hijackers were in the rear of the plane.

Meg and Dan Lehay made their way toward the front of the plane. From across the forward business-class cabin, the remaining hijacker guarding the business-class passengers saw Dan coming and raised his weapon. Before Meg could take a shot, three sharply dressed passengers in blue blazers with University of Southern California and American flag lapel pins took advantage of the distraction and leapt from their seats. As quietly as they could, the USC men beat the crap out of the hijacker.

Meg quickly moved into the center aisle and called Dan Lehay over to her. "From what I can guess, there's no more than two of them guarding first class. We need to get up there and arm the mayor and Bob Lawrence. If you can distract them, I think I can take both of them out."

"Are you that good a shot?" he asked.

"For all of our sakes, I'd better be."

"What do you want me to do?"

"First, we're going to pass your weapon up to those guys in the blue blazers. I'm sure one of them will be able to handle it. You'll then walk up your aisle to first class and walk directly in. Hopefully that will confuse the hijackers and that's when I'll do my thing."

"That's it?" asked Lehay.

"That's it. But don't just stand there. Act lost or sick or something. Do whatever you can to help confuse them. When I start firing, get down on the ground."

"Try to shoot straight, okay?" said Dan Lehay as he took a deep breath, squared his shoulders, and walked past the galley and into the first-class cabin, praying the entire way that Meg Cassidy would be able to pull it off.

The minute he entered first class, both of the hijackers snapped to. *At least there were only two of them.* So far Meg was batting a thousand.

The hijackers told him to put his hands up.

"What you do here?" one of them asked in broken English.

"Ah, well, you see," replied Lehay, trying to mask his fear and grasping in his mind for something, anything, to say to distract the hijackers. "We're all out of Colombian coffee back in business class and—"

Colombian coffee? The two hijackers couldn't understand what they were hearing. They turned to look at each other, and that was when Meg sprang from the opposite aisle. Her first shot went wide, but she ran straight at them and kept pulling the trigger until both men were lying on the floor in a pool of blood. Once again, the passengers began screaming.

Quickly she made her way to the mayor and Bob Lawrence. Meg recounted what had happened as she handed over the two submachine guns she had slung over her shoulder. As she was finishing her story, Dan Lehay appeared, armed to the teeth like a Mexican bandido.

Meg told Lehay to watch the aisle and turned back to the mayor and Bob Lawrence. "Any ideas?" she asked.

"First and foremost," said Lawrence, "we have to see to the safety of the passengers on this plane."

"I agree," said the mayor, "but let's keep in mind one

thing. The only language these people understand is"—he paused as he pulled the slide back on his submachine gun— "nine-millimeter."

Before anyone could respond, an enormous explosion rocked the back of the plane and was followed immediately by automatic-weapons fire.

21

When Harvath and the CIA SAS team landed at the old Cairo airport, it took them only fifteen minutes to unload their weapons pallets from the cargo hold of the United 747-400. Morrell had anticipated every eventuality. In addition to the standard equipment the team would need for the takedown of the hijacked aircraft, the pallets also contained a host of concealable gear they could use, on the off chance the hijackers changed their minds and allowed a maintenance crew on board to service and restock the plane.

One of Harvath's favorite "sneaky" weapons was the extremely short H&K MP5K submachine gun covertly mounted in a toolbox, which could be fired via a button on the toolbox's handle. He had used one years ago in Turkey, where a prominent American businessman and his family had been taken hostage. In this instance he'd had the weapon mounted inside a briefcase, and when he showed up for the exchange, all of the kidnappers thought he was carrying the ransom money. Their expressions of shock and surprise barely registered on Harvath as he took out every last one of them. They never saw it coming. When the rest of Harvath's team stormed the building, there was nothing left for them to do but help escort the businessman and his family safely back to the U.S. Embassy.

After strapping on his body armor, Harvath stuffed every pocket he had with extra clips of ammunition. The CIA had spared no expense. Not only were the weapons top-of-the-line, but so was the tactical gear. All of it had come from BlackHawk Industries out of Norfolk, Virginia. Harvath placed several flash bangs into a hip pouch, then wrapped the support strap of his low-slung black nylon assault holster around his right thigh. He glanced around at the SAS team, all dressed in Delta Force's black, fire-retardant Nomex fatigue uniforms, as he was, and knew he was going to have to watch his own back when the takedown took place. None of these guys were going to take care of him. That was fine by Harvath, because as far as he was concerned, not only could he outshoot and outmaneuver all of them, he could also outthink them.

Harvath did one last check of his equipment. Though the locked and cocked H&K USP pistol at his side was an excellent backup, the hope was that any shooting would be done quickly with his MP5. Transitioning weapons mid-assault normally meant things were not going well. To that end, he used a magazine "doubler" for the MP5 to secure two thirty-round magazines together for fast and easy changes. He checked the submachine gun's laser sight and then bent down to strap on his kneepads.

Though Morrell had said not to bring anything with him at all, Harvath still brought along his favorite combat folding knife—a Benchmade 9050 automatic.

The stainless-steel blade featured a razor-sharp edge and a needle-sharp point that swung into place with the push of a button. Harvath had no idea whether he would need it, but he felt good just knowing he had it with him. He clipped the knife into a vest pocket and realized that it also felt good knowing he had found a way to disobey one of Morrell's direct orders.

As it closed low and fast, Harvath could make out the distinct rotor noise of a MH-60 Black Hawk helicopter. The men gathered their gear and made their way to where the helicopter was preparing to land. Within three minutes of touching down, the Black Hawk was loaded and once again airborne, rushing Harvath and the SAS team the twenty-five miles to the new Mubarak International Airport.

Through the open side doors of the darkened Black Hawk, Harvath could taste the dry desert air. He slipped on his night-vision goggles, often called NODs—short for Night Optical Devices—and watched through glowing green lenses Cairo's chaotic jumble of decrepit mud dwellings and crisp modern buildings slip rapidly beneath them as they sped through the night sky. In a matter of minutes, it would be show time. Scot felt the familiar quickening of his pulse and tightening of his muscles. He was like a racehorse chomping at the bit, ready to explode from the gate.

Scot, like everyone else, tuned his Motorola to the same encrypted frequency and listened via his headset as the Delta Force commander sitting next to Morrell relayed the codes and radio frequencies that were being used for the operation. He did one last check of his gear as the Black Hawk flared and came in for a landing on the far side of Cairo's new international airport. The helicopter had covered the twenty-five-mile distance from airport to airport in just over ten minutes.

A group of Suburbans sped across the tarmac toward the Black Hawk and pulled up as the team was unloading the last of their equipment. The gear was quickly transferred to the oversized black SUVs, and the men grabbed whatever seats they could find. Harvath recognized a Delta Force operative behind the wheel of one of the Suburbans and jumped in the passenger seat next to him. The man was a no-BS guy from Brooklyn who had a gift for getting to the point. He was also an incredible shot. Everyone referred to him as Bullet Bob. Scot knew him from Delta's Special Operations Training facility at Fort Bragg.

"Harvath? What the hell are you doing here?" asked the man, surprised to see him.

"I've crossed over to the dark side, Bobby," said Harvath in an exaggerated, monster theater voice as the Suburban raced toward the terminal.

"So, you're doing black ops for the CIA now? What the hell happened to the Secret Service?"

"I'm still Secret Service, but these CIA guys are so fucked up, I got asked to come along and give them some pointers."

"Well, if you came to give them tips on killing, you're going to be preaching to the choir."

"That's what I'm afraid of. This group is very 'Tango'-centric. There's no question that the passengers in this op are not a priority for them. Where are we going to be?" asked Harvath.

"We're actually in the terminal—at the EgyptAir clubroom, a few gates down from where the plane is."

"Isn't that a little dangerous?"

"It depends on what your definition of 'dangerous' is. It gives us perfect access. All of the windows in the airport are reflective, like those two-way mirrors in interrogation rooms. We can see them, but they can't see us. If they take a pot shot and hit anything, it'd only be through sheer luck."

As they neared the terminal and began to slow down, Bob spoke again. "Well, here we are, Mubarak International."

Harvath looked up at the immense white marble structure rising out of the desert sand and hoped that it wouldn't be covered in blood come morning.

Bob helped Scot unload his gear from the back of the Suburban, but didn't bother to offer the CIA guys any help. It was obvious he cared for them even less than Harvath did.

Inside the terminal, Morrell and some of the other men were already waiting. He did a head count and once everyone was together, they made their way upstairs to the EgyptAir clubroom.

The room was tastefully decorated with leather sofas and a green-and-blue patterned carpet that was supposed to represent the Nile. Large potted palms stood in every corner, and all of the tables were carved from rich black marble. Scot knew a couple of the other Delta operatives in the room and nodded in their direction. They returned the greeting as the others went about their business.

The Delta Force commander, after a short conversation with Morrell, instructed the room to settle down and then began his briefing. The order from on high was to end the standoff. An Egyptian officer, presumably a member of the 777 unit, translated for his colleagues. The majority of the briefing covered information that had already been relayed to Harvath and the CIA SAS team en route. The Delta commander used a map of the airport and pointed out where his snipers had been placed and where one of the SAS snipers was to be positioned. Teams were assigned for the takedown and team code names were established. The Egyptian, 777 unit would bring up the very rear of the takedown. They would enter opposite the American team assigned to breach the rear of the aircraft, but only after the Americans were already inside.

Harvath couldn't believe his ears. They were actually going to let the Egyptians get a piece of it! He looked toward Morrell to communicate his disapproval, but Morrell ignored him. Bullet Bob rolled his eyes and then shook his head, demonstrating that he thought as much of the idea as Harvath did. Somewhere, somebody was playing politics and it had absolutely no place in a situation of this magnitude. At least Harvath was going to be breaching the front of the aircraft. He wouldn't have to worry about a bullet in the back from one of the Egyptians. *No, but he might have to worry about one from one of the SAS operatives.*

After all of the elements of the takedown had been clarified, the briefing was adjourned and the men were dispatched to their positions. Morrell's sniper team headed off toward the control tower with an enormous, silenced FNH Hecate II fifty-caliber sniper rifle. With an effective range of over two thousand meters, Harvath knew there wasn't much that those boys weren't going to be able to hit.

He and Morrell made their way with the rest of their team down the concourse to an access stairway next to the gate where the hijacked plane was parked. Inside the stairwell, half of the team descended to wait behind a door that gave out onto the tarmac, while the rest of the team went up. At the top of the stairway, just behind the door that opened out onto the roof, Morrell was true to his word. When they got into formation for the assault, Scot was first in line with Morrell right behind him. *At least this way*, he figured, *if he did get shot in the back, he'd know who to haunt.*

Harvath tried to relax and focused on his breathing. He looked at the SAS men surrounding him, every one of them cool as a cucumber. In fact, despite the still, warm air of the stairwell, there was not a single bead of perspiration on any of them. *Goddamn freaks*, Harvath thought to himself. *The CIA must have removed their sweat glands — probably at the same time they removed their personality glands.*

After drying the moisture from his forehead with the back of his sleeve, Scot glanced at the luminescent dial of his watch. They were T minus ten minutes and counting. When the "Go" command came over their earpieces, both teams would quietly exit their respective doors. The downstairs team, code-named Alpha, would sneak beneath the belly of the plane and, via a collapsible stainless-steel ladder, frame a C4 ribbon charge right beneath the floor of the 747-400's workout room. Harvath and Morrell's team, code-named Bravo, had a similar, but more difficult task.

Bravo Team's duty was to cross the terminal roof and lower themselves down onto the top of the Jetway. One of the SAS members, now hiding inside the Jetway, would quietly maneuver it as close to the aircraft as possible. Using suction cups, the Bravo Team would scale the side of the 747 to the very top, above the upper-deck lounge, where they would frame their own shape charge and enter through the ceiling.

The magic of explosives was that they always sought the path of *most* resistance. This meant that the charge placed on the belly of the plane would blow straight up and the charge placed on the roof above the upper-deck lounge would blow straight down. The demolition charge itself looked like gray-colored Fruit Roll-Up, only thicker. The goal was to blow right through the skin of the aircraft, through any wires or anything else that might get in the way, and create a big enough opening for the team members to enter through.

Everyone on the ground knew that the longer they waited to attack, the more the hijackers would be anticipating it. Most likely, the hijackers had rigged the main forward door of the aircraft, and possibly several others, with a satchel charge designed to trigger an enormous explosion if anyone attempted to enter through those points. Though the SAS team could easily have blown that door off its hinges from a safe distance away and not gotten hurt, the hijackers were not very likely to foresee the team coming from above and below. This would help give them the element of surprise so desperately needed in an action of this type.

As Alpha and Bravo detonated their quarter-inch ribbon charges, creating a deafening explosion and disorienting pressure change throughout the aircraft, other teams would be breaching several doors on both sides of the plane via mobile staircases on the tarmac.

It was Harvath's sincere hope that with his superb speed and marksmanship, he could take out as many of the hijackers as possible and prevent the loss of any passengers or crew members.

He opened the stairwell door in front of him just a crack to let in some fresh air and was immediately greeted by the faint sound of automatic-weapons fire. Though the sound was heavily muffled, when two windows were blown out on the left side of the upper deck, it became obvious to all that the shots had come from inside the aircraft.

Morrell radioed the Delta commander and relayed what they had heard. Harvath and the rest of the team were deathly quiet. Their hands tightened around the grips of their MP5s as adrenaline coursed through their veins.

Suddenly, without warning, every light in the airport, both inside and out, was extinguished. *Someone had jumped the gun.*

22

Harvath and the rest of the team immediately switched on their NODs. Morrell did the same as he hailed the Delta commander and demanded to know why the lights had been shut off before the agreed to time. Speed, surprise, and overwhelming force of action were the key to a successful takedown, and surprise appeared to have been all but taken away from them.

Finally, the Delta commander radioed back that the 777 unit had jumped the gun and weren't responding to his orders to hold up. On a separate channel, they had given the command in Arabic to airport staff to kill the lights and were currently zooming across the tarmac on their mobile staircase.

"Fuck!" was the next thing to come out of Rick Morrell's mouth. Harvath wanted to say, *I told you so*, but choked it back. Now wasn't the time.

Morrell finally recovered and gave the "Go" command for the teams to move out. Harvath pushed the door all the way open and, crouching low, ran across the gravel-covered roof, followed by the rest of Bravo Team. He dropped noiselessly onto the top of the heavy Jetway and ran forward as the SAS man inside began maneuvering it closer to the plane.

Before Harvath got all the way to the end, a hail of gunfire erupted from the cockpit and the Jetway stopped moving. He and the rest of the team were sitting ducks.

Harvath hit the deck and prepared to return fire, but even with the NODs on, couldn't see anyone through the foil-covered windows of the cockpit. There was no telling if the hijackers were holding any flight crew in there with them. Harvath didn't want to risk killing one of the pilots.

Morrell called frantically over the radio to get the Jetway moving again, but his man below was not responding. One of the Alpha operatives reported from below the plane that the Jetway's navigation station had been riddled with bullets and it looked like they had a man down.

Once again, the first thing that came to Morrell's lips was, "Fuck!"

This party was going ugly early. It was obvious to Harvath that Morrell was quickly coming to the end of his command ability, and there was no way he was going to sit with his ass hanging out in the wind on top of the Jetway waiting for Hashim Nidal or one of his guys to pick them all off. It was time to take control.

Harvath activated his throat mike and called over the radio to the Delta sniper team. "Tick Tock One, Tick Tock One, this is Bravo Team, do you copy?"

"Roger that, Bravo. This is Tick Tock One. We copy," came the voice of Bullet Bob.

"I've got a VUP in the cockpit, but he may have flight crew with him. I need you to pin him down. Throw some of that heavy lead in there nice and high."

"Roger that, Bravo Team. 'Very unfriendly person' in the cockpit, possible friendlies present. I'll see what I can do to pin him down. Tick Tock One out."

Harvath next radioed the SAS sniper team to take out the plane's auxiliary power unit mounted in the 747's rear fuselage. His hope was that it would disrupt power within the plane and shut off the interior lights.

"Who the fuck is this?" demanded the CIA sniper.

"This is Norseman," replied Harvath, "now take out that APU!"

"I don't take orders from you, Harvath."

"Do it now!" broke in the voice of Morrell, who must have finally found his balls rolling around somewhere on top of the Jetway. Next, he focused his attention on Harvath, "We need to get somebody down to that navigation station and get the Jetway up against the plane."

"No time," answered Harvath, who crawled past Morrell and back up the Jetway.

"Harvath! Harvath! What the fuck are you doing?" hissed Morrell.

Scot ignored him and kept crawling until he was alongside the team's designated demolition man, none other than the operative he had elbowed in the mouth in Jerusalem.

"Give me your demo sack," said Harvath as he reached for it.

"What the hell for?" he asked, pulling the bag out of Harvath's grasp.

"I've got a plane to catch. Hurry up."

"No way. That's not the plan," responded the man.

Harvath hated it when people refused to cooperate, especially disagreeable people. "So much for team spirit," he said as he pinned the man's hand in a sophisticated joint lock, quickly retrieved the demo sack, and slung it over his back along with his MP5. As Harvath was sliding his gloved hands through the specially designed fittings of the black polymer climbing cups, Rick Morrell crawled over.

"What the hell's going on here?" he asked.

"Beats me," said Harvath.

"I don't know what you're up to, Harvath, but—"

"What *we're* up to is making a jump for that plane."

"Are you crazy?" responded Morrell. "There's no way we'll make it. It's too far away. I'll get one of the Alpha Team guys up to get us closer."

"There's no time. We go now."

"Bullshit. We go when I say, and I say we get the Jetway closer!"

"Sorry. No can do," said Harvath as he got up and took off running down the Jetway.

He bounded down the roof of the Jetway and ran as hard as he could while Bullet Bob tore up the hijacked 747's cockpit with half-inch rounds. At the very end of the Jetway, Harvath pushed off with all his might and flung himself out into space toward the big bird.

When he hit, he hit hard, but true to all the propaganda from Fretwell Industries, the suction cups didn't fail and he was now adhered to the aluminum skin of the plane. Using the *grip* and *release* buttons on the sides of the suction-cup handles, he quickly pulled himself up to the top of the plane. It was similar to the hull climbing he had learned in his SEAL days, only a lot drier. Once atop the plane, instead of turning left and heading toward the bubble, he turned right and ran toward the tail.

Morrell's voice could be heard immediately through his earpiece. "Harvath! What the hell are you doing? The plan was to make for the bubble and breach there."

"That was the old plan," replied Scot. "Now we're going to do things the way they should be done."

"Harvath, you've gone too far—"

"So have the Egyptians. From what I can see from up here, it's only a matter of minutes before they arrive, and they've got a head start on the Delta boys. Do you want them doing the takedown or us?"

"Us, of course," replied Morrell.

"Good. Then we do it my way," replied Harvath as he reached the tail-end section of the airplane and fished the ribbon charge from the demo sack. From what he had memorized about the 747–400's layout, he knew he was above an open area in economy class with four lavatories and no passenger seating.

"Okay, we do it your way, but I want you to know I am not happy about this," said Morrell.

"And I am? Just instruct Alpha Team of the change and to wait for my signal."

"Will do. Hold a sec—"

"What's up?" asked Harvath.

"It looks like Tick Tock Two knocked out the APU. Behind the window shades the plane has gone totally dark."

"Perfect. I'm framing my hatch. Have Alpha get ready to blow the belly."

"On your mark."

Harvath thought about what his next move was going to be. Every single terrorist between the tail end of the plane and business class was going to be his responsibility once he blew his hole and jumped inside. He pulled what he always referred to as "Man's best friend," the roll of duct tape he never traveled without, from his pocket and pulled up the suction-cup devices sitting next to him. Wrapping the tape beneath the handles and around his legs, he quickly secured the devices to the back of his calves. Harvath activated the cups to "grip" and then radioed Morrell. "This is Norseman."

"Roger, Norseman," came Morrell's voice.

"Is Alpha Team on line?"

"Roger that," came the voice of Alpha Team's leader.

"We go on my mark. In three . . . two . . . one . . . Now!"

Harvath's explosion kicked in first, followed by a devastating concussion from the bottom of the aircraft. He pulled out two flash-bang grenades from his hip pouch, jumped across the gaping wound in the plane's skin, and slammed the suction cups around his calves against the exterior aluminum. With his legs secure, he readied his MP5, chucked the flash bangs into the plane, and swung into the hole headfirst.

He was hanging by his legs with his head pointing toward the floor, so everything he saw was upside down, but a properly tuned laser sight on an MP5 never lied. He took out two hijackers at the rear of the plane, and as two more, about fifteen rows up, began shooting, he nailed them as well.

Harvath pulled his knife from his vest and cut himself free of the suction cups. He swung his legs over his head, hit the ground on his feet, and quickly made his way up the port aisle yelling in English and Arabic for the passengers to get down on the floor of the plane.

Two more terrorists came shooting at him down opposite aisles, and Harvath quickly took them out with perfect shots to the head. A massive explosion rocked the front of the plane, followed by multiple bursts of submachine gun fire as smoke began filling the main cabin. For a moment, Harvath wondered if the front door had indeed been rigged and if maybe Morrell and the rest of Bravo Team had breached it. That was impossible; Harvath had the demo sack and nobody in their right mind would have touched that door with their bare hands. The only way through it was to blow it. It had to have been something else. Harvath looked behind him and didn't see the 777 unit. Could the Delta boys have beaten them to the plane? He couldn't tell.

Harvath kept making his way forward. He picked up two more hijackers, armed with Beretta model 12S submachine guns and emergency flashlights, and blew them away. More smoke began to fill the cabin as another explosion and more gunfire rocked the front of the plane. A few passengers had opened emergency window exits and were now fleeing as fast as they could scramble over one another.

As Harvath ran forward, the rows of seats stopped and he found himself in a somewhat open area. Out of instinct, he dropped to the ground, just as shots sliced by his head from the economy-class galley. Within seconds, a wave of smoke passed, and through his NODs, Harvath could make out another hijacker swinging his weapon from left to right, trying to reacquire his target. Harvath didn't give him the opportunity. He drilled a bullet straight through the hijacker's brain. Another hijacker appeared right behind him, and Scot dropped him without a second thought.

Harvath couldn't figure out why he hadn't seen any of

the Alpha Team members working their way toward him. Taking advantage of the lull in the action, he pulled the first of the doubled magazines from his weapon and slammed the second into place. He swung his MP5 from right to left, the laser sight slicing eerily through the smoky darkness. All around him he could hear the screams of passengers as they tried to evacuate the plane.

An explosion from the rear starboard door of the plane signaled the arrival of the Thunderbolt 777 force to the party. The danger factor had just increased exponentially.

Harvath knew the only way to avoid heavy civilian casualties with these jokers now on the scene was to make sure that all of the hijackers had been taken out. With his laser sight arcing from side to side, Harvath crept forward into the business-class section of the plane. Just as in the economy class, passengers were scrambling to get to any available exit. It was absolute chaos.

As he neared the carpeted stairs that connected the lower-level workout facility with the main level and upper deck, Harvath saw two bodies slumped together across seats 16 A and B. Carefully, he rolled the top body off the one beneath. There was blood everywhere. The man on top was of Middle Eastern descent and had been shot in the throat. *But by whom?* Harvath wondered. He still couldn't see or hear any trace of the Alpha Team.

Beneath the Middle Easterner lay the almost lifeless body of another man, who appeared to be a passenger. He had taken two rounds to the chest, but was still alive—barely. Harvath found a blanket nearby and after folding it, quickly applied it to the man's wounds as a makeshift pressure bandage.

"Is he okay? Is he alive?" came a voice from behind him in the aisle.

With his MP5 up and ready, Scot whirled and locked the little red dot of his laser sight onto the forehead of one of the female passengers. Harvath couldn't believe his ears. With almost all of the passengers running for their lives, this woman wanted to know if another passenger was going to make it.

"He's pretty bad. Come over here and keep the pressure on this blanket. Don't let him lose any more blood."

Georgia Bormann did as she was told, and as she took over for Harvath, a faint whisper escaped Bernard Walsh's lips. "Find Meg. Help her."

Harvath had no idea what the man was talking about, nor did he have time to figure it out. The aircraft was not yet secure. Hashim Nidal was somewhere on board. Scot could smell him. This wouldn't be over until he had him in his sights and made him pay for all of the killing he had been responsible for.

With Bormann tending to Walsh, Harvath made his way to the carpeted stairwell. Carefully, he looked over the railing down toward the workout facility. Between choking waves of smoke, he could see three bodies lying motionless on the ground. Part of Alpha Team was down. As much as Harvath wanted to help them, he couldn't. There were still hijackers aboard and it was his job to find them.

He decided to move forward, up to the first-class section, and as he passed the main forward door, he noticed that it was indeed wired with explosives. He took a red paint marker from his pocket and drew a fat **X** on the door's porthole-style window, warning any teams on the other side not to use the door, as it was rigged from the inside with explosives.

When Harvath got into the first-class section, he looked from right to left with his NODs and was amazed. It was completely empty. No United CEO, no Chicago mayor, nothing. His first thought was that maybe they had all evacuated. As he was sweeping the cabin again with his night-vision goggles, he heard, "Now!"

Immediately, he was blinded by a powerful emergency flashlight that had been turned on him. Once again, he reflexively hit the deck. It took him a moment to clear the spots from his eyes, but when his vision returned, he could see that the first-class passengers had been hiding behind their seats waiting in ambush. Now he looked up at no fewer than six submachine gun muzzles pointing down at him.

"Drop your weapons. Do it now!" commanded Harvath, raising his MP5.

"Identify yourself," said one of the voices.

"Delta Force. Now, put that flashlight and your weapons down. I'm not going to tell you again," said Harvath as he pushed himself to his feet. With his right hand still holding his MP5, he used his left to tear a Velcro'd piece of fabric from his right upper arm area. Underneath was a bright red, white, and blue American flag.

"We're here to get you out," he continued. "Is everyone okay?"

"Everybody's okay," said Mayor Fellinger, who tilted his head in Meg Cassidy's direction. "Thanks to her."

Even through his goggles he could tell the woman was beautiful. She had been put through the ringer, but she was still gorgeous. He tore his mind away from the vision in front of him and got back to business. "I don't know how you got those weapons," he said, "but I want you to set them down."

"*Set them down?*" said the United CEO, confused.

"There are Egyptian commandos entering the aft of the aircraft as we speak. We don't want any of you folks to get confused for hijackers and shot," replied Harvath. "Now drop those weapons and get yourselves down on the ground between the seats. This thing isn't over yet. Don't move until someone comes for you."

"And what about you?" asked Meg Cassidy, her eyes riveted on Harvath.

"Me? I've got a bone to pick with someone whose parents should have practiced better birth control. Now, everybody on the floor."

After a moment of studying the mix of sheer determination and icy calm written across his face, Meg followed suit with the rest of the people around her, setting her weapon on a nearby seat and getting down on the floor.

Harvath made his way out of first class and back through business class to the stairs that led to the upper deck. When takedowns came, hijackers traditionally fled to what they believed was the safest place on the plane—the cockpit. Though cockpits on all planes had been significantly fortified after September 11, there wouldn't be enough fortification in this plane's cockpit to prevent Scot Harvath from getting in and getting what he wanted. He swore to himself that the only way Hashim Nidal and any of his remaining men were going to be leaving this plane was feetfirst.

As Scot climbed the stairs, he noticed that the walls were charred and pitted. Small pieces of shrapnel littered the carpeting. It appeared as if a fragmentation grenade had gone off in the stairwell. That must have been one of the explosions he had heard after breaching the rear of the aircraft. It seemed too dangerous a weapon for the Alpha Team to have used in a hostage situation. Then Harvath was reminded of what the CIA team's top priority in this mission was. Still, a frag grenade was excessive, even by Morrell's standards.

Before reaching the top landing, Harvath pulled a flash bang from his vest and hurled it over the railing into the upper-deck lounge. He averted his eyes, waited for the detonation, and then sprinted up the remaining stairs and stormed onto the upper deck. Right at the top of the stairs, he almost tripped over the dead body of another Middle Easterner. He figured it was a hijacker and guessed that this had something to do with how the passengers in first class had gotten their weapons.

He cleared the lavatories, the galley, and then searched behind every seat, as well as the bar. He found the bodies of two more Middle Easterners as well as a large Caucasian man who appeared from his clothes to be American. Harvath pegged him as an air marshal or one of the mayor's bodyguards. His build and style of dress screamed law enforcement, and knowing how good the air marshals were at blending in with other passengers, Harvath figured the man had been one of Mayor Fellinger's police bodyguards.

Throughout his search, Harvath kept one eye on the cockpit door, ready for it to spring open at any minute.

When he got to the thick outer flight-deck door, he

could see up high where the half-inch, fifty-caliber rounds from Bullet Bob's sniper rifle had penetrated clean through the cockpit and had probably kept flying through the upper-deck area. The question now was how to breach the door? He could blow it with a ribbon charge, but if there were flight crew on the other side, they might end up seriously injured. That was a risk Harvath would have to take. Injured was better than dead any day of the week. He reached into the demo sack and was about to remove the explosive when he heard a noise and the cockpit door began to open.

Scot leapt back, his MP5 raised and ready. The first thing to appear was a hand covered in blood, gripping the outer edge of the doorframe. Harvath could just make out an aviator chronograph watch strapped to the man's wrist. In an instant, the full form of a man in a flight crew uniform was visible as he stumbled out of the cockpit and fell to the floor. He was badly injured. Scot checked his pulse. It was weak, but steady. He hated to leave the man, but he needed to sweep the cockpit. It only took a moment. Both the captain and the first officer were dead.

There was the faint thumping of boots from the stair-well in the lounge and Harvath spun to see a Delta Force team cresting the landing and fanning out across the upper deck. A disjointed chorus of "Clear . . . clear . . . clear . . ." rang throughout the upper deck as the Delta team swept for any hidden hijackers.

Harvath stepped forward, identified himself to the team leader, and said, "I've got a man injured here."

The team medic raced over and produced a small bag and began tending to the flight crew's injured navigator.

Once Harvath felt sure the man was in good hands, he approached the team leader. "Did we get Nidal?"

"I've got no idea. It looks like a fucking shooting gallery down there. We've got several Alpha Team members down, a badly injured flight attendant, one passenger with multiple gunshot wounds, and about three hundred plus other passengers jumping out of any exit they can find. They're all running around the tarmac in the dark. At this point, there's no telling where your guy is."

Harvath's blood ran cold.

Harvath was just about to ask why the lights hadn't been turned back on yet, when all of the airport lighting came to life. *There's that Egyptian efficiency*, he thought to himself. A moment later external power was attached to the aircraft and the interior lights came back on as well. The upper deck looked exactly like a war zone.

When Harvath made his way down to the vestibule outside the lower-level workout facility, Morrell was already on-scene triaging his men.

"How are they doing, Rick?" asked Harvath.

"One of the guys lost a couple of fingers, but for the most part just superficial injuries to exposed arms and legs. The vests and those Kevlar helmets saved them."

"What happened?"

"Apparently, when Alpha Team breached from down below, there was a short firefight through the stairwell, and then the hijackers dropped a concussion grenade followed by a fucking frag."

"Jesus. I thought that's what it was," said Harvath.

"These guys were very well trained. They only went for chest or head shots and didn't waste a second between ejecting spent clips and inserting fresh ammunition into their weapons. They knew how to handle themselves in a firefight."

"Did we get them all? What about Nidal?"

"Too hard to tell at this point. They were dressed just

like civilians from what we can tell. Delta's still evacuating passengers."

"Have you secured the perimeter?"

"Of course we have. We'll isolate all of the passengers to make sure none of the hijackers are trying to mix in with them. We'll go through them one by one. God, this thing turned into a goat fuck," said Morrell.

"It could have been a lot worse. Next time, let's leave the Egyptians at home."

Morrell didn't like *I told you so*'s, no matter how veiled they were, and let Harvath know it. "You know what? If I have anything to say about it, there won't be a next time. That crap you pulled up on the Jetway was totally unacceptable."

"What are you talking about?" said Harvath, growing angry with Morrell as well.

"I'm talking about you assaulting one of my men, commandeering his demo sack, and making a jump for this aircraft. All against my orders."

Scot lowered his voice, but gave it to Morrell with both barrels. "Against your orders, my ass. You couldn't fucking think straight up there. The Egyptians jumped the gun and it threw your whole plan out of whack. Face it. For all the training you and the rest of your SAS monkeys think you have, hostage-rescue situations require a more delicate touch than you're capable of. Had we waited for you to come up with another plan, who knows how many of the passengers would be dead right now. Be glad this turned out as well as it did."

"What I'll be glad about is confirming that we have taken out Hashim Nidal. I just pray that we got him, so that our little special working relationship here can be over."

"I can't wait to get rid of you either."

Harvath turned to walk up the stairs, but had to wait for a group of passengers being led by a Delta operative to come down. As he looked up, Scot recognized the faces as those he had seen earlier in first class.

"Great, what the hell is this?" said Morrell to the Delta operative when he reached the bottom landing.

"These are the VIP passengers from first class and those who were involved in a direct standoff with the hijackers. We've been instructed to see to their secure evac and get them to the EgyptAir clubroom for debriefing. It's a madhouse upstairs, so we're taking this group out Alpha Team's rabbit hole and down the ladder."

The Delta operative didn't wait for Morrell's permission; he didn't need it. He already had his orders. He politely but forcefully indicated with his weapon that Morrell should back up, and then he waved his group toward the exercise facility.

As Meg Cassidy made her way down the stairs, Scot could tell that his original assessment of her had not been wrong. She was definitely beautiful. She had also definitely been through the ringer. Her eyes were glazed over and she was shaking. As she neared the bottom step, she faltered and fell forward right into Harvath.

He deftly moved his weapon out of the way and caught Meg with his left arm. He helped her regain her feet, but knew that if he let go of her, she would fall to the ground like a rag doll.

"Are you all right?" Scot asked.

Meg didn't respond.

"What's happening? Is she okay?" came the voice of Mayor Fellinger as he broke ranks and came back to see what was going on.

"I think she might be in shock, sir," said Harvath.

"Wait a second. I know you, don't I?" he asked.

"Yes, sir, we met about a year ago in Chicago at a party fund-raiser."

"That's right. I remember you now. You were on President Rutledge's Secret Service detail, correct?"

"Yes, sir. Agent Scot Harvath."

"I guess I shouldn't ask what a U.S. Secret Service agent is doing all the way in Cairo with a Delta Force team, should I?"

"Probably not. You do have quite a memory, though, Mr. Mayor."

"I never forget a face. Let's hope Meg here doesn't either."

"What do you mean?" asked Harvath, who motioned to one of the Delta guys at the top of the stairway to throw a blanket down to him.

"From what I've been told, no one has found the two hijackers dressed in black jumpsuits. They were the ones running the show. They wore masks, but Meg said she saw the face of one of them. She also said she shot him in the head. She's an amazing woman. We all owe our lives to her."

The Delta operative upstairs whistled to get Scot's attention and threw him down a couple of blankets. Harvath wrapped them tightly around Meg as he continued to help hold her upright. For her part, all Meg could do was stare straight ahead. Scot quickly took her pulse. He wanted to know who this woman was and what role she had played in helping to subdue so many of the hijackers. But it would have to wait.

"She's going to need medical attention," said Harvath.

"If she's seen who I think she's seen," broke in Morrell, "she's going to need to be debriefed first."

Meg stiffened under Scot's arm. It was very subtle, but Harvath felt it nonetheless.

"Back off, Rick. The first thing this woman needs is medical attention, and that's the first thing she's going to get."

Ex-Army and now a career politician, Mayor Fellinger could smell a pissing match coming a mile away, and diplomatically stepped in. "Agent Harvath, I'd like it if you could see your way clear to escorting us off the plane and helping Ms. Cassidy get the medical attention she needs. The president and I go way back, and I am sure he would appreciate any assistance you can give us. That is of course"—Fellinger paused to look directly at Morrell—"if you can be spared."

Morrell had no idea why people liked Harvath. In his opinion, the guy was nothing but trouble and he would be glad to be rid of him. "Fine. Go ahead," he said. "But I want to know where this woman is at all times, and once she receives medical treatment, I want to talk to her. Understood?"

"You're all heart," said Scot as he pushed past Morrell into the exercise facility.

The room looked like a bomb had gone off in it, which was pretty much what had happened. Alpha Team's ribbon charge had blown a rectangular hole clean through the underside of the airplane and up through the floor of the exercise room. Weights and splintered cables were scattered everywhere. Exercise bikes and treadmills were overturned, and all of the plate-glass mirrors, which once covered the walls surrounding the room, were now shattered.

Harvath helped direct Meg Cassidy through the maze of twisted metal and broken glass that littered the floor, and then gently lowered her down the ladder to Mayor Fellinger.

When Scot hit the tarmac, he wasn't surprised to see soldiers and police everywhere. The perimeter was so tight, not even a scorpion could have sneaked through. If Hashim Nidal was not already among the dead and was somehow trying to hide among the passengers, he'd be nailed for sure. There was no possible way he could get out of this one.

24

Hashim Nidal was a fool. Trying to have his way with the American woman was an unwise and unprofessional act. She may have been beautiful and may have represented everything he hated about America, but he had allowed his desire to consume him. By molesting the American woman, half-witted Hashim had brought consequences upon them that could never have been foreseen. Though he had been warned once, he still could not help himself, and that had cost them dearly.

Hashim's masked comrade had discovered him lying on the floor of the upper deck, where the American woman had left him to die. Praise indeed belonged to Allah in that the bullet had not entered his skull, but had just grazed him. It had been enough to make him lose consciousness and he had bled profusely, but he would live. The scar it would leave would hopefully serve as a reminder to him of his foolishness. His mistake had cost the organization not only millions, but tens of millions of dollars, which could have been smuggled out of the airport along with them.

It was only through sheer force of will that Hashim's accomplice had been able to neutralize the Alpha Team and successfully drag him to their hiding place deep within the bowels of the plane. They had underestimated their enemy, and because of it, all of their months of planning and training were ruined.

Now they had no choice but to wait. All of their soldiers were dead. It was a calculated loss. Contrary to what they told their devout followers, they had suspected that the plane might never leave Cairo and that many might die. As part of their contingency plan, they had prepared for either an assault or the need to create a diversion themselves by detonating several charges throughout the plane, but not so soon. They had hoped to ransom at least one of the VIPs. Either the mayor or the airline CEO. One ransom would have helped their cause incredibly, but to get paid both would have been an answer to their prayers. They needed the money desperately and now they were left with nothing, less than nothing in fact, because the execution of this mission had been expensive. With America's war on terrorism waging, it seemed that everything these days was very, very costly.

Hashim's impulsiveness would one day be the ruin of the organization. Abu Nidal had not worked as hard as he had to have it torn asunder by his idiot son.

Hours passed, and finally Hashim Nidal and his accomplice felt themselves moving. A forklift removed the crate from the cargo hold and transferred it to a flatbed trailer with several other matching containers. Everything was being done under strict military supervision. Though armed teams had swept the cargo bay repeatedly once all of the passengers were off the plane, they were still leaving nothing to chance. The crates were driven to a customs warehouse adjacent to the terminal along with all of the passenger luggage from flight 7755.

Customs broker Farouk Negim was waiting in the warehouse, flanked by one of his company's most important clients, Dr. Abdel Mandour, curator of Cairo's Egyptian Museum, and Dr. Kamal el Aziz, Egypt's government minister of antiquities. They had been camped out in the warehouse manager's office since the hijacking had been announced the previous afternoon. As part of the cultural exchange between Chicago and Cairo, Chicago's Field Museum was loaning the Egyptian Museum a pair of mummies that had been removed from Egypt over a hundred years ago. The Egyptian Museum planned to study the mummies and then put them on display.

The fact that all of the containers had been sitting in the cargo hold of the 747-400 since yesterday afternoon troubled all but one of the men, who now exited the warehouse manager's office and quickly made their way toward the incoming airport trailer truck.

The truck was met by Egyptian soldiers and a blond man, an obvious westerner, in a pin-striped business suit.

"Whoa, whoa, whoa," said the blond man as the three Egyptians approached the trailer. "This area is off-limits. No one gets in here."

"Who are you?" demanded Dr. el Aziz.

"*Who am I?* I'm Tom Ellis of the United States Embassy and this is a crime-scene investigation involving American property."

"Well, I am Dr. Kamal el Aziz, Egypt's government minister of antiquities, and this crime, which happened on Egyptian soil, also involves priceless Egyptian property, which has been languishing in unacceptable conditions. We are here to remove those containers in particular and get them back to the Egyptian Museum as soon as possible."

"*We?* Who's 'we'?" asked Ellis.

"This is our customs broker, Farouk Negim, and Dr. Abdel Mandour, curator of the Egyptian Museum."

"Gentlemen, I am sorry, but those containers are not going anywhere until we have had a chance to thoroughly investigate them."

"You will pardon my asking, Mr. Ellis," began Dr. Mandour, "but what is it exactly you wish to investigate?"

"We want to make sure that no one has stowed away in them and that they don't contain any evidence that might have to do with the hijacking."

"That is impossible," replied the museum's curator, who was completely unaware of what the containers truly held.

"So you say, but until I'm convinced, those crates are not going anywhere."

Dr. el Aziz did not like the man's tone and stepped away from the group to place a call on his cell phone.

"Mr. Ellis, do you wish to know what is in those crates?" asked Dr. Mandour, who was just as ignorant as his colleague, Dr. el Aziz.

"You betcha, and I plan to find out."

"Let me save you the trouble. The crates contain two ancient mummies, their two wooden boxes, and two rather extraordinary sarcophagi."

"Let's hope, Doctor, that that's all they contain."

"Surely, Mr. Ellis, you do not intend to open them here."

"Yes, I do."

"That simply cannot happen," said Dr. Mandour.

"Really. And why not?"

Dr. Mandour did not have the energy for this. He had been waiting since yesterday afternoon to claim the containers and had not gotten a wink of sleep all night. His wife had called him incessantly, believing he was using the hijacking as an excuse to see another woman. Finally, the poor man had to turn off his cell phone. No, the curator definitely had neither the energy, nor the patience for any of this.

"Mr. Ellis, let me show you something, if I may," said Dr. Mandour, taking the clipboard from the customs broker and guiding Ellis toward the crates. "These crates, as you can plainly see, have all been stamped and stenciled as 'Enviromentally Controlled.' The top of each one has been locked with a rubber seal under the strictest of conditions at Chicago's Field Museum. Inside, a substance called silica gel has been added to temporarily maintain the proper balance of humidity. The key word here, Mr. Ellis, is *temporarily*. Because of the risk to the artifacts from our modern-day air, we can only open these containers within a special facility at the Egyptian Museum—"

"And that is exactly what is going to happen," said el Aziz, the minister of antiquities, who flipped the top down on his cell phone and returned to the group.

"What are you talking about?" said Ellis.

"Mr. Ellis, I know it is very early, but if you would kindly call your ambassador at his residence, you will find that not only has he already spoken with my government, but that he will instruct you to impede us no further."

Ellis called the American ambassador, of course, and was furious when told to back down. Dr. el Aziz then shouted orders in Arabic to both the soldiers and the warehouse workers. A semitrailer from Worldwide Customs Brokers International was backed into the warehouse, and the Egyptian Museum's containers were loaded without further delay.

Once the semi was loaded, Dr. el Aziz offered to treat Dr. Mandour to breakfast before he returned to the museum to open the crates. Dr. Mandour accepted and the pair departed in the minister's chauffeured Mercedes.

Farouk Negim finished signing the paperwork and climbed into the semi's passenger seat next to his driver.

Tom Ellis was fuming. "Mr. Negim," he called snidely through the open window. "Beware of the mummy's curse."

Farouk Negim didn't bother to respond. He simply instructed his driver in Arabic to proceed. Once they had cleared the customs warehouse and were on the road leading from the airport, he smiled to himself. *Mummy's curse, indeed.* He knew full well that the occupants of his crates were not at all cursed. If anything, they were blessed, and they had showered riches upon him and his counterpart in Chicago, the likes of which neither had ever before seen in their long careers of smuggling.

25

Bernard Walsh, the navigator, and the badly beaten flight attendant were immediately choppered to El Salam International Hospital, but Rick Morrell had other plans for Meg Cassidy. After Harvath had escorted all of the VIPs to the EgyptAir clubroom, Morrell magically appeared with his SAS medic in tow. They made a beeline for the leather couch where Scot had laid Meg down and was conducting a cursory assessment.

"Okay, Harvath, we'll take it from here," said Morrell, who indicated to the medic to take Scot's place. The SAS man was apprehensive. He was already sporting two butterfly bandages above his eye and had no desire to add to them. He didn't want to be anywhere near Harvath.

Morrell sensed his operative's trepidation and said, "Clear the way, Harvath. I've got some questions for this woman."

"I'm sure you do, but she's in no condition to talk. I told you, she needs medical attention," replied Harvath.

"Why do you think I brought my medic with me?"

"Listen, Rick. I can appreciate that you want to find out what she saw, but she needs to be seen by a real doctor in a real hospital."

"If she was that bad, why didn't she go out on the chopper with the other wounded?"

"Because when the Delta medic triaged the injuries on

the plane, there were plenty more serious than her. They were barely able to squeeze your injured men into the Black Hawk along with the civilians. Now, we need to get an IV started on her, and then—"

"What we need," said Morrell, cutting Scot off, "is a description of the man she saw. I've got every person from that flight being held in a containment area. If Hashim Nidal is among them and she can ID him, then that's what we need done."

"And what if he's not?"

"Then she's going to need to view the bodies and tell me he's among the dead."

"Jesus, Morrell. We don't even know the extent of her injuries and you want her to sit through a lineup of hundreds of people? For Christ's sake, the woman can't even speak. What's she supposed to do, blink once for *yes*, twice for *no*?"

"If that's what it takes."

"Well, that isn't going to happen. An As-Salam ambulance has already been called."

"*As-Salam?* You mean El Salam."

"No, I mean As-Salam. It's a private ambulance service. If you dial Egypt's version of nine-one-one, they only send out a public ambulance that'll transport to the nearest hospital. I figured we would want her to be taken to the El Salam hospital where the other injured are."

"No way. If she's not talking now, I want her close when she starts. Have her taken to the Anglo-American Hospital."

"But that's not close. That's the other side of town."

"It's close to the embassy, and that's where I want her."

"Fine," said Harvath, anxious to be rid of Morrell so he could tend to Meg Cassidy. "I'll ride over in the ambulance with her."

"No you won't. I'll send one of my people to keep an eye on her. I want you down in the containment area conducting interviews right now. And don't try to buck me on this one."

Harvath knew why Morrell wanted him interviewing the passengers. As a matter of fact, there were probably two reasons. Number one, it was tedious as hell and Morrell wanted to stick it to him. Number two, it had been scientifically proven that the highly and specially trained U.S. Secret Service agents were exceptionally capable of detecting microexpressions. These were facial expressions that manifested themselves when a person was under psychological stress, such as from lying, harboring an intent to do harm, or, most pertinent to the current situation, trying to conceal one's true identity. The expressions lasted for only a fraction of a second and were therefore incredibly difficult to detect. The Secret Service had never revealed how their agents were trained to pick up on these subtle facial cues. It was a closely guarded secret and part of what made the U.S. Secret Service the greatest protective force in the world. Obviously, Morrell planned to get his money's worth out of Harvath.

The interview process was long and drawn out. At one point, Harvath thought they had a hit, but it turned out to only be a passenger hiding the fact that he was smuggling American cigarettes and whiskey in his suitcase. Judging by the looks on the faces of the Egyptian customs officers, Harvath figured the contraband would never make it as far as the evidence locker.

Once all of the passengers had been interviewed, Scot wandered over to the adjacent hangar, where the bodies of the hijackers were lined up along the floor, covered by tarps. He looked each one over. What he saw didn't surprise him. The bodies were all those of Middle Eastern men in their twenties to thirties, with dark hair, dark skin and eyes. He was sure that if he went through their pockets, each would have a copy of the Koran. Harvath felt for the Muslim people. Islam was an honorable religion that was unfortunately rotting from within. Like it or not, the radicals gave all Muslims a bad name.

In fact, if blame had to be laid for the modern decay of Islam, the Saudi royal family was the perfect group to begin pointing the finger at. In an attempt to shore up their sovereignty, the Saudis had helped to promote one of the most radical forms of Islam, which an overwhelming majority of the world's Islamic terrorists followed.

Harvath continued to look at the bodies, wondering if one of the men was Hashim Nidal himself. Something—he didn't know what—told him he was wasting his time.

Scot was interrupted by a Delta operative, who told him that the Delta commander wanted him in the EgyptAir clubroom for a debriefing. When Harvath arrived, Morrell and his people were nowhere to be found. "Where's the SAS team?" he asked.

"Back at the embassy. They took the mayor and Bob Lawrence with them," said the CO.

"What about Ms. Cassidy?"

"They were going to take her to a nearby hospital for further observation."

"And the debriefing?"

"We've already got a statement from Morrell, so I guess they plan to do their own debriefing at the embassy."

"That's just great. What about the rest of the passengers? What if there's a hijacker mixed in there, after all?"

"Apparently, a few consular affairs officers have already been dispatched from the embassy to sift through them once again."

Consular affairs officer was one of the CIA's smokescreen titles for U.S. Embassy employees who were really covert, CIA in-country operatives.

"Those guys are as thick as thieves," said Harvath.

"Yup, and they don't play well with others."

"Tell me about it. I've gotten to see it firsthand."

"That's exactly what we are going to talk about," said the CO as he gestured for his men to take their seats. "All right, let's get this coffee klatch rolling. I've got a feeling the after-action report from this job, especially Agent Harvath's actions, will be studied for a long, long time."

When the debriefing was over, Bullet Bob and some of the other Delta operatives were preparing to take the remainder of the SAS team's gear over to the embassy and they offered Harvath a ride. As far as Scot could tell, his job at the airport was done. Morrell had left without giving him any further instructions, so the embassy sounded like as good a place as any to find out what their next move would be. Harvath retrieved his duffel from the back of Bullet Bob's Suburban, changed back into his civilian clothes, and tucked his pistol into his waistband beneath his shirt.

26

Cairo was an amazing city. The official population was around eleven million, but when outside workers streamed into the city during the day, the numbers shot up to between sixteen and seventeen million. It was an eclectic mixture of old and new. Donkey-drawn carts shared the streets with shiny new Mercedes as men in business suits shouldered their way down sidewalks with men dressed in the traditional robes known as galabiya. Egyptians referred to Cairo as Umm al-Dunya, "the mother of the world," and Harvath was no stranger to it. He had been here many times. It was a city that you absolutely loved or hated, and Harvath loved Cairo. Though he wasn't crazy about Egypt's politics, that didn't stop him from appreciating its people and their incredible culture.

The row of Suburbans sped down the paved street, passing side streets that were nothing more than sand. Sand was everywhere here, and dealing with it was part of life in a desert. Egyptians went so far as to wrap bed-sheets around their parked cars to help keep them free of it. It wasn't pretty, but it was practical, and that was the mentality of the Egyptians. They did the best with what they had.

The team slowed down as they got further into the city and were caught in the snarl of one of Cairo's inevitable traffic jams. As far as Harvath could see, there was nothing ahead, but a sea of aging Fiat and Peugeot sedans. Drivers leaned on their horns rather than using their blinkers to indicate lane changes. A family of six, piled into an old 1940s motorcycle complete with sidecar, sneaked past them on the right.

At el-Geish Square, Harvath could make out the Gate of Conquests and told Bullet Bob to pull over.

"What for?" he asked.

"I'm gonna get some breakfast," replied Harvath.

"Why don't you wait until we get to the embassy and have something there?"

"Because I'm hungry now. Listen, find Morrell and tell him I stopped off for a bite and that I'll be there shortly."

Bullet Bob radioed the other drivers and the caravan came to a stop. Harvath got out of the Suburban and walked around to the driver's side window to thank his friend. He stuck his hand in and they shook.

"What's this? No baksheesh?" asked Bullet Bob.

Baksheesh was slang for "tip."

"Sure, I'll give you a tip," said Harvath. "Don't drink with the blacksmith's wife. You're liable to get hammered."

Bullet Bob winced as if he were in pain. "God, that's a bad joke," he said.

"Hey, nobody's perfect," replied Harvath.

"I hope you're packing more than that lousy sense of humor."

Harvath raised the front of his shirt a fraction and displayed the butt of his forty-five-caliber.

"Good. Watch your back. If we don't see you at the embassy, give me a shout the next time you get near Fort Bragg. Our tour is up, and we're rotating back at the end of the week."

"Will do," said Harvath. He stood back as Bullet Bob gave the order to move out, and the Suburbans rolled off toward the embassy.

The Gate of Conquests was the northern gateway of a fortification that once encircled the original center of Cairo. Harvath loved this part of the city. In addition to bringing his favorite knife from home, Harvath had also brought along a couple of hundred dollars. While he respected Morrell's black op's policy of not bringing any ID with him, he had learned early on that carrying extra money was never a liability. In an escape-and-evasion situation, his watch and any money he had could always be used to help buy his way to safety.

Harvath found an exchange machine and traded some of his U.S. currency for Egyptian pounds. It wasn't the best rate in town, but all he needed was a little walking-around money.

He continued south until he found himself in the bazaar known as the Khan El-Khalili, which was once a meeting place for caravans traveling from Asia to Africa. The present-day Khan El-Khalili was a warren of winding streets and twisted alleyways. The narrow passageways were filled with boutiques, carts, stalls, and workshops making and selling all manner of goods imaginable—white and green marble chess boards, black alabaster statues, wooden boxes inlaid with mother-of-pearl, intricate mosaics, faded tapestries, bright silk carpets, gold jewelry . . . there was no end, it seemed, of what was for sale here.

Harvath followed alleys bearing the names of trades their tenants once specialized in—Al-Khayameya, for tent makers, Al-Fahhamin, for coal traders, and Al-Nahhassin for coppersmiths. As he traveled this last alley, the sound of present-day smiths could be heard as they pounded their hammers against shiny sheets of copper and brass. The air was heavily scented with spices and the flowers from nearby perfume shops.

On El-Fishawy, Harvath stopped at the famous teahouse, Fishawy's, and ordered a rich Turkish coffee and a couple of small herbed spinach pies to eat. He sat outside and watched the men across from him smoke the traditional *shishah*, or water pipe, as shopkeepers with buckets and mops washed the entryways and sidewalks in front of their stores. The smoke from the apple-flavored tobacco mingled with the lemon scent of cleaning solution and rose into the sky, further intensifying the already fragrant ambience.

Proficiency in a foreign language, just as in shooting, was a perishable skill, and while Harvath trained on several firing ranges in and around Washington D.C. on a weekly basis, he had not had many occasions to speak Arabic since leaving the SEALs. From what he could decipher from the newspaper of the man sitting next to him, the hijacking of United Airlines flight 7755 was the lead story of the day, followed by the Islamic world's ever increasing outrage with Israel. There was an overwhelming distrust of the Jewish state, especially as it had made no progress in its investigation into the Hand of God organization. Accusations were running rampant that Israel was actually behind the terrorist attacks. Not surprisingly, Iran, one of the most volatile powers in the region, had begun canceling leave for its soldiers and was pledging its full cooperation and support to the Palestinians, as well as the rest of the Arab world, if war with Israel broke out.

Through the open window, the café's television, which had served as nothing more than background noise, now caught Harvath's attention as it replayed a news conference from Cairo, taped earlier that morning. Though the participants were speaking English, an Arabic voice translated for the station's Egyptian audience and was given more volume. The two simultaneous languages made it difficult to understand. Harvath asked the waiter to turn up the volume.

Doctors stood behind a makeshift podium with a piece of paper taped to it that read, "Anglo-American Hospital." It was obvious that this hospital didn't do a lot of news conferences and that they wanted everyone to know who they were. Standing in the background were Mayor Fellinger, Bob Lawrence, and several other suits, who Scot guessed were either with the airline or the embassy. The press conference was already in progress and a British doctor was saying, ". . . was brought here by ambulance early this morning and is now in stable condition. We expect her to make a full recovery. Her prognosis is very good." Harvath figured the man was referring to Meg Cassidy and was positive when he added, "As to the patients transported via helicopter to El Salam International Hospital, at this point I am going to turn the podium over to Mr. Tom Ellis, of the U.S. Embassy here in Cairo, who can address that issue further. Mr. Ellis?"

"Thank you, Dr. Hill," said Ellis as he took control of the podium. "Good morning, ladies and gentlemen. At this point, I do not have much information for you, but what I can tell you is this: Six people in total were transported to El Salam International Hospital this morning, as Dr. Hill mentioned. These individuals were wounded either during the hijacking itself or during the raid upon the aircraft. Three have already been treated and released. Another remains in serious, but guarded condition, while two others are in surgery at this moment. As I get more information, of course I will be happy to share it with you, but at this point, we are withholding names until we have been able to contact their families. As Mr. Lawrence mentioned earlier in the press conference, United Airlines has set up a one–eight-hundred number back in the States for families of passengers wishing to know the status of their loved ones.

"As you might have heard, it has been reported that passengers assisted in wresting control of the aircraft away from the hijackers." Harvath was surprised that the powers-that-be were going public with this information so early. He set down his coffee and leaned forward to hear the television better. "I can confirm for you that these reports are, indeed, true. In fact, a large portion of the credit is to be given to a lone female passenger, the one being attended to by Dr. Hill and his staff here, who subdued several of the hijackers single-handedly and then, with the help of fellow passengers, held the plane safe until military personnel were able to secure the situation."

The small conference room where the press conference was being held erupted in a roar of questions from the press. Ellis held up his hand to silence them. "At this point we are not going to reveal this woman's name. As I said, we are trying to contact the families of those who were injured first. The last thing we want is for family members to hear about their loved ones from their televisions rather than personnel from the State Department who are equipped to answer questions and help provide any assistance that might be needed.

"I will say that this woman's ability to have such an impact upon the outcome of this situation not only speaks volumes about her courage, but also speaks volumes about the ineptitude, lack of organization, and lack of leadership on the part of the hijackers. When this event first began to unfold, there was serious concern, as there always is in a situation of this nature, about the level of expertise and determination of the hijackers. What we've learned is that they were not a highly trained cadre, but rather a disorganized band of amateurs. In the wider world of terrorist events, this group was obviously not very well trained."

Harvath couldn't understand what he was hearing. This Ellis guy, who had CIA written all over him, was putting a literally *unbelievable* spin on what had happened. The men who committed this hijacking were anything but incompetent. They were highly motivated and extremely well trained. Why was Ellis saying these things?

"These facts notwithstanding," continued Ellis, "both the U.S. and Egyptian governments take the crimes committed in connection with the hijacking of United Airlines flight 7755 very seriously. We are confident that we will apprehend all of the people involved in the planning and execution of this act of cowardice. To that end, we are asking the international community for its help in identifying this man, Hashim Nidal." Ellis held up a computer-generated composite sketch.

"He is the ringleader believed to have masterminded

and orchestrated the hijacking. This sketch was developed with the assistance of an eyewitness, and we feel . . ."

Harvath had gone from not understanding what he was hearing, to not believing it. Obviously, Meg Cassidy had helped the CIA develop a composite sketch of Nidal. If they were circulating a sketch, that could mean only one thing. Somehow he had gotten away. But that was impossible. Security at the airport had been airtight. The only way he could have gotten out of there was in cuffs or a body bag.

Something bad was going on, and the only thing Harvath knew for sure was that whatever it wās, it had Rick Morrell's dirty little fingerprints all over it.

27

Harvath quickly found a taxi on the edge of the Khan El-Khalili, but it seemed to take forever to reach Garden City and the U.S. Embassy. Once he had paid the driver and exited the cab, the first thing he noticed were the Marine guards in full tactical gear. What had normally been a sight reserved for instances of heightened security was now an everyday occurrence. Security, especially for U.S. embassies abroad, was taken very, very seriously.

After explaining to the Egyptian police officers guarding the embassy's outer perimeter that he could not present identification because his wallet and passport had been stolen in a mugging, he was finally allowed to approach the main gate. It took slightly less time to explain his real situation to the American Marines at the entrance to the embassy, but it was still an ordeal. He was watched very closely by one heavily armed Marine while the other made a quick series of phone calls. Eventually, an embassy staffer appeared and escorted him deep within the complex to a secure, soundproofed conference room known in intelligence-speak as the "Bubble."

Seated at the table were Bob Lawrence, Mayor Fellinger, some of the men from Morrell's SAS team, and several suits whom Harvath, once again, didn't recognize.

Fellinger was the first to acknowledge Scot as he was admitted into the room. "And here's our other hero."

Harvath smiled at the mayor and nodded politely to

Bob Lawrence. None of the SAS members paid him any attention, so he returned the favor. One of the suits stood and offered Harvath his hand.

"Agent Harvath, I am Randall Gray, assistant Cairo CIA station chief."

"Nice to meet you," said Harvath, shaking the man's hand. "You want to tell me what's going on?"

"Actually, we're just finishing the mayor's and Mr. Lawrence's debriefings. They will be leaving within the hour."

"Flying United, of course," said Scot.

"Damn straight," said Lawrence. "We're picking up the other 747 from the old Cairo airport and flying it back to Chicago. I want the world to see that we got back safely. Too many people in the U.S. are still terrified to travel, especially internationally. This whole thing has been a PR nightmare. We need to get ahold of it, and quick."

"Speaking of quickly getting ahold of this thing," said Scot. "What was with that press conference from the Anglo-American Hospital?"

"At present, I am not at liberty to answer that," said the assistant station chief.

"Not at liberty? You do understand by whose authority I am operating, don't you?" asked Harvath.

"I've got a pretty good idea, yes. Listen, Agent Harvath, it's not that I don't want to answer your question; it's that I honestly can't. Things have been evolving very fast this morning."

Scot looked at Randall Gray and sensed the man was being honest with him. "Well, if you can't give me some answers," he said, "then who can?"

"I would imagine my boss, Tom Ellis, can."

"And where might I find him, short of CNN?"

"He's still at the Anglo-American Hospital debriefing Meg Cassidy."

"Is Rick Morrell with him?"

"Yes, he is."

"Then that's where I'm going. Gentlemen," said Harvath with a polite nod toward the mayor and Bob Lawrence, "have a safe flight home. I'm very sorry about all of this."

"So are we," said the mayor. "We're just glad that we had you to help get us out of it."

"It's what I was trained to do," said Scot.

Both Lawrence and the mayor gave Scot their business cards and told him if he ever needed anything, all he had to do was call.

"I'll get someone to drive you," said the assistant station chief.

Harvath appreciated the gesture and began to believe that maybe not everyone at the CIA was a total asshole after all.

When he reached the embassy's motor pool and saw his driver, he started to have second thoughts. Leaning against the car with a cup of coffee and looking more like a Chippendales dancer than a CIA operative, was Gordon Avigliano—the kid who had couriered the CIA's Hashim Nidal file to Harvath's apartment back in Alexandria.

He was so engrossed in drinking his coffee that he didn't notice Harvath had come up alongside him until he said, "*Al salaam a' alaykum.*"

Avigliano nearly jumped out of his skin. "Holy shit," he

growled as he tossed the cup into a nearby garbage can. "You can't do that to a person."

"Well, I just did," said Harvath, shoving past him and opening the driver's side door. "Keys."

"Wait a second, I'm supposed to be driving you."

"You can't even courier documents properly. What makes you think I'm gonna let you drive? Besides how many times have you been in Cairo before?"

"None. This is my first time. But I've got a map."

"Learn on someone else's time, Gordo. Now toss me the keys."

Avigliano threw Harvath the keys and walked around to the passenger side and got in. As they shot out of the embassy gates, Avigliano attempted to make conversation. "Have you got some sort of problem with me?"

"Not specifically. My guess is that you are somehow tied to Operation Phantom, but aren't one of the heavy hitters. You're the new guy and, being low man on the totem pole, get to courier documents and drive guys like me around. Things got hot over here with the hijacking, and you got called in as part of the backup for Rick Morrell and the rest of the team. How am I doing so far?"

"Let me see," answered Avigliano, "classified, classified, restricted, and classified."

A broad smile swept across Harvath's face. "Have you had any military training?"

"I did three years with First Ranger Battalion."

"What made you decide to leave the Army and hook up with the CIA?"

"Better pay grade and it looked like more fun."

"And now you're on the Agency fast track."

"I can handle it."

The pair made their way along the Nile and at the el-Tahrir Bridge crossed over to Gezira Island, where the Anglo-American Hospital was located. Harvath found a parking space about a block away, and he and Avigliano made their way toward the building.

The one-hundred-bed Anglo-American Hospital was more than a century old and badly in need of a face-lift. To its credit, the atmosphere was welcoming and the staff very friendly. With one of Morrell's SAS men standing guard outside, Meg Cassidy's room wasn't hard to find. The man stretched his thick arm across the door the minute he saw Harvath.

"If you wanna keep that arm," said Harvath, "you'd better lower it."

"No admittance, Harvath. Boss's orders," replied the powerful-looking operative.

Before Scot could respond, Avigliano piped in. "Jerry, it's okay. Rick and Tom should be expecting him."

"Do I care? My orders are no one gets in while the debrief is going on."

"Stop being such a prick, Jerry, and just knock on the goddamn door, would ya?"

Harvath was impressed. The kid might have potential after all. In fact, Harvath worried that Avigliano was actually starting to grow on him.

The burly operative relented, and after a couple quick raps, the door opened a crack and Rick Morrell peered out. "What is it?"

That was the only opportunity Harvath needed. He

slipped past the sentry and shouldered the door open. Morrell caught it with his head.

"For fuck's sake, Harvath," he grunted as he rubbed his forehead. "You're like a bull in a china shop. Shit, that hurt."

"Maybe it'll keep you honest," said Harvath. "Now, I want to know what's going on here."

"We going to have a problem with this guy?" asked the sentry, his muscular body filling the doorframe.

"You might if you don't turn around and close that door—" began Harvath, who was immediately interrupted by Tom Ellis.

"No, Jerry. Everything's okay. Why don't you and Mr. Avigliano wait outside."

When the door was closed, Tom Ellis turned to Harvath and offered his hand. "I'm Tom Ellis, director of consular affairs—"

Now it was Harvath's turn to interrupt. "And I'm the tooth fairy. Pleased to meet you," he said as he shook the man's hand.

Rick Morrell shook his head in disgust.

Upon hearing laughter, Morrell and Ellis turned, revealing Meg Cassidy, who was sitting upright in her hospital bed, attached to an IV.

"You're looking much better," said Harvath. "Funny how some fluids will do that for a person."

"I want to thank you, Agent Harvath," she said, "for saving our lives."

"First of all, you can call me Scot. And secondly, from what I hear, Ms. Cassidy, the people on that plane owe their lives to *you*."

"I guess I didn't have much choice."

"What you did took a lot of courage. People are alive because of you. I was just saying to someone not too long ago," said Harvath as he threw a disapproving glance at Rick Morrell, "that this whole thing could have been a lot worse."

"Well, I want to put it behind me. All of it."

"No one can blame you for that."

Ellis interrupted again. "Ahem," he said as he cleared his throat. "Agent Harvath, could we have a word with you in private please?"

"The tooth fairy's work is never done. Will you excuse me, Ms. Cassidy?"

"Only if you'll stop calling me Ms. Cassidy and call me Meg," she said with a smile that warmed him all over.

"Fair enough. Meg, it is," said Harvath as he smiled at her in return.

Harvath followed Tom Ellis and Rick Morrell down the hall and was shown into the same small conference room that had been used for the press conference earlier that morning. The piece of paper with *Anglo-American Hospital* printed on it was still taped to the podium. Morrell closed and locked the door behind them.

"Agent Harvath," began Tom Ellis, "I know you're not much for playing by the rules—"

"What I'm not much for, Tom, is bullshit," replied Scot.

"Neither am I, so on that front we should get along fine. Now, in my capacity here in Cairo as—"

"CIA chief of station?"

"Yes, that is my capacity. I hope you understand that as Meg Cassidy is a civilian, presenting myself to her as chief Cairo station officer could be uncomfortable."

"And having the U.S. Embassy send over their 'chief consular affairs officer' to debrief her on a hijacking is supposed to somehow put her more at ease? You guys crack me up. You live in your own little world, you know that? We have one sharp lady in there, and I bet she saw right through you."

"Well, whatever the case may be, I'm sure any doubts she had about my capacity with the U.S. government were answered by your referring to yourself as the 'tooth fairy,' so we can set that one aside."

"Fine with me," said Harvath. "I just want to get to the bottom of this."

"Good. To do that, though, we need to enlist the help of Ms. Cassidy. She's the only one who can positively ID Hashim Nidal, so instead of encouraging her to put everything behind her, like you were doing back in her room, we need to encourage her to work with us. It's the only way we'll be able to nail him," said Ellis.

"I don't understand what the problem is here."

Ellis was exhausted. He had been going full throttle since the hijacking had started and was desperately in need of sleep. He leaned wearily against the edge of the podium and said, "We lost him."

"I figured as much. How?"

"Well, there's no question that Meg Cassidy saw his face. He had taken her up into the bubble of the plane and was going to rape her and God knows what else. She put up a struggle and was apparently assisted by one of Mayor Fellinger's bodyguards, who had been tied up in one of the upper-deck lavatories, but managed to get out. He was killed as he plowed into the guy with his hands still cuffed behind his back.

"Cassidy used the distraction to get away from Nidal and grab his weapon. He slashed at her with his knife, nicking her ankle, and she shot him in the head. She then capped a couple of the hijackers, gathered their weapons, and made her way downstairs, where she capped a few more and got up to the first-class section with Mayor Fellinger and Bob Lawrence. She told us that there had been explosions and gunfire, but it all happened so fast, she can't put together a comprehensive timeline."

"I'm not surprised," said Harvath, a degree of awe creeping into his voice. "What amazes me is that she was able to pull the whole thing off by herself. But where does losing Nidal come into play here?"

"Like I said, she swears she shot him in the head."

"Where in the head? Between the eyes?"

"No, higher up."

"How does she know she hit him?"

"She says he went down. She thought she saw blood too."

"A description such as that, does not a confirmed kill make," replied Scot.

"Unfortunately, we agree, so we photographed all of the faces of the dead hijackers from the takedown. We also videotaped all of the passengers and crew who were being held in the containment area for the interviews."

"And?" asked Harvath.

"And nothing. Not one of them rang a bell with her. She remembers Nidal, all right, says she could never forget his face. We worked with her via an encrypted laptop with a sketch artist back at Langley and came up with the composite we showed during the press conference."

"By the way, what was that all about?"

"We're convinced he escaped somehow with one of his lieutenants, who was probably assisting him."

"What are you talking about?" asked Harvath.

"Cassidy has said, and other passengers have confirmed, that there were two hijackers dressed in black jumpsuits, who kept their faces covered the entire time—except for in the bubble when Cassidy saw Hashim's face."

"And who was this other masked hijacker?"

"We believe it was a very high ranking member of the organization. I only use the word *lieutenant* as a figure of speech. We don't know who he was."

"But why were they wearing masks and not the other hijackers?"

"I think they realized they had more to lose."

"Yeah, but how do you get a bunch of other people to participate in a hijacking after you've told them 'Hey, by the way, we're going to be wearing masks to protect our identities, but none of you guys can'?"

"Who knows? Maybe the others were fanatics who were prepared to die. Maybe they were promised protection or new identities after the hijacking. There's no way to tell. The one thing that's for certain is that the non-masked hijackers were spaced throughout the cabins as regular passengers and therefore had no choice."

"How do our masked hijackers fit in, then? They couldn't have gotten on board with masks on. You've already got the security tapes from O'Hare International. Let's have Meg review each of the passengers that way."

"We already have. Everyone is accounted for."

"So what are you telling me? Hashim Nidal and his lieutenant are ghosts?"

"Maybe 'Operation Phantom' wasn't such a bad name after all," injected Morrell.

Harvath ignored him and said, "Let's forget for a moment the fact that it was predominantly Egyptian military guarding the perimeter, how do you suppose they escaped?"

"This is where I get really pissed off," said Ellis. "I think we had them in our hands and were forced to let them go."

"Wait a second, Tom. You had them in your hands? What do you mean? When?"

"I've got a team going over the plane as we speak, but here's what I think happened. The 747-400 was designed to be easily reconfigured. Lavatories and galleys can be moved to different parts of the aircraft, and whole classes of seating can be moved about."

"I know all of this. What's your theory?" said Harvath.

"This flexibility also applies to the workout facility. Normally, everything beneath the main cabin level on a 747-400 is for cargo, but United is trying to offer more perks on its long-haul flights to compete with other carriers. If at some point United decided they didn't want to offer this perk on a particular flight or they wanted more cargo room, they could off-load the exercise equipment, pop out the walls, and that would be that."

"I still don't see what you're driving at."

"The walls of the exercise room can only be removed from the cargo side. With the right tools, it's not very difficult at all. As a matter of fact, there are certain sections where you can take out just one panel—"

"Enough for a person or persons to gain access to the aircraft from the cargo hold?" asked Harvath.

"Exactly."

"So you think Nidal and his lieutenant had been stowed away in the cargo hold and waited until the plane landed before making their move?"

"Yes. Their weapons and explosives were probably hidden there as well."

"And you think they returned to wherever they were hiding when the takedown happened?"

"That's when I think we had them right in our hands and lost them."

"I thought the cargo hold was thoroughly searched, just in case."

"It was, but there were several crates that we didn't get to look into."

"Why not?"

"There were a couple of mummies being shipped from the Field Museum in Chicago to the Egyptian Museum here in Cairo as part of an exchange program. There were two mummies, their wooden boxes, and the sarcophagi—all shipped in separate crates."

"So you searched the crates, right?"

"We couldn't. I was actually at the airport supervising the search and had the minister of antiquities and the museum's curator breathing down my neck about not exposing the artifacts to the air. The crates were supposedly hermetically sealed in Chicago, and there was risk of accelerated decay if they were opened outside one of the museum's contained laboratories."

"Did you at least x-ray the crates?"

"I didn't get a chance. The minister of antiquities and the curator were freaking out because the crates had been sitting in the cargo hold of the plane on the tarmac for so long. They thought the items might be irreversibly damaged because of the temperature or humidity or something."

"What happened to them?"

"The minister of antiquities got on his cell phone with someone in his government who called our ambassador, who told me to release them. When it comes to antiquities, the Egyptians are pretty serious."

"So somehow Nidal and his lieutenant used the crates to sneak in and out of the plane?"

"I'm positive. Earlier this morning we picked up a police report that there had been a shooting at the Egyptian Museum."

"Let me guess," said Harvath.

"I'll save you the trouble," replied Ellis. "Apparently, the minister of antiquities and the museum curator went out for breakfast while they waited for the customs broker to load the crates at the airport and deliver them to the museum. We put a tail on the truck, just in case, but it drove straight to the museum and never made any other stops. The minister and the curator apparently returned from breakfast, got checked through security, and were last seen making their way down to the contained lab where the crates had been placed. Two hours later, a lab technician showed up and found both of them shot in the head. They were on the floor in front of two heavily insulated crates, each with several bottles of oxygen and related gear inside."

"There must be surveillance monitors in the museum."

"There are, but not in the lab itself. The closest camera

was in the hall. Security tapes showed what looked like the minister and the curator leaving the lab and exiting the building through a side entrance. What was interesting, was that the curator seemed to lean against the minister as he walked. We didn't get a clear shot of either of the faces. They were very careful."

"So, that's it then. Somehow Nidal and his lieutenant used the crates to get away from the airport, killed the minister and the curator, changed into their clothes, and left the museum by a side door. Doesn't seem to be much room for doubt on this one. What about the customs broker?"

"The Egyptians haven't been able to find him yet, and even if they do, who knows how much the guy knows, if anything at all."

"Is that why you went public with a news conference?" asked Scot.

"We had to make some fast decisions. If Hashim Nidal was making a run to get out of the country or using a local safe house, we wanted to at least throw up a net to try to catch him. We had to do something. We're too close to let him slip through our fingers again."

"But what about the other stuff, about this being a band of untrained individuals and all that? What happened on that plane was no amateur night, I can assure you. These guys knew what they were doing."

Now Morrell chimed back in. "We hoped that through the news conference we could not only get a tip that could help capture Nidal, but also discredit and potentially embarrass him, as it were, on the world stage. People working with him or thinking of hiring him, might not want to be associated with him if he's shown to be incompetent."

"That's a long shot," replied Harvath.

"Yes," said Ellis, taking over control of the conversation once again. "But it's one of the few shots we have. We are taking it to this guy, and his organization, on all fronts. We've already added him to the FBI's most wanted list and expect confirmation shortly from the State Department that any information leading to his arrest or capture will qualify under the Rewards for Justice program."

"So the message to the world is going to be that this guy is a bumbler, but we're worried enough about him to offer millions of dollars for his arrest or capture?" asked Harvath.

"Not only is he a bumbler, but a lone civilian, a woman no less, was responsible for thwarting his hijacking. That's the most damning fact, and the one we hope will seriously demoralize his organization and impede his ability to carry out further actions."

"Having your ass handed to you by a woman is probably the pinnacle of shame for a guy like this," offered Morrell.

Harvath was silent and that made Morrell nervous. "You've spent time over here, Harvath. You know how these people think. Avoidance of shame is a major motivator in their culture. You don't agree this is going to be a serious blow to the guy?"

"I think it'll be a serious blow to his ego, and yes, I think it will damage his reputation some, but not enough to keep money and support from flowing in his direction."

"That's the other concern," said Ellis as he straightened up and stopped leaning on the podium. "Had he been able to ransom Mayor Fellinger and Bob Lawrence, that would have been twenty million dollars right there. Had the Egyptians fully delivered on Abu Nidal's frozen assets, that would have been almost another five million. What the hell does he need that much money for?"

"And," added Morrell, "have we been able to stave off whatever it is by foiling this hijacking?"

Harvath pondered a few moments before responding. "I'll tell you this right now. I have no idea what this guy is up to, but from what I've seen so far, if he wants the money bad enough, he'll find another way to get it. And I think he wants it bad enough. If anything, the only thing we've done is slowed him down."

"Well, that's better than nothing," said Ellis as he crossed the room and unlocked the door, indicating that their meeting was drawing to a close. "Now we need to figure out what his next move is going to be and make sure we're one step ahead of him."

"Something tells me," responded Harvath as Morrell followed Tom Ellis out the door, "that we'll hear from Hashim Nidal before he hears from us."

As if on cue, an enormous explosion rocked the opposite side of the hospital and sent a concussion wave racing down the hallway.

28

The violent force of the blast ripped through the open doorway of the conference room and sent all three men flying backward. Harvath was the first to recover. He couldn't tell if Morrell and Ellis were okay, and frankly, there just wasn't enough time. He had to get to Meg Cassidy. The explosion was no accident. Scot was sure of it.

Even before he had been informed of Hashim Nidal's escape, something about Ellis's news conference had made Harvath uneasy. Now he knew what it was. It was the piece of paper taped to the podium. Scot looked behind him, and miraculously there it was, still taped in place, though the podium had been flipped over. The sign told the world where the woman responsible for foiling the hijacking was being treated, Cairo's Anglo-American Hospital. Instinct kicked in, and before Harvath knew it, he was already on his feet and out the conference room door.

The hallway was quickly filling with thick black smoke. Many of the fluorescent lights along the corridor ceiling had come loose and hung at angles resembling sinking ships, as they sputtered and shot red-hot sparks onto the bland linoleum floor. Overturned supply trolleys, IV trees, and crash carts littered the hall. The incessant blaring of the fire alarm and the spray from overhead sprinklers made the scene even more chaotic and more difficult to navigate. Staff members and patients alike held surgical masks and wet towels to their mouths to help them breathe as they began assisting each other toward the exits. It took a few moments before Harvath was finally able to locate Meg Cassidy's room.

Remarkably, he found both Gordon Avigliano and the beefy CIA sentry, Jerry, unhurt inside. When Harvath entered the room, both of the men had their weapons drawn.

"Are you guys okay?" asked Harvath.

"We're fine. What the hell was that?" asked Avigliano.

"It was a bomb of some sort. Probably a car bomb. How's Ms. Cassidy?"

"I'm okay," came the woman's voice from the hospital bed.

"What about Morrell and Ellis?" asked the sentry.

"They were standing in the doorway of the conference room down the hall when the blast hit. To tell you the truth, I don't know how they are. You need to go take a look. Gordy and I will look after Ms. Cassidy."

"Will do," said the sentry, who soaked a hand towel in water and then crouched low beneath the smoke as he ran from the room.

"I thought you two were standing guard outside," said Harvath as he carefully removed Meg Cassidy's IV from her arm.

"We were," replied Avigliano. "Jerry had orders to physically check on Ms. Cassidy every half-hour. He had come in the room to see how she was doing and I was in the doorway when the explosion happened."

"Gordo," said Harvath as he threw the young CIA man the keys to their car, "I want you to bring the car around to the back of the hospital. There's probably a service entrance of some sort. We'll meet you there."

"What about Morrell and Ellis?"

"There's no time for them. That explosion was a little too coincidental and I don't—"

"Believe in coincidences," said Avigliano, finishing Harvath's sentence for him. "Neither do I."

"Good, then get going. We'll meet you in back."

Avigliano didn't bother to look for a towel to cover his face. He knew time was of the essence and sprinted from the room. Meg already had her legs swung over the side of the hospital bed.

"Are you going to be okay?" said Scot.

"Do you think that explosion was somehow meant for me?" she asked.

"Now is not the time to find out. We need to get you out of here to someplace safe. Do you think you can make it?"

"I think so. Scot, are we in danger?"

"I don't know, Meg," he said as he slung his left arm around her waist and helped her up. "Let's just focus on getting out of here, okay?" She was a little unsteady on her feet and leaned heavily against his chest. He helped her to the sink, where he soaked a small hand towel for each of them before they left the room.

A raging fire was rapidly spreading throughout the small hospital. People were trying to run through the corridor, but stretchers and wheelchairs were causing mini, yet deadly, versions of the ubiquitous Cairo traffic jam. With a couple of well-placed hip-checks against the gridlocked stretchers, followed by commands barked in both English and Arabic, Harvath managed to get the frenzied flow of patients and staffers moving again. Judging from the distance they had traveled, Harvath figured they weren't far from the stairwell they needed. It was then that a hospital patron wearing a surgical mask caused Harvath to stop dead in his tracks.

Though the figure was across the smoke-filled corridor and was dressed in the traditional galabiya robes, Harvath still knew who it was. It was those eyes. Eyes so silver they bordered on black. They were the eyes of the assassin he had faced in Macau who had killed Sammy Cheng. They were very same eyes that Schoen had described seeing in Israel and that the old gypsy woman in Bern had attributed to the Devil. They belonged to Hashim Nidal himself, and Harvath was sure of it.

For a sliver of a second, Scot was torn. His Secret Service training had taught him that fighting was best left to others because his job was to see to the safe evacuation of his protectee. His SEAL training, though, had taught him that if you have a shot, you *take* the shot.

The struggle between an offensive reaction and a defensive one was no struggle at all. Hashim Nidal was too important to let go. It was obvious that he had come to the hospital looking for Meg. He was risking everything to come and finish her off. But, if anyone was going to be finished off, it was Nidal and Harvath would do the finishing.

Scot dropped the wet towel covering his mouth and drew his pistol from his waistband. "Get down!" he yelled as he forced Meg to the floor.

He spun hard to his right and for a moment lost the figure in the billowing smoke of the corridor. Several distinct cracks from an AK-47 told him that Nidal had seen him as well. The bullets tore up the wall to his left.

Scot swung his weapon toward where he thought the shots had come from, but the smoke was still too thick to see. The already frenzied mob of people trying to escape the hospital began screaming in terror at the sound of the gunfire. There were just too many of them. Harvath couldn't risk taking the shot, not until he knew he had Nidal directly in his sights. The AK-47 burst forth with another deafening fusillade of fire.

The rounds were thankfully well off their mark. Harvath rose from where he had been shielding Meg with his body and swept his pistol from left to right. For no more than an instant, the curtains of smoke parted and Harvath strained to pinpoint Nidal's eyes. As the curtains swept back together, he thought he had a lock and pulled the trigger of his powerful handgun, letting loose a devastating deluge of fire.

Right away, he knew his shots had been wasted. Nidal was using the smoke to his advantage and had moved before Scot had even fired a single shot. It was now Nidal's turn, and Scot knew what was coming. With his powerful arms, he pulled Meg Cassidy to her feet and urged her on toward the stairwell. If Nidal was using the smoke for cover, so could they, but they needed to get moving, fast.

Just as Harvath had predicted, Nidal swept his assault rifle in a wide swath of flaming lead, tearing up everything in its path. Scot and Meg made it into the stairwell just as a half dozen rounds chewed up the emergency exit door behind them.

There was no need to urge Meg to run faster. She had found her stride and despite all of the punishment her body had been through, she was moving faster than Harvath. In his defense, it was quite a job barreling down the stairs in front of them while simultaneously keeping an eye out behind for Nidal or any of his accomplices.

When they hit the lower landing, the door for the service entrance was right in front of them. Harvath ran past Meg, slammed his hip into the horizontal, stainless-steel bar, and the door crashed open. As instructed, Gordon Avigliano was right there waiting for them. He was scanning the surrounding area with a silenced Ingram model 10 submachine gun.

"Where the hell did you get that?" asked Harvath as he bundled Meg into the backseat of the car.

"I told you. This is my first visit to Cairo. I wanted to be prepared."

"Do you always travel like that?"

"Sure. I bring my Pepto, hot water bottle, and plenty o' firepower."

Scot shook his head and got into the driver's seat. He really was beginning to like the kid.

When Avigliano was in and had slammed the passenger side door, Harvath peeled out. They drove north then crossed the Nile and headed south along en-Nil Street. Scot took advantage of its sparse traffic to pick up as much speed as possible and deftly weaved in and out of the relatively slow-moving vehicles. When they passed the el-Gala and el-Gama Bridges, Avigliano, who had been studying his map of Cairo, decided it was time to speak up. "Ah, Scot?"

"I'm a little bit busy right now, Gord," replied Harvath, who pushed the embassy car faster and faster through the ever-thickening Cairo traffic.

"I can see that, but is there any reason we haven't crossed back over to the Garden City side of the river yet?"

"Because we're not going to Garden City."

"You do know that's where the embassy is, don't you?"

"Where are we?" asked Meg Cassidy as she started to crawl up onto the backseat.

"Meg," said Scot, who could see what she was doing in his rearview mirror, "I want you to stay down on the floor back there. We're not out of the woods yet. I'll let you know when you can get up." Harvath then turned his attention back to Avigliano. "We're not going to the embassy."

"We're not?" said the CIA operative, confused.

"Nope," replied Harvath. "Now, when we slow down, which is inevitable in Cairo traffic, I want you to have that door of yours ajar at all times. Keep one hand on the door handle and one hand on your weapon, which should be off safety. You understand? I want you to be able to spring from this car at a moment's notice. You got me?"

"Yeah, I gotcha, but where are we going?"

"Do you have a cell phone on you that works over here?" asked Harvath, ignoring the operative's question.

"Yes, why?"

"Give it to me," said Harvath as he fished Bob Lawrence's business card from his pocket.

Avigliano handed Scot his phone as Harvath drove the car up onto the sidewalk to get around a group of cars stopped at a red light. Avigliano braced for impact, but they made it through the intersection without incident. As Harvath maneuvered the car back into the street, he dialed Bob Lawrence's cell and prayed that as an international CEO, the man also had a phone that worked in Cairo.

Lawrence picked up after the second ring. "Bob Lawrence," he said.

"Mr. Lawrence, Scot Harvath here," said Scot as he once again pulled the car up onto a sidewalk to get around a group of cars stopped at a red light. Avigliano braced for impact again and closed his eyes. Harvath was either incredibly brave, or incredibly insane. Avigliano couldn't yet tell which one it was.

"Agent Harvath, when I said keep in touch, I didn't think I'd be hearing from you so soon. What can I do for you?"

"Have you taken off yet?"

"No. We're just boarding the aircraft now. Why?"

"I was hoping I could hitch a ride with you."

"We're not going to D.C., we're returning to Chicago."

"Chicago's fine—"

Harvath was interrupted by Avigliano, who said, "What the hell are you doing?"

"Hold on," said Harvath, as much for Avigliano's benefit as for Bob Lawrence's. He swung the wheel hard to the left, and the car spun onto the Giza Bridge. "I have a special passenger with me who I think will be very glad to get back to Chicago."

"Is this our friend to whom we owe a very deep debt of gratitude?" asked Lawrence.

"You can't take her on that plane," broke in Avigliano.

"Indeed it is," said Harvath, who then pressed the phone against his chest and turned to the CIA operative and said, "The embassy is the first place Nidal would expect us to take her. Morrell and Ellis fucked up with that news conference and led him right to her. I am not going to give him a second chance. This is the right thing to do."

"If you ask me—" began Avigliano.

"I'm not," said Harvath, who then held the phone back up to his ear and said, "Sorry about that, Mr. Lawrence. The two of us would like to fly back to Chicago with you if that's okay."

"Of course it's okay. What about the embassy, though?"

"This whole transport operation is on a need-to-know basis, and the embassy doesn't need to know right now."

"I hear you loud and clear. We'd be happy to give you a ride back. As a matter of fact, it's the least we can do. Is there anything else you need on our end?"

"Please have your pilot alert the tower that you are awaiting two last-minute passengers. We're in an embassy car with diplomatic plates. As long as security knows we're coming, we should be able to sail through."

"Any idea how long you'll be?"

"We're on Salah Salem Street right now, heading toward the airport. We'll be there as soon as we can."

"Good enough. We'll wait for you."

"Our friend will also need a change of clothes," said Harvath. Meg was still wearing her hospital gown.

"I'm sure we can find something for her."

"Thank you, Mr. Lawrence. We'll see you when we get

there," said Scot as he punched the *end* button and tossed the phone back to Avigliano.

For his part, the young operative now knew better than to argue with Harvath. He sat back and tried to survive the ride as he wondered how the hell he was going to explain the situation to Rick Morrell.

29

Harvath had thought he would sleep all the way back to Chicago, but instead, spent most of the trip talking with Meg Cassidy. She was a fascinating woman—very driven, very outgoing, but underneath it all there was something else. There was a vulnerability that Scot could sense and which he was sure Meg shared with few people, if any at all. No, the image she portrayed and wanted everyone to see was the superachiever, a woman who had her act together and did anything she set her mind to.

For Meg's part, she saw in Scot Harvath all of the things that most women immediately noticed in him. He was handsome, intelligent, and had a great sense of humor. Those were all excellent qualities in Meg's book, but what she really liked about him was that he made her feel safe. From the moment he had placed the blankets around her on the hijacked plane and had helped her to the EgyptAir clubroom, she somehow believed that no one could harm her with this man around. It had been a long time since she had felt that way. No matter how many self-defense classes she took, no matter how near the gun on her nightstand, after her attack, she had never really felt safe again. Meg had learned that she could rely only on herself, but the weight of that responsibility never allowed anyone else to get close. Scot Harvath, though, made her think of changing.

When the plane landed at Chicago's O'Hare International Airport, security was tight, and the flight was met by a contingent of Chicago's top cops. The area outside the security checkpoint was crowded with media. While Bob Lawrence and Mayor Fellinger stopped to make statements to the press, Scot and Meg quietly stole away with the rest of the crew.

Meg tried to convince Harvath to stay a few days in Chicago. Though he was tempted, both by his love for the town and his growing interest in Meg Cassidy, he knew he needed to get back to D.C. He couldn't keep avoiding the president and the White House forever. Besides, Bob Lawrence had arranged for a private plane to fly him back to Washington.

Because the plane was going to be leaving from Meig's Field, not far from where Meg lived downtown, Lawrence had also arranged for a limo to get both of them into the city. Scot and Meg decided that though they were wiped out, there still was enough time to grab a late lunch, and they had the driver swing them by Gino's Pizzeria on Rush Street.

Scot liked Meg's style. Here was this popular, powerful Chicago businesswoman who could have had a table at any restaurant in town and she wanted to go for pizza. Not just any pizza, mind you, but the best deep-dish pizza Chicago had to offer at one of Harvath's favorite places in town.

Meg's face still bore discernable marks where she had been struck by her attacker. Harvath wondered if she had chosen the dimly lit, graffiti-plagued restaurant out of a hope that nobody she knew would see her, but then he watched her order. She waved away the menus when the waiter approached. She didn't need a menu because she already knew exactly what she wanted. With Scot's permission, she ordered for both of them. Meg hadn't suggested Gino's so she could hide out. She actually liked eating there. If it weren't for the fabulous shape she was in, Scot might have thought she was a regular.

To finish it all off, Meg asked the waiter to bring them two of the coldest Sam Adamses they had. Once the waiter had left the table, Meg said that it was a shame that Gino's didn't serve Moretti beer. She knew that deep-dish wasn't exactly authentic Italian pizza, but she really liked the way a cold Moretti went with even quasi-Italian food. The fact that Meg liked Morettis, not to mention even knew what they were, raised Scot's interest in her even further. Meg explained that in college she had spent her junior year studying in Rome. She loved everything Italian, except the drivers. It was the only country she had ever seen where people passed speeding ambulances because they thought they had more important places to be. Other than that, it was wonderful—the art, the history, the people, the food . . .

And on and on it went, the two of them falling into easy and boundless conversation, as if they had known each other for ages. Finally, Scot glanced at his watch and realized he had to get going.

Meg rode in the limo with him down outer Lake Shore Drive to Meig's Field, where they lingered uncomfortably before shaking hands good-bye and Scot boarded the private jet. As the ground dropped away and the plane banked out over the sailboat-dotted waters of Lake Michigan, Harvath turned his thoughts away from Meg Cassidy and toward what the future held in store for him back in D.C.

* * *

By the time the jet touched down at Ronald Reagan International, Harvath knew he had to address his job situation with the Secret Service, and the sooner, the better.

He caught a cab for the short ride back to Alexandria and, after emptying the stack of junk mail from his mailbox, climbed the stairs to his apartment. He removed the hair from the upper-right corner of the doorframe, less confident in this security measure ever since Rick Morrell had slipped into his place undetected to drink his beer and short-sheet his bed. Because he hadn't taken any bags with him to Cairo, there was nothing to unpack. So much the better. He was exhausted. He'd gone longer without sleep in the past, his Navy SEAL training had seen to that, but as adept as he was at operating on little to no shut-eye, he also knew that sleep was a weapon that sharpened the mind and fine-tuned the reflexes. Whatever the rationale, at this point Harvath didn't care. He was just glad to be home. After leaving a message for Secret Service director Stan Jameson, who had already gone home for the evening, Scot was happy to get undressed and slide into his own bed for a night of well-earned sleep.

Harvath awoke early the next morning semirested and refreshed. He put on shorts, a T-shirt, and his Nikes. He was glad he got up when he did. The air outside was still cool and not overly humid.

He ran to a café he frequented in Old Town, ordered a house brew, and found a quiet table, upon which someone had left a copy of *The Washington Post*. He set his coffee down and turned the paper over. Front and center was a picture of Meg Cassidy with the headline, "The Woman Who Saved Flight 7755." Scot sat down and began reading the article. The details were sketchy at best, but Meg was being credited with leading the passenger revolt that helped bring the hijacking to an end. There was no mention of Hashim Nidal and another hijacker escaping.

So, the cat was officially out of the bag. Meg was being heralded as an international hero. She had been extremely courageous and deserved the praise, but Harvath wondered if it was such a good idea to go public with her identity while Nidal was still at large. He tried to console himself with the thought that Hashim Nidal was half a world away and hunting down Meg Cassidy would not be worth his while. Or would it?

Now that Meg's full name, occupation, and location were out in the open, she made a much easier target. Scot made a mental note to speak to Gary Lawlor about protection for her back in Chicago and then finished his coffee before heading back to his apartment.

When he got home, there were two messages on his voice mail. The first was from Director Jameson. The president would be returning to the White House tomorrow afternoon and wanted to see Harvath personally. A time had been set, and Jameson said he would be there as well. Harvath knew that the meeting would be about his new position as director of Secret Service Operations at the White House and how soon he would be expected to start. Ever since the former head of White House Sercret Service Ops, Bill Shaw, had been arrested for his involvement in the president's kidnapping, an interim director had been minding the store until Harvath could move into the position and take over full-time.

The second message was from Frank Mraz, the deputy director of the CIA's Directorate of Operations. *God, what a title*, thought Harvath as he reminded himself who Mraz was. The message was succinct and to the point. Mraz wanted to see Scot at Langley today for a debriefing on everything that had happened in Cairo. The Agency would send a car for him at nine o'clock. Business casual attire was fine and the Agency would see to his lunch.

Business casual? Lunch? Mraz made it sound more like a social invitation than a debriefing. Harvath hopped in the shower, shaved, and then put on one of his dark Brooks Brothers suits with a white shirt and gold tie. He didn't know what Mraz's game was, but he wasn't about to let the CIA dictate to him how to dress. He had half a mind to pack his own lunch, but decided against it. He'd been to Langley before and they had a relatively decent cafeteria. Buying him lunch was the least the CIA could do, especially as he was going to fill them in on all of the mistakes their "Special" Activities Staff had made over the past two days.

Even though he knew he'd never be allowed into the building with it, he brought along the H&K USP pistol he had been issued in Cairo. It was just another way to reiterate to Mraz that Harvath didn't trust him or anyone working for him.

The last thing Harvath did before leaving his apartment was call Lawlor's office regarding a protective detail for Meg. Neither Lawlor, nor his secretary were in, so Harvath left a message on his voice mail.

At precisely nine o'clock a navy blue Ford Crown Victoria pulled up in front of Harvath's building. The driver didn't have to bother ringing the bell. Scot knew the man would be right on time and he was already waiting for him. Normally, Harvath would have sat in the front seat and made conversation with whoever was driving, but this guy didn't look like much of a talker, so Scot sat in back. As it turned out, he was right. The driver didn't say a single thing during the entire drive to Langley.

The silence suited him just fine. It was a beautiful summer day, and Harvath sat back and watched the gently rolling countryside through the smoked windows of the car as they made their way northwest along the Potomac.

When they arrived at the main entrance of the sprawling CIA campus, the driver pulled into the employee lane. At the cinderblock checkpoint, black-clad, submachine-gun-toting operatives from the Office of Security Operations checked the driver's identification and gave the entire vehicle the once-over. The Central Intelligence Agency was more vigilant about security now than ever before. For every security measure a visitor or employee of the CIA saw, there were hundreds more they didn't. For instance, Harvath knew that unseen behind the bulletproof, tinted glass of the checkpoint house was a fully armed and armored tactical unit ready to meet any assault head-on.

They were outfitted with nothing but the best weapons, including .45 and .357 pistols with hollow-point Hydra-Shok bullets; H&K 21E fully automatic machine guns, effective out to half a mile; custom-made Robar .50-caliber sniper rifles capable of knocking out aircraft, vehicles, and even terrorists at well over a mile; M249 Squad

Automatic Weapons, known as SAWs; M203 40-millimeter grenade launchers; as well as shoulder-fired antiaircraft and antitank missiles. There were also the concrete-and-steel bollards recessed just beneath the surface of each lane resting upon high-tensile industrial-strength coils that in a fraction of a second could be "popped" up in case a car tried to rush through the checkpoint and into the CIA's compound.

Once cleared at the main entrance, the driver proceeded to the underground parking garage of the Old Headquarters Building, where he was again required to show his ID before being allowed to enter. The car rolled down the concrete ramp and once the driver had parked, he opened his door and motioned for Harvath to follow. They passed through a series of steel fire doors and emerged into a small service corridor and another security checkpoint. This time, Harvath was also asked to present identification and to sign in. Next, he was instructed to pass through a metal detector, which immediately went off.

Slowly and with a wide grin, Harvath unbuttoned his suit coat and drew it back to reveal the butt of his semiautomatic. "Just like my American Express card. I never leave home without it." No one laughed.

Harvath carefully withdrew the weapon and handed it to the security guard, who ejected the magazine, cleared the chambered round, and handed the whole lot over to Harvath's driver. In the next machine, an explosives "sniffer," Harvath was required to stand still as small puffs of air were bounced against his clothes and returned to the machine for analysis.

"You guys get HBO on this?" asked Harvath.

Again, none of the security staff said a word. Harvath figured they had probably had the same sense-of-humor-gland removal that Morrell's people had had.

After Harvath had been handed his ID badge, the driver led him into a waiting elevator and punched the button for the sixth floor. "So this is it? We just zip right up in the elevator?" asked Harvath as the doors closed and the elevator began to rise. "No tour? What about the Berlin Wall Monument? Or the sculpture in the New Headquarters courtyard? You gotta promise me you'll at least walk me through the directors' portrait gallery on our way out. Okay? You promise?"

"Shut the fuck up," replied the rather surly operative.

Finally, Harvath had gotten to him, and he smiled to himself.

When the doors of the elevator opened, they walked down a short hall and entered the CIA's highly vaunted Counter Terrorist Center, known as the CTC. Predominantly windowless, the center was composed of groupings of hundreds upon hundreds of cubicles. Street signs proclaiming, "Osama bin Lane," "Saddam Street," and "Qadhafi Qourt" informed passersby what area of expertise they were entering. *So the CIA did have a sense of humor after all.*

Signs and placards were everywhere with pictures of the smoking World Trade Center on one side, a badly damaged Pentagon on the other, and in the middle a billowing American flag with the words "Let's Roll." Harvath knew that coffeepots percolated around the clock and dedicated CTC operatives often slept on mattresses laid out in the hallways. This was one of the key nerve centers in America's war on terrorism, and it looked every bit the part. For a moment, Harvath almost felt guilty for razzing the always serious CIA, but then he changed his mind. Yes, they had a tough job to do, but so did he. People who took themselves too seriously not only were no fun, but could also be very dangerous.

The CTC had been established in 1986 by then-CIA-director William Casey. The idea was to bring together the Agency's four directorates to address terrorism and to coordinate the Agency's efforts with other law enforcement agencies. The CTC monitored the whereabouts of known terrorists around-the-world, twenty-four hours a day, 365 days a year. Agents from the FBI, Department of Defense, the National Security Agency, and elsewhere were also stationed at the CTC. It was a warren of intelligence officers, psychiatrists, explosives experts, hostage negotiators, cultural, religious, and language experts—all of whom aided in the gathering and analyzing of intelligence and the running of covert operations both at home and abroad.

The center, though widely criticized for some of its dramatic misses, had had several significant hits. The CTC was responsible for linking the 1988 bombing of Pan Am flight 103 over Lockerbie, Scotland, with Abu Nidal and several Libyan agents, for uncovering Saddam Hussein's plot in 1993 to assassinate former president George Bush, and had continued to be extremely instrumental in assisting both domestic and foreign intelligence agencies in the arrests of countless terrorist operatives.

Harvath was shown to a small, perfectly soundproofed conference room off "IRA Avenue." Inside, Frank Mraz and two other operatives were already waiting for him. The driver spoke quietly to Mraz as Harvath took a seat. An attractive young woman entered and placed a tray with two carafes of coffee, mugs, cream, and sugar down on the table. Once she and the driver had exited, Mraz called the meeting to order.

"Okay, Agent Harvath" he began, "let's start from when you arrived on the ground in Cairo."

"As long as this is going to be for the record," replied Harvath, clearly and deliberately so that the operative who was transcribing the session, in addition to tape-recording it, could get everything right, "let's start with when I received Rick Morrell's less-than-adequate notice that we were going to Cairo in the first place."

Mraz nodded his head, and so it went for the next several hours until they broke for lunch. Harvath detailed his account of what had happened up to, during, and after the takedown of the hijacked airliner. He pulled no punches and presented a critical assessment of Morrell's handling of the operation and its subsequent fallout. Though it was obvious that he didn't personally care for the man, Harvath kept his remarks about Rick Morrell strictly professional.

When it was time for lunch, copies of the day's menu were passed around the table, and Mraz placed their order over one of the conference room telephones. The men were given a brief chance to stretch their legs and use the rest rooms while they waited for the food to be delivered. The operative transcribing the session escorted Harvath to and from the men's room. At first, Harvath believed it was because Mraz had ordered him to keep an eye on him, but it soon became apparent that the guy just wanted to hear more.

"We really don't get a lot of opportunities to meet people engaged in actual takedowns," said the man. "I'm honestly impressed with what you did."

Not another one, thought Harvath to himself. If he kept bumping into half-decent CIA guys, he was going to have to rethink his opinion of the entire agency.

Once they had all finished lunch, the Q-and-A session continued, and Harvath was every bit as blunt as in the beginning. Mraz asked a lengthy set of questions about why Harvath did not seek out Morrell's direction after the hospital bombing and why he didn't return with Meg Cassidy to the U.S. Embassy in Cairo. He wanted to know about everything Harvath and Meg had discussed from the moment he helped her escape from the hospital to the moment the two of them parted at Chicago's Meigs Field. Mraz then ordered dinner and had a series of questions about Harvath's assignment in Hong Kong and how the assassin he had seen in Macau fit in with what he had seen and heard in Bern, Jerusalem, and Cairo.

It was well past ten o'clock in the evening by the time Mraz finally called the debriefing to a close, but not without informing Harvath that he might elect to bring him back at some point in the future for further questions if he saw fit. As long as it was at some point in the future, Harvath didn't care. Right now, he was sick of answering questions. All he wanted to do was get home, have a beer, and hit the sack. Though he had had one night of semi-decent sleep, he was still on edge. After an intense operation, it often took a few days before he completely calmed down.

As they filed out of the room, Mraz reminded Harvath to keep his CIA-issued pager with him in case Morrell wanted to get ahold of him. Harvath knew that the beeper only served to keep up the pretense that Morrell and the CIA's Directorate of Operations were cooperating with him, but he had made this point very clear in his debriefing and didn't see the need to beat a dead horse. Besides, he was too tired.

Out in the hallway, Harvath was stopped by the operative who had been doing the transcribing. "On behalf of the CTC, I want you to have this," said the man as he handed Harvath one of the center's highly coveted lapel pins. It bore the image of a ski-masked terrorist angrily waving a rifle with a red line crossed through him. "It's none of my business, but there are obviously some people within the Agency you don't exactly care for. We're an organization like any other, and it takes all kinds to make it work. I'm not trying to make excuses for anybody. As a matter of fact, from what I heard in there, we're fortunate to have you working with us. Just remember that we're all on the same side and all want the same thing. Some of us just have a different way of going about it."

"That's precisely what has been worrying me about this whole operation," said Harvath as he shook the man's hand and thanked him for his gift.

30

The following afternoon, Harvath arrived early at the White House for his meeting with the president and the director of the Secret Service. He wanted to reacquaint himself with the lay of the land. As he moved from office to office, there was no shortage of staffers and fellow Secret Service agents who were happy to see him. Harvath had always been well respected and popular around the White House, but after he had saved the lives of both President Rutledge and his daughter, Amanda, his reputation had taken on mythic proportions. Though he had made brief visits to the White House since the kidnapping ordeal, he had been largely unaccounted for as he continued his search for those involved. All but an enlightened few were under the impression that he had been on an extended leave of absence due to the injuries he had suffered rescuing the president. Harvath did nothing to dissuade his friends and coworkers from that opinion.

In the duty room, Harvath found the three people he was looking for. Sitting around one of the square Formica tables drinking coffee and enjoying their break were Agents Kate Palmer, Chris Longo, and Tom Hollenbeck. All three had been on active duty with Harvath when the president's kidnapping had taken place and had been equally involved in the frantic search and rescue efforts for their fellow agents and the civilians trapped beneath the avalanche triggered by the kidnappers.

Hollenbeck was the first to see Harvath standing in the doorway. "Whoa!" he roared. "Would ya look at what the cat dragged in." Both Palmer and Longo turned to see whom Hollenbeck was talking about.

Harvath walked up to the table and set down the biggest box of chocolates any of them had ever seen. "Good afternoon, lady and . . ."

"I think the word you're looking for is *gentlemen*," said Longo after Harvath's pregnant pause.

"No. The word I am looking for is definitely not *gentlemen*," he said as he put an affectionate hand on Kate Palmer's shoulder. "Palmer, I brought these back from Switzerland for you. I remember what happened when you came back from Europe one time and left some chocolate in here."

"Yeah, all of you pigs ate it," said Palmer.

"Not me," said Longo, who had already opened the box and was choosing his favorite pieces. "I hate chocolate."

"What did I tell you, Scot? Never trust anyone who says they don't like chocolate," replied Palmer as she yanked the box away from Longo before he could remove any more pieces.

"You were all very helpful to me during the situation, and I thought the least I could do was bring something back for you from overseas." "Situation" was how the staff around the White House quietly referred to President Rutledge's kidnapping.

"Hey, you brought the president back safely and that's the best thing any of us could have asked for," said Hollenbeck.

"Though chocolate runs a close second," offered Palmer as she began sorting through the box.

"Speaking of seconds," continued Hollenbeck, who had been named interim director of White House Secret Service Operations. "When are you coming back to work? I'm starting to get tired of keeping your seat warm for you."

"Don't listen to him," said Longo. "You could stay away for another six months and it wouldn't bother him a bit. I think the power has gone right to his head."

"There's nothing worse than people who only feel bitterness and jealousy as their betters zip past them on the ladder of success," replied Hollenbeck.

"See what I mean?" responded Longo. "And you know what? On top of it all, he's become quite arrogant."

"*Arrogant?* Me? Palmer, you've got to come to my defense here. Tell Harvath I am the same old Tom Hollenbeck you've always known and loved."

"Well," she began slowly, "*loved* is a pretty strong word."

"Okay then, *known*," he replied.

"Jeez, Tom—wait I'm sorry—Jeez, *Mr. Interim Director*—that is the way you told us all to address you, isn't it?" she joked.

"I can't believe this," cried Hollenbeck. "Every time I turn around, another knife in the back!"

"Well, I'm glad nothing's changed around here," said Harvath as he joined his friends at their table.

They made small talk until it was time for Harvath's meeting. When he got up to leave, Palmer asked, "So, what's the deal? When are you coming back to work?"

He was as honest with her as he could be and said, "Right now, I don't know."

They all shook hands and wished each other well a Harvath left to make his way to the situation room downstairs. It wasn't unusual for President Rutledge to conduct his more sensitive meetings in this room. It was one of the few places in the entire building where he knew he wouldn't be disturbed unless there was a dire emergency or matter of grave national consequence.

Though both of the Marines standing guard outside the situation room knew him, they still closely examined the credentials hanging from around Harvath's neck. Even a facility as secure as the White House had decided that it could use a few improvements. Nothing was left to chance, and things were done strictly by the book. After waiting a few moments outside, Harvath was told he could enter. He heard a click and then the faint hiss of the situation room's seal and door lock being released.

The first person to stand and greet him was President Jack Rutledge himself. "Scot, it's good to see you," said the president as he offered him his hand, which Harvath shook carefully. He was happy to see the president using it again. The kidnappers had cut off one of his fingers and sent it to the former vice president as a threat.

"It is good to see you too, Mr. President," replied Harvath. "How is the hand?"

"So far so good. We'll see how I do when pheasant season rolls around. That'll be the real test."

"You outshot so many of us last year, Mr. President, we were hoping you might take up a different sport. It's embarrassing for a lot of the agents that you can shoot better than they can."

"You weren't embarrassed, though, were you, Scot?"

"No, sir."

"And why was that?"

"Because I brought down three more birds than you did."

"Ah, ah. Let's tell the truth here. You only brought down two more than me. The third one, *supposedly* went down somewhere in the woods. As it was never found, you couldn't rightfully count it, could you?"

"No, Mr. President. I couldn't. But I know I hit that bird. If I'd only had a better dog—"

"Stop right there, Agent Harvath. I spent a lot of money and a lot of time training those dogs, and I won't have you disparage my fine pedigreed animals."

"Fine pedigreed animals? No offense, Mr. President, but Crackle is so lazy, he won't even chase cars. He just sits on the South Lawn and jots down license plate numbers."

The other attendees gathered in the situation room began laughing. It was a brief but welcome respite. They hadn't had anything to laugh about in a while. Harvath had gotten the last word and the president knew it. He slapped him on the back and showed Harvath to his seat. "I believe you know the rest of the gentlemen present," said the president as he motioned around the table. Indeed he did.

Harvath nodded in turn to FBI director Sorce, CIA director Vaile, Homeland Security director Dreihaus, Secret Service director Jameson, and deputy FBI director Gary Lawlor. Harvath had been expecting to meet with just the president and Director Jameson to discuss his new White House position. With all of the additional people present, he had a feeling he was here to discuss something entirely different. Part of him wondered if he was going to be taken to task for spiriting Meg Cassidy out of Egypt, but he knew he had done the right thing and decided not to stress about it. Harvath knew President Rutledge didn't like to waste time and would get to the point soon enough.

"First of all," began the president, "I want to commend Agent Harvath for what, in my opinion, was a job extremely well done. I've read the after-action reports of both the Delta and SAS commanders and think you prevented a very bad situation from getting worse. It's precisely this ability to assess and appropriately react to hostile situations that has made you such an asset to the Secret Service and the White House."

Harvath was uncomfortable with such fulsome praise, especially when bestowed by the president in front of so many other people, but he accepted it humbly. "Thank you, Mr. President."

"Now, moving forward," continued the president. "I will be convening a meeting this evening of the National Security Council to discuss the escalating tensions in the Mideast and tightening the net around Hashim Nidal by applying direct pressure to anyone who is known to be harboring or assisting him, or any other members of his organization. I don't want to talk right now about how this hijacking happened. I plan to take that issue up later. What I do want to talk about is how we're going to get Nidal back in the crosshairs before he pushes the Middle East into all-out war. With that said, I'm all ears."

CIA director Vaile cleared his throat and waited for the president to nod in his direction before he spoke. "Mr. President, as you are aware, it was the CIA who gave birth to Operation Phantom and who initiated the hunt for—"

"Director Vaile, the clock is ticking. Don't waste my

time telling me things I already know. How are we going to stop Hashim Nidal before he strikes again?" commanded the president.

Vaile's nuts were in a vise. Not only had his agency been behind the curve in discovering the existence of Hashim Nidal, but they had let him slip through their grasp in Cairo. If Vaile wasn't very careful, the vise would begin to tighten real quick.

"Pinpointing the whereabouts of Nidal and his base of operations so we can take them out is the highest priority of all our agents right now, both at Langley and in the field."

"Which brings us to Ms. Meg Cassidy, correct?" asked the president.

Upon hearing her name, Harvath leaned into the table.

"Exactly, Mr. President," continued Vaile. "As she is the only known person outside of his organization to have ever seen him and survived, she is of the utmost importance to the success of Operation Phantom."

"So what's the problem?" asked the president.

"Yesterday, we sent operatives to Chicago to conduct a follow-up with her—"

"And?"

"Well, as I explained to you previously, Mr. President, Ms. Cassidy is reluctant to cooperate."

"Do you suppose *The Washington Post* piece had anything to do with it?" asked Harvath.

"Agent Harvath," said Vaile as he turned in his chair to face him, "*The Washington Post* article is part of a calculated effort to discredit Hashim Nidal on the world stage and thereby—"

"Destabilize his organization, which will hopefully slow him down long enough for us to nail him. I know you thought all of this out very well, but did you ever think about what Meg Cassidy wants? Have you asked her if she wants to be front and center in your PR blitz?"

The president discreetly signaled for Harvath to back off and Scot immediately fell silent. Director Vaile, though, continued with his justification, "Frankly, being a high-profile PR person, we didn't figure Ms. Cassidy for someone who shied away from media exposure, of any kind. What's more, it isn't as if we, or she, have any choice in the matter. Our psychological operations people are convinced that the PR angle will help and that it needs to remain an adjunct of any ongoing strategy we pursue."

"I am sure your people are doing the absolute best they can," said the president as he steered the conversation away from Meg Cassidy and toward other pressing elements of the operation. "Let's talk about a timetable and what assets you need called into play."

When the president concluded the meeting, he thanked the participants for coming and asked FBI deputy director Lawlor and Agent Harvath to remain behind.

Once the other members had left the room and the door sealed shut behind them, the president spoke once again. "I hope you both know me well enough to know that I am not a fan of back-biting or infighting. I don't approve of it in my party, and I don't approve of it within our intelligence community. That being said, what I am most concerned about here is results. This doesn't leave this room, Agent

Harvath, but I'm not as impressed with Director Vaile's operations as I might lead him to think.

"The world has become a much more dangerous place over the last several weeks. The Hand of God attacks have pushed the entire Mideast region to the brink of war. This morning I was briefed by the chairman of the Joint Chiefs who presented me with a stack of satellite photos showing that Iran, Syria, and Egypt have realigned troops and equipment on their borders indicating a potential attack on Israel.

"It's like a puddle of gasoline and everyone is dancing around with lit matches—including the Israelis. What worries me the most is that Hashim Nidal's organization has made it clear they intend to drop the first match. That's all it would take at this point to set things off, and we have no idea where he is or what he is planning.

"If the CIA wasn't so deep into this investigation already with so many assets in place, I would seriously think about putting you in more of a leadership position. As it stands now, though, this is going to have to remain the CIA's show, so I am going to ask you to try to cooperate with your fellow operatives." The president could see Harvath was about to speak up and raised his hand again to stop him. "As I said, I read both after-action reports. I don't take issue with anything you did. As a matter of fact, I wouldn't change a thing, but I do want you to start respecting their chain of command. You can walk softly and still carry a big stick, just lighten up from using it on CIA personnel all the time. Okay?"

"Yes, Mr. President. I understand," replied Harvath.

"Good. Now, I want to tell you why I stopped you from

going after DCI Vaile on the Meg Cassidy issue. In a nutshell, we need Meg Cassidy's help."

"I don't understand what the problem is," said Harvath.

"The problem," answered the president, "is that Meg Cassidy doesn't want to cooperate with us."

" 'Us' who? The United States Government?"

"More to the point, the CIA."

"That shouldn't be a problem. Don't make her work with them."

"And who would you suggest she work with?"

"Delegate the task of identifying Hashim Nidal to another agency like the DOD," replied Harvath. "We've got a war going against terrorism, so having her interface with the Department of Defense would make complete sense. It'll upset the CTC people a bit, but all they were going to do was have her sift through pictures and descriptions from the world's top terrorist databases anyway. The DOD can access those.

"You begin at the top and work your way down. For starters, there's the German *Kommissar* system. That one has backgrounds on countless suspected and known terrorists worldwide, including photographs, fingerprints, dental records, voiceprints, and a ton of other data. All Defense has to do is narrow the parameters of the search so she's not reviewing material she doesn't need to see.

"Next on the list, like it or not, the CIA will have to allow the DOD access to their DESIST database. There's also the State Department's international terrorist database, and then the FBI's Terrorist Information System. If there's a record of this guy anywhere, they'll find it."

"That all makes perfect sense, but unfortunately it's

not that easy," said the president. "First of all, we don't have time to transfer the investigation to another agency and secondly, we're not just talking about sitting Meg Cassidy in front of a computer monitor and flashing digital mug shots at her. The CIA needs to recruit her."

"Recruit her? What for?"

"Director Vaile feels they're close to nailing the exact location of Hashim Nidal's base of operations."

"So then we insert a Special Ops team to direct fire, bring in some fast movers, and smoke the entire place. End of story."

"Nope. Not *end of story*. We will need confirmation that we have not only devastated his training camp, but that we are taking out the man himself. For that we need a positive on-site ID, and Meg Cassidy is the only person who can make that identification."

"But she's a civilian."

"Which is precisely why the CIA needs to train her. She's going to have to insert with a team, go along as they conduct the operation, and get out."

"And that team would be Operation Phantom under the command of Rick Morrell."

"That's it."

"Well, now I'm not so confused anymore. Not only is it extremely dangerous, but it's got to scare a civilian half to death."

"That's probably not the only reason this is distasteful for her," added Lawlor.

"Now is probably a good time for you to contribute your part, Gary. Why don't you go ahead."

"Thank you, Mr. President," responded Lawlor before

continuing. "Scot, as the president said, the CIA's reasons for approaching Ms. Cassidy were sound, but their methods weren't. From what I have been able to gather from the CIA's inner agency reports—"

"I don't want to bog us down, but before we go any further, can you please explain what the FBI's interest in Meg Cassidy is and why the FBI's deputy director is reviewing CIA inner agency reports?" asked Harvath.

Lawlor looked to the president, who nodded his head. "I am not directly operating on this in my capacity as deputy director right now."

"Then how are you operating on this?"

"As part of the FBI's restructuring, the president has suggested the creation of a unit to implement what is being referred to as our new strike-first policy. While I will consult with the FBI from time to time, I will report directly to the president," said Lawlor.

"About what?"

"In a sense, I'm a consultant at this point, trying to help figure out how to better defend our country. There are certain operations, such as Operation Phantom, that I have taken an interest in. The president has agreed to let me be involved in a supervisory capacity. That's all I am going to say at this point."

Harvath knew Lawlor well enough to know not to push for more information. Even as a Secret Service agent granted an extreme amount of latitude by the president of the United States, he was not on a direct need-to-know basis on this one, and so he kept his mouth shut.

Lawlor took Harvath's silence as an indication to continue and did. "From what I can gather, Morrell put the squeeze on Meg Cassidy for information on Nidal the minute he discovered she had seen his face."

"I can verify it. He wasn't about to let her alone until I stepped in. I had to fight to get her medical attention."

"Okay, I've skimmed the lengthy transcript of your debriefing at Langley with Frank Mraz yesterday, so I understand you spent most of the flight back to Chicago talking with her. You then had lunch together and she saw you off?"

"That was it. She had caught a couple of naps on the plane and was pretty tired. So was I. That was pretty much it."

"Do you think she likes you?" asked Lawlor as he placed his elbows on the table and leaned in toward Harvath.

"*Likes me?* What does that have to do with anything?"

"A lot, potentially."

"I suppose so. But I think it was nothing more than appreciation."

"I think it might be more than that."

"Even if it was, which I doubt, so what?"

"Scot, we need Meg Cassidy on board immediately. The CIA wants to get her started with their File of International Terrorist Events right away. Their analysts are hoping that with her help, they can crawl a little bit deeper into Nidal's head and forecast his future behavior."

"Maybe they should try sending her flowers."

"Nothing they do at this point is going to work. She doesn't trust them. She thinks they used her as bait with that attack on the hospital."

"In a sense," said Harvath, "they did use her as bait."

"There was no way they could have ever expected

Nidal would come gunning for her. They figured he had gone to ground or was trying to make his way out of the country. On top of it all, they had reliable information from Ms. Cassidy herself that she had shot him."

"They still should have expected it. I would have. You expect the unexpected in this business. By the way, did you get my message about protection for Meg Cassidy?"

"Yes, and we were already one step ahead of you. The Chicago field office is keeping an eye on her."

"Good."

"Listen, Scot, as far as all of this is concerned, we can't change what the CIA has done. That's in the past. What we need is to convince Ms. Cassidy to work with us now, and that's what we want you to talk to her about," said Lawlor.

"Me? What do you want me to tell her? I can't stand Morrell and his people."

"That's precisely it."

"Excuse me?"

"Think about it. Meg Cassidy knows you don't harbor any warm and fuzzy feelings for the CIA. What's more, you saved her life and saw that she was safely taken care of. You're the perfect person to convince her. She'll trust you."

"You want me to use that trust against her?"

"Look at the bigger picture here. Thousands, maybe hundreds of thousands of lives could be riding on this. We have no way of telling. We don't want you to shanghai Meg Cassidy. On the contrary, she needs to participate of her own free will. We want her to see things from your perspective—why you're doing this and what's at stake for you personally."

"I don't think she'll relate to my motives," said Harvath as he reflected on them.

"We know that you're motivated by a deep love and concern for your country. Most of the staff at the White House still joke that Mel Gibson had to come to you to get the rights to use the name *The Patriot* for his movie."

Harvath hated that joke. He didn't see himself as any more patriotic than any of the other people he had served with in the SEALs or in the Secret Service. Asking Meg to put her life on the line to prove her patriotism didn't seem like a fair proposition.

"All we're saying," continued Lawlor, "is that you should be honest with her. If you don't care for Morrell and his people, feel free to let her know. This is a woman who can smell a spin from a mile away. Just don't go too over the top. We trust you to say what is necessary to bring her in."

"As a civilian," injected the president, "she would also be eligible for a portion of the reward on Nidal. It would be done quietly, but it would be available to her if she wanted it, nonetheless."

"I don't think that would matter to her," replied Harvath.

"Whether it matters or not, she deserves to know it exists," said the president.

Harvath thought about Lawlor's proposal for a moment before asking, "Would I participate in her training?"

"As the president said," answered Lawlor, "this is the CIA's baby, but I can't see why you wouldn't participate, can you, Mr. President?"

"I can't either," replied the president. "There is nobody

I trust more or who is more capable than you to see to her safety. Let's not forget, this is a highly unprecedented and potentially explosive operation. We're taking a civilian and fast-tracking her through training so that she can participate in a top-secret covert operation. When it's all said and done, I want Meg Cassidy delivered home without so much as a scratch on her. This is an American hero we're talking about here. The public would be outraged if any harm came to her. You do whatever it takes. We're asking a lot from this woman, and I want you to protect her with the same degree of vigilance you would protect me. And, lest we forget why we're even having this conversation, I want Hashim Nidal to cease being a problem for us, and the rest of the world."

That was all Scot Harvath needed to hear. He had been given a direct order by his commander in chief. It was not a question of *if* he could convince Meg Cassidy to come on board. He absolutely had to. Hashim Nidal was to be taken out and Meg Cassidy returned home without harm. The president had handed him quite an assignment. The only question Harvath had at that point was, "When do I leave?"

"Tonight," said Lawlor as he slid an envelope with cash and plane tickets across the situation room table to him.

31

Harvath's ride into downtown Chicago wasn't as fancy as it had been a couple of days before. He grabbed a Continental airport shuttle, which dropped him across the street from the Ambassador East Hotel. Once he was settled, he put in a call to his contact at the Chicago FBI field office. Nick Wilson was an old friend whom Harvath had worked with several times in the past. Wilson explained that Meg Cassidy was at her cottage in Lake Geneva and that he had new information he was sure Harvath would be interested in hearing. They made plans to meet for drinks, and then Harvath hung up and dialed Meg's number in Wisconsin.

A few moments later, he had her on the phone. "You're back in town?" she asked.

"Yes, and I need to see you," replied Harvath.

Meg was guarded and realized he probably had not come back just to see her again. This was business. "I take it this isn't a social call."

"I'm afraid not."

"Were you sent here to try and change my mind about things?"

"Believe it or not, my instructions were to explain to you what *my* motivation is, but for what it's worth, I'm not sorry I got sent back."

"Really?"

"Yeah, I love Chicago. It's the one town that won't let you down."

"Uh-huh," she said, disappointed that he hadn't cited her as the reason he was happy to be back. This was ridiculous. What was she doing? He was here to try and persuade her to team up with the CIA. He had been sent on official business, and she needed to get that through her head.

"How about dinner? It's on me. What time will you be back in the city?"

"I'm spending the night up here. I won't be back in the city until tomorrow morning."

"Well," said Harvath as he scribbled on the pad on his desk, "that's going to make dinner a bit difficult then, isn't it?"

"How about breakfast?"

"That would work. Do you want to eat here at the hotel? I'm staying at the Ambassador East."

"Let's meet at Mitchell's on the corner of North Avenue and Clark Street around eight. This way I can drop my car at my place and meet you over there. It's an easy walk for both of us."

"Great, I'll be looking forward to it."

"I wouldn't be too excited about it if I were you. I've already made my position on this very clear."

"I understand, and whatever you decide, I'll respect. I just want a chance to talk with you about it. I think we see eye to eye in many ways on this subject."

"I don't think you know the half of it."

"Well, you can fill me in tomorrow morning. Okay?"

"Fine then. I'll see you at Mitchell's around eight," and with that, Meg Cassidy hung up the phone.

Harvath was already sitting at a table in the Ambassador East's famed Pump Room when Nick Wilson entered. They made small talk while waiting for their drinks, and then, once the waitress had left the table, Wilson got straight to the point. He removed a large manila envelope from his briefcase and spread several grisly Chicago Police Department crime scene photos on the table in front of them.

"This guy's been torn apart," said Harvath as he sifted through the pictures.

"Just his throat," replied Wilson as he took a sip of his drink and used the straw to draw Harvath's attention to the wounds.

"Who the hell was he?"

"Serial rapist the Chicago PD had been after for some time."

"What's this have to do with Meg Cassidy?"

"She's the one who did that to him."

Harvath couldn't believe it. As he picked up the photos to study them more closely, Wilson held up his empty glass and signaled the waitress. "You want another?" he asked.

"No," answered Harvath. "When did this happen?"

"A couple of years ago. Apparently, Ms. Cassidy had been jogging through Lincoln Park one night a little bit later than she should have. It was dark and she got jumped by this scumbag. According to the report, she screamed, but nobody was around to hear her. He pinned her down and shoved something in her mouth to gag her. She fought back, though, hard. Clawed at him and everything."

"What happened?"

"*What happened?* She went for his windpipe, dug her nails in, and ripped the guy's throat out. That's what happened."

"You're joking, right?" said Scot.

"Hell, no. She killed the guy."

"I can't believe it."

"Believe it. The cops did DNA testing on the stiff and found that he was the serial rapist they'd been looking for. She was lucky. He'd put most of his victims in the hospital. One even died."

"Nick, why wasn't this in her file back in D.C.?"

"It never saw the light of day. Her father was a career cop and well liked to boot. He obviously had some pretty good juice with the department to hush this all up. The only thing that ever got announced was that the police had found the body of their serial rapist, and that it was suspected he'd been killed in some sort of drug deal gone bad. That was it."

"How'd you get your hands on it?" asked Harvath.

"Headquarters was pretty intent on us finding out everything we could about her. We were told to leave no stone unturned. Why they were so interested in her, I don't know, but mine is not to reason why, you know?" Wilson waited for the waitress to set his fresh drink down and depart before he began speaking again. "I've got a friend at the Chicago Police Department. He's been there a long time and has an even longer memory. He owed me a couple of favors. You know how the game works."

Harvath nodded his head. He did know how the game worked. As he studied the crime-scene photos yet again, a lot of things about Meg Cassidy became clearer. The question now was, with everything she had been through, how in the world could he convince her to team up with the CIA?

32

Harvath awoke early the next morning and decided to go for a run along the lakefront. The weather was cool, with a bit of a chill in the air—unusual for Chicago in August. Most likely, there was a storm moving in. He ran as far as Belmont Harbor and after a few minutes of admiring the yachts and sailboats, turned south and ran back through Lincoln Park. At North Avenue, Harvath could see the restaurant where he and Meg would be having breakfast. Out of habit, he jogged slowly by the eatery, checking everything out, and then ran back to the Ambassador.

After a quick shower, he flipped on Fox News while getting dressed. The lead story was about a suicide bomber who had detonated himself inside a crowded Tel Aviv hotel and killed over twenty-two people, including an Israeli cabinet minister. The al-Aqsa Martyrs Brigades were once again taking credit for the bombing, stating that it was another retaliation for the Hand of God attacks. The violence was continuing to spiral out of control. Many countries were beginning to pull out all nonessential diplomatic personnel from Israel.

Three major U.S. attempts to get the peace process back on track had failed miserably. Harvath could tell the problems in the Middle East were wearing terribly on the president. Shuttle diplomacy wasn't working either. No matter whom he sent to the region, no matter how many meetings they had, the situation only seemed to worsen. Many in Washington were beginning to believe that some sort of war was inevitable. Smack in the middle of the media maelstrom, though, was Ali Hasan, who continued to call for peace and an end to the violence.

So far, Hasan was still extending an olive branch, which boded well for the pending European peace summit, but Scot dreaded what might happen if events forced Hasan to drop the olive branch and pick up a rifle, and this only made his assignment more critical.

Harvath arrived at Mitchell's a half hour early and chose a booth in the back corner. A stocky waitress ambled over and when Scot informed her he was waiting for someone to join him, she poured him a cup of mediocre coffee and left him alone. Harvath passed the time by reading a copy of the *Chicago Tribune*.

When Meg arrived, everyone turned toward the door to look at her. Harvath couldn't tell if it was because she was so attractive or because of all the press she had been receiving from the hijacking. He figured it was probably a combination of both. Though it had only been a few days since he had last seen her, she was even more beautiful than he remembered.

It took Meg a few moments to work her way back to the booth, as she was stopped every three feet and asked for an autograph. When she finally made it to the table, Harvath greeted her with a warm smile. "It seems somebody is quite the celebrity."

"It isn't all it's cracked up to be," said Meg as she slid

into the booth across from him. "I've got so many requests for interviews and talk show appearances I'm going to have to actually hire a publicist."

"Do you know any good ones?"

"One or two," said Meg, returning his smile as she picked up the menu and was silent.

Harvath could tell that Meg was waiting for him to speak. The niceties were behind them and it was time to get down to business. Scot looked around to make sure no one was eavesdropping before beginning. He remembered the president's and Gary Lawlor's instructions to be as candid as possible and said, "You know why I'm here, and all things considered, I appreciate your meeting with me."

So this really was about what happened in Cairo, period. Meg was disappointed that she had allowed herself to reserve some glimmer of hope. It was against her better judgment, and now she inwardly chastised herself for it. "I'm happy to meet with you," she said.

"I want you to know that the president himself asked me to come and see you—"

"To change my mind, right?"

"No. I told him that if you had already made up your mind, we should respect that. You're a busy woman. You've got a company to run, commitments. I totally understand where you're coming from, especially after everything you've been through." He stopped and took a sip of his coffee before continuing. "I came because I want you to know why I'm involved with all of this . . ."

Harvath hesitated as he searched for the right words. He was about to walk onto the very thin ice of discussing top-secret information with someone who didn't have proper clearance, but Lawlor and the president had both said they trusted him to say the right thing and so he offered, "Do you remember when the president was kidnapped last winter?"

"Of course. Who wouldn't? It was everywhere," replied Meg.

"Well, what wasn't reported was that I was the leader of the presidential advance team on that trip. The president's security, as well as that of everyone around him, was my responsibility. The day the kidnapping took place, I was skiing with the president's daughter and just narrowly saved her life."

"That was you?"

"Yes, that was me. Out of all the immediate protective detail agents, I was the only one lucky enough to survive."

"That must have been an incredible thing to deal with."

"It was and it still is. The men that died were my responsibility. Many of them were good friends of mine. I made them a promise that day that I wouldn't let their deaths go unpunished."

"And does the hijacking and the man who attacked me have something to do with the president's kidnapping?"

"We believe Hashim Nidal is behind the killing of several American operatives involved in the search for the president, as well as several brutal terrorist attacks around the world which have resulted in hundreds more people being killed. He has to be stopped."

"You mean by killing him?"

"If necessary, yes."

"Scot, I'm going to ask you a stupid question."

"Go ahead."

"Have you ever killed someone?"

Harvath was silent.

"Of course you have. You've obviously been trained to do it. I haven't, and I hate it. I hate that I took someone else's life."

"But you did it in self-defense."

"That still doesn't make it any easier."

"Meg, you did what you *had* to do. It was your life or theirs. Don't you see that?"

Meg turned her eyes away from Harvath and focused on her menu. "You talk like this is something people face on a daily basis."

"In the world I live in, they do. Listen, there are people like me, or better yet, as much as I don't care for him, Rick Morrell, who do face the decision to kill or be killed on a frighteningly regular basis. They do it so that the rest of the people in this country can live their lives without ever having to make that kind of decision. In a perfect world, you never would have been drawn into this. Your flight never would have been hijacked and you never would have been called on to make that terrible decision. You made a choice, though, the right choice, and because of it you and hundreds of other people are alive."

"But it didn't end there," said Meg, looking up. "I can't walk away from it. I can't just put it behind me like I did the—" She broke off and was silent again.

"The last time?"

Meg locked eyes with Harvath. "What are you talking about?"

"I know, Meg."

"Know what?"

"I know about the man who attacked you while you were jogging that night in Lincoln Park. I know you fought for your life and as a result, he lost his. I know you didn't ask to be attacked, just like you didn't ask to be on a plane that was hijacked. It was late, it was dark, and you must have been scared as hell. Your instincts took over, and because of you, other women were saved from being subjected to the same horror or even worse."

Meg searched Scot's eyes for an explanation of how he possessed knowledge of her most closely guarded secret. "I guess I shouldn't be surprised, but who told you?"

"I can't say," he replied.

"Yes, you can. My own government trusts me enough to join the CIA, but not enough to tell me how they discovered something I thought had been buried long ago where no one would ever find it?"

"The government knows nothing about this, and as far as I'm concerned they never have to. It was self-defense."

"You're goddamn right it was," said Meg, the anger evident in her voice. "Do you know what I have had to live with since that attack? Can you imagine the guilt? The fear? Feeling that I was responsible for everything that happened? The only consolation I had was that the man who had attacked me was gone and nobody would ever know what happened that night."

"Nobody does know."

"Hello? Are we having the same conversation here? You know."

"Meg, your secret's safe with me."

"My secret is anything but safe. If you know, how many other people know?"

"I promise you. No one else will know. I will personally see to it that the source is plugged up for good, okay? You can trust me."

"Trust you? I don't even know you. I don't know any of you. As a matter of fact, I have half a mind to press charges for going public about me and almost getting me killed at the hospital in Cairo."

"Wait a second," said Harvath, a hint of indignation creeping into his voice. "Don't lump me in with Morrell and the rest of his team. I don't blame you for being upset—"

"How sweet of you."

Harvath ignored her sarcasm and continued. "I did not for one moment like how those guys handled things."

"So why didn't you do something about it?"

"First of all," said Harvath leaning across the table, "this has been the CIA's ball game from the start, and secondly, I did do something—twice!"

"Twice?"

"I can assure you that it's not standard operating procedure to storm a plane alone, but while those guys were standing there trying to figure out what to do next, I took the initiative and breached that plane from the rear, on my own."

"I had no idea—"

"I was also the one that rushed to the Anglo-American Hospital the minute I saw the CIA's hastily conceived press conference. I didn't like the fact that they were telegraphing your whereabouts to the surviving hijackers. I'm also the guy that told Morrell to jump in the lake when he wanted to question you right after the hijacking and I thought you needed medical attention. So, don't put me in the same category as those clowns."

Meg was quiet for a moment as she thought about what Harvath had said to her. "I'm sorry," she replied. "You really don't care for them, do you?"

"Not much, but they're the ones in charge and I have to abide by the president's wishes."

"Does that mean they call the shots?"

"In a sense."

"What's *that* supposed to mean?"

"It means that the president has asked me to cooperate with them, but if I disagree, I'm doing what I think is best."

"Why bother working with them at all?" asked Meg as the waitress arrived with their food.

Scot waited for the waitress to disappear again before continuing. "What I want is results. To get those results, I have to work with Morrell and his people. The CIA is the best-equipped agency to handle this operation. The man we're looking for is very dangerous—"

"No kidding," said Meg as she speared a piece of melon with her fork.

"That's right *no kidding*. Meg, this guy has been able to unite numerous terrorist organizations around the world under one banner. Whatever his reach might have been originally, it's been increased a hundredfold, and so has his capacity to hurt people. I won't sit back and let another innocent life be lost. This guy has got to be stopped, and if it means I have to work with Rick Morrell and the CIA to do it, then I will."

"Why do I have to become part of all of this?" asked Meg, though she knew the answer.

"You already are part of it. You've seen Hashim Nidal's face."

"And I gave the CIA a full description."

"But that's not enough. You're the only person who can positively ID him, Meg."

"Can't you just send some people wherever you think he is, do what you have to do, and then let me identify him from photos once it's all over?"

"I wish we could, but we can't. For all we know, there might be a hundred or more people with Nidal when we track down his whereabouts. We can't just fire missiles at them, wait until the smoke clears, and then whip out the camcorder. There could be nothing left of him to ID. What's more, this is going to be a covert surgical-strike team that needs to get in and out fast. If there were any other way to do it, I wouldn't be sitting here right now having breakfast with you."

"Thanks a lot."

Harvath hadn't meant to hurt her feelings, but he needed to press on. "We need on-site confirmation of his identity before we take action, and you're the only person that can do that for us. We have to be absolutely sure that we have got the right man. The CIA can't do this without you."

"The CIA almost got me killed. I feel like they used me for bait."

"You're right. They did."

"So I'm nothing more than a means to an end as far as the CIA is concerned?"

"Basically."

"That's great. You really know how to inspire confidence in a girl."

"Meg, what I'm trying to tell you is that you matter to me and you very much matter to the president. It's not just the CIA that needs you; your country needs you. Right now you're the only person who can help us nail Hashim Nidal. He's already put the United States on his list. First he takes care of Israel, and then the terror begins here. It could happen right outside this restaurant, and it will happen if we don't do something."

"How do I know I'll be safe?"

"Because you have one thing tipping the odds dramatically in your favor."

"What's that?"

"Me. If you agree to come on board, you and I will be joined at the hip. The president knows what an incredible sacrifice this is for you and he wants you to know that every effort is being made to protect you."

"So, he's sent his best man to do the job?"

Harvath flashed his most irresistible smile. "I guess you could say that."

Meg tried to ignore it and changed the subject. "What am I supposed to do about my company? My clients?"

"The CIA is trying to pinpoint the whereabouts of Nidal as quickly as possible. Surely, you've got people who can handle things while you're gone."

"Maybe. It's just tough to up and leave everything for God knows how long."

"I know it's hard. If there was any other way, believe me—"

"You wouldn't be sitting here having breakfast with me. I caught that part earlier."

"You'll also be eligible to receive a substantial portion of the reward. Of course, all of this is classified and you're not allowed to discuss it with anyone."

"I'm going to be late for work."

"Fine. Why don't I get the check and we can talk about it on the way to your office."

33

Nick Wilson and his partner were the two FBI agents on Meg's protective detail that morning, and Harvath stopped outside the restaurant to chat with them in their car. He explained that he and Meg would be walking to her office and that the two agents could go pick up breakfast and meet them there.

Despite the thickening storm clouds, it was still a beautiful day to be walking in Chicago. A cool breeze was keeping the humidity down, and there was a tangible electricity in the air as the sky grew darker. Meg pointed out places of interest as they walked, and though Scot wanted to press her for an answer, he could tell walking and talking about other things was Meg's way of working her way through to a decision.

When they arrived at the Beckwith Realty Building, Meg invited Harvath up to see her offices. It was a reasonable invitation, as Meg had yet to voice her decision, but in truth, neither of them was ready to say good-bye. As the elevator made its slow ascent, Meg leaned over and punched a button for one of the intermediate floors.

"What's up?" asked Harvath.

"I forgot to get coffee. You don't mind, do you? It'll only take a second."

"As long as it's good coffee, I don't mind."

Meg laughed. "It's good coffee, all right. Much better than what my assistant Judy's got waiting up in the office. Trust me."

The elevator doors opened and Meg showed Harvath to a stairwell that exited onto the alley behind her building. Around the corner was a Starbucks.

In the amount of time it took Meg to get her thermos filled and paid for, it started raining. Harvath was standing at the front of the shop looking out the window. "Lovely weather you have here in Chicago," he said.

"Hopefully, we'll get a little of this up in Lake Geneva. My grass needs it badly."

"I only wish I'd brought an umbrella."

"I thought you guys were supposed to always be prepared."

"That's not the Secret Service; that's the Boy Scouts," teased Harvath.

"I'm sure that makes the president feel real safe. Here, we'll use this," said Meg as she handed Harvath part of a newspaper to cover his head with. "You ready to go?"

"It looks pretty wet out there."

"I thought SEALs liked the water."

Immediately, Harvath's antennae went up. "I never told you I was a SEAL."

"No, you didn't."

"So how did you know?"

"I have my sources. This one was temporarily stationed in Cairo. He seemed to know you quite well. Said you did a little training together—that is, I assume, when you weren't barhopping and chasing young ladies."

A smile crept across Harvath's face. "Lemme guess. Did this source have a Brooklyn accent by any chance?"

"Maybe," said Meg, with a coy smile.

Bullet Bob, Harvath thought to himself. "Well, regardless of what fairy tales your source might have told you, I have no problem with getting wet."

"Good, neither do I. Let's get going."

On the count of three, the pair ran from the coffee shop and down the street. When they got to the alley behind Meg's office building, it was already filled with large puddles, so they decided to stick to the sidewalk and run around to the front.

When they turned the corner and were only fifty feet from the entrance, a huge explosion rocked the Beckwith Realty Building and shook the ground beneath them. Harvath pulled Meg behind the safety of a parked car as broken glass rained down on top of them and an enormous fireball climbed into the black sky. It took Harvath only a moment to realize that the car they were using for cover belonged to Nick Wilson and his partner, who were supposed to be meeting them upstairs at Cassidy Public Relations.

Meg looked up and screamed. The blast had come from directly inside her corner office. Right away, Harvath knew it was no accident. And had they not gone for coffee, both of them would have been killed in the explosion.

"Oh, my God, my office! I have to get up there," yelled Meg, her ears ringing from the blast.

Harvath grabbed her face in both of his hands and turned it toward him. His ice blue eyes bore into hers as he said, "No way. Whatever that was, it was meant for you. We're not going up there."

"But Judy . . . My staff," was all Meg could say.

Harvath raised himself from behind the cover of the parked car where they were hiding, and looked up and down the block for any signs of people who might be injured and in need of assistance. His eyes swept past a motorcycle messenger and almost kept going, but something made him stop and look back.

That was all it took. Their eyes met and instantly, each knew who the other was. Before Harvath could draw his gun, the terrorist was firing up the motorcycle.

"Stay here and wait for the police," Harvath said to Meg.

"Why? What's going on?"

"Just do it!" he yelled as he ran across the street toward the half-moon driveway of the opposite office building. Underneath the canopy was a man waiting out the rain on his motorcycle.

"I need your helmet and keys, now," said Harvath as he ran up to the man and flashed his Secret Service credentials.

"But, this is my Ducati, dude."

Harvath pulled out his gun and said, "Your choice."

The man handed his helmet and keys right over.

Harvath reholstered his gun, pulled the helmet on, and fastened the Velcro chin strap. In an instant, he had the bright red motorcycle throbbing to life. He revved the rpms into the red and popped the clutch, laying down a trail of rubbery fire under the canopy. When he hit the street, the bike fishtailed underneath him on the wet asphalt and threatened to tear loose, but Harvath got it back under control. Almost a full block ahead of him, he saw his target turn left onto State Street.

Rocketing down Hubbard, Harvath blew the stop sign and pulled an incredibly hard left on State that sent the bike shooting out of control through the intersection. He narrowly missed slamming into the side of a northbound green-and-white Chicago Transit Authority bus complete with a billboard encouraging young men and women to join the Army for excitement. *The Army? How about the Secret Service?*

Harvath chased Nidal three blocks north, where he turned and headed east. By this time, Harvath was only a half block behind and closing the distance fast. Nidal pulled out of the street traffic and raced up the sidewalk. Harvath followed right behind. Because of the wet conditions, Scot lost control several more times and thought for sure he was going down, but mercifully he got things under control at the last second. There was no doubt that this ride was taking years off his life.

When the dueling motorcycles hit Michigan Avenue, Nidal removed a Micro-Uzi from beneath his jacket. Harvath saw the weapon, but not before Nidal let loose with a rolling wall of nine-millimeter lead that tore through several cars and shop windows on both sides of him.

Harvath desperately wanted to unleash his own weapon, but as he was right-handed, to do so meant he would have to let go of the gas—something he couldn't do at this point if he hoped to keep up with Nidal. Though he was good at shooting with his left hand, he wasn't *that* good.

They continued racing east, with Harvath trying at every chance to overtake Nidal. At the next intersection, he turned south and Harvath followed right behind. They crossed the Chicago River and Nidal headed toward the lake, but then slammed on his brakes and pulled a U-turn, rocketing down onto lower Wacker Drive.

The pair were now out of the rain and on dry pavement. Harvath gunned the Ducati for everything it was worth. They darted around astounded commuters at speeds over ninety miles an hour. Even if Harvath could have removed his Secret Service issued SIG Sauer, there were too many innocent people within his field of fire.

At the next bridge, Nidal pulled an almost impossible right turn and shot beneath upper Michigan Avenue, then grabbed the first left. Harvath let go of the handle bar and reached behind with his left hand. He unholstered his SIG Sauer P229, swung it around, and let several rounds fly. All of them went wide of their mark, except for one, which barely missed hitting Nidal and instead took out his entire taillight assembly.

Nidal took another sharp left and sped down a dark service ramp toward the river. When Harvath hit the ramp seconds later, he could smell the noxious odor of brake smoke and melted tires. His entrance was greeted with another tidal wave of nine-millimeter rounds, two of which caught the front of the Ducati and sent him into an irrecoverable slide. Harvath ditched the bike and crashed end over end in a painful roll down the concrete ramp. When he finally came to a stop, he pulled the helmet from his head and saw the bike totaled against the far wall. Because his adrenaline was still pumping, he had yet to feel the effects of the fall, but he knew it was just a matter of time before the pain set in.

It took Harvath only a moment to find his gun and when he did, he pointed it down the ramp as he slowly picked his way to the bottom. He was inside some sort of underground service entrance. Train tracks ran off to his right and electric and gas company trucks were parked pell-mell beneath the dim fluorescent lighting. There was neither sight nor sound of Hashim Nidal until a loud roar ripped through the underground tunnel. Harvath recognized it right away—marine engines.

He ran toward the murky daylight coming from the end of the service tunnel, where a small indoor-outdoor marina opened up onto the river. The marina master was yelling as Nidal finished untying a swift thirty-eight-foot Baja and sped away from the partially covered pier. The only other thing in the water when Harvath reached the dock was a thirty-foot twin-screw Cigarette Mystique, which thankfully had the keys in it. Apparently, the marina master had prepped both boats for optimistic owners who hoped the weather would clear so they would get a nice day out on Lake Michigan. It looked as though they were going to have to make other plans.

As Harvath slammed both throttles forward and adjusted the trim tabs to help pop the Cigarette out of the hole, the rain hit him full force in the face. It reminded him exactly of Macau. Except this time he was chasing the silver-eyed assassin by boat instead of by car. That was fine by Harvath. Knowing water the way he did gave him the edge.

Nidal wisely avoided the locks that opened onto the lake, knowing full well he'd be a sitting duck, and headed west. Just after the Merchandise Mart, he swamped a Wendella sight-seeing boat and managed to sneak around it as it turned sideways. Harvath had to slow down considerably to get around the boat, and it cost him valuable time.

Reaching the north-south fork, Nidal steered his boat as if he was going to go north under the Kinzie Street Bridge, and then swung the Baja hard to port and aimed it due south. Once again, he withdrew his Micro-Uzi and fired, the rounds tearing up the bow of Harvath's Cigarette. Scot ducked beneath the wraparound windshield to avoid being hit and, when he looked up again, realized he was perilously off-course. He jerked the wheel hard to starboard, sideswiping a construction barge parked on the east side of the river, and tore up the left side of his boat.

The howling wind and pounding rain made it impossible to see, much less aim, but Harvath had little choice and fired away. He had no idea if his shots were finding their mark or not. If they were, the Baja showed no signs of slowing. They passed beneath the Lake, Randolph and Washington Street Bridges, the sound of their roaring engines reverberating off the façades of the concrete-and-glass buildings that fronted the river.

At the Adams Street Bridge, Harvath saw a searing white light race from Nidal's Baja and strike the engine compartment of another sight-seeing boat floating just off Union Station. He had never figured Chicago boaters for safety nuts, but apparently whoever owned the Baja kept a flare gun aboard, and the wrong person had found it. Nidal managed to get around the sight-seeing boat just as an explosion rocked through the engine compartment and blew a gaping hole in the hull. Passengers jumped, screaming, into the water as the boat quickly caught fire. Once again, Harvath had to pull back on the throttles, and once again, he lost valuable time.

After Harrison Street, the Chicago River opened up into a long straightaway. If he was going to catch Nidal, this would have to be place to do it. He tried to coax every ounce of speed he could from the Cigarette, and around Taylor Street, it looked as if the effort was paying off. Through the torrential rain, just ahead, he could make out the stern of Nidal's Baja.

The gap was closing, but something was wrong. It was closing too fast. For a moment, Harvath let himself believe that one of his rounds had hit home and had caused the Baja to slow, but when he realized what was really happening, the searing bolt of a flare was almost on top him. He turned the Cigarette hard to port and played right into Nidal's hands. Though the flare missed, rounds from the Micro-Uzi ripped down the starboard side of the Cigarette. Smoke began pouring from the starboard engine, and Harvath had no choice but to shut it down.

Running on one engine now, he pushed the remaining throttle as far as it would go and headed right for Nidal before he could load another flare and come around for a second attack. Harvath raised his SIG and pulled the trigger repeatedly until he heard the empty click of the spent magazine. In one fluid motion, he ejected the old clip and slammed in a fresh one, but it was too late. With Harvath operating on only one engine, Hashim Nidal had more horsepower and could easily outrun him. The driving rain had cut visibility down to nothing. With alarms buzzing and engine warning lights flashing, Harvath backed off on the remaining throttle and limped down the river, hoping against hope that maybe he'd catch a break and still be able to come across Nidal.

The only thing Harvath came across was the Baja abandoned just before Chinatown. Once again, the silver-eyed assassin had vanished into the storm.

34

By the time Harvath made it back to the Beckwith Realty Building, the fire department had the blaze all but extinguished and the police had established a command center in the lobby of the office building across the street. It was there that he found Meg, still being interviewed by police.

As he crossed the marble lobby toward where she was sitting, she could see that his clothes were soaked through. Though the look on his face said it all, she still had to ask, "Did you get him? Is he dead?"

"No," Harvath replied. "I didn't get him and he's not dead."

Meg had been hoping, praying, for Scot to return safely, but with a completely different report. "This is never going to end, is it?" she asked as tears began to well up in her eyes. "He's going to hunt me down and he won't stop until he's killed me."

"They're not going to hurt you. I promise you."

"But they already have. Hurting the people I care about is the same as hurting me."

"How are the people in your office? Have you heard anything?"

"Two people are dead."

"From your staff?"

"No, it was your friend and his partner from the FBI. They were apparently in my office when the bomb went off. Judy was outside at her desk. She's at the hospital now. Why is this happening? Why can't he just leave me alone?"

Harvath's jaw tightened. Two more people he knew had lost their lives. Wherever he went, Hashim Nidal left a trail of dead bodies in his wake. He had a long list to answer for, and Harvath was going to make him pay for every name on it. The sooner, the better.

"Excuse me," interrupted a young detective who identified himself as Daryn Gasteire. "Who are you and what are you doing in here?"

"It's okay, detective. This is Agent Harvath. The one I was telling you about."

"Are you the gentleman who was outside with Ms. Cassidy when the explosion happened?" asked Gasteire.

"Yes, I am," said Harvath as he fished his Secret Service credentials from his pocket and showed them to the twenty-something detective. Gasteire appeared too young to have already made the rank of detective, especially in a city like Chicago. He had a youthful arrogance to him that grated on Harvath's nerves. It was obvious the detective was attracted to Meg and had taken it upon himself to watch over her. Despite her beauty and outward show of strength, there was something about Meg Cassidy that made men want to protect her.

The detective also reminded him of Gordon Avigliano, and Harvath remembered that he hadn't liked the young CIA man at first either. He would try to forgive the detective's tone, but forgiveness had never been one of Harvath's strong suits.

"You want to tell me what you saw?" continued Gasteire.

"To tell you the truth, no," replied Harvath. "The two agents that died up there were friends of mine. I want you to tell me what *you* have."

Detective Gasteire tried to be polite. "I'm sorry about your friends, but try to see things from my perspective. A bomb explodes in the office of one of Chicago's now most-famous citizens, who single-handedly helped rescue the mayor and the CEO of United Airlines during a hijacking, a motorcycle chase ensues down numerous streets and side-walks, followed by a boat chase down the Chicago River, I've got two deceased FBI agents, countless civilian injuries, an untold amount of property damage, and stand-ing right in front of me are a prime witness and copartici-pant in the chase, and you want me to fill *you* in on what *I* know? Forget it. I am going to ask you again nicely to answer my questions."

"Or else what?" asked Harvath, his anger getting the better of him.

"Let's just say, I have a way of easily losing my patience," replied Gasteire, his smile never faltering.

Harvath fished a card out of his wallet and handed it to the detective. "I'd like to say I appreciate your position, Detective, but my investigation takes precedence here. Call the gentleman on that card and he'll tell you the same thing."

"What's the deputy director of the FBI have to do with an agent of the U.S. Secret Service?" asked Gasteire.

"This may sound rude," said Harvath as he lowered his voice, put his hand on the detective's shoulder, and forcibly steered him away from Meg Cassidy, "but it's none of your fucking business. This is a federal investigation and I don't have time to dick around with you. Now, I've also got Mayor Fellinger's card in my wallet, and you can feel free to call him if you want, but he's going to tell you the same thing."

"The mayor? Bullshit," said Gasteire.

Harvath pulled Fellinger's card from his wallet and handed it to the detective. "Now, you decide who the hell you want to call and get on with it. Let's go. Chop, chop."

Gasteire removed a cell phone from his pocket and angrily walked to the other side of the lobby to make his calls as Harvath turned back to Meg. "I'm so sorry about all of this, Meg. Even though we were being cautious, we never really believed he'd come all this way after you."

"If we hadn't gone out for coffee," said Meg as her body started to shake again despite the warm, wool blanket one of the firemen had draped around her, "we'd probably be dead right now." Her eyes were glazed and she was looking off into the distance at nothing in particular.

Harvath put his arms around her and they stayed that way for several minutes until Meg's shivering began to subside and Detective Gasteire returned, his attitude only slightly improved. "I've called both the FBI and the mayor's office. They told me to give you any cooperation you need. So what do you want to know?"

"What have you and your men been able to piece together?"

"It's going to be a bit longer before the fire department can get in there and do a thorough investigation, but based on what survivors told us and what the firefighters saw upstairs, the explosion came from Ms. Cassidy's office."

"Any idea what caused it?"

"None yet, but we're working on a pretty good assumption right now."

"Which is?"

"A lot of deliveries had been flooding Ms. Cassidy's office—flowers from fellow passengers on the hijacked plane, gift baskets, et cetera," said Gasteire as he referred to his notes. "According to Ms. Cassidy's receptionist, several reporters had tried to gain access to her office by posing as delivery people. Word was sent to the building's front desk that all packages were to be left there and someone would come downstairs from time to time to pick them up. There were to be no visitors allowed upstairs."

"Makes sense to me," said Harvath.

"Well, early this morning, a delivery person matching the description of the messenger you chased, arrived with a large gourmet basket, which was left at the building's front desk. The receptionist claims that when she retrieved the basket and saw that the card bore the return address of the mayor's office at City Hall, she placed it directly in Ms. Cassidy's office. A call by one of my colleagues has revealed that the mayor sent no such basket, so we're now assuming that it contained a bomb of some sort."

"What about the security tapes?" asked Harvath.

"No good. You're free to look at them, but the suspect never removed his helmet. He kept it on the entire time."

"Anything else?"

"Units have recovered the stolen motorcycle and powerboat used by the suspect. We've impounded them both and will go over them completely for prints, hairs, and fibers. We've also got teams retrieving shell casings from where they fell on the streets and sidewalks during your chase."

"Anything else?" asked Harvath, sensing they'd arrived at yet another dead end in their attempts to stop Hashim Nidal.

"Not really. I was told that after finding the suspect's boat abandoned near Chinatown, that you phoned your contacts at the FBI and filled them in on what happened. All federal, state, and local law enforcement agencies, as well as the border patrol, customs agents, and Coast Guard, have been placed on high alert in connection with a very discreet APB. This has something to do with the hijacking, doesn't it?"

"Why do you say that?"

"I might look young, Agent Harvath, but I'm not stupid. People like Meg Cassidy don't normally develop the kind of enemies who blow up offices and then escape in a hail of automatic-weapons fire. Besides, someone just brought me this from the fax in my car," said Gasteire as he held up the CIA's sketch of Hashim Nidal. Meg felt a wave of revulsion wash through her at the sight of it.

"The last time I saw this face was during a press conference from Cairo after the hijacking, wasn't it?" said the detective, pressing Harvath for confirmation of his assumption.

"You could be right, but I don't suppose the powers that be want that spread around," said Harvath.

"No, they don't. The mere mention that a terrorist wanted only days ago for a hijacking in Cairo has somehow managed to slip into this country, blow up an office building in Chicago, and kill two FBI agents would cause widespread panic."

"If it's any consolation, the man in that picture is not who you're looking for."

"He's not? Then why was I sent this?"

"Because that's who the government believes was behind the explosion this morning."

"And you're saying the government is wrong?"

"Yes."

"Based on what?"

"I saw him."

"Wait a second. From what I understand, the suspect's face was completely covered with a helmet."

"It was."

"Then how can you say this isn't the same person?"

"Because I saw his eyes."

"You what?"

"I saw his eyes. It was a different person. It was someone who works with the man the government is looking for."

"Are you sure?"

"These are eyes like no eyes you have ever seen before; they're—"

"Silver," interrupted Meg, "and they can grow as black as night in an instant."

Meg had thrown Harvath for a loop. "How did you know that?" he asked.

"On the plane. When Nidal first accosted me, the man with the silver eyes stopped him."

"How come you didn't tell anybody this before?"

"I did, but everyone seemed to be more interested in what I saw upstairs in the lounge when I pulled Nidal's mask off."

"What exactly did this man do?"

"When he saw what Nidal was trying to do to me, he got very upset. Some angry words went quietly back and forth, and then Nidal backed down—for the time being. I went back to my seat, and it wasn't until later that he reappeared and forced me upstairs."

Every one of the passengers on flight 7755 said the brown-eyed man gave all the orders, but what Meg was claiming took place between the two hijackers didn't make sense. If Nidal was in charge, why did he back down? There had to be something more—something they weren't seeing. A nagging suspicion began to tug at the edge of Harvath's mind.

"Did anything else happen? Anything else at all that you can remember or didn't think was significant?" he asked.

"No. Not really," she lied. She held back the fact that she had been incredibly drawn to the hijacker's luminescent silver eyes, had felt herself drowning in them, and that when he touched her cheek with his gloved hand, she felt an odd feeling of awe mixed with gratitude. She had heard it referred to once as Stockholm Syndrome—when hostages begin to identify with their captors, but Meg knew her reaction was something more than that. She was ashamed of her feelings and felt it best to keep them to herself.

"Okay, then I want to focus on getting you someplace safe," said Harvath.

"Even though I never gave you an answer about what we discussed this morning?" Meg was choosing her words carefully in front of Gasteire.

"That doesn't make any difference. Your safety is the number-one priority here."

"So I guess this means I don't get to ask any more questions," injected Detective Gasteire.

"I'm afraid you're right," said Harvath. "There's really no more either of us can tell you anyway."

"Whether that's true or not, we may never know."

"Trust me, Detective, if there was anything we knew that could help you, you'd have it."

"Then I guess that's it."

"Not exactly. There is one more thing."

"What?"

"We need one of your officers to give us a ride."

"I have to check out the boat over by Chinatown anyway. Where do you need to go?"

"We're going back to Ms. Cassidy's place on Astor Street to pack up some of her things—"

"No, we're not," said Meg. "We're going to check in on Judy and the others at the hospital. Then we can go to my place."

Harvath didn't like it. "I don't think that's such a hot idea, Meg."

"And why not?"

"Because at least with your apartment, we can send in a team to sweep first. The hospital is too large, too public a place. Our friend might be expecting you to put in an appearance there."

"Then you come up with a way to get us in without him knowing. Until I see my people, I'm not going anywhere else with you."

· Scot could see that she was serious. He thought for a moment and then pulled Detective Gasteire aside. Fifteen minutes later, Harvath and Meg had discreetly climbed into an ambulance via a lower-level loading dock and were on their way. Gasteire met them at one of the seldom-used alley entrances of Northwestern Hospital's main facility. He provided them with surgical scrubs, long white lab coats, paper hats, and booties. Harvath was happy to get out of his wet clothes. He fastened his belt around his waist so he could continue to carry his gun and placed the rest of his belongings in the deep pockets of the lab coat. Everything else was left in the waiting ambulance.

Gasteire escorted them from room to room. Several of Meg's staff were already close to being discharged and sent home. She spent time with two men who would probably be staying in the hospital through the week and promised their families that they would receive the absolute best care. Harvath was moved by Meg's loyalty to the people that worked for her.

The last patient they visited was the most distressing and the one Meg was most concerned about, her assistant, Judy. Meg didn't want to go into the room alone and so asked Scot to come in with her. Burn Unit rules were some of the strictest around and with good reason, few patients were as prone to infection and the deadly complications it could bring.

Harvath and Meg scrubbed as if they were going into surgery and donned new paper caps, booties, and disposable paper gowns. They were also required to wear gloves and masks—the biggest risk being an infection transmitted via the respiratory system. Detective Gasteire sat outside their door holding Harvath's SIG and other personal belongings.

At the sight of her good friend, Meg Cassidy began to cry. Because of her charred lungs, Judy was enclosed in a plastic oxygen tent and on a ventilator. The area where the flesh of her chest and arms had been burned away was covered in some places with a thick white salve and in others with wet-to-dry bandages soaked in a special saline solution. Morphine for pain and antibiotics to fight infection were intermingled with her IV fluid. Judy's eyes were closed, and it was hard for Meg to tell if she was sleeping or not. Harvath, though, knew that the woman was on so much pain medication that she was in a state much deeper than sleep.

All Meg wanted to do was take her friend's hand and tell her everything was going to be okay, but that was impossible. Nothing was allowed to breach the patient's oxygen tent. Though they were only inches apart, the inability for them to physically connect made Meg feel as if a chasm hundreds of miles wide lay between them.

She pulled up a chair next to the bed and let the tears roll down her face. She had neither the strength nor the desire to wipe them away. Judy's chest rose and fell to the mechanical rhythm of the ventilator.

This is all my fault, Meg thought to herself. *All my fault*.

She remembered Judy's face floating before her during the hijacking. She remembered wanting to believe that Judy, who kept her crazy life in order and doted on her like a daughter, somehow was her guardian angel. *If it hadn't been for her lousy coffee, I would be lying in that bed right now, or worse*.

Meg leaned in as close to the oxygen tent as she dared and whispered, "You really are my guardian angel. I love you so much, Judy. Everything is going to be okay. I promise."

When Meg Cassidy stood up and crossed the room to

leave, she locked eyes with Harvath, who had been respect-fully standing against the far wall. "I don't care what I have to do, or where I have to go. That animal has to be stopped. I don't want him harming another human being."

Harvath waited before opening the door. "So you're in?"

"You're goddamn right I'm in. And you tell the president he can keep his reward money."

35

"Giant Killer, Giant Killer. This is Stork One requesting clearance," said the pilot of the luxuriously appointed Falcon 900 passenger jet. The air traffic control moniker was intimidating to say the least, but that was exactly its purpose.

The airspace over the CIA's highly secretive training facility known as Harvey Point, or more simply the Point, was restricted. The Washington Sectional Chart, which every pilot flying in and around the area would have aboard, specifically stated that clearance to pass through Restricted Area R-5301 could only be obtained by contacting "GIANT KILLER" on the indicated frequency. Failure to do so would result in the scrambling of a contingent of the most-advanced tactical fighter aircraft in the world, Lockheed Martin F-22s, quietly stationed with the Fourth Fighter Wing at nearby Seymour Johnson Air Force Base.

Interestingly, there was no depiction at all of a Harvey Point runway on the sectional chart. This was highly unusual as far as sectional charts were concerned because military airfields were never omitted. Even the CIA's airstrip at Camp Peary, Virginia, was clearly depicted and labeled.

Stork One was immediately cleared and given instructions on how to land.

The Point itself was just that—a stubby finger of land

that curled out into the murky water where North Carolina's Perquimans River met the Albemarle Sound. Thick-trunked cypress trees overgrown with heavy Spanish moss stood silent vigil over the sixteen hundred acres of poisonous-snake-infested swamp on which the CIA's facility sat. Locals claimed that the area had once been ruled by Blackbeard the pirate, who had buried his treasure somewhere in the vicinity. It was all the locals could publicly claim, because it was the only thing they were really sure of.

Nine miles southwest of the sleepy town of Hertford, the road abruptly ended at a sign that read, "Harvey Point Defense Testing Activity." Officially, it was known as a remote Pentagon post, but ever since its inception in 1961, just weeks after the Bay of Pigs fiasco, area residents believed it to be some sort of base for the CIA. Explosions from the Point could be heard and felt for miles around as windows shook and walls sometimes cracked. Strange-looking helicopters often swept in low from the skies overhead, while blacked-out transports conveyed unknown passengers quickly through town in the middle of the night. All sorts of old cars, buses, SUVs, and limousines were seen entering on flatbed trucks, only to be carried out later either riddled with bullet holes or burnt to nothing more than charred hulks, or both. The locals had, indeed, pegged Harvey Point correctly, but they didn't know the half of what went on there.

The Point was where the CIA's hard-core paramilitary training took place. Personnel were schooled in explosives, paramilitary combat, and other clandestine and unconven-

tional warfare techniques. While the "Farm" at Camp
Peary was where CIA personnel earned their stripes and
learned their tradecraft, the Point was where a chosen few
received a Ph.D. in serious ass-kicking.

The personnel invited to the Point weren't only limited
to American CIA operatives. In the past fifteen years, the
CIA had provided counterterrorism training to several
American Special Operations groups, as well as foreign
intelligence officers from more than fifty countries, including South Korea, Japan, France, Germany, Greece, and
Israel.

As the Falcon 900 jet banked and came in over the
water for its landing, Harvath watched Harvey Point's
runway magically materialize out of the dense cover of
foliage. He knew it was only a trick of the landscape, but
an uncomfortable feeling swept over him, nonetheless.
Nothing was ever what it appeared to be with the CIA,
and Harvath wasn't looking forward to being a guest on
their turf.

The plane touched down and taxied over to an aircraft
parking revetment. When the copilot opened the Falcon's
door, the cabin immediately filled with the muggy, swampy
air that Harvey Point was famous for. Harvath and Meg
descended the metal stairway and found Rick Morrell on
the tarmac waiting for them in front of a blacked-out Suburban.

"Thank you for coming, Ms. Cassidy," he said. "I know
you've been through a lot, and we want you to know that
your country appreciates your cooperation. I hope your
flight was comfortable."

"Yes, thank you," replied Meg.

"Well, if you'll follow me. We'll get you settled in." Morrell took Meg's bags and loaded them into the back of the Suburban. He didn't offer to help Harvath, nor did he even acknowledge his presence.

"What? No kiss? Not even a, *honey, I missed you?* I'm going to start thinking you don't care," said Harvath.

"I don't," responded Morrell as he helped Meg into the Suburban and closed the door behind her. "You've stepped on a lot of toes wiseguy. There are more than a few people at the Point who don't like you, so as long as you're on my playing field, you'll keep your mouth shut and watch your act."

"If that's your idea of a warm welcome, it's no wonder this resort has yet to rate five stars."

Morrell climbed into the driver's seat and expected Harvath to hop into the passenger seat next to him. Instead, Scot got in back and sat next to Meg, effectively reducing Morrell to chauffeur status. Morrell wanted to tell Harvath off right then and there, but he had been warned to be on his best behavior around Meg Cassidy.

For a while, it had looked as if they were not going to be able to bring her in, but somehow, Harvath had managed to swing it. That made Morrell dislike the Secret Service agent even more. Meg Cassidy was integral to the operation, that much was true, but Harvath was barely palatable baggage and would be treated as such.

They drove past a lodge, a gym, and a conference center before pulling up in front of a low-rise barracks-style building.

"Not exactly the most glamorous accommodations in the world, but I'm sure you'll find it very comfortable," said

Morrell as he hopped out of the SUV and went around to open the door for Meg. After retrieving her bag, he led them up a short flight of stairs and into the main door of the building. "Meals are served at the lodge, but there's also a fully stocked kitchen at the end of the hall here. There's a lounge with a big-screen TV, but you also have a television in your room.

"Okay, here we are. Ms. Cassidy, this is your room, number eleven, and you're over there," he said to Harvath as he jerked his head at the door across the hall.

"Would you be so kind as to hold my calls? It's been a long day."

Morrell ignored Harvath and said, "You'll find your training schedules on your desks, as well a listing of when meals are served at the lodge. The conference center runs movies every night as long as there are no classes using the building. On Friday afternoons we normally do a barbecue, weather permitting, and then there are pickup softball games on Sunday—"

"When do we get to roast marshmallows and tell ghost stories?" interrupted Harvath.

Meg was trying her hardest to be polite, but started to laugh. She didn't feel like laughing, not after everything that had happened to her, but she couldn't help it. It was cathartic and she let it come.

Morrell had a short fuse and was trying to keep his temper in check. "We host a lot of international guests here, and it is the Agency's wish that we convey a healthy and appealing American image. They like to call it *hearts and minds*; I call it bullshit. We're not here to play games, and you'd do well to remember that."

"Duly noted. Anything else?" asked Harvath, glad that Meg was still smiling.

"Yes," said Morrell as he fished two ID badges from his pocket. "These are to be worn at all times. If you're caught without one, you'll be detained, and it'll be my responsibility to come and get you. I don't want to have to come get you—*either* of you," he stressed, staring at Harvath. "You are not to speak with anyone other than me and the rest of my team. We all have rooms in this building—"

"Which one's yours?" asked Harvath.

"Not a chance," said Morrell. "Ms. Cassidy, if you should need anything from me, there's a phone in your room or you can use any of the facility phones and dial the operator. Wherever I am, I'll be found and will return your call as soon as possible."

"Got it. Thank you," said Meg politely.

"I want to remind you both that this is a highly classified operation," continued Morrell. "We've done our best to isolate you, but should you choose to do something like use the gym or see one of the films, you will most likely come across other trainees. If you do, you are not to provide your names, personal history, or any information about the operation you're involved with. Is that clear?"

Harvath and Meg both nodded their heads.

"Good. Now, you were both relieved of your cell phones and the in-room phones do not dial off the facility. If you feel you need to make a call, you are to contact me. If I feel the call is warranted, I will make arrangements for you to place said call. Is that understood?"

Once again Scot and Meg both nodded their heads.

"It may seem like I'm being a bit excessive—"

"You? Excessive? Never," said Harvath.

"—but this is for your safety, Ms. Cassidy, and the security of this installation."

"I understand," said Meg, trying to make up for the ground she saw Harvath losing with Morrell every time he opened his mouth.

"That seems to be it, then. Tomorrow's going to be a very busy day, so I suggest you get something to eat and get a good night's sleep. If there's anything you want that we don't already have in our kitchen here, just let me know and I'll see what I can do."

"Do you have any beer in there?" asked Harvath.

"We don't allow alcohol on the Point," replied Morrell as he opened Meg Cassidy's door and placed her bag inside.

Bullshit, was what Harvath wanted to say, but he kept his mouth shut and slung his bag into his room and closed the door behind him.

Ten minutes later, Meg knocked.

"What's up? You're not homesick already, are you? It's only the first night of camp," said Harvath.

Meg tried to force a smile.

"Laugh and the whole world laughs with you, cry and the CIA has you right where they want you," said Scot.

"Doesn't it bother you that they don't seem to like you very much?"

"Who? Morrell and company? Are you kidding? They love me."

"They sure seem to have a hard time showing it."

"That's okay. As long as you and I get along, that's all I care about."

"So far so good, I guess."

Harvath could tell by the tone of her voice that she was still upset and was reaching out to him. While he couldn't go back in time and change what happened, he could at least try to take her mind off of things. "You 'guess'? I'll have you know there are many out there that consider me excellent company."

"Out where? At Harvey Point?"

"You might have to go a bit further afield than that, but my legions of fans do exist."

Meg was quiet.

"What about dinner? Are you hungry?" asked Harvath.

"Not really."

"Sure you are. We'll eat in. The kitchen's stocked, and I'll even cook."

"I think I'll just turn in early."

"Meg," said Harvath as he took her hand in his, "it's been an overwhelming past couple of days for you, I know, but we're going to come through this with flying colors, I promise you."

"You sound so sure."

"I am. Listen, I understand what you're feeling and I want you to remember something." Meg was silent. Harvath gently lifted her chin with his other hand until she was looking him in the eyes. "You are not alone in this. I'm going to be right next to you every step of the way. No matter what happens, you'll only have to look over and there I'll be."

"You promise?" asked Meg as she wiped away the

beginnings of the tears she was so desperately trying to keep at bay.

"I promise."

Finally, she couldn't hold back anymore and the tears came on full force. Harvath wrapped his arms tightly around her and held Meg Cassidy as she cried.

She felt so good in his arms—her hair against his neck, the smell of her skin. Harvath knew he was in dangerous territory. Eventually, the tears stopped, but neither wanted to break the embrace. Finally, Meg stepped back and reached for the box of Kleenex on his desk. "Able to take out a plane full of hijackers, but cries at the drop of a hat. What a lethal combination, huh?" said Meg, drying her eyes and feeling slightly embarrassed.

"I think you're just hungry," answered Harvath, realizing their moment had passed, angry with himself for what he was feeling. "What about dinner?"

"I guess I could eat something."

"That's the right attitude. Let's see what's in the kitchen," said Harvath as he swept his hand in front of him and indicated that Meg should lead the way.

While Harvath rummaged through the cabinets, Meg had the base operator track down Rick Morrell. She requested he check on the condition of her people still in the hospital back in Chicago. Five minutes later, Morrell called back. The news was good. Their conditions remained guarded, but improved, especially Judy's. Meg was relieved to hear it. They were overdue for a piece of good news.

As she hung up the phone, Meg filled Scot in on what she had been told. She then resolved that no matter how long it took, no matter what she had to do, she wouldn't rest until Hashim Nidal had been put out of business.

Harvath nodded his head in agreement and went back to preparing dinner. Meg Cassidy had turned the corner, and that was good, but she had no idea what still lay ahead of them.

36

The next morning, Meg was up before anyone else. She was in the lodge reading the morning paper by the time Harvath finished working out and had found her. "So what's it going to be today?" he said as he sat across from Meg and placed two cups of coffee on the table. "Horse-back riding or sailing lessons?"

"I wish," replied Meg. "I have a physical scheduled, so I'll have to pass on the coffee for now."

"Pass? Why?"

"They're going to do a blood draw, and I am supposed to have had nothing to eat or drink except water since midnight."

Harvath took a sip of his coffee and made a face. "Don't worry, the coffee's not that great."

"You're just saying that to make me feel better."

"Yeah, you got me. It's actually pretty good. The DEA guys probably bring it up from South America. So what fun does Camp Harvey Point have in store for you later?" asked Harvath as he withdrew his copy of Meg's schedule from his pocket. "Ooh, there's a fitness assessment after lunch. Somebody planned that one well."

"They sure did. What kind of a torture farm is this? No food after midnight and then once they do let me eat, they've got a fitness test planned right after it?"

"I know it might seem *excessive*," said Scot, mimicking

Rick Morrell, "but I can assure you this schedule exists for your safety and the security of the facility."

Meg smiled. Harvath was glad to see her doing better.

"What's on tap for tonight?" she asked.

"Well, it looks like that's going to depend upon how long they keep you looking at mug shots."

"Mug shots? Is that what this undetermined block of time is set up for this afternoon?"

"Yup. They're going to have you review pictures and descriptions of known and suspected terrorists from some of the world's biggest databases."

"Sounds like fun."

"As long as you're in an air-conditioned room, count your blessings. I can't believe how hot it is down here."

"And humid," added Meg.

"How'd you sleep last night?"

"Great, why?"

"So your air conditioner works fine?"

"It did last night. Didn't yours?"

"No," said Harvath, a sneaking suspicion creeping over him. "For some reason, mine's on the blink."

"Why don't you ask Morrell to look into it for you."

"I would, if I thought it would actually do any good."

"Well, maybe if you weren't such a smart-ass to him, he'd be willing to help you."

"You don't know Rick Morrell the way I do."

"I don't need to. He's a person, for crying out loud, and wants to be treated with respect."

"I agree, but respect is not a given; it has to be earned."

"*Men!* Everything is a competition with you."

"That's not true," said Harvath, who noticed that Morrell had entered the lodge and was making his way over to their table. "Listen, try and find out for me what room Morrell is in today, would you please?"

"His room? Why?"

"Never mind, just try to find out, okay?"

"Sure, but—"

"Good morning," said Morrell as he neared the table and smiled at Meg as sincerely as he was capable of. "I trust everyone slept well?"

"Like a baby," offered Harvath. He knew the reason his AC didn't work was somehow Morrell's doing, but he wasn't going to give him the satisfaction of complaining.

"Ms. Cassidy, are you ready for your physical?"

"The sooner it's over the sooner I can eat. Let's go," said Meg.

"Good. Agent Harvath will meet you back here for lunch."

"I'll see you later, okay?" said Scot. "I'm going to go over to the arts-and-crafts cabin to make my mom either a cutting board with a secret compartment for microfilm or a key chain that shoots poison darts."

Morrell was fed up, but he tried not to show it. "Ms. Cassidy, if you're ready, I'll drive you over."

Meg said good-bye to Scot, and once she had walked away from the table, Harvath caught Morrell by the arm. "You make sure you take care of her, understand me?"

"Yeah, I understand you," said Morrell, jerking his arm out of Harvath's grasp. "Relax."

"Like you take care of your eyes, Ricky. I don't want anything to happen to her."

"For fuck's sake, Harvath, I'm taking her to get a physical. It's not like we're disarming land mines."

"I'm talking about in general. I'm setting the ground rules for the training and the operation right now."

"You?"

"Yeah, me. Meg Cassidy is not expendable, so you figure that into your planning. Got me?"

"You have a thing for this woman, don't you?"

Harvath avoided the question and simply responded, "Her safety is the number-one priority."

"Number one for you maybe, but number one for me is the successful outcome of my mission."

"You'd better find a way to reconcile the two, because I'm here to see that nothing happens to her."

"I thought you were here because you wanted to see us nail Hashim Nidal."

"That too," said Harvath, "but not at the expense of this woman's life."

"Understood. Are you finished now?" asked Morrell as he impatiently glanced down at his watch.

"Just about. You guys need to realign the profile on Nidal."

"What? You're joking right?"

"No, I'm one hundred percent serious. There were two masked hijackers on that plane. I think Meg saw the lieutenant's face and not Nidal's."

"Based on what?"

"She said she saw the one you're calling the lieutenant, tell off Nidal."

"Harvath, Meg Cassidy barely remembers anything of what she saw."

"That's not true. She had trouble putting together a coherent timetable of the events during her struggle with the hijackers."

"Same thing in my book. Listen, the man Cassidy saw without his mask was the one issuing all of the orders during the hijacking. I have eyewitnesses who will back that up. This man was also wounded by Cassidy and had to be assisted in his escape from the plane. Are you telling me that we've got it wrong and Hashim Nidal would risk his freedom, or possibly worse, his life, to help a lieutenant escape?"

"If that lieutenant knew enough to bring him down, yes."

"Then why not just kill the lieutenant? Why go to all that extra trouble?" asked Morrell as he glanced once more at his watch.

"Who knows? Maybe there's honor among thieves, after all. Maybe the lieutenant was very valuable to him or had information buttoned down somewhere as an insurance policy. There's a million possible reasons."

"Yes, but only one makes sense. The face Cassidy saw belonged to Hashim Nidal, period."

"Revise the profile, Rick."

"What, and go solely by a set of eyes? Because that's all anyone has seen of the other hijacker."

"It's a good start."

"It's a waste of time. Just like this conversation is. We've got the right man and we're not diverting our focus."

"You're making a mistake."

"And you're free to leave any time you like," said Morrell as he began walking away. "You'll excuse me, but I've got a schedule to keep."

37

It didn't take long for Meg's training at Harvey Point to grow monotonous. It was based upon intelligence the CIA had been able to gather from its Indonesian sources, who believed Hashim Nidal's base of operations was on one of the Moluccas Islands, formerly known as the Spice Islands.

During the day, Meg worked with Rick Morrell and his sniper teams, learning how to identify and call out targets. In the evenings, they would do the whole thing all over again, only this time aided by night-vision devices. Meg's free time was never her own. She was plonked down in front of monitors and subjected to hours of images relating to suspected and known terrorists. It soon became overwhelming. Despite her resolve, everything began getting to her—the heat, the humidity, the insects, the incessant training schedule . . . Morrell had planned everything down to the minute. They went through the same drills over and over again until the execution was perfect, and then they did them again.

They practiced amphibious assaults launched from both the Perquimans River and the Albemarle Sound. Meg grew accustomed to speeding silently across the top of the water in the black rubber Zodiacs, only to slip over the side hundreds of yards from shore and have to swim the rest of the way in.

Meg turned out to be an excellent swimmer. As a matter of fact, there wasn't much that Morrell and his men had thrown at her that she couldn't handle.

Harvath understood Morrell's need to repeat drills over and over again. The goal was to become so accustomed to them that they became second nature. Under the stress of a real operation, you would know what to do automatically and the "fog of war" would have a far lesser impact. On the flip side, though, nobody ever knew how an operative was going to perform in combat until that operative actually saw combat.

Harvath had no doubts that Meg would come through, but what bothered him was that the training Morrell had laid out for her was extremely limited. Morrell didn't even plan to issue her a weapon, and in Harvath's mind, that was a mistake. Teaching her simply to keep up and keep out of the way was not good enough.

By not giving Meg better counterterrorism training and not allowing her to carry a weapon, Morrell was making her overly dependent on the rest of them. If she was going to be one of them, she needed to function just like everybody else—she needed to have the self-confidence of knowing she could operate on her own if she had to.

In addition, there was a change in Meg's personality that was troubling Harvath. While he thought it might be the frustration of the repetitive training schedule and the hurry-up-and-wait scenario that they were all facing as conflicting reports continued to pour in about Hashim Nidal's whereabouts, there was a chance something else was involved. Over the nine days they had been at the training camp, her temper had grown shorter and shorter, with the smallest things setting her off, and Harvath wanted to know why.

When they finished their training that night, Scot told Meg he had a surprise for her and to knock on his door in an hour. At the appointed time, she knocked, and when the door opened, she was greeted with an unexpected sensation.

"You finally got your air conditioner fixed," she said as she walked into Harvath's comfortably climate-controlled room.

"Not exactly," he said with a smile as he pulled a large bucket filled with ice and Corona beers from underneath his desk. "Compliments of our fearless leader, Mr. Richard Morrell."

"Wait a second. He fixed your air conditioner *and* gave you a bucket full of beer? That doesn't sound right. What's going on here? I thought there was no alcohol allowed at the Point."

"There isn't," said Harvath, his smile turning to a mischievous grin as he popped open two of the bottles and handed one over to Meg.

"So where'd it come from?"

"Morrell. Just like I told you," he said as he took a long swallow of the ice-cold beer, letting his words hang in the air.

"How many of these did you have before I got here, because you're not making any sense."

"I just got them."

"How could he have just given them to you? I thought he and his men went into town tonight."

"They did."

"Then what gives?"

"What *takes* might be a better question."

"So, these *weren't* given to you?" asked Meg, slowly catching on.

"Very good, Ms. Cassidy. They'll make a CIA operative out of you yet."

"How'd you get into his room? Wait, better yet, how'd you find his room?"

Meg sat down in a chair and made herself comfortable. This was a story she couldn't wait to hear. If Harvath had one-upped Morrell, it would be priceless.

"Chocolate?" asked Harvath as he produced a family-sized bag of M&M's.

"You bet," said Meg taking a handful. "I assume these were his too?"

"The guy's got a sweet tooth like you wouldn't believe. Always has, ever since I've known him. You should see all the stuff in his room."

"So you did get in there! You've got to tell me how you did it."

"Well, nobody, I mean nobody, would tell me what room he was in. I knew it was here in the building, but that was it. I even tried to scam the operator without any luck. Finally, I wondered if he might just lead me to his room himself."

"But he always makes sure we're on our floor before he disappears again."

"As much as I don't care for a lot of his tradecraft, I figured it would be really hard to track him. Plus if he caught me, it would have been a little embarrassing."

"So how'd you do it?" asked Meg as she leaned forward and grabbed another handful of M&M's.

"Do you remember a few nights ago when we used that paint to mark our trail?"

"The kind that only shows up with the night-vision goggles?"

"That's the stuff. I stole a can of it before we went out on our maneuvers last night. Remember how I jumped out of the Suburban before you and Morrell?"

"Yes."

"Well, I poured a little on the steps outside."

"And after tucking us in, he walked through it and made his way to his room?"

"Yup."

"But what about—"

"The night-vision goggles?"

"Yeah, I thought we were supposed to turn them in with the rest of the gear."

"I did. I just pulled them back out of the case when nobody was looking."

Meg was having such a good laugh she had to set her beer on the floor for fear of spilling it. "You have got to show me his room," she said.

"When we finish the beers, I will. Enjoy the AC while you can. I think you're going to find Morrell's room very uncomfortable."

"You switched air conditioners?"

"Um-hum."

"That's classic."

"I'm not done yet."

"Oh, no?"

"Nope, there's something else I owe him."

"What's that?"

"Do you know what short-sheeting is?"

"Are you kidding me? This isn't my first summer camp experience."

"Well, I take it a step further."

"How?"

"We're going to short-sheet him, but we're also going to take out all but two of the supports from his mattress frame."

"When he gets into bed, he's going to hit the floor?"

"Yep, and when he realizes he's been short-sheeted, he's going to hit the ceiling."

Once again, Meg started laughing. After another beer, she confided in Harvath that it felt good to laugh because she hadn't been feeling herself lately and didn't know why. When asked what her symptoms were, Meg stated that she'd almost completely lost her appetite, had tons of energy, and seemed to get angry at the drop of a hat. Sometimes she even got the shakes coupled with what felt like heart palpitations. She figured it had something to do with the vitamin supplements she was being given, but when she asked the CIA doctor about it, he had told her it was just stress and not to worry about anything.

"You're being given vitamins?" asked Harvath skeptically.

"The doctor prescribed some stuff that first day we got here. Remember when I had the physical? I think you had arts and crafts," said Meg, giggling.

Harvath didn't want to alarm her and so smiled and asked, "Can I see the vitamins you're taking?"

"Nope," she said as she took another long swig of beer.

"Why not?"

"I don't have any on me. They give them to me at breakfast in the morning. I think that's why Morrell is so adamant about me not being late. There's always one of the doctor's assistants there."

"I've seen him. I just figured they were checking in to make sure you were feeling okay."

"Yeah, he does that too. Asks a lot of questions."

"Questions like what?"

"Like do I feel happy, sad, angry . . . You know, things like that."

"So it's more emotional than physical?"

"They ask physical questions, but for the most part, it's emotional."

"Interesting," said Harvath, letting the subject drop, but not before asking, "Would you mind doing me a favor tomorrow?"

"Sure, as long as you agree to do me one."

"What do you need?"

"Hand me another beer."

Harvath laughed and popped the top on another Corona.

"How come you don't have any limes for these?" asked Meg.

"That's what we get for ripping off someone with no class."

Meg started laughing again. "So what do you want me to do?"

"I want you to palm your vitamins tomorrow." Harvath gathered up a handful of bottle caps and began to show her. "Lift your hand to your mouth and pretend to pop them in—"

"I know what palming is, Scot, but why? Is there something wrong with them?"

"I don't know. I wouldn't worry about it. Just bring them to me tomorrow so I can check them out."

"Fine. Consider it done. God, this beer tastes good."

"Twice as good since we didn't have to pay for it," said Harvath.

By the time they made it to Morrell's room, both Scot and Meg were feeling no pain. They short-sheeted his bed and removed all but two of the bed frame supports, and in a fit of sophomoric genius, decided to take all of the left shoes from his closet and scatter them around the Point.

When they finally made it back to their rooms an hour later, they knew there might be hell to pay, but neither of them cared. As they said good night, Meg wrapped her arms around Harvath. She planted a deep kiss on his lips and Harvath did nothing to pull away. This time, it was Harvath who finally broke their embrace, and Meg retreated into her room and locked the door for the night. It was the best she had felt in she couldn't remember how long. While she fell asleep smiling, Harvath took a long time before drifting off, worried that things between them might be going too far. They had been at the Point for only a little more than a week, and there was no telling how much longer they would be working together. He couldn't let anything develop between them that might jeopardize the operation.

38

At breakfast the next morning, Meg Cassidy's slight hangover from several Coronas and way too many M&M's didn't do much to improve her mood. When the doctor's assistant doled out her vitamins, Meg palmed them just as Harvath had asked, and returned with them to the table.

Scot looked through the multicolored tablets and shook his head.

"What is it?" asked Meg.

"You've heard of better living through chemistry?"

"Yeah, so?"

"Well, this is better soldiering through chemistry."

"What are you talking about?"

"I'm sorry to tell you, but these aren't all vitamins."

"Excuse me?"

"I'm no pharmacist, but I'm pretty sure I recognize one of these little guys."

"Which one," asked Meg as she leaned in and stared at the pills in Harvath's hand.

"This one," he said as he rolled an oblong capsule off to one side of his palm. "They call them *Unkies*."

"What the hell's an *Unkie*?" asked Meg as she rolled the pill around with her finger.

"You know how they say, 'The Lord loves a workin' man'? Well, we used to always say 'Uncle Sam loves a fightin' man.' Some adjunct of the Special Operations community a ways back came up with an anabolic steroid derivative which was supposed to safely increase strength and stamina, but had the nasty side effect of putting a mean edge on people's tempers."

Concern was etched across Meg's face. "Were there any other side effects?"

"Like regular steroids, they could mess up your complexion with acne and that kind of stuff."

"Anything else?"

"Nothing you need to worry about."

"You know what?" said Meg, anger sliding into her voice. "I'm getting pretty sick and tired of people deciding what Meg Cassidy should and shouldn't worry about. I want you to tell me, right now, what the other side effects were!"

"Don't get pissed at me. I didn't prescribe these."

"You're not answering my question."

"Fine. The biggest side effect was that your testicles could shrivel up," said Scot as he wondered how that one was going to sit with Meg.

"So there are potential reproductive side effects?"

"As far as I know, only if you have testicles," said Scot, trying not to laugh.

"You think this is funny? This is *not* funny. This is my body we're talking about here. I didn't give any of these goddamn CIA mad scientists permission to monkey around with my body. What the hell are they thinking?"

"I think they're thinking they want you a bit more aggressive."

"*Aggressive?*" repeated Meg, her voice now incredulous.

"They want you to be a real eat-glass-and-drink-gasoline kind of gal. They don't want you falling apart crying on the battlefield if things get tough."

"So are you telling me you support this?"

"Absolutely not," said Harvath in all seriousness. "No one but you has a right to decide what goes into your body."

"You're goddamn right," said Meg. "What is it with you men?"

"Hey don't lump me in there again."

"Oh, who cares? You're all the same, always trying to control women's bodies!"

Meg was reaching critical mass, and just as Harvath was attempting to calm her down, Rick Morrell entered the lodge. He was fuming, obviously intent on a heated confrontation over the pranks that had been played on him the night before. Little did he know that Meg was even hotter under the collar than he was. Before Harvath could stop her, she jumped from the table and made a beeline straight for him.

"Get out of my way," said Morrell as Meg approached him. "My beef's not with you, it's with Harvath."

"You'd better think again, mister. Your beef is most definitely with me. Just who the hell do you think you are?"

Morrell had obviously never been confronted by an extremely angry woman before. He had no idea how to handle the situation. If Meg Cassidy had been a man, it would have been easy, but she wasn't. So, Morrell did what most men normally did in a situation like this and just stood there with his mouth agape and a stupid *what'd I do?* expression on his face.

"Do you get off on controlling people? Is that what this is all about? Is it?" railed Meg. "You have got to be the ultimate micromanager, you know that? I'll have you know that I am NOT one of your operatives, and I will not—"

Morrell, having recovered some of his sense of dignity, interjected, "Why don't you just calm down?" BIG mistake number one.

"Calm down? Calm down?" screamed Meg, even angrier now. "Of all the arrogant, chauvinistic . . .You just snap your fingers and expect little ole me, the woman, to just do as you say. Is that it?"

"Ms. Cassidy, I don't know what the problem is—"

"The problem appears to be that I'm not aggressive enough for you. Is that it correct? Is *that* what the problem is here, Mr. Morrell?"

"I have no idea what you're talking about. Whatever this is, you are obviously overreacting." BIG mistake number two.

Out of nowhere, Meg Cassidy hit the enormous CIA operative with a very well-placed right hook. While it didn't send Morrell slumping to the floor, his knees did buckle, and he was sure everyone in the room had seen it.

"Now that's overreacting! I hope it was aggressive enough for you," said Meg as she sidestepped Morrell and left the building.

Harvath was right behind her. On his way out the door, he couldn't help but take a shot at a dazed Morrell. "You've got a hell of a way with the ladies, Ricky. A hell of a way."

39

The lone assassin entered Saudi Arabia just as before, via a series of intermediaries and paid conspirators along the Yemeni border. As with the previous mission in Medina, the objective was the same—wreak maximum terror and maximum devastation. This time it would be at Mecca, the very heart of the Muslim world.

The silver-eyed terrorist carried neither identity papers nor documents that could be linked to the Hand of God organization. Saudi Arabia would know the Hand of God had been on their soil only if the mission was successful. Should the assassin be killed or captured along the way, the authorities would never comprehend the full picture. Neither the most vigorous of interrogations nor the most thorough of background checks would reveal anything. In essence, the highly skilled operative was nothing short of a ghost—a wraith borne straight out of the Saudi royal family's worst nightmare.

It was widely known that King Fahd had abandoned the title of "His Majesty" for "Custodian of the Two Holy Mosques," a reference to the mosques of Medina and Mecca. Tying himself to the holy sites and his people's faith was a desperate attempt to tighten a slipping grasp on the legitimacy of his monarchy. As the importance of Muslim clerics grew in the daily lives of the Saudi people, less reliance was placed upon the king. The less the people relied upon their king, the greater the threat that one day they would wake up and decide they did not need a king anymore. Fahd and the royal family could easily wake up one morning and find themselves on the outside looking in, exactly as the Shah of Iran had. It might take more work to get rid of the Saudi royal family, but it was amazing what a populace, especially one infused with religious fervor, could do when their minds were set to a task. This was the ever-present reality the Saudi monarchy lived with and feared, day in and day out.

As guardian of two of the holiest sites in the Muslim world, King Fahd took his responsibilities very seriously and had beefed up security at pilgrimage sites around the country. For Fahd, it wasn't a question of if the Al-Haram Mosque at Mecca, the holiest place on earth to Muslims, akin to what the Vatican was for Catholics, would be attacked, but when. It was the final jewel in the triple crown of terror that he knew the Jewish Hand of God organization had planned. They had made the battle personal by murdering his son, Prince Khalil, in Paris and he was bound and determined not to let them succeed in any further efforts to harm any part of the Muslim world under his protection.

The king had dispatched increased numbers of police, as well as members of the Saudi National Guard, the Special Security Force, and even members of the elite Special Warfare Unit to watch over the great mosque at Mecca, as well as other holy sites along the great pilgrimage trail. His efforts, though, were all for naught.

After murdering Prince Khalil in Paris, the assassin had traveled to Montpellier by train. There, it was a short car ride to the seaside home of Jacques Thevenin. Thevenin had been a member of France's fabled counterterrorism team known as the GIGN. In 1979, the Saudis had called in the GIGN to help dislodge several hundred armed Muslim extremists who had taken over the sacred mosque at Mecca and who were holding thousands of pilgrims hostage in the sixty square kilometers of tunnels and passageways beneath the mosque.

Through a thoroughly detestable little man, known as the Troll, who dealt in the purchase and sale of highly classified information, the assassin discovered that against strict operational policy, Thevenin had kept the plans of the 1979 takedown of the mosque, as well as detailed blueprints of the tunnels beneath, as a souvenir.

Thevenin was still a relatively young man, only in his mid-fifties, but he had gotten soft and careless. To his credit, he did put up some resistance, but only a token amount. The assassin had only begun to fillet his left foot, with a long fishing knife from the kitchen, when Thevenin gave up the location of the plans for the takedown and the schematics of the tunnels. The man also provided the assassin with updated security measures being employed by the Saudis, to which he was privy, having been hired by their government in the last several years as a security consultant.

This last bit of information was an unanticipated bonus. Thevenin had proffered it in the hope that he would be able to save his own life. The hovering specter of death had a way of encouraging dramatic confessions and efforts at bargaining. This was precisely why, whenever possible, the assassin didn't kill instantly. So much more could be gained by taking one's time.

When the skin up to Thevenin's knees was peeled back and most of the flesh had been cut away, the assassin realized the man had nothing more to give. It wasn't that Thevenin hadn't tried. He had offered a wealth of information, but none of it was useful to his inquisitor. The assassin removed a long garrote wire from the backpack resting against the chair to which Thevenin had been duct-taped, and wrapped it quickly around the man's throat. The razor-sharp wire cut into the former counterterrorism operative's neck as if it were nothing more than a wheel of soft Camembert cheese.

Thevenin's schematics turned out to be even more helpful than the terrorist had thought they'd be. Not only were the tunnels beneath the Al-Haram Mosque accurately detailed, but structural comments littered the diagrams as well. It only took the assassin one visit inside the labyrinth of passages to understand that the attack would be a huge success.

Knowing where all of the security measures were made the assassin's job that much easier. The terrorist was able to proceed at a relatively leisurely pace, confident that none of the Saudi security forces knew what was going on beneath the mosque and its grand courtyard.

The assassin placed bombs strategically throughout the tunnels and enhanced their deadly force by adding aluminum azide, magnesium azide, and bottled hydrogen. While normal high explosives had a velocity of at least three thousand feet per second, these bombs would detonate with a velocity of over fifteen thousand. To add to the devastation, the assassin also lashed canisters of sodium cyanide to the bombs directly beneath the mosque in the hope that the fumes would vaporize and be sucked up into the ventilation and air-conditioning systems, as well as the stairwells and passenger tunnels—killing scores more.

The assassin knew that there was a reason what was about to happen had to happen. No longer blinded by youth and naiveté, the assassin saw the world as it was, stripped of all its pretense. It had been a mistake to think that some of those people were different. They had no hearts. They were incapable of feeling. They were not even people. They were animals who deserved to die. And they would die. All of them. It was only a matter of time.

As much as the terrorist wanted to stay to watch the explosion and its deadly aftermath, training and a strong instinct for self-preservation dictated leaving the country as quickly and as quietly as possible.

The assassin stopped at a postbox and deposited a letter to each of the most widely read Arabic dailies, *Ar-Riyadh* and *Al-Jazirah*. By the time these letters were received, the damage would already be done and the world would be closer to embracing the inevitable.

40

In a remote corner of North Carolina's Fort Bragg stood a high Cyclone fence patrolled by heavily armed soldiers. On the other side of the fence lay one of the most secure counterterrorism training facilities in the world—Delta Force's famed headquarters and multimillion-dollar Special Operations Training facility.

The facility was known by many different nicknames. Some called it SOT for short, while others, because of the original stucco siding, called it the Fiesta Cantina. The real comedians liked to refer to it as Wally World, after the amusement park in the Chevy Chase movie *Vacation*, or the Ranch, because of early Delta Force operatives' penchant for chewing tobacco and wearing cowboy boots. Whatever name was used, there was no escaping the fact that it was the most impressive complex of its kind.

The Ranch boasted a wide array of training areas. There were large two- and three-story buildings used for heliborne inserts and terrorist takedowns; indoor and outdoor live-fire ranges, as well as ranges for close-quarters battle, combat pistol, and sniper training; Delta's Operations and Intelligence Center; staging grounds where mock-ups of structures in different terrorist scenarios could be constructed; and a host of other facilities and training areas too numerous to list. Simply put, the Ranch was where the best of the best came to train, and that was the reason Harvath had chosen it.

As a former SEAL, Harvath and his charge would have been welcome guests at SEAL Team Six's training facility located in Dam Neck, Virginia, but there would have been too many questions asked. Having been on-site for the hijacking in Cairo, Delta already knew about Operation Phantom and Hashim Nidal. Plus, Delta had everything they needed right at Fort Bragg. SEAL Team Six was always jetting off someplace or other to train. They climbed oil rigs in the Gulf of Mexico, parachuted in the Arizona desert, practiced boarding tankers in Southern California, and sharpened their close-quarters battle skills at Eglin Air Force Base in Florida. Total-immersion training with Six was too widespread and would have taken too much time. Every second Harvath had with Meg Cassidy needed to be as efficiently spent as possible.

When Meg had sucker-punched Rick Morrell in the middle of the Harvey Point lodge, Harvath knew he had to get her out of there. Not only was she suffocating under the routine, she wasn't getting everything she needed in the realm of counterterrorism training. Even though she was a civilian riding along on a government operation, she was traveling with experienced soldiers and needed to learn the ropes as quickly as possible. Harvath had hoped that Morrell and his men would teach her, but when it became apparent that they weren't going to, he marched over to the Point's communications center and was cleared by Morrell to make two phone calls.

The first call was to Gary Lawlor, who had been appointed his liaison and, for lack of a better term, supervisor, for Operation Phantom. Once Harvath had explained the situation and had gotten Lawlor's approval, Harvath made his second call. Within forty-five minutes, he and Meg Cassidy were packed and standing on the Harvey Point helipad as an MH-60K Special Operations helicopter, piloted by members of the 160th Special Operations Aviation Regiment, or SOAR, touched down and took them aboard. Also known as the Night Stalkers, for the pilots' unparalleled ability to fly over all kinds of terrain in all kinds of weather using only night-vision devices, SOAR was attached to Delta Force specifically for the purpose of aviation support and getting Delta's "guys in the skies."

Harvath hadn't expected a tearful farewell from Morrell and didn't get one. He simply ferried Scot and Meg to the helipad in his Suburban, asked for their ID badges back, told Harvath to stay close to his beeper, and then drove off. Harvath had pulled some major strings and knew Morrell was seething about it, but didn't care. The man was not running his operation correctly, and Harvath was not about to stand by and see Meg miss out on training that might save not only her life, but also the lives of her teammates. Meg Cassidy was going to get the best training the United States was capable of.

When the helicopter touched down at the Special Operations training facility at Fort Bragg, Bullet Bob was waiting. He stood off to the side of the helipad with several of the Delta Force operatives who had been part of the takedown in Cairo. When Harvath and Meg stepped out of the helicopter, Bullet Bob lifted a walkie-talkie to his mouth and said, "Let 'em rip, T-Bone."

From a nearby demolition range came the sound of a twenty-one-gun salute—all done with explosives. *There is nothing like guys who enjoy playing with demo*, thought

Harvath. And so the tone for their time at the Ranch was set.

Meg Cassidy was again pushed to her limits day in and day out, but always by intelligent instructors who clearly articulated and explained the goals of the exercises.

In concert with Bullet Bob and several Delta instructors, Harvath had come up with what they believed was a thorough yet turbocharged curriculum in counterterrorism training. She was instructed in the use of weapons, including stun grenades and flash bangs; close-quarters battle, also known as CQB; room-clearing techniques; self-defense and hand-to-hand combat; land navigation; small boat operation; encrypted radio operation; and basic first aid. She excelled in everything, except the training that involved heights.

Rappelling, fast roping from a hovering chopper, and land qualifying for parachute jumping were the most difficult training sessions of all. Meg even refused to get into Fort Bragg's vertical wind tunnel to simulate free fall unless Harvath was with her. She was deathly afraid of heights and practically had to be dragged to every session kicking and screaming. It was important to have Meg acclimated to all situations that required her to deal with heights, just in case. But, as the operation profile didn't call for anything along those lines, Harvath eventually backed off the exercises.

Meg's training was rounded out by spending time with female members of Delta, affectionately nicknamed by the men as the Funny Platoon. Members of the Funny Platoon were experts at infiltrating foreign countries to conduct reconnaissance and intelligence gathering. Harvath figured that they could give Meg special insight into the experience of being a woman involved in covert operations.

He and Meg had been at the Delta facility for two weeks, when she entered the cafeteria one day and found him in the back, reading the paper. Harvath was engrossed in a story about the bombing at Mecca and how Jordan was currently amassing armored divisions along Israel's borders. Not only had the death toll from the Hand of God attack been staggering, but the group had struck at the most sacred Islamic site in the world. Thousands of worshippers outside the Holy Mosque had been killed when the center of the courtyard exploded in flames and collapsed, while thousands more inside had perished as a result of the vaporized cyanide. The explosion had taken with it the Ka'ba, a square stone, wood, and marble building, which Muslims considered the most holy structure in Islam—believed by some to have been the first house of worship, originally built by Adam, and of great importance in the life of Muhammad.

The article explained that even though the previous attacks had been horrendous, the bombing of Mecca was seen as an absolutely unforgivable assault upon the Islamic world. Even liberal and moderate Arabs, so heavily relied upon to keep the peace in the Middle East, were now calling for an all-out war against Israel.

A million scenarios ran through Harvath's mind as to how Hashim Nidal could now definitively push the region into all-out war, and he didn't like the United States's chances of stopping any of them.

"Were you looking for me?" asked Meg as she put a gentle hand on Harvath's shoulder and sat down next to him, interrupting his thoughts. She was wearing a gray T-shirt with "ARMY" emblazoned across the chest and a pair of black fatigue pants. Her hair was pulled back in a ponytail, and she wasn't wearing any makeup. She didn't need to. All of the outdoor training had tanned her skin to a deep, rich brown, which enhanced her beauty even more.

Harvath tried to pull his mind back to business. "Yeah. I heard from Washington last night. It looks like the CIA might have new information on Hashim Nidal's whereabouts. What do you think? Are you ready?"

Meg had done extremely well and had excelled at almost everything she had been taught, but classroom proficiency was not a reliable indicator of real-world performance.

"Ready? You bet I'm ready. Look at this," said Meg as she flexed her bicep before twisting the lid off a bottle of Gatorade and taking a long drink.

"That's all well and good, but what about up here?" asked Harvath as he tapped a finger against his temple.

"To tell you the truth, I don't think you could cram any more knowledge in there."

"You've really been fast-tracked through this stuff. If we had more time—"

"But we probably don't. Don't worry. I've got it all down. Honestly, I'm good to go."

Harvath had his reservations. "Meg, it takes months to learn this stuff and years to perfect it. You've been here two weeks. I don't want you getting overconfident in your abilities. If this thing goes according to plan, we'll be in and out without encountering any—"

"Hostile fire or dangerous situations which might necessitate calling upon my newfound skills. Scot, I know all this. You sound like an old lady. I am one hundred percent ready to go."

Meg had done well, and, unfortunately, she knew it. But, she had also become a little too cocky, and that was dangerous. Harvath worried that he might have created a monster. She'd been thrown in at the deep end and had proved she could swim, but that was in the pool. The next test would be the open ocean itself.

"You've done a good job," said Harvath as he reached for his coffee.

"*Good job?* I've done a *great* job."

"Easy there. I don't want this going to your head. There's a big bad world outside the Ranch, and it's a completely different place. Out there, the bombs are real, the bullets are real, and people die—" Harvath's admonishment was abruptly halted by the sound of his pager going off.

"What is it?" asked Meg as Harvath studied the display.

"The big bad world. Time to see how well you've learned."

41

The black Gulfstream V-SP jet raced through the frigid, high-altitude air above the Atlantic Ocean at Mach .80. With an uninterrupted range of 6,750 nautical miles, the aircraft was more than up to the task Rick Morrell and the Operation Phantom team had set for it.

After responding to Morrell's page, Harvath and Meg were choppered from Fort Bragg back to the airstrip at Harvey Point. The sleek, dark as night jet, courtesy of the CIA's Air Branch, was waiting for them on the runway when they arrived. Morrell was barking orders left and right as his operatives loaded the plane with gear. When Harvath and Meg hopped out of their Special Operations helicopter, Morrell shouted over the roar of the rotors that clothes had been left for them in the adjacent hangar and that they should get dressed as quickly as possible. Much to Harvath's surprise, he found boots and fatigues waiting for them in a desert-camouflage pattern—not jungle. The uniforms made no sense for assaulting a tropical island in Indonesia.

Once the plane had leveled off, Harvath unbuckled his seat belt and made his way back to where Morrell was sitting. The Gulfstream V-SP was one of the most technologically advanced long-range jets in the world and through recent design enhancements, had been able to increase cabin volume by more than twenty percent. Baggage capacity had also been increased by twenty-five percent, and

Gulfstream's exclusive second pressurized bulkhead allowed unrestricted access to the baggage compartment during flight.

"Rick," said Harvath, "can I get a word?"

Morrell typed in a few more keystrokes and then closed the lid of his encrypted laptop. "What do you want?"

"I'll give you three guesses and the first two don't count."

"I'm not in the mood for games, Harvath."

"Neither am I, so let's cut to the chase. Where are we going and why are we dressed in desert camo? I can tell from the plane's eastward flight path that we're not going toward Indonesia, unless we're taking the long way around."

"No, we're not. We're going to Libya."

"Libya?" repeated Harvath quietly.

"Yeah. We've received new intelligence that Nidal is going to be there."

"What kind of intelligence?"

Morrell gestured to the empty seat across the table from him and Harvath sat down. "You want some coffee?" asked Morrell as he removed a thermos from a bag on the seat next to him.

"Sure. Thanks," said Harvath as Morrell poured some into a small, Styrofoam cup and handed it across the table.

Morrell tightened the lid on the thermos and set it back down next to him before speaking again. "You're familiar with the fact that the U.S. government has been monitoring several suspected Abu Nidal Organization bank accounts around the world?"

"I was under the impression that we had frozen them all," said Harvath as he took a sip of coffee.

"For the most part, we have, but we left a couple semi-frozen."

"What do you mean by *semifrozen?*"

"We had assets at certain banks, human assets, and we quietly leaked word in ways that were sure to get out to Hashim Nidal's people that these assets could be had for a price."

"And in exchange, the assets would provide access to the frozen funds?"

"Exactly. Knowing that the FRC was desperate for money, we thought we could smoke out a couple big fish."

"And?"

"We got a hit. Two days ago in Helsinki."

"What happened?"

"An FRC operative contacted our agent at the Bank of Finland and arranged an immediate meeting. It happened so fast we almost didn't have time to organize the grab."

"But you got him. Can he ID Nidal?"

"No," said Morrell, shaking his head and taking a sip of coffee. "Unfortunately he can't."

"Did he have any useful information?"

"Big time. This guy was involved with organizing an upcoming meeting between Nidal and a wealthy Saudi. He gave us the time, place . . . everything except what they'll be serving for dinner."

"How credible do you think the information is?" asked Harvath.

"Very."

"Based on what?"

"The man was extremely uncooperative. The information was extracted under duress," said Morrell.

"Would this be of the physical or chemical variety?"

"I'm not at liberty to answer that. Suffice it to say that my superiors believe the intelligence is quite reliable."

"And you think the meeting is still a go, even though this guy has been pulled out of action? Don't you think his superiors might be a little suspicious when he goes missing?"

"Technically, he's not out of action. He's in a hospital in Helsinki, the victim of a horrible car crash. Among his many injuries is a broken jaw that needed to be wired shut, and he's pumped so full of sedatives, nobody could get anything coherent out of him even if they wanted to. His room is being kept under surveillance, but other than that, his friends and associates are free to come and visit. There was even a write-up in several of the local papers about the crash. As far as we're concerned, there's no reason for his superiors to suspect anything other than an unfortunate accident."

"And he's going to remain incommunicado until the meeting with Nidal and the Saudi is finished?"

"Yup, at which point the Finns will take him into custody for a host of immigration violations. He's not going anywhere."

"Let me guess," said Harvath, setting down his empty cup, "we're on our way to crash Hashim Nidal's rendezvous with the Saudi."

"Correct."

"What do we know about the Saudi?"

"Not much, unfortunately. Our guess is that he is a potential investor in the organization."

"Where in Libya is the meet taking place?"

Morrell took his laptop off the table, removed a large map from a cardboard tube, and unrolled it in front of them. He made a circle on the map with a blue pencil and said, "Here, on the western edge of the country. About a hundred and seventy-five miles south of an abandoned Libyan city called Ghadames."

"In the Ubari Sand Sea?" asked Harvath, leaning in to get a better look at the map. "There's nothing there but—"

"Sand?" said Morrell, smiling.

"Nothing but."

"Well, it would seem that Abu Nidal's son is a bit of an entrepreneur cum philanthropist."

"How so?" asked Harvath, playing with his empty Styrofoam cup.

Morrell opened up his thermos and poured them both more coffee. "There seems to be a growing trend with wealthy Muslims in Libya. They foot the bill for creating oasis towns in outlying areas of the country. The town is usually named after the family and a large mosque is built, a school, gas stations, a meeting hall, maybe a hotel, tract housing for the workers who cultivate the land—"

"Yeah, but you first need water. That's the basic building block of life in the desert."

"Get this. The families pay for extensive government surveys to locate potential stores of water beneath the earth. When they have found one and all necessary arrangements have been made with the government, they bring in massive drilling equipment and go to work."

"What's in it for them?" asked Harvath, searching for a catch.

"On the surface, they claim their small oasis towns provide a better life for their poor Libyan brothers and sisters who have crowded into the country's bigger cities looking for work. Little is mentioned of the fact that as they own the entire town, the revenue from everything from fast-food restaurants to pharmacies is quite lucrative."

"What if they find oil while looking for water?"

"It's a windfall for the family and the government."

"Why haven't the oil companies jumped all over this?"

"The Tham Oil Company has been involved in some of the joint Libyan-Egyptian oasis projects, but by and large, the chances of finding oil in a lot of the locations is a long shot at best."

"But it's one hell of a goodwill maneuver, especially if the Nidal family needs a place to hide. It's not easy to harbor terrorists these days, even for an international pariah like Gadhafi."

"You're right, it isn't. But he still does it. Especially when the terrorists make themselves useful to him."

"What happened to the Indonesia angle?"

"That's why Nidal has been so hard to track. With all of his terrorist affiliations, it's been difficult to nail down exactly where he is. We still believe he has his hands in some goings-on over there, but we now believe that he constructed this oasis town as a cover for his training camp and base of operations," replied Morrell as he pulled out a large manila envelope.

"But how could you guys have missed that?" asked Harvath, though he was actually somewhat reluctant to rub the CIA's nose in another screwup.

"The oasis development project is something Gadhafi has been very high profile about. We kept tabs on it, but since he wasn't hiding anything, we figured there was nothing to hide. You can look at these yourself," said Morrell as he spread several labeled satellite photos across the table. "It all looks exactly like what it is supposed to be—the construction of small towns in the desert."

"What about this one? Do they all have airstrips?" said Harvath as he tapped one of the photos in front of him.

"The ones that were developed with private money from individual families had the occasional idiosyncrasies: disgustingly large houses, enormous swimming pools, luxury multistoried bungalows for guests . . . Our analysts got used to seeing stuff like that."

"Yeah, but airstrips?"

"Harvath, you know as well as I do that having your own plane is a status symbol, no matter where in the world you live. It's the ultimate representation of freedom."

"But out of all these pictures, Nidal's is the only oasis town with an airstrip this big. And look at all of these support buildings."

"Unfortunately, we didn't pick up on it until recently. We had no idea he was involved with this oasis town."

"How could you not?"

"Because it's all being done through another Muslim family with a different name. We had no idea he was attached. In fact, if Gadhafi was ever pressed on the issue, he could probably make a strong case that he didn't know it either."

"Plausible deniability."

"Exactly."

"But if Nidal's so strapped for cash, why would he be pumping money into a sandy real estate development deal?"

"For the same reasons we've already discussed. Eventually, the town will turn a profit and provide a steady stream of income. Secondly, with all the itinerant labor brought in to work the fields, it's the perfect cover for moving terrorism recruits in and out for training. And finally, the success of the oasis development program makes Hashim Nidal's host look good, and that goes a long way in helping to ensure Gadhafi's continuing blanket of asylum."

"Being the boss of your own town in the middle of the desert must carry with it a certain amount of political weight too."

"The CIA predicts that the towns will develop into their own little fiefdoms. In the long run, they might turn out to be more of a headache for Gadhafi than he ever imagined."

"For now, at least one of those towns looks like it's going to be a headache for us. What's the plan?"

Morrell gathered up all but the most relevant Ubari Sand Sea oasis satellite photos and placed them back in the envelope. "The name of Nidal's town is the *Hijrah Oasis*. Hijrah is an Arabic term that refers to—"

"The Prophet Muhammad's journey from Mecca to Medina. It means 'to leave a place of persecution in search of sanctuary or religious freedom.'"

"Then you also should know that the term can mean 'leaving a bad way of life for a better or more righteous way,' which is how we think it is being applied in this case. Nidal has brought in a very radical fundamentalist cleric to run the mosque. Either Gadhafi doesn't know about it, or doesn't care, but it's another reason we think this whole thing is going to come back to bite him in the ass eventually."

"As far as I'm concerned, Gadhafi can go screw himself. I'm in this for Nidal."

"As are we," replied Morrell, who used a wax pencil to circle a building on one of the photos. "But we also want his training camp taken out."

"Are you sure that's it?"

"No, and that's another one of our problems. We haven't had enough time to do extended reconnaissance. We're going to need to get in there and recon it ourselves. The last thing we want to do is take out a hospital or an orphanage or something. Gadhafi would have a field day with that one and milk the worldwide PR for all it was worth. We need to be able to pinpoint where the training is happening and, if possible, what they're training for."

"Sounds like a pretty tall order to me."

"Tall order or not, that's our mission."

"It seems the parameters of this operation are being stretched a bit."

"Harvath, like I've told you before, if you don't like it, you're free to leave at any time. As a matter of fact, there's an exit right there," said Morrell as he tipped his wax pencil in the direction of the forward cabin door.

"You're not getting rid of me that easily, Ricky. Besides, I want to see Nidal taken out just as badly as you do. Let's get down to brass tacks. I've got three questions. How do we get in? How do we do it? How do we get out?"

"Our infiltration is still *in flux.*"

"What do you mean *in flux?*"

"Originally, we thought we'd go in via Algeria's border with Libya, but Gadhafi's all of a sudden doing military exercises in that area."

"Do you think there's a connection?"

"No. He does these border defense drills all the time. This is just bad timing. We're still working on it. If the Algerian angle falls through, I've got a backup."

"Such as?"

"We've still got several hours until we get there," said Morrell. "Let's see what shakes out between now and then."

"What about taking out Nidal?"

"It's by the book, just like we trained. Meg Cassidy will ID him, and the snipers will earn their checks. Simple as that."

Harvath wished things were that simple in the real world. He could see from Morrell's face that he was worried too, but Harvath let it slide for now. There was no sense putting any more stress on Morrell than was obviously already there. Instead, Harvath asked for an answer to his third question. "And how do we get out?"

"If we're able to insert via helicopter from Algeria, that's the same way we'll do the extraction."

"And if not?"

"We've got a contingent of FAVs at an airbase in Sicily. I've already dispatched several of my men to load them onto a C-130 and drop them into the Ubari Sand Sea, not far from the Hijrah Oasis."

Harvath had worked with FAVs, or more appropriately, Fast Attack Vehicles, before. They looked like dune buggies on steroids and were awesome pieces of machinery. The knobby-tired, 2100-pound FAVs could reach speeds in excess of eighty miles per hour cross-country and could clear sand berms over six feet high. They came complete with a fifty-caliber machine gun and forty-millimeter grenade launcher forward, as well as a 7.62 machine gun to cover the rear. Strapped to the roof rack of each FAV was an antitank-and-antiaircraft missile. Though the vehicles were made to carry only three people, two extra passengers could be transported in the wire-mesh equipment baskets welded to each side of the vehicle. All in all, the FAV was an extremely efficient way to get around and extremely deadly for any opponents.

"It seems like you've thought of everything," said Harvath in an attempt to be reassuring.

"You and I both know you can never think of everything," said Morrell with a wry smile.

Harvath smiled back. It was a rare moment of camaraderie between the two men. "What's the timetable on this? Are we going to be able to go through some run-throughs in country before the actual assault?"

"Negative. The meeting's set for tomorrow night."

Harvath couldn't believe what he was hearing. "*Tomorrow night?* What time?"

"About eleven P.M. local time."

"That's nuts. We'd have to get in place *tonight.*"

"I know."

"Jesus, any other surprises?"

"I hope not. Listen. I want to ask you a favor."

"What?"

"I want you to keep Meg Cassidy as calm as possible until we go in. I'd rather not discuss the operational details with her just yet, especially as we haven't been able to nail everything down."

"As long as you don't ask her to fast-rope out of one of

the helicopters, I think she'll be fine. She's not too fond of heights."

"So I've heard. Just try and keep her calm up there, and keep her mind off of things for the time being. Okay?"

"Fine by me. Is there a movie on this flight?"

"No, and no prime rib either. I stocked the plane myself, so I know. You've got your choice in the galley of MREs or we loaded a couple of pizzas on board."

"I think I'll go with the pizza," said Harvath as he stood up. "Did you bring any beer?"

"Beer? What are you, crazy? I wouldn't bring beer on a mission."

Harvath shrugged his shoulders as if to say, *It never hurts to ask*, and made his way back up to the front of the plane to see if Meg was hungry for pizza.

When he returned from the galley with two hot slices for each of them, he noticed that Morrell had joined his nine-man team in the back of the plane for a discussion. He knew Rick was holding back something about the execution of the mission. He didn't know what it was, but something was off. Harvath tried to push it out of his mind as he settled in for lunch and the long ride ahead.

42

Two-and-a-half hours out from Libyan airspace, the Gulfstream jet began to descend and Rick Morrell called another
meeting. An hour earlier he had given Harvath, Meg, and
the rest of the SAS team a full mission briefing. Morrell covered everything from the encrypted radio frequencies they
would use, to GPS coordinates, land contour formations,
code names, and the contents of their weapons packages.
The two items he had left out were the methods of infiltration and extraction. As the team members gathered in the
rear of the aircraft this time, it looked as if Morrell was ready
to complete the picture.

"According to our intelligence, it doesn't look like the
Libyan military exercises along the Algerian border are
going to be letting up anytime soon. I had hoped to insert
via helicopter from Algeria, but that's no longer an
option," said Morrell.

"So how are we getting in?" asked Harvath.

"We're going to hop and pop."

"No, seriously. How are we going in?" repeated Harvath.

"I am serious."

"But right now we're descending. Are you going to try
and get us in under their radar in this jet?"

"No. We're going to go in through the normal air traffic
lanes with a commercial IFF signature so we don't raise
Libya's suspicions. We're descending now to below ten

thousand feet so we can get everyone started on masks with one-hundred-percent oxygen."

"And then what?"

"We climb to just over thirty thousand."

"Then we hop and pop?" asked Harvath.

"That's the plan. We'll be under canopy for a little over a half hour, but it's going to put us right on the money."

"You're forgetting one thing," said Harvath, hinting in Meg Cassidy's direction with his eyes.

"If there was an easier way to do this, I would," replied Morrell.

Meg, who had been listening, but not understanding any of the exchange, finally spoke up. "What are we talking about here?" She had a bad feeling she wasn't going to like the answer to her question.

"There's been a decision made on the infiltration, Meg," said Harvath.

"How are we going in?"

"It's a technique called HAHO. A high-altitude, high-opening parachute jump."

Meg's face immediately drained of all color. "Exactly how high are we talking about?"

"We'll be exiting the aircraft above thirty thousand feet. Ten to fifteen seconds later we'll pop our chutes and glide down to the sand dunes behind the Hijrah Oasis. A piece of cake," lied Harvath. He knew HAHOs were one of the most dangerous insertion techniques ever conceived of.

"Why is the plane going down?" asked Meg, growing more nervous.

"The plane is descending so we can use masks to begin

breathing pure oxygen. It will help flush most of the nitrogen from the bloodstream and tissues."

"What if I don't want the nitrogen flushed from my bloodstream and tissues?"

"Have you ever been scuba diving?"

"Yes, but—"

"This is very similar. There are going to be pressure changes when we jump, and we're all going to be on oxygen on the way down. It's just a safety precaution to help prevent any decompression problems."

"Scot, I can't do this. I *won't* do this."

"Meg, look at it this—"

"No. One minute we're training to beach on a small tropical island by swimming in from a rubber Zodiac, and now you want me to jump out of an airplane at over thirty thousand feet. I'm not doing this."

"Ms. Cassidy," interjected Morrell, "you did the wind tunnel and ParaSim at Fort Bragg, didn't you?"

"Yes, but—"

"This is no different."

"I'd say it's a hell of a lot different, and I'm not doing it."

"Ms. Cassidy, if there were any other way, believe me, we'd be doing it, but there isn't. Hashim Nidal is conducting his meeting tomorrow night and we must be in place. We have no other choice.

"Now, there will be a radio inside your helmet and we'll all be able to keep in touch during the jump. We'll talk you all the way in. I know you practiced landings at Fort Bragg, and this will be just like that."

"You're still not listening to me. Find another way because I am not jumping out of this plane."

"What if I jump with her?" asked Harvath.

"What are you talking about?" replied Morrell.

"We'll go tandem."

"A tandem HAHO? No way."

"Why not?"

"For starters, you'd only be able to carry half the amount of gear."

"Then reconfigure the loads. Your men are tough guys. They can handle a little more weight."

"We're talking about over two hundred pounds of food, water, ammunition—"

"—medical supplies, communications gear . . . I know what goes in the packs, Rick. Figure it out, or else you'll be leaving the plane without us."

"Scot," said Meg, "I can't do it."

Harvath took her hand in his, not caring what Morrell or any of his men thought of it. "Yes, you can, Meg. You *can* do this. We're going to do it together. I told you I wouldn't let anything happen to you, and I don't intend to let you down, especially while we're both sharing a parachute."

The entire plane was silent. After several tense moments, Meg halfheartedly returned Harvath's smile, nodded her head. The mission was a go.

43

Harvath kept a very close eye on Meg for the next two hours as they inhaled aviators' breathing oxygen. This was the preferred oxygen for jump operations, as other forms, such as medical oxygen, contained too much moisture and could freeze up in the regulator, the hoses, or the mask during the jump and make it impossible to breathe.

He watched for any potential signs of hypoxia caused by the decrease in ambient pressure as they ascended. At thirty thousand feet, the air pressure was close to being only one fourth of that at sea level. The other factor Harvath was concerned with was psychological. Even though they were going to be locked together for the jump, Meg was still incredibly frightened. Harvath had seen otherwise self-confident operatives freak out and start to hyperventilate due to claustrophobia brought on by having their heads and faces covered with a helmet and oxygen mask. Scot kept speaking to Meg in soothing tones, encouraging her to relax.

The entire plane had been depressurized to acclimate the team for the jump. Over their fatigues, all of the members wore extreme-cold-weather jumpsuits. Though cumbersome, the superinsulated suits not only would keep the team members warm during their jump, but also had the added benefit of radar absorbency, which would allow them to glide across the sky without being detected by enemy radar.

At the two-minute warning, the team transferred from the jet's oxygen console to the portable bottles strapped to their chests. They double and triple checked not only their weapons and equipment, but also each other one last time for any of the telltale signs of hypoxia: slowed reactions, euphoria, cyanosis—a bluish tint to the skin on lips or under fingernails—overconfidence, or lack of life in the eyes.

The cabin lights were switched over to jump lighting, and the jet was filled with an eerie red glow, punctuated by stabs of neon green at the ankles of each team member. Chem-lights had been taped to boots so team members could locate each other in the dark and avoid potentially deadly collisions.

Icy, subzero air blew across the open doorway as the Operation Phantom team lined up. Rick Morrell determined the order and had placed Harvath and Meg smack in the middle. As soon as Morrell gave the signal to jump, the line of bodies in front of them lurched forward, but Meg's legs refused to move. She willed herself to follow, but it was no use. Either her brain was refusing to give the command, or her body was refusing to obey it. Whatever the case, it was imperative for the team to stay together and that could only happen by jumping at precise intervals. Harvath wrapped his arms around Meg, lifted her clear off her feet and made for the open door.

At the last minute, Meg tried to reach out and grab something to prevent their leaving the plane, but it was no use. Harvath's grasp was too strong.

The frigid air burned their faces as they accelerated toward their terminal velocity of one hundred twenty miles per hour. Harvath glanced at his altimeter and watched the luminescent dial sweep off their rapidly increasing descent. "It's okay. Everything's okay," he repeated over the radio to Meg. Harvath figured the temperature was at least thirty-five degrees below zero. It took only seventeen seconds to descend to twenty-seven thousand feet, but to Meg Cassidy it felt like a lifetime.

When Harvath pulled his silver rip cord and deployed the ram-air, high-glide-ratio parachute, the expertly packed material shot straight and high into the air and then snapped into an enormous square double canopy overhead. Though Harvath had told her he was about to deploy the chute and she had been forewarned about the jolt, Meg had no idea the shock would be so intense. It was like riding in a falling elevator, which had just found the basement. She knew the intense stab of pain she felt was nothing compared to what Harvath must be feeling. He had borne the brunt of the shock and had told her in the plane that he would probably be sore for several days. It was always like that with HAHOs.

The deafening rush of air that they'd heard as they hurtled through the night sky was now gone. It was replaced by a silence unlike anything Meg Cassidy had ever experienced, and the view was absolutely incredible.

Harvath was appreciating it too. Between glances at his altimeter and the positions of his teammates, he took in the beautiful starlit vista over the sea of desert far below. It never ceased to amaze him how peaceful the world looked from this height, even when he knew he was inserting into hostile territory.

The team formed a vertical column in the sky, each

parachutist seeming to rest on top of the next. The lowest man in the airborne totem pole acted as the navigator, using a compass, GPS device, and barely visible terrain features to guide them into the drop zone.

They floated for forty miles, and a little over a half hour. Despite their high-tech jumpsuits and insulated Gore-Tex gloves, each of them was numb to the bone with cold. As they descended, the air began to gradually get warmer. At twelve thousand feet, they removed their oxygen masks and were able to breathe normally. The navigator continued to correct their course based on changes in wind speed and direction, until finally the signal came across the encrypted radios that they were coming within range of their DZ.

Meg fought the reflex to stiffen her legs as the ground raced up to meet them. At the last moment, Harvath pulled down hard on the parachute toggles, dramatically slowing their descent. They touched down in the soft sand and immediately rolled to their left. Harvath pulled in the rest of the chute and unbuckled Meg from where she was attached to his harness. The rest of the team members were already burying their parachutes and Chem-lights in the sand.

"Now that wasn't so bad," whispered Harvath with a smile as he finished covering their chute with sand and checked Meg's equipment.

"Not at all," she replied. "I can't decide which I liked more—my heart beating through my chest or my teeth nearly cracking from almost forty minutes in the freezing cold air."

"You'll warm up. Wait'll we get walking. It's actually

pretty warm in the desert tonight. It just takes your body a while to heat back up."

Harvath did one last check of his own gear and scanned the horizon with his night-vision goggles before he and Meg joined the rest of the team. It was already well past one in the morning local time. It would take them at least two hours, maybe three, to hike into the rocky hills above the oasis, where they would wait until tomorrow night. They could sleep during the daytime, but for now they needed the cover of darkness to hide their movements. Not a moment could be wasted. When the team was gathered together, Morrell gave the order to maintain complete radio silence and then signaled them to move out.

The deep desert sand, coupled with the heavy loads Morrell's men were carrying, made for extremely slow going. Free of his tandem rig with Meg, Harvath had taken more than his share of weight off the packs of the other guys, but they still slogged along. It wasn't until the team hit firmer terrain that the pace noticeably picked up. It didn't matter that they were hiking at a steep grade up the hillside. Everyone was thankful just to be off the sand.

Morrell's man on point gave the full-fist hand signal to stop, and the column came to an immediate halt. Team members took up defensive firing positions as Morrell and the point man explored a small cave behind a low over-hang and several large boulders. A moment later Morrell reemerged and gave the command to set up camp. Two of the men unshouldered their packs and set out to re-connoiter the rest of the area. Morrell set up his encrypted Motorola portable satellite communications system, while one of the men positioned a field antenna on the rock overhang.

"Welcome to the Plaza," said Harvath as he helped Meg into the cave. They found a relatively smooth area on the ground toward the west wall and unpacked only the gear they would need for the time being. Extra food, water, and equipment would be placed in a nearby hide site, in case they had to exit the cave in a hurry. The last thing they wanted to do was leave behind any clues that would tip off the Libyans or Hashim Nidal that they were in the area.

Meg unwrapped one of the three-thousand-calorie MREs and asked, "Can you eat this cold?"

"Cold or hot, it doesn't matter," replied Harvath as he laid out a poncho liner for each of them to sleep on.

"You have to boil it in the package if you want it hot, though, right?"

"Yeah, but toxic chemicals leach off the wrapping, so you have to toss the water out afterward. It's a waste of good water and that's something you never do in the desert."

"But there's an oasis just around the corner with plenty of water."

"And probably plenty of people who would be more than happy to let Nidal know we're here. Let's just say Jack and Jill will not go down the hill and will not be fetching a pail of water. Your MRE is already unwrapped, so you eat it cold."

Meg took a cautious bite and made a face right away. "God, this is terrible. How do you guys eat this stuff?"

"I've eaten much worse."

"I can't imagine worse than this."

"There is, believe me. You don't want to hear about it."

"Well, with all of the advancements the military has made in weapons and technology, you'd think they could at least spend a little time in the food department."

"Now you're starting to sound like a true soldier, Cassidy," responded Harvath. "Let's check your weapons."

Most of the men, except for the snipers, were carrying next-generation Heckler & Koch G11 caseless ammunition assault rifles. Though the G11 was an excellent weapon, Harvath and Meg carried H&K's G36 modular weapon system, which, because of its collapsible stock, was effective both at longer ranges and in close-quarters battle. Harvath always liked to be prepared for anything.

He was explaining how to fieldstrip the weapon and the importance of keeping everything free of sand when Morrell came back inside the cave followed by one of his men.

". . . and I think it just froze up," said the man.

"Those devices are supposed to be rated to extreme cold," said Morrell as Harvath and Meg stopped what they were doing to listen to the conversation.

"There are ones like that, but because we were deploying in a desert theater, we never thought we'd need anything arctic rated."

"What's up?" asked Harvath.

"Our Marty is nonoperational," said the operative.

"Your what?"

"Marty McFly," said Morrell. "That's what we call our micromechanical flying insect. It's a spin-off of a project the Navy code-named Robofly."

"You mean those tiny drones with the miniature fuel

cells that can literally be a fly on the wall to gather intel?" asked Harvath.

"The same," answered Morrell. "We think the cold from the jump screwed ours up."

"Why would you drag one of those along on a sniping mission?"

"Washington wants to know who the Saudi is. They thought if we could get the mini-drone in close enough, we could ID him."

"Jesus, anything else we can do while we're here?" asked Harvath. "Maybe we can pick a few villages and help vaccinate some kids on our way out."

"I know. I know," said Morrell.

"So do I," responded Harvath. "The more elements you try and add to a mission, the greater the chances it's going to turn into one big GoFu."

"What's a 'GoFu'?" asked Meg.

"A Goat Fuck, ma'am," said the operative who was trying to fix the mini-drone.

"Rick, there are already too many elements involved here, what with taking out Nidal and you being given the additional task of reconning the training camp. Be smart. Let's not add anything more. Mark my words. Out here, anything that can go wrong, will go wrong, and it will screw our day major," said Harvath.

"Consider them marked," replied Morrell as he turned back to help the operative with the drone.

44

The time difference between the east coast of the United States and Libya was six hours. By the time Harvath and Meg had organized all of their gear and gotten to sleep, it was after midnight for them back home and almost sunrise on the Ubari Sand Sea.

Harvath had offered to post one of the four-hour guard shifts, but Morrell declined, saying he had more than enough men to cover the rotations. Harvath drifted into one of his deep trancelike states while Meg slept in interrupted, fitful bouts. At one point, she awoke with a start at the sound of bells, but Harvath was quick to cover her mouth. A herd of goats from one of the oasis farmers had wandered close to the mouth of the cave. Meg looked around and saw that every member of the team had his weapon drawn and was ready to kill the goatherd, should he be unlucky enough to stumble across them, but nothing happened. The goats moved on, and the team eventually stood down.

After a while, Meg gave up trying to fall back asleep. Thoughts of what lay ahead filled her mind, and there was no way she could completely relax.

Morrell had brought along two two-man sniper teams as part of the operation. The men who had gone out to recon the area had confirmed the distances to where they assumed the target would be, and the sniper teams were now quietly quizzing each other on ballistic charts. "At five hundred meters in ten-to-twelve-knot winds, how far will a three hundred Win Mag drop?" said one of the men.

The spotter from the other team responded, "Considering the drag coefficient on a three hundred Win Mag, it'll be seven inches off, right to left," and so the conversation continued. It was completely over Meg's head. All she knew was that there were at least seven more hours till sunset and God only knew how many more before Morrell would give the order to move out of the cave so they could take up their positions and await Hashim Nidal.

Meg turned to Harvath to help pass the time. Normally, he would have been concerned with keeping an operative's head in the game, but he realized Meg needed distraction. She didn't want to think about what lay ahead. She needed to talk about something else . . . anything else.

Harvath asked questions about her family and growing up in Chicago. He asked about college and starting her own business. He even spent some time trying to explain the philosophy of true country music, which could be summed up as, "three chords and the truth"—my wife left me, my dog ran away, I lost my job . . . He had no idea if Meg appreciated his position, but she laughed nonetheless.

Darkness had just fallen when Morrell finally made his way to the back of the cave where Harvath and Meg were still talking. "Saddle up," was all he whispered before gathering his gear and heading outside.

Sounds from the distant oasis could be heard floating on the mild breeze that stirred the loose sand all around them. Harvath and Meg took their places in the middle of the column, and after a final weapons and equipment check, the team set off for their positions overlooking the Hijrah Oasis.

They picked their way over the boulder-strewn hillside with extreme caution, careful not to make even the slightest sound. Though the entire team was wearing throat mikes, no one dared break radio silence. As they crested the hill, the oasis came into full view. A perfectly still, oblong pool of water seemed to magically spring up from the desert sand like a forgotten mirror and reflect everything around it. An amazing array of flowers and vegetation, including young date and palm trees, surrounded the tiny desert lake and spread outward for hundreds of meters, adding brilliant touches of color to the otherwise barren landscape.

Many of the buildings shown in the satellite photos, once only a hodgepodge of unimpressive gray boxes, were now completely visible. Vegetation hung from windows and over the edges of makeshift balconies. To people who had no idea of the real purpose of this oasis town, it could easily have been mistaken for a modern-day Garden of Eden.

On a small promontory jutting out into the dark water, obviously a place of great honor and ceremony, stood a large bedouin-style tent. Torches lit a path to the open panels of striped fabric that billowed in the desert wind. Robed figures trudged back and forth from covered trucks, preparing for the meeting between Hashim Nidal and the Saudi, while other robed figures stood quietly by, clutching Kalashnikov assault rifles.

All of a sudden, loud music erupted from a boom box in the back of one of the trucks, and the men setting up the tent cheered. The Operation Phantom team hit the deck and searched for cover. Morrell clutched his throat mike and snapped, "What the fuck is that?"

The operatives were all silent. After listening for a few moments Harvath whispered, "Flashlight."

" 'Flashlight'? I didn't see any flashlight. I'm talking about that goddamn music."

"It's the name of the song. 'Flashlight,' by Parliament. They may hate us, but they love our music."

"Fuckin' no-taste ragheads," spat one of the operatives.

"Actually," whispered Harvath, " 'Flashlight' is considered far and away a seventies funk classic."

"Both of you shut up," commanded Morrell. "Obviously, our real players haven't arrived on the scene yet. Let's get into place."

Morrell gave the signal for the team to split up, and the members fanned out in separate directions. Two men went off to recon the suspected training camp as the sniper teams took up strategic positions overlooking the striped tent. Harvath and Meg were directed to stay behind a large outcropping of rocks while Morrell took several more men and his operative who had somehow managed to repair the mini-drone further down the hill.

Harvath scanned the scene below with one of the next-generation AN/PVS starlight scope systems he and Meg had been given to identify Hashim Nidal with. The music seemed to have had the desired effect. The men were now unloading the trucks at a much improved pace. Harvath noticed that not all of them were dressed in robes. Some wore civilian clothes, and one even had a Chicago Bulls T-shirt on. He loved the hypocrisy of it all—*The U.S. is the Great Satan, but Michael Jordan? He's number one!*

The radio silence was interrupted when Rick Morrell whispered, "Marty away." Harvath and Meg both tried to locate the mini-drone through their starlight scopes, but at half the size of a wine cork, it was next to impossible to see.

For a moment, they heard what sounded like the beginning strains of "Kung Fu Fighting"; then an irate and obviously very senior member of Hashim Nidal's staff began yelling at the men near the tent and the music was immediately turned off.

The wind picked up, and rough sheets of sand blew across the narrow streets of the oasis town. The workers wrapped their kaffiyeh headdresses across their faces to keep the sand out of their mouths and noses. Over the plastic earpiece wedged deep within his ear, Harvath heard one of the operatives say, "We've got an inbound aircraft."

As Harvath turned his eyes to the north, he could make out the lights of a small plane off in the distance. A moment later, the landing strip lit up like a Christmas tree. The man taken into custody in Helsinki had indicated that the Saudi would be arriving via private jet and he was right on time. That meant Hashim Nidal couldn't be far behind.

One of the sniper teams quietly hailed Meg and asked her to call out various points and distances around the tent. Meg pressed her face against the rubber blinders of the starlight scope and synced with both spotters to make sure they were on the same page. She didn't dare remove the device from her face. Her vision was now acclimated to the greenish glow, and the last thing she wanted to do was expose her eyes to any of the blowing sand. The mission could not afford her missing the target.

She was still scanning the area around the tent when

another voice came over the team's earpieces and said, "Two convoys approaching target area."

Meg knew that one of the convoys approaching from the direction of the airstrip would belong to the Saudi, while the other would most likely belong to Nidal. She noticed her hands were shaking, and she tried to steady them by resting her elbows on the boulder in front of her.

"You okay?" asked Harvath, whose eyes were also glued to the scene unfolding through his starlight scope.

"A little nervous."

"That's good. It's to be expected. Just ID Nidal to the snipers the way we practiced it. You're going to do fine."

"I hope so. I want this to be over with."

"It will be soon enough. Don't worry. It looks like the convoys are about to enter the perimeter."

The voice came back over their earpieces. "Convoys entering perimeter. All teams stand by."

Two sets of Land Rovers came to a stop twenty meters away from the tent. As the doors to the vehicles opened, another gust of wind erupted, sending sharp blasts of sand in all directions. The men momentarily retreated into their vehicles until the wind passed, then reemerged with their kaffiyehs drawn tightly across their faces, like the guards and workers.

"Wild Onion, have you identified the target?" came the voice of one of the spotters over Meg's earpiece.

As Meg was from Chicago, Morrell had assigned her a code name based on what the Native Americans had originally called the Windy City.

"Target not yet identified," said Meg as she strained to get a better view through her starlight scope.

Seconds passed and the men moved toward the tent, their bodies bent against the force of the wind and blowing sand.

"Wild Onion," came the voice again. "Do you have the target?"

"Negative. Target not yet identified."

The men had now covered half the distance to the tent and would be inside within the next ten seconds.

"Wild Onion. You must identify the target before they're out of view."

"I'm trying," said Meg desperately, more to herself than anyone else. "They're all dressed alike and I can't see their faces."

"It's no good," said Harvath over his throat mike as he watched the men finish filing into the tent.

"Target pool out of view," came the voice of one of the sniper team spotters. "Awaiting instructions."

"Damnit," hissed Morrell over the team's earpieces. "Stand by."

Meg pulled the starlight scope from her face and slid down against the large boulder. "I blew it," she said.

Harvath slid down next to her and put a hand on her shoulder. "You didn't blow anything. Nobody could have called that shot. Their faces were completely covered."

"So what do we do now?"

"You don't want to know."

"Yes, I do," said Meg as she wiped the perspiration from her palms onto her fatigues.

"I think Morrell's probably got no choice but to light that tent up like a roman candle."

"If he does, how are we going to know for sure we got Nidal?"

"We might never know for sure, but we also might never get another chance like this."

"In Chicago, you told me you wouldn't just fire missiles into a bunch of people. You said you couldn't. You said you *had* to know for sure you got him."

"If Morrell decides to take out that tent, I would have to agree with him. It's a good tactical decision."

"But there's innocent people in there."

"Meg, calm down. The people in that tent are anything but innocent."

"Are you absolutely sure about that? Do you know for a fact that the people helping set that tent up and who are probably serving a meal inside right now aren't some hapless workers from the oasis town?"

"No, but this is a numbers game. We have to be willing to sacrifice a few for the benefit of the many. And better it be a few of theirs, than many of ours."

"What about their families?"

Harvath was beginning to lose his patience. "What about *your* family? What if Hashim Nidal had been responsible for killing someone you cared about? How about your assistant, Judy? Do you want to let this guy slip through our fingers again only to hurt more innocent people than we might?"

"Of course not. But I want to know we did everything we could to nail him before another innocent person dies."

"Well, you can sleep like an angel. Your conscience is clear. We did do everything we could."

"No we didn't."

"What are you talking about?" said Harvath.

"It doesn't matter if Nidal's face is wrapped up tight.

After what he tried to do to me on that plane, I'd know him just by his eyes."

"You can't make out anybody's eyes from up here."

"You're right. But, from down there I could," said Meg as she pointed her index finger over the water of the oasis and toward the tent.

45

This is, without a doubt, the mother of all bad ideas, said Harvath to himself as he and Meg Cassidy crept around the outer edge of the oasis toward the tent. Meg had convinced Morrell of her plan in no time. Of course it wasn't a very tough sell. It seemed Morrell would sacrifice anybody and anything to accomplish his mission.

Harvath had gone along with Meg's idea for one simple reason. If they had chosen to stay back and annihilate the tent from a distance, there would been no way of confirming that they had actually taken Hashim Nidal out. Sure, everyone inside would be dead, but what if Nidal had had a change of heart at the last minute and had sent someone else to conduct the meeting in his place? The other thing that bothered Harvath was that he was not so sure Nidal was who everybody thought he was.

It only took Harvath about two seconds longer than Morrell to realize that they didn't have any other choice, and so he made his way with Meg into the darkness.

They were under cover of the two sniper teams the entire way. Their circuit took a painfully long time and was made even worse by the intermittent wind that kicked up enormous clouds of sand.

They had been creeping around the edge of the lush oasis, using the thick groves of palm trees for cover, when fifty meters away from their objective, Harvath held up his hand for Meg to stop. With two fingers, he pointed at his own eyes and then motioned toward the front of the tent. Meg shook her head *No*. It was no good. She wouldn't be able to identify Nidal from this distance, not even with their night scopes. She wanted to be closer. She signaled Harvath that they should sneak nearer to the tent. Harvath immediately shook his head. *Negative*. They were already much closer than he had wanted to get.

Harvath indicated that they would stay where they were and wait. With two short abrupt movements, he again pointed at his eyes and then at the tent. Meg got the picture, but she didn't like it. She again shook her head *No*. Harvath didn't care what she thought and he firmly pointed to the ground at their feet. He was lowering from his crouched position to his knees and preparing to lay in behind a clump of tall oasis grass when Meg took off. It was the last thing Harvath had expected.

He engaged his throat mike and whispered, "Meg! Damnit! Get back here. You're going to get killed!"

Meg either didn't hear or didn't want to hear, because she kept moving at a running crouch closer toward the tent. Harvath had no choice but to go after her.

"What the fuck is going on down there?" rasped Morrell over his earpiece, but Harvath didn't pay any attention. His only thoughts were on stopping Meg before she went too far.

She was no match for him, especially in the soft sand. She had swung out toward a pile of discarded crates when Harvath caught her around the waist and tackled her to the ground.

"What the hell's the matter with you?" snarled Harvath as he rolled her over to stare her in the face.

"*With me?*" whispered Meg. "What's the matter with *you?* I told you I couldn't see anything from where we were. I had to get closer."

"And I told you *no.*"

"We're here now, so let's make the best of it."

"No way. We're getting out of here."

"You've gotta be kidding me," said Meg as she rolled over and prepared to get back up.

"The hell I am. We've got absolutely no sniper support here."

"We don't need it. We're safe here. If we can get over behind those crates, I can get a good view of Nidal when he leaves the tent. Then the sniper team can take him out. Nobody will be looking for us over there. Once the shooting starts, we'll sneak back out and around the oasis."

"That plan is almost as bad as coming down here in the first place."

"But it will work."

"It might work," said Harvath.

"It will," replied Meg. "Trust me."

"Trust *you?* Taking off like you did, you just lost my trust. From now on, you do exactly what I say. You understand me?"

"Does that mean we're staying?"

"Are you going to do what I say?"

"Yes."

"Then we're staying."

Meg thanked Harvath, but he ignored her as he quietly radioed to Morrell their new intent. Morrell didn't like the fact that Harvath and Meg were where the rest of the team couldn't see them, but he agreed with their plan nonetheless.

Harvath signaled to Meg to remain completely quiet as they silently crawled forward toward the stack of discarded crates. Halfway there, first one, then several figures began to emerge from the tent. Harvath didn't need to tell Meg what to do. She froze, then slowly brought the night scope up to her eyes. The men had exited the tent between gusts of wind and, believing that the sandstorm had passed, did not bother covering their faces.

"The party is breaking up," said Harvath quietly into his throat mike to the rest of the team.

"Copy that. Awaiting your ID," responded one of the sniper teams.

Harvath crawled over so that he could lie right next to Meg. He was angry that they hadn't been able to make it to the cover of the crates before the men began exiting the tent. "How's the view?" he whispered into Meg's ear.

Meg rocked her outstretched hand from side to side as if to say, *So, so,* and then pointed her thumb straight down. Her voice barely a whisper, she leaned toward Harvath and said, "I'm getting backs of heads and the occasional profile. This is no good. We've got to get behind those crates."

Harvath didn't like it. It was too risky. Though they were halfway there already, it still seemed a long way off. What's more, they'd be that much further away from the oasis and the fire support the sniper teams could lend them if they were seen. But, Harvath knew they had no choice. Scot tapped Meg on the shoulder and indicated for her to quickly follow him, which she did.

Men were now filing out of the tent at a steady clip, and the eyes of the armed guards were busy surveying the entire area. With the night scope again pressed tight against her face, Meg peered out from behind the crates and focused on a tall man in a striped robe as he exited the tent and looked around. When the man unknowingly glanced in their direction, Meg could see his eyes. *It was him! Hashim Nidal.* As Meg was about to engage her throat mike and call in the target, she was struck hard with the butt of an assault rifle against the back of her head and everything went black.

46

When Harvath awoke with a throbbing headache, the first thing he noticed was the stifling heat. It made him feel as if he were in an oven. There was no telling how long he had been out, or where he was. He assumed that he was somewhere within the oasis town. The tiny room was completely black. The floor he was lying on was hard-packed sand and reaching out either arm he could touch the walls, which were some sort of stone. He did a quick inventory and wasn't surprised that all of his weapons had been taken away, as well as his Rolex.

Something with way too many legs crawled across his thigh and he quickly brushed it off. He jumped up and, guessing at where the creature was, raised his foot to smash it. He brought his boot down and heard the satisfying squish of a direct hit.

Despite the good-night kiss he'd been given by one of Nidal's men, physically, he was doing okay. He wished he could be sure of the same for Meg. There was no telling what they were doing to her. A woman like Meg was quite a trophy. Being captured as an enemy would all but guarantee the unthinkable.

Harvath stood for hours, leaning against the wall of his cell. He could hear the sound of gunfire and occasional explosions. Men shouted to each other in Arabic. He listened hard, but the voices were too muffled for him to discern exactly what was being said. At times, it was completely quiet and Harvath figured the men had either stopped for prayers, or had gone off somewhere to eat. Finally, from the other side of the rough wooden door securing his cell, there came the sound of metal scraping upon metal. The heavy bolt was drawn back, and the door was slowly opened.

The late afternoon sunlight exploded into the dark cell and burned so bright that Harvath had to shut his eyes. Several heavily armed men grabbed his arms, shackled his hands in front, and roughly shoved him outside.

Harvath had to hold up his hands to shield his eyes, but soon the sun dimmed, and he could see he was in a large shaded courtyard. When he looked up, he saw that he was not in a courtyard as much as a canyon the length of at least two football fields. An opaque woven fabric, the color of the surrounding steep rock walls, was stretched far overhead from end to end. *That explains why this place has never shown up on any satellite photos*, thought Harvath to himself.

The canyon floor was broken up into different training areas. There were firing ranges, makeshift shoot houses, the charred hulks of numerous types of automobiles, various ambush and attack scenarios . . . You name it and Hashim Nidal had it. It made the monkey-bar footage from Osama bin Laden's training camps look like child's play in comparison. This setup was extremely sophisticated, and though Harvath had no idea where he was, it was obvious he wasn't in the oasis town anymore.

At the end of the canyon was an enormous stone edifice carved directly into the wall of rock. It reminded Harvath of Petra, the two-thousand-year-old rock-carved city in Jordan. The carvings were incredibly intricate, and the façade looked like the entrance of an enormous palace.

Abruptly, Harvath's captors steered him toward a discolored section of the canyon wall. The pockmarks in the rocks told him all he needed to know. If he had any doubt about what lay in store for him, when one of the guards offered him a cigarette, the picture was perfectly clear.

Two of the guards fired rounds at Harvath's feet to see if he would jump. He didn't. Not even a flinch. If they were going to kill him, he didn't intend to add to their pleasure by going soft.

The captain of the guard stepped away from his men and walked up to Harvath. He was carrying a Russian Makarov. He raised his robed arm and placed the pistol against Harvath's forehead. As he did, Harvath could see that he was wearing his missing Rolex. The man smiled with a mouth full of yellowed teeth and then pulled the trigger.

Harvath harbored a strange feeling that he had not been brought all this way to be killed. These men were nothing but low-level peons amusing themselves at his expense until their boss called. Well, now it was Harvath's turn.

His reaction undoubtedly surprised the captain and his men. Instead of blubbering for his life or pissing his pants, as many poor souls before him had probably done, Harvath just smiled. He smiled big and wide, then kneed the captain right in the pistachios.

"Now the camels in the village will be safe for the rest of the day," said Harvath in Arabic.

A couple of the captain's men could not help but

chuckle. The captain, though, was enraged and, as soon as he caught his breath, dove for Harvath.

Shackling Harvath's hands in front had been a dumb idea. It didn't take long for Scot to overpower the captain and lock him in a choke hold with the restraints. The man kicked like a mule as Harvath began to squeeze the life out of him. His men looked on stupidly, not knowing what to do. One of the captain's kicks eventually connected with Harvath's left thigh, and the two men fell to the ground and continued to wrestle.

Finally, a hail of bullets tore up the sand only millimeters from the men's heads. Whoever was firing at them was either extremely lucky or extremely accurate. Harvath was tempted to crush the captain's windpipe, but let up on the pressure and looked up to see who had fired the shots. Astride a beautiful black Arabian was a perfect match for the man Meg Cassidy had described as Hashim Nidal. With his kaffiyeh, flowing white robes, and the elaborate tassels on his mount, he looked more like someone out of *Lawrence of Arabia* than a cold-blooded terrorist.

"Enough!" shouted the man from atop his horse.

Harvath was loath to surrender his advantage. The man pointed his weapon down at him, and Harvath knew he had little choice in the matter. He let the captain free, and as the man rolled out of his prisoner's grasp, he delivered a hard elbow to Harvath's ribs.

"We're not finished yet," groaned Harvath.

Two other guards yanked him to his feet and pushed him painfully toward the stone façade at the rear of the canyon.

As Harvath was shoved along, he kept his eyes open

and tried to take in everything that was going on around him. If he ever got out of this situation, he wanted to be able to report in the greatest detail possible what he had seen.

The guards led him up a massive series of stone steps and through the main entrance of the enormous edifice. The interior was amazing. At least a hundred columns soared over six stories to the perfectly domed ceiling, which contained a grand oculus exposing the sky high above. Intricate mosaics adorned the walls, and the floors were covered in marble tiles so highly polished they shone like mirrors. The acoustics were perfect. Even the slightest whisper from across the immense rotunda reverberated back with absolute clarity. All throughout the structure, natural light radiated from a series of mirrors and additional holes carved in the roof of the building.

Harvath was marched through a narrow apse to a low doorway along another colonnade. One of the guards knocked twice upon a heavy wooden door and waited until he was directed to enter. When the direction came, the guard pushed the door open and motioned Harvath inside.

This room was much darker than the series of hallways they had been navigating, and it took a moment for Harvath's eyes to become adjusted to the low level of light. The wooden floors, paneled walls, and bookcases were all a deep mahogany. Thick, splintered beams of the same color ran at intervals along the ceiling. Several chairs sat in front of a large wooden desk, and in the corner stood an actual fireplace. The room looked like something out of a medieval British abbey. The walls were covered with photographs, many of which, from what Harvath could make out from where he was standing, were not of Arabs, but of Anglos. One in particular caught his attention. He was trying to figure out why the photo had captured his interest when a small door opened at the back of the room and several figures appeared. The first, much to Harvath's relief, was Meg Cassidy. She was also incredibly relieved to see Scot and ran right to him.

Though his guard tried to stop him, Harvath reached out for her. "Are you all right?" he asked as he looked her over. There were no apparent signs that she had been harmed.

"I'm okay. But this is all my fault. I'm so sorry," she replied as she laid her head on his chest, wishing the entire nightmare would just disappear.

"This isn't your fault, so don't worry about it. They haven't done anything to you, have they?"

"Mr. Harvath, contrary to what you might think, we are not barbarians," said a man standing in the doorway that Meg had just come through. Harvath recognized him immediately. It was the man who had broken up his fight with the captain of the guard outside. Meg squeezed Harvath's arm, and it was the only signal he needed.

"There are millions of people around the world who would disagree with you," said Harvath, letting go of Meg so he could face the man and the other figure who had joined him. The other person's face was covered in the traditional Arab kaffiyeh, but there was something familiar about him. "How do you know my name?" he asked, though he was sure that Meg had told them. It would have made sense to question her first. She was the weakest of the pair and could be broken much easier.

"I know more than just your name," said the man as he took a seat behind the large desk. "Your government should not have sent a woman, a civilian no less, to do a soldier's job." The man's English had a thick Middle Eastern accent.

"Considering that she foiled your hijacking, you hardly seem qualified to comment on the abilities of women," said Harvath with a smile.

The man signaled his guard, who brought the butt of his rifle hard into Harvath's stomach. Scot doubled over in pain as Meg screamed. She tried to intervene, but another guard grabbed her arm and pulled her away to the other side of the room.

"I believe that is what the British call *witty repartee*, no? I can assure you I do not find it amusing at all. Do not forget, Mr. Harvath, who is in control here," said the bearded man as he removed his kaffiyeh and set it on the desk in front of him.

"And who would that would be?" asked Harvath as he struggled to his feet.

The man gave another command with his hand, and the guard struck Harvath once more; this time on his shoulder as he was trying to regain his balance. Harvath fell to his knees and, though he tried to stifle it, a deep groan of pain escaped his lips. Meg screamed for them to stop.

"We can do this as long as you wish, but I am not a very patient man, Mr. Harvath. You have information I want, and we will get it out of you sooner, rather than later."

Harvath looked up from where he knelt on the floor and said, "The only thing you have even the slightest chance of getting out of me is a very serious beating. I'm not telling you anything."

The man stood up from his chair and removed a long knife from inside the folds of his robe. He spoke as he began to make his way around the desk, "You will find, Mr. Harvath, that I am quite good at getting what I want with a knife."

"First of all, it's *Agent* Harvath to you, and second of all—" Harvath was interrupted by an unseen backhand from the guard.

Harvath tasted blood in his mouth and spat onto the guard's robes, saying in Arabic, "Let your mother clean that up for you."

The guard was incensed, and as he raised his rifle to bring it crashing down upon Harvath's head, a voice rang out from the back of the room.

"Enough!" it shouted. It was a woman's voice, but it hadn't come from Meg Cassidy.

47

The covered figure in the back of the room unwound a dusty kaffiyeh to reveal the face of one of the most beautiful women Scot Harvath had ever seen. Her long black hair tumbled down to her shoulders and framed the near perfect features of her face. She appeared neither Middle Eastern nor western, but somehow a mystical combination of the two that came together to form an otherworldly beauty.

Immediately, Harvath was drawn to her eyes, which had momentarily flashed deep black, but were now returning to an almost platinum color. *The assassin!* But she was a *woman*. Harvath didn't believe what he was seeing.

In perfect English with a hint of a British accent, she said, "You must forgive my brother. He is sometimes overzealous in his approach, but his intentions are admirable."

"Do not patronize me," spat the bearded man as he rolled up the sleeves of his robe so he could go to work on Harvath.

"Me? A simple woman? Patronize you? Oh, Hashim, please, do not think me so insubordinate," said the woman with a feigned curtsy.

The truth hit Harvath, hard. It took only a moment to sort it all out. "All this time that we were looking for Abu Nidal's son," he said, "and we should have been looking for—"

"His daughter, Adara Nidal," said the woman as she locked eyes with Harvath and made another curtsy, this one much more genuine.

"*Adara*," repeated Harvath. "Interesting name. It's Arabic for 'virgin,' isn't it?"

"And to the Jews, it means 'fire.' "

"Your father certainly was creative in naming you two."

The bearded man raised his knife and nodded toward the guards, who tightened their grip on Harvath. "We are wasting time."

"Leave him alone," Meg screamed.

"Of course," said Hashim, stopping in his tracks and turning to face Meg. "Mr. Harvath is very brave. He is a soldier and is most likely no stranger to pain. You, on the other hand, are different." Hashim Nidal ran the flat of his blade along Meg Cassidy's cheek until the point rested just underneath her eye. He applied just enough upward pressure to cause an involuntary fluttering of her lids.

"What do you want?" growled Harvath, struggling against the grip the guards had on him. "She doesn't know anything."

"Everyone knows something, Mr. Harvath. The question is how to arrive at the information, and I think I have found a way to make you more cooperative."

"Don't you touch her," snarled Harvath.

"You are commanding me?" said Hashim as he ran his hands over Meg's body.

"You will not defile that woman here. Not in my presence," said Adara.

"I will do what I like, where I like," replied the brother as he lowered his blade and ran it along the inside of Meg's thighs. Tears were now streaming down her face. The nightmare had once again returned.

"I'm not going to tell you again," warned Harvath. This was a torture worse than anything they could have dreamed for Meg, and Scot knew it. He strained against his captors with all of his might, but they held fast.

"Mr. Harvath, you are in no position to tell me what to do. As I told my sister, I do as I like, where I—"

His rant was interrupted by Adara, who, slipping unseen across the room as her brother's attention was riveted on Meg, landed a searing blow to the side of his head.

Enraged, the man spun on his sister, but she spoke first. "Your indiscretions have cost us dearly. I will not permit another. Agent Harvath will tell us what the Americans know about our plans. I guarantee you."

"You forget yourself, sister," said Hashim. His eyes smoldered and his face was flushed with embarrassment at being so demeaned.

"I forget nothing. Your place is not to disagree with me. Our father made clear—"

"Our father was a sick old man."

"How dare you?" hissed Adara. "You have sworn your loyalty and obedience."

Hashim Nidal hated to be seen taking orders from a woman, but he backed down. There was no question left as to who was in charge. He glared at his sister, who never broke eye contact. She commanded the guards in Arabic, and as Scot and Meg were herded out the opposite door, Hashim called after them in English, "We have only just begun. I will come for each of you later."

And I'll be waiting, thought Harvath.

48

The minute the guards locked Harvath in his room, his evasion-and-escape training took over. He needed to find something, anything, that could be used as a weapon or aid in their escape, and he needed to find it before Hashim Nidal came back for them.

Whoever had retrofitted the guest room as a glorified holding cell had done an extremely good job. Everything was either bolted to the floor or the wall. The holes that served as windows were barred from the outside, there were no accessible light fixtures, no springs in the mattress or the bed frame, and there wasn't even any glass in the bathroom.

An hour later, Harvath's search was interrupted by the sound of his door being unlocked. His time was up. He would have to face Hashim empty-handed.

When the door opened, he saw Meg standing in the hallway flanked by the same guards from earlier that day. "Where are we going?" he asked in Arabic. One of the men just motioned him outside with his assault rifle. Harvath shook his head, *No.*

The other guard grabbed a handful of Meg Cassidy's hair and yanked hard, causing her to cry out. Harvath gave in and came out of his room.

He and Meg were paraded down several hallways to an elaborate dining room. Muted frescoes adorned the walls, and a large chandelier hung from the arched ceiling. Two candelabras on a sideboard provided additional light. Sitting at the head of the long, rough wooden table eating her dinner was Adara.

"Quite lovely, isn't it?" she asked as the guards marched Scot and Meg to the head of the table and then took up positions behind them. "This whole complex was once a secret stronghold of the Knights of Saint John of Jerusalem. Colonel Gadhafi presented it to my father as a gift."

"Pretty generous guy," said Harvath.

"You'll find that generosity is a cornerstone of our culture. In fact, I am prepared to make you a very generous offer. But first, you must be hungry. How would you like something to eat?"

Adara Nidal rang a small silver bell next to her wine-glass, and a servant appeared. She gave him instructions in Arabic, and he quickly set two more places at the table.

"Please, sit," she said.

"We're not interested," replied Harvath.

"Please do not be impolite, Agent Harvath. You would do well to take advantage of my generosity. The alternatives are not very pleasant."

A rifle barrel jammed in his back encouraged Harvath to accept the woman's hospitality.

"Excellent," she said. "Yes, you sit there, Agent Harvath, and Ms. Cassidy will take the seat here next to me."

As Meg took her seat next to Adara, she noticed, a faint scent that she thought she recognized. Her thoughts, though, were disrupted when their hostess raised the bottle in front of her and asked, "Ms. Cassidy, may I pour you some wine? It's quite nice. A Frascati. Wine of the popes, they say. This is a Santa Teresa Superiore, one of the best."

"No thank you," replied Meg.

"That's too bad. What about you, Agent Harvath?"

"I'm not thirsty, thank you. Besides, I thought alcohol was forbidden by the Muslim faith."

"It is," answered Adara as she refilled her glass. "But there are certain pleasures in life which I am unwilling to forgo."

"Did your father know you drink?" asked Harvath.

"I don't wish to talk about my father. I would much rather talk about us. It has been quite an odyssey, hasn't it? You have followed me around the world."

"Indeed. Macau, Bern, Cairo, Chicago," said Harvath, rattling off the cities.

"And let's not forget Jerusalem," added Adara.

Harvath was taken completely off guard. How did she know about Jerusalem? The icy grip of death had been on the back of his neck, and he hadn't even felt it. He tried not to show his surprise. "*Jerusalem?* I haven't been there in a long time."

"Please, Agent Harvath. Let's not play games. At one point I stood right behind you. Had you been paying attention, you could have smelled my perfume. What were you doing there? What was your assignment? Were you sent to kill me? If so, you did a very bad job."

"If I had wanted to kill you, you would be dead, believe me," said Harvath, trying to use the illusion that America knew more than it did to his advantage. "I wasn't there to kill you. We wanted to know more about your operation. Why don't we talk about what you and your brother are planning."

"We have many plans, Agent Harvath. Many of which are the same, and many of which are not. We are two completely different people."

"You don't seem that different to me."

"Oh, yes, we are. And we always have been. When we were very young, my father used to play a game with us called Alquerque. I was quite skilled at it. Hashim was not. It demands a mind adept at strategy, which my brother does not have. I beat both my father and my brother repeatedly. Eventually, Hashim refused to play. My father spent nights on end playing Alquerque with me, virtually ignoring Hashim. It drove him mad with jealousy, and he tried to find other ways to impress my father and gain his attention."

"Did he find anything?"

"No. I always ran faster, jumped farther, and even shot better than he did. The point of the matter is that the only thing my brother surpassed me in was his love for Islam. My father saw it as a means of uniting people. I saw it as a boring, profitless pursuit, and had no time for it."

"It would seem your ability to speak English is another area in which you surpass your brother."

"My father sent me away to private boarding schools and eventually on to university at Oxford. By living in the West, I learned the ways of the West. Understanding the disposition of your enemy is one of the most necessary elements in conquering him."

Something clicked in Harvath's mind. Like picking a lock, a tumbler had fallen into place. It had something to do with Ari Schoen, but he didn't know what it meant. He just felt he was onto something. "Your father seemed to think of everything."

"I have him to thank for all of this, really," said Adara as she swept her arm and took in the room. "He realized early on that Hashim's love of Islam alone would not be enough to carry on everything that he had built, everything that he had worked so hard for. My brother is not a thinker. He is not a planner. He is ruled by his passions, and passions can be dangerous. Make no mistake, though, Agent Harvath. My brother may be a fanatic, but there's one thing he's fanatical for above all else—family. He'd die for me if he had to. Of that, I'm sure."

"That's interesting, especially since the organization was put into your care."

"Why?" said Adara as she took another sip of wine.

"Isn't it obvious? You're a woman."

"That was the added brilliance of my father's plan. Not only was I the most capable of doing what needed to be done, it was a move that would never be suspected by our enemies."

Harvath decided to change tack. "And Israel is one of those enemies?"

"Of course Israel is one of our enemies. It is our greatest enemy. Israel and all those who support it, especially America," she said.

Harvath could actually see her eyes darkening and turning color right in front of him. He had hit a nerve. A big raw one. "So the change in management hasn't altered the family's position on Israel."

"Nothing will ever change our position on Israel! We

were born with a hate for all of its people. It is in our blood."

"Nobody is born hating anything. You have to learn to hate. Who taught you? Your father?"

"You know so little. You know nothing of me and what my life has been. My father tried to teach us about the Jews. My brother took to it faster and with more conviction than I did. I had to learn the hard way."

"The hard way?" asked Harvath. "I don't understand."

"It is not for you to understand!" snapped Adara. There was a flash again of her eyes as they throbbed dark as night.

Calming herself, she turned her attention to Meg Cassidy as the servant reappeared with a large serving dish. "Ms. Cassidy, I can understand your saying no to the wine, but please do not say no to the main course. Having spent most of my life in the West, I am not partial to the dishes of the desert. It is extremely difficult for me to find the ingredients I need here. But, the difficulty only adds to the flavor of the food. If you try it, I think you will find this to be the best truffled lobster risotto you have ever had."

Harvath knew it was important for them to keep their strength up, so he answered the question in Meg's eyes with a nod of his head. The servant spooned out large portions onto each of their odd hand-painted plates, and they began to eat.

Soon, Adara Nidal began putting direct questions to Harvath about his operation. He knew it was only a matter of time. She wanted to know the extent of the United States's knowledge, how closely they were working with the Israelis, and who else was aiding them in their hunt to bring down the Abu Nidal Organization.

Harvath deftly parried and avoided every question. Adara was nearing the end of her patience. "Agent Harvath, you are testing the limits of my hospitality. Only if you cooperate can I provide you with good treatment."

"As captives," said Harvath as he waved off more food from the servant.

"Not as captives, as my guests. You would be shown every courtesy."

"Really? For how long?"

"Only time would be able to tell."

"I thought so."

"Agent Harvath, I know Ms. Cassidy possesses limited knowledge of your operation and your country's overall involvement, but if you do not cooperate with us, you've seen that my brother is not above using her to loosen your tongue."

"If you or your brother lay a hand on her, I guarantee it will be the last thing either of you ever do."

"Idle threats, the last refuge of a beaten man," said Adara, shaking her head.

"That wasn't a threat. It was a promise, and it was anything but idle."

Adara pushed herself back from the table and stood. "You do not frighten me, Agent Harvath."

"I should."

"Nevertheless, you do not. I will give you the rest of the night to think about what I have offered you. Either you choose to cooperate, or I will hand you *both* over to my brother in the morning and he will do things his way. The choice is entirely up to you. The guards will show you to your rooms."

With that, Adara Nidal turned and left the dining room. The guards stepped forward and escorted Scot and Meg back to their rooms. Just as they reached their doors, Harvath turned to Meg one last time to tell her everything was going to be all right. This time, though, it was different. She knew by looking in his eyes that he didn't really believe it.

49

When the guards locked Harvath back in his room, he knew he'd been blessed with the rarest of opportunities—a second chance. He went over the room again inch by inch, searching for anything he could use as a weapon. Out of frustration, he walked into the bathroom for the third time, and that's when inspiration struck.

It took several hours of digging at the grout with his fingernails, but Harvath finally was able to loosen one of the large square tiles and then remove it from the wall. He scored the back of it as best he could by rubbing the tile continuously across one of the metal flanges used to bolt his bed to the floor. Once the tile was scored, he placed the guide cut over the edge of the bed frame and punched down on the tile with his blanket-wrapped fist.

The tile broke perfectly, leaving a jagged, sharp edge. Harvath worked the bottom of the tile against the metal flange a little longer, fashioning a makeshift handle, which he then wrapped tightly with strips of cloth torn from his sheets.

He took a moment to sit back on his mattress and admire his handiwork. It wasn't pretty, but by prison-shiv standards, he had created quite a formidable weapon. Judging from the night sky outside his window, there were only a few more hours until daylight. Harvath didn't even want to begin to imagine what morning and Hashim Nidal might have in store for them.

A loose plan had begun forming in his mind. He tried to quiet all of the competing thoughts whirling in his head and focus on how he was going to get them out of this. If anything happened to Meg Cassidy, he'd never be able to forgive himself. She had suffered more than enough already.

A loud explosion broke Harvath's meditation and drew him across the room to the window. It was soon followed by another explosion and then another. They all sounded as if they were coming from the other side of the compound.

At first, Harvath wondered if the terrorists were doing some sort of oddball nighttime training, but discarded that idea when the lights dipped twice and then went out. The room was completely black, except for the faint glow of moonlight streaming in through the window. Harvath heard a commotion in the hallway and crossed from the window to that side of the room in three quick strides.

He pressed his ear up against the door and heard what sounded like retreating footsteps. He tried the handle of his door, but it was still locked from the outside. He couldn't be sure if Morrell had arrived to rescue them, but something was definitely happening.

He kept his ear against the door for several more minutes, but heard nothing. The explosions continued outside, but at wider intervals. They seemed to be coming from different directions.

With his shiv at the ready, Harvath finalized his plan. It wasn't the best one he'd ever conceived, but he figured trying it was a lot better than waiting for Hashim and his men to come take him down to the dungeon torture chamber that he knew in his bones this place possessed. If Morrell was somewhere outside, he'd need all the help he could get.

Scot began pounding on his door and calling out for the guard. He would keep the shiv hidden underneath his shirt until he could get close enough to one of the men and take him out. He would then try and take out the second guard and free Meg Cassidy. He calculated the odds and didn't like them, but they were a whole lot better than the potential alternative. The bottom line was that Adara and Hashim Nidal were never going to let Harvath or Meg leave the compound alive.

When he stopped pounding and pressed his ear up against the door again, he heard the faint sound of footsteps. Seconds later there was the sound of the bolt on the other side being drawn. Harvath had had no idea someone was that close. The footsteps had sounded much further off. He decided he would let the guards find him doubled over and maybe they would think he was ill. If he could get at least one, if not both of them, to lower his defenses for just a moment, that would be all the time he needed. He jumped back and readied his weapon.

The door swung open and blazing flashlight beams pierced the darkness. Then they turned off. Harvath could just make out several large forms entering the room in classic buttonhook fashion. They fanned out and cleared the room and bathroom area in less than five seconds. Harvath had no idea what was happening. He was surrounded by three heavily outfitted men in tactical gear with helmets and armed with silenced Mark Eleven Mod Zero assault rifles.

"Somebody order room service?" asked one of the men, whose face was covered with a black balaclava.

Harvath recognized the voice immediately. *It was Gor-*

don Avigliano! "Where the hell have you guys been?" asked Harvath.

"Long story," replied Avigliano. "I'll tell you in the car. Where's Ms. Cassidy?"

"Straight across the hall."

Avigliano handed Harvath a silenced forty-five-caliber H&K Special Operations Command pistol and some extra ammunition. Mounted on the rail beneath the barrel was a SureFire tactical light complete with pressure switch. With the pressure-sensitive switch affixed to the pistol's grip, you could activate the beam when, and only for as long, as you needed it.

"You look like shit," said Avigliano.

Harvath wanted to say that the Nidal family health spa left a lot to be desired, but he bit his tongue. The men formed an assault column known as the Conga Line, with each operative covering a different angle with their weapons.

Avigliano drew back the bolt on Meg Cassidy's door and cautiously pushed it open. Before he knew what was happening, Meg was flying at him with a large vase held high above her head. Since he was decked out in full tactical gear, she couldn't tell Avigliano was one of the good guys. He tried to blind her with the beam from his flashlight, but it was too late. Meg Cassidy had already locked on.

Avigliano raised his rifle just in time. The vase shattered against it sending shards of porcelain, water, and flowers in all directions.

One of Avigliano's teammates quickly wrestled Meg to the ground. "Ms. Cassidy, my name is DeWolfe. We're part of the Operation Phantom team. We're here to get you out."

Meg struggled underneath the large man, who had taken her down and pinned her arms behind her back in the blink of an eye.

"Where's Scot?"

"Scot?" asked DeWolfe.

"Harvath. Norseman," said Meg as she struggled to break free of the man's powerful grip.

Harvath came into the room and tapped DeWolfe on the shoulder. He let up on Meg. "I'm right here. Are you okay?" asked Harvath.

"Why the hell did he have to do that?" she asked as the men quickly swept the rest of the room.

"It was for your own protection."

"My protection?"

"It's just the safest way to do things. They didn't want you hurting them or yourself. I would have done the same thing."

"Thanks. I'll remember that."

"Can we do this later, Meg? Right now, let's focus on getting out of here."

"Roger that," said Avigliano from behind Harvath. "Let's beat feet."

"Where's the rest of the team?" asked Harvath as the men prepared to go back into the hall.

"This is it," replied Avigliano.

"What do you mean, 'this is it'?"

"We dropped in with the FAVs. Morrell instructed us to follow the truck you'd been loaded into after you got captured. Once we found out where they had taken you, we radioed back. The team was going to rendezvous with us, but Libyan soldiers are crawling all over the place. Nidal must have called them in. Morrell and the guys made it back to their FAVs, but got cut off. They couldn't get around the Libyans to get here and help out."

"So you pulled this off yourselves? Just the three of you?"

"And against orders. Morrell told us to pull out."

"*Pull out?*"

"He didn't want to risk it. He wanted to wait until we had regrouped before doing anything."

"I'm glad you didn't listen to him. Thanks for coming," said Harvath.

"The party's not over yet. I'd hold your *thank-you's* if I were you. Let's get out of here first."

"Amen. Let's roll."

The team snaked down the hall past the dining room. Suddenly, Avigliano held up a fist, signaling the team to come to an immediate stop. DeWolfe drew up shoulder to shoulder with Avigliano, and when Harvath and Meg's two guards came running around the corner, DeWolfe and Avigliano popped them both with silenced rounds to the head. The men fell straight to the ground, and their rifles clattered on the dark stone floor. Harvath wanted to grab their weapons, but as they weren't silenced, he knew they couldn't use them.

Avigliano waited several seconds before signaling that it was all clear to move out. As they passed the two lifeless forms sprawled on the ground, Harvath felt cheated. One of the guards was the man who had struck him several times while they were in the study. That feeling disappeared two minutes later when they entered the compound's enormous columned rotunda and Harvath saw a certain man before anyone else did.

It was the captain of the guard whom he had fought with the day before. The man had an AK-47 and was playing peekaboo from behind a pillar halfway across the room. There was no time to warn the rest of the group. In a fraction of a second, they would be trapped in his line of fire.

Harvath took a running slide across the slick marble floor and repeatedly pulled the trigger on his silenced H&K. The powerful gun bucked in his hand and tore huge chunks of stone from the column behind which the captain of the guard was hiding.

Avigliano and the rest of the team fanned out in all directions as they tried to shield Meg Cassidy and simultaneously spot any additional shooters.

As Harvath's slide came to a stop, the captain fell forward from behind the shelter of his column. He had taken two bullets to the chest and another through his left eye.

Once Harvath had replaced the spent magazine, he carefully approached the man and rolled him over. Definitely dead. Harvath retrieved his Rolex and went through the man's pockets until he found his knife too. "Now, we're finished," said Harvath to the dead man. "Say hi to Allah for me, asshole."

DeWolfe booby-trapped the body with two fragmentation grenades and rolled the dead man onto his stomach.

Harvath rejoined Avigliano, who had moved the team toward the entrance of the building. "How are we getting out of here?" asked Harvath.

"If we go out and pull a hard right, there's a narrow slot canyon. We've got a FAV stashed at the end of it about a mile-and-a-half down."

"Won't there be a little resistance outside?"

"Tons, but we've got that handled," said Avigliano as he drew a small transmitter from his pocket. "On three. One. Two. Three!"

Avigliano depressed the red and green buttons on his transmitter, and the team ran outside. Explosions ignited at the far end of the canyon, back toward where Harvath had first been held. The canyon floor was littered with dead bodies—the victims of previous explosions. There were still many men left, and they seemed to be running in all directions. It was mass chaos. Trucks drove this way and that, some men apparently fleeing, some trying to help put out the fires and locate the cause of the many explosions. Avigliano and DeWolfe silently took out several terrorists as they made their way to the canyon.

Fifteen yards in, Avigliano's third operative, a muscle-bound comedian named Carlson, removed two claymore mines from his backpack and handed one of them to Harvath. Where the claymore usually read, "Front Toward Enemy," Carlson had made a slight change. He had placed a long piece of masking tape with writing on it that read, "Have a Nice Day." Carlson flashed Harvath a thumbs-up and moved to the other side of the narrow canyon. Once the devices were set, the two men ran to catch up with the others.

Thirty seconds later they heard the sound of the fragmentation grenades detonating inside the rotunda. Someone had found the booby-trapped captain of the guard. Harvath hoped that Adara and her brother had stumbled across the body together, but he doubted they'd been that lucky.

The signature *clack-clack-clack* of AK-47 fire erupted from behind them in the canyon. Adara Nidal's men were hot on their trail.

The canyon was the most dangerous part of Avigliano's escape plan, as it acted like a funnel, channeling all of the terrorists' fire right at them. The only thing they could do was keep on running.

They then heard the sound of the claymores detonating behind them. Hailstorms of steel ball bearings propelled by the exploding hunks of C4, showered anyone within fifty meters in front of the antipersonnel devices. Agonizing screams followed from the few men who had actually survived, but had been torn to bits. This bought the team a little time, but not much.

Avigliano worked his radio, calling in their status, as his long legs kept propelling him forward. "Big John, Big John. This is Point Guard. We have the package. I repeat. We have the package. Kick the tires and light the fires. Point Guard out."

Harvath mouthed, *Big John?* to DeWolfe, who was running alongside Meg Cassidy and who answered, "That's our exfil," short for *exfiltration*.

It seemed to take an eternity to run the almost mile and a half, but suddenly, the canyon ended and opened up onto a wide, barren plain. Avigliano and his men quickly removed the camouflage netting that disguised their Fast Attack Vehicle.

"Where's the other FAV?" asked Harvath.

"That's it. There aren't any other ones," said Carlson as he handed Harvath and Meg encrypted radios with headsets. "We're going tisket-tasket."

Harvath knew what that meant. He and Meg would be

riding in the supply baskets on either side of the vehicle. Harvath quickly helped Meg secure her radio and then belted her into one of the baskets.

"She knows how to use one of these, right?" asked DeWolfe as he handed Meg his Mod Zero.

"I'm a fast learner," replied Meg, who grabbed the weapon with her right hand and held out her left for extra clips of ammunition.

Harvath hopped in the opposite basket and strapped himself into the modified shoulder straps. Carlson tossed him his Mod Zero, and in less than a minute they were rolling.

Avigliano was behind the wheel with DeWolfe sitting next to him manning the Mark 19 grenade launcher. Up top, Carlson had his choice of either the forward .50-caliber machine gun or a 7.62 millimeter covering their rear. In addition, he carried one Stinger antiaircraft missile as well as an AT4 antitank missile. As it turned out, they were going to need everything they had.

50

With an added fuel bladder, the FAV had a range of approximately five hundred miles. The amount of terrain Avigliano and his team had already covered to locate Harvath and Cassidy, coupled with the fact that there were now five people riding in the FAV, as opposed to the customary three, made for a drastic reduction in the vehicle's range.

The exfiltration plan called for the team to rendezvous with a Boeing MH-47 Chinook helicopter, code-named Big John. Flying low to avoid Libyan radar, the blacked-out copter would touch down in the uninhabited desert just south of the Tunisian border, drop its rear cargo door, and the team would drive the FAV right up the ramp. Then they would lift off and disappear like shadows in the night. That was the best-case scenario.

The northern edge of the Ubari Sand Sea was a combination of flowing sand dunes and rock-strewn gullies known as *wadis*. The FAV hammered the terrain, racing straight up numerous steep dunes and tearing straight down the opposite sides. After they crested what DeWolfe said was the last major dune on their topo-map, Harvath caught a flash of something in the distance. Engaging his lip mike, he said, "Contact. Eleven o'clock."

DeWolfe, the FAV's navigator, pulled a pair of night-vision binoculars out of a bag strapped down next to him. Though the team were all wearing night-vision goggles, the binoculars afforded greater range.

"What do you have?" asked Avigliano.

"Looks like five Land Rovers, each with 7.62s mounted up top. I'd be willing to bet they're Libyan regulars."

"Have they seen us?" asked Avigliano.

"Looks like it. They're changing course right now."

Upon hearing that piece of good news, Carlson, sitting in the rear, only had one response, "Fuck."

"What's going on?" asked Meg.

"Little change of plans," said Harvath.

"Hold on, everybody," yelled Avigliano as he pulled the wheel hard to the right and steered the FAV in a new direction.

"We don't have enough fuel for this, Gordo," said DeWolfe.

"We're just going to have to set a new rendezvous point with Big John."

"Big John is already coming deeper into uncle Mu'ammar's backyard than he wants to."

"Tough shit. He's going to have to come in further," said Avigliano.

"Roger that. Should we tell him we've got company?"

"You bet your ass. Tell him it's going to be a hot exfil."

DeWolfe picked a location five miles ahead and radioed the coordinates to Big John.

No longer concerned with fuel consumption, Avigliano pinned the accelerator to the floor. An enormous sand dune loomed in front of them, and they took it at full speed.

As they hit the top of the dune, they found themselves in midair. Instead of a gradual descent down the other side, the dune was backed up against the rugged slope of an incredibly steep drop-off leading into a deep wadi. The FAV launched off the dune and hung in the air for what seemed like an eternity, before crashing onto a treacherously inclined hill of loose and shifting rock.

Avigliano strained against the wheel, trying to prevent the FAV from flipping over. Jagged boulders reached out on both sides and attempted to tear the vehicle to pieces. Avigliano finally got control, but only for a few moments. He attempted to steer it toward the floor of the wadi, but something was wrong. He thought for a moment that the problem was due to the unstable scree that they were driving down. He gave the FAV more gas, then more still. It picked up speed, but it had stopped responding to the steering wheel altogether.

A small dune appeared to their left, and almost as if of its own accord, the FAV headed right for it. Avigliano tapped the brakes, but in the wash of loose rocks, that only sent the back end fishtailing out of control as they continued to pound down the hill.

"Brace yourselves!" he yelled. "We're going in hard!"

Hard was an understatement. Seconds later, they hit the dune at full speed. Shoulder belts dug into flesh and heads snapped forward, then came racing back. The steering wheel saved Avigliano, but DeWolfe was not as lucky. Despite his shoulder harness and helmet, he hit his head hard enough to be knocked unconscious. Carlson slammed his left shoulder against the fifty-caliber machine gun. After the HAHO jump and the beating he had taken at the hands of Adara Nidal's guards, Harvath was sore all over, but no one area seemed to be any worse now than before the crash. He unbuckled himself from the basket and ran around the FAV to Meg who was already undoing her own straps.

"You okay?" asked Harvath.

"Aside from the fact that my rear end feels like I've been on a two-year trail ride, I guess I'm doing okay. My shoulders hurt like hell from that harness, though."

"But nothing's broken? You're not bleeding?"

"No. No breaks. No bleeding."

"Good. Let's help the others."

Harvath and Avigliano removed DeWolfe from the FAV, careful to support his neck and shoulders in case he had suffered any spinal trauma. Carlson got himself out of the FAV while Harvath hopped back in and tried to back the vehicle off of the sand dune.

The tires began to catch, but the right front wheel wasn't responding. Harvath laid on the pedal a little heavier as Avigliano ran to his side of the vehicle. He signaled Harvath to take his foot off the gas while he examined the wheel.

"We snapped the CV shaft. This thing's not going anywhere," said Avigliano as he stood up and dusted the sand from his fatigues. He checked his GPS and continued, "Let's get some cover, and I'll call in Big John."

No sooner had Avigliano spoken than a wall of bullets tore up the ground all around them.

Three of the Libyan Land Rovers had taken up positions above them, and the occupants were firing into the wadi with their 7.62s. Everyone took cover behind the ditched FAV.

"Is this any way to treat visitors to their country?" remarked Carlson.

Avigliano was already calling in Big John to their position.

"Big John is on his way. We just need to hold them until he gets here," said Avigliano.

Meg, who had been taking a look at Carlson, said, "I think he's got a broken collarbone."

"I break bones. I don't get mine broken," said Carlson as Harvath slid over to him.

The minute Harvath applied pressure to Carlson's left collarbone area, the pain was so intense the man almost blacked out.

"Well, bone crusher, this time you're the breakee," said Harvath as he instructed Meg on how to make up a sling for Carlson.

With DeWolfe still unconscious, that left only Harvath, Avigliano, and Meg to hold off what would soon be five Land Rovers full of Libyan soldiers.

Harvath swung out from behind the FAV with his Mod Zero and, setting the fire selector to *single*, took several well-aimed shots. Two Libyans, dumb enough to be standing in front of their Rovers looking down into the small canyon, were hit. Though their wounds might not have been fatal, it showed the rest of the soldiers that Harvath and his team were a force to be reckoned with.

It didn't take the Libyans long to regroup. Soon, machine-gun fire rained down on them from both sides of the canyon. The other two Land Rovers had arrived and took up positions on the high ground on the other side of the wadi.

During a lull in the firing, Harvath unhinged the 7.62 from the back of the FAV. He would have liked to have taken down the fifty or the Mark 19, but it would have been too difficult. He grabbed as much ammo as he could, and when he let loose with it, all of the Libyans, on both walls of the wadi, ran for cover.

Avigliano called Big John for an ETA, but he was still twenty minutes out. According to an AWAC the U.S. had in the area, the team had bigger problems. Two Libyan helicopter gunships were en route to their position.

"Ah, Scot?" said Avigliano.

"I'm kinda busy, Gordo," said Harvath as he let loose with another deafening volley from the 7.62 machine gun.

"We're going to have company real soon," said Avigliano once Harvath stopped to reload the 7.62.

"Animal, vegetable, or mineral?" asked Harvath as he readied new ammunition.

"Aerial. We've got an AWAC monitoring our situation. It looks like two Alouette helicopters."

"Complete with twenty-millimeter cannons, rocket pods, and surface-to-air missiles?" said Harvath as if it were a standard sight in the desert.

"Probably a good chance of that."

"How far out?"

"Five minutes. Tops."

"What did Carlson say when the Libyans first spotted us?"

" '*Fuck*'?" asked Avigliano.

"Yeah, *fuck*."

Harvath let loose with another long burst of fire along both sides of the ridge before turning back to Avigliano. "How's DeWolfe?"

"He's still out."

"All right then. Here's the deal. You and Meg are going to have to move him."

"*Move him?* Move him where?"

Harvath took another glance around and found what he was looking for. "That outcropping. Twenty meters to our left. I'll lay down cover fire for you. Once you're there, you'll be safe."

"What about you?"

"I'm going to take care of those inbound helicopters."

"Are you crazy?"

"Nope. I'm going to send Carlson over to the far side of the wadi to cover my left flank. You and Meg will cover my right from that outcropping. Those Libyan birds will have no choice but to fly right down the center of the canyon. They expect us all to be right here huddled behind the FAV. That's what the pilots will be targeting. Between you, Meg, and Carlson, the soldiers up above won't be able to get a shot off. We've got one Stinger and one AT4. I'm hoping that will be enough to do the trick."

"And if it isn't?"

"Big John better beat his ETA."

Harvath explained his plan to the others, and everyone made ready. When there was a pause in the Libyan machine-gun fire from the ridge above, Harvath gave the "Go" command. He rolled out from behind the FAV and swung the big 7.62-millimeter machine gun back and forth across the top of wadi, spraying the Libyan Land Rovers full of lead. Once Gordy and Meg had gotten DeWolfe safely to the outcropping, he laid off the trigger and rolled back behind the safety of the FAV.

The next thing he needed to do was unstrap the missiles

from the roof rack. Harvath activated his lip mike and said, "Let's keep it to short bursts to save on ammo. I need to get the Stinger and AT4 off the roof. When I count to three, give them something to chew on, okay? One. Two. Three!"

Carlson started firing first, followed by Avigliano and then Meg. They were each at separate sides of the wadi, with Harvath and the FAV stuck right in the center. He wasted no time and used the distraction for all it was worth. He quickly climbed into the backseat and unfastened the straps that secured the two shoulder-fired missiles to the roof. With one in each arm, he jumped out of the vehicle and hid back behind the defunct front wheel.

"Cease fire," commanded Harvath over their encrypted radio. "Now, let's let them come to us."

The wait wasn't as long as it seemed. The Libyan helicopters made it to their location ahead of schedule. Harvath kneeled on the ground less than two feet away from the FAV. The minute the choppers swung into the narrow valley, he could hear their cannons chewing up the canyon floor. With his right hand on the Stinger and the parallel trails of bullets racing toward him, Harvath followed a procedure so well known to him he could do it in his sleep.

First, he primed the system by clamping down on the lever that lit the battery and charged the ignition system. He waited as the two helicopters grew closer and closer with every passing second. The rows of cannon fire seemed to only be yards away when Harvath yanked the Stinger from the ground next to him and slapped it onto his shoulder. He centered the first chopper in the Stinger's viewfinder and depressed the large button on the front of the launcher tube, uncovering the seeker head of the missile.

A tone indicated he had target lock as the missile began to grumble inside the tube. Harvath reflexively looked behind him to make sure all was clear, and with no one behind him and nothing close enough to reflect the exhaust blast, Harvath squeezed the trigger and said, "One away."

A cloud of white gas erupted from the back of the tube as the Stinger raced toward the Libyan helicopter. By the time the pilot realized what was happening, it was too late. The rocket slammed into the first chopper and turned it into a torrent of fire and debris that rained down onto the floor of the wadi. Fearing another missile attack was right behind, the second French-made Alouette pulled up and out of the narrow canyon. They had caught a break, but Harvath knew it wouldn't last long.

51

Harvath adopted the lowest profile he could as machine-gun rounds slammed into the dune-buggy-like frame of the FAV. For a moment, he had toyed with the idea of trying to physically drag the nose of the vehicle around so that they could answer the Libyan soldiers with some forty-millimeter grenade rounds from the Mark 19. That idea, though, even in Harvath's book, was pure suicide.

"How's everyone doing on ammo?" asked Harvath over his Motorola, during a lull in the shooting.

"There's never enough at a time like this," said Carlson.

"I take it you're running low. How about you and Meg, Gordo?"

"I don't suppose in the spirit of fair play, the Libyans would be willing to toss a little down here."

"Are you kidding? They're more than happy, as long as it's delivered via the end of their rifles," quipped Carlson.

At least morale hasn't suffered, thought Harvath.

"We do have some good news," offered Meg Cassidy.

"We can all use some of that," replied Harvath. "What is it?"

"DeWolfe is awake."

"How's he doing?"

"He's a little groggy, but it doesn't look like he's suffered any serious injuries. Arms and legs work, and he thinks he'll be able to walk."

"Ask him if he's hungry," interjected Carlson over his headset.

There was a pause, and then Meg came back. "He says he's got the stomach to eat if Carlson has the balls to go get the pizza."

"I knew it," said Carlson. "He's fine."

"How far out is Big John, Gordo?" asked Harvath.

"Ten minutes until they're on-site."

"Tell them to hurry up. Any minute now, that other . . . Scratch that. They're back."

Off in the distance, Harvath could distinctly hear the remaining Alouette helicopter as it lined up for another run down the canyon. Seeing their buddies blown to bits had scared off the pilots of the second craft, but Harvath had known it wouldn't last. He also knew that this time, the Alouette would come at them with everything it had.

Just as the helicopter entered Harvath's field of vision, the pilots killed their lights. The thunder of the rotors reverberated off the canyon walls as the attack helicopter sped toward them. Harvath had anticipated their move and had grabbed the helmet and night-vision goggles DeWolfe had left behind in the FAV.

He flipped the goggles down, and the night now glowed an eerie green as he got a fix on the speeding Alouette. Its twenty-millimeter canons and machine-gun pods were blazing, and he knew it was only a matter of seconds before the pilots loosed their air-to-surface missiles.

The two major drawbacks to Harvath's remaining AT4 antitank missile were that it was made for tanks, not aircraft, and that the weapon had no optics on it at all. Harvath did the best he could to line up his target, and without a second thought, let the powerful missile fly.

The bright ignition flash, as well as the phosphorus gas stream that followed the weapon as it streaked toward the Alouette, sent the pilots into immediate evasive action. They banked the helicopter into a steep turn, but it wasn't steep enough. The missile ripped into the craft's tail section and detonated, shearing away the rear rotor. The Alouette spun wildly out of control for several seconds until it careened into the high wall of the wadi and exploded, sending shards of searing metal in all directions.

As the Libyan soldiers bolted for cover, Avigliano ran over to Harvath and began yanking things out of the vehicle. "We're going to have to blow the FAV in place," he said as he threw a small bag to Harvath. "Big John says uncle Mu'ammar's got more men heading in our direction, and it looks like they're scrambling jets out of Tripoli."

"Super," said Harvath. "What else could go wrong?"

"How about this? With all the heat, Big John can't land in the wadi. They're dropping a rope and we're going out FRIES."

"Ask a stupid question . . ." mumbled Harvath as he unzipped the bag, knowing full well what he'd find inside.

FRIES was a military acronym for Fast Rope Insertion/Extraction System. Harvath had learned the technique when he was in the SEALs, where it was called SPIE, short for Special Purpose Insertion and Extraction, but no matter what you called it, there was one thing Harvath knew for sure—Meg Cassidy was not going to like it.

Harvath pulled out two nylon FRIES harnesses from the bag and asked, "How about some Valium?"

"I thought you were a tough guy," said Avigliano as he finished placing his explosive charges throughout the FAV.

"It's not for me. It's for our friend, Ms. Cassidy. She's afraid of heights."

"Then I suggest you don't tell her until the very last possible moment. I'll cover you with the 7.62. Get over there and get her geared up."

Harvath flashed Avigliano a thumbs-up and took off toward the outcropping the minute he heard the heavy machine gun open up.

DeWolfe was feeling well enough to be taking shots at the Libyans with his Mod Zero and helped lay down enough cover fire for Harvath to get across to their end of the wadi. As soon as he got to Meg Cassidy, he handed her one of the FRIES rigs.

"What's this?" she asked.

"A harness. Now watch how I put mine on, and do the same," replied Harvath.

"What do I need a harness for?"

"Safety."

"Safety for what?"

"Meg, I really don't have time for this now. In case you haven't noticed, there's people up there trying to kill us."

"Scot, what the hell is going on?"

So much for not telling her, he thought. "The helicopter can't land in this area. They're going to lower a rope for us. You clip your harness to it and it pulls you up."—*with everybody else, and we fly away beneath the helicopter like five fish on a stringer,* but she'd realize that soon enough. That harness was their only ticket out of Libya.

"Like when the Coast Guard picks up somebody out of the water and reels them in?"

"More or less," said Harvath. He hated not being completely truthful with her, but he knew it was the only way Meg would go along with things.

"Which one? *More* or *less?*" she demanded.

"Take your pick. Listen, we don't have time for this. Our helicopter is going to be here in a matter of minutes and we both have to be ready to move, so watch me closely and do exactly as I do."

Harvath finished tightening his FRIES harness and inspected it, then inspected Meg's and DeWolfe's. Everyone was good to go. He radioed Avigliano, who told him to stand by. Big John was less than a minute away.

It was amazing to Harvath that he could not yet hear the enormous Chinook, but that was part of the pilots' M.O. If things went well, you had no idea they were there until they were right on top of you.

Soon enough, the roar of the big MH-47's rotors was all you could hear. That, and the deafening fire from the Dillon Miniguns, manned by door gunners on both sides of the helicopter, who were throwing down deadly blankets of fire.

As Big John made repeated passes to strafe the Libyan soldiers, Carlson ran out into the wadi with pockets full of Chem-lights to mark their makeshift landing zone. Once Avigliano got the word from Big John that he was coming in to drop the rope, the team made their way toward the LZ.

There was a loud, blowing wind as the Chinook swept in, flared, and then hovered above the wadi. Sheets of sand hitting the rotors gave off sparks making them appear greenish white in the night sky.

One of the Chinook's crew kicked the heavy FRIES rope out the door, and Harvath and the rest of the team let it hit the ground and stay there for several seconds. Because helicopters weren't grounded, they generated a tremendous amount of static electricity, which made it necessary to allow the rope to discharge the current before touching it.

Loops were staggered along the thick rope, and Harvath took up the first position, where he rapidly locked his harness in with a heavy metal D ring. Out in the open, even with the heavy fire from the door gunners up above, they were all still sitting ducks. Next on the line came Meg, then Carlson, DeWolfe, and finally Avigliano. Once everyone was clipped in, Avigliano blew the FAV with a remote detonator. He then signaled the pilot with an infrared beam, and the Chinook began its quick ascent.

The key to a hot FRIES extraction was to keep one hand on the rope and the other on your weapon, so you could return fire at the enemy. Harvath, DeWolfe, and Avigliano, along with the gunners in the MH-47, gave the Libyans every single thing they had. With a broken collarbone, it was all Carlson could do to hold on, and it made him madder than hell that he wasn't able to shoot anybody.

Meg Cassidy's sheer terror of the FRIES extraction was rivaled only by her newfound hate for Scot Harvath. By the time they had crossed the Tunisian border, she had vowed to herself not only to never trust him again, but never to speak to him either.

52

The new United States Embassy in Tunisia's capital, Tunis, was located at the intersection of the La Marsa Highway and the road to La Goulette—literally *the gullet*, which connected the Gulf of Tunis to Tunisia's main seaport. The sprawling, intricately landscaped compound occupied approximately twenty-one acres and included a chancellery, guardhouses, motor pool, commissary, low-rise office building, warehouse, shops, Marine barracks, recreation center, and embassy staff town houses. All U.S. Embassy operations for Tunisia were headquartered there. Some might wonder why the U.S. needed such a large compound in Tunisia, but Harvath knew the answer.

The embassy served as a major intelligence-gathering center. Its off-limits areas, with raised floors and next-generation satellite listening-and-surveillance equipment, ran at a frenetic pace day and night as operatives tried to stay three steps ahead of everything that was happening in "their corner of the world." From this forward outpost, the United States monitored, collected, and processed sensitive information regarding most of the Mediterranean, North Africa, and the Middle East. Almost the entire staff was on either the NSA's or CIA's payroll, and it was no surprise to Harvath that after their extraction from Libya, this was where they had been brought for debriefing.

It had been intense. Though Harvath tried to interject on his behalf, Gordon Avigliano took quite a verbal beating from Rick Morrell for coordinating the unapproved rescue operation. To Avigliano's credit, he shielded his two fellow operatives from most of the heat and claimed sole responsibility for disobeying a direct order from his superior. Harvath was seeing, yet again, a different side to the CIA and, in particular, the Special Activities Staff. He was beginning to think that his earlier assumptions about the group as a whole might have been wrong.

The debriefing was an endless session of finger-pointing and shouting. Harvath was repeatedly blamed for screwing up the operation by going in too close and getting captured. Though Harvath claimed that they had acquired excellent intelligence, Morrell would hear nothing of it. Morrell was certain that even if Abu Nidal had a daughter, there was no way she would ever be put in charge of his organization. At best, the whole scenario, stated Morrell, was established to put Harvath off-guard to get information from him that would be useful to Hashim Nidal.

Round and round the debriefing went until Harvath was excused from the room so Morrell and his men, along with the Tunisia CIA station chief, could finish the meeting in private. Harvath didn't like being shut out, but it had also been over forty-eight hours since he'd had any sleep. As he got up to leave, he asked for access to one of the embassy's other secure conference rooms to make a telephone call.

"If you're looking for a secure line," responded the station chief, "you can use the STU in my office."

Harvath wanted a secure telephone unit, all right, but he also wanted to be in a room where he was guaranteed no one would overhear his conversation. "I need to make a report to the president. I'm sure you can appreciate my desire to keep the conversation private."

Once an aide had shown him to the secure conference room and the double doors had locked behind him, Harvath made himself comfortable at the head of the table and picked up the STU. He dialed Gary Lawlor's direct number at FBI headquarters in D.C. by heart.

"Deputy Director Lawlor's office, may I help you?" Lawlor's assistant, a woman Harvath had known for years named Emily Hawkins, picked up on the second ring.

"Emily, it's Scot Harvath. Is Gary in?"

"Hi, Scot. Where in the world are you?"

"U.S. Embassy, Tunis. I'm on the STU. I don't mean to be short, but I need to talk with Gary right away."

"He's not here right now."

"Where is he? Can you patch me through to his cell?"

"He's with the president at the White House. They're in the situation room. I can put a call in and interrupt if it's that important."

Harvath thought about it for a second. He needed to talk to Lawlor and find out what was going on back in Washington, but the last thing he wanted to do was interrupt a meeting with the president. "Any idea when the meeting is supposed to end?"

"It could be a while. The FBI arrested three terrorists this morning in D.C. who were plotting to detonate a dirty bomb. Apparently, they were one of Hashim Nidal's sleeper cells, and there's reason to believe other attacks were planned to go off at the same time in multiple cities around the country."

"Did they say when the attacks were supposed to happen?"

"The only thing being said right now is that they were in the advanced planning stages and that radioactive and bomb-making materials were discovered at two of the men's apartments."

"As soon as you talk to Gary, please have him contact me at the embassy here."

"Will do. You take care of yourself."

"You too."

Harvath reset the STU and dialed his home phone in Alexandria. The last message on his voice mail was a series of discordant digital tones, which signaled he had messages waiting on his secure cell phone. Once again he reset the STU, and this time dialed his digital phone, which had been left behind in Alexandria, per Morrell's orders. He had one message waiting. Harvath pressed 1, to play the message.

"Agent Harvath, this is Ari Schoen. I have been trying for some time to get hold of you. I have been hesitant to leave a message, but I think it is of the utmost importance that we speak. Please return my call. You already have my number."

Schoen? After what Frank Mraz had said about him possibly being involved with the Hand of God attacks, Harvath had decided to avoid him. But what if he wasn't involved? What if Schoen was one of the good guys? What if Mraz was wrong? What if Mraz wasn't telling him the truth?

Harvath figured there was no harm in calling Schoen back and seeing what he had come up with. He dialed the secure number Schoen had given him. After several rings, the voice with the pronounced lisp answered, "Thames &

Cherwell Antiques." Another tumbler fell into place in Harvath's mind.

"Ari, it's Scot Harvath. I received a message you might have information for me."

"You are on a secure line?"

"Trust me. I could not be any more secure than I am right now."

"Agent Harvath," lisped the voice. "It is good to hear from you. I was beginning to wonder if you were ever going to contact me again. I thought we had an agreement. A sort of quid pro quo."

"I apologize, Mr. Schoen. I have been . . . how shall I put it?—very busy of late."

"So I've heard. You haven't been pestering any of our mutual friends in Libya lately, have you?"

Nothing amazed Harvath anymore, especially in the world of intelligence, but even so, Schoen had some incredibly well-placed sources if he had already heard about the Operation Phantom attempt in Libya. If Schoen knew enough to mention Libya, then he probably had at least part of the bigger picture. Harvath decided to play along. "Funny you should mention Libya, Ari."

"I'm guessing," said Schoen, "that you were unsuccessful in completing your assignment."

"Why would you say that?"

"Well, if you had, you would never have bothered returning my call."

"Touché."

"So you were unsuccessful, then."

"Not completely."

"What do you mean?"

"We learned something quite remarkable. We have reason to believe that the Abu Nidal Organization is not headed by his son, but by his—"

"Daughter," completed Schoen.

Harvath was completely shocked. "How did you know?"

"It's a very long and complicated story, Agent Harvath. Did you actually see her? The one with the silver eyes?"

"Yes, I did, but how did you—"

"Where is she now? Is she still in Libya?"

"She has probably already left."

"Do you know where she was going?"

"We don't know that yet. Listen, if you knew there was a daughter involved with all of this, why didn't you say so?"

"Have you told the CIA what you discovered?"

"Of course," said Harvath.

"And what was their response?"

Harvath began to see why Schoen might have been holding back on him. "Though they didn't say it in so many words, they think it's nuts. They don't believe Abu Nidal would have turned the organization over to a daughter, even if he had one. What's more, they said none of Nidal's men would ever take orders from a woman."

"And by now you know about both the sister and the brother?"

"Yes."

"Good," said Schoen as a long pause occupied the scrambled phone line.

"Good? Is that all you can say? This isn't exactly quid pro quo."

"I can say the same for you, Agent Harvath. You have not been fully forthcoming with me either. Where have they gone?"

"I don't know. What I do know is that despite what I told them, the CIA is still focusing on Hashim, the brother," said Harvath, trying to fit the pieces together in his mind.

"Let the CIA chase him. He's not the one you want. It's her."

"And you want her too, don't you, Ari?"

"I want her more than you will ever know, Agent Harvath."

"Then tell me what you know."

"It is not much, but maybe it will prove useful. Abu Nidal had a longtime friend and financial partner—an extremely wealthy Moroccan named Marcel Hamdi. We had him under surveillance in Marbella, Spain, where his yacht, the *Belle Étoile*, left the Puerto Banus two days ago. I'm going to have my people post the surveillance materials for you within a web site we occasionally use."

"What does that have to do with Nidal's daughter?"

Schoen was a very bright man and no stranger to manipulating people. He was sure that the CIA had informed Harvath that they believed he was connected to the Hand of God attacks. He had to play his hand very carefully. If he could stall Harvath long enough to get the cooperation he needed, then nothing else would matter. And the way to do that was to tell Harvath almost everything he knew.

"Hamdi is like a second father to her. We intercepted a communication that we thought might have been from her, but couldn't be sure. Then the *Belle Étoile* left Marbella heading east. Yesterday, Hamdi stopped in the open ocean and was met by a seaplane. One of his bankers from the Palma de Mallorca branch of Deutsche Bank boarded the yacht with two large suitcases for him. Those suitcases contained over fifteen million U.S. dollars, cash. From what our sources tell us, Hamdi and the *Belle Étoile* are headed for an island somewhere off the southern coast of Italy."

"Where? Sicily? Sardinia? Corsica? Which island?"

"That's the problem, Agent Harvath. At this point, we have absolutely no idea."

53

Harvath tried to connect Schoen's new dots as he walked back to the staff town house where he and Meg were staying. The door to her room was slightly ajar and as he looked in, he could see she was sleeping. It was just as well, she probably still wasn't speaking to him. He walked quietly down the hall to his room, popped several Tylenols, and fell asleep the minute he hit his bed.

Later that afternoon, Harvath awoke to the smell of fresh brewed coffee. When he entered the kitchen, he found Meg sitting at a small table dressed in civilian clothes and reading a day-old copy of *The International Herald Tribune*.

"Did you get a good sleep?" she asked, folding the paper and setting it on the counter behind her.

"Good enough for now. Is that coffee I smell?"

"Yup, Starbucks even. I got it at the commissary, along with some croissants and a paper. Help yourself."

"You get the clothes there too?"

"No, an embassy staffer brought them over. I guessed at your sizes. Yours are on the chair in the hall."

"Thanks."

"You're welcome."

"So, you're talking to me again?" said Harvath as he found a cup and poured himself some coffee. The kitchen window had a nice view of a small courtyard outside.

Meg paused before responding. "You could have told

me what was going to happen. I kept waiting for the helicopter to reel us in because you made it seem like it was going to be like one of those Coast Guard rescues. You lied to me."

"Let's just say I didn't paint the full picture."

Meg tore off a small piece of croissant before responding. "I guess I owe you a thank-you."

"I guess you do."

"Well, thanks."

"Well, you're welcome," said Harvath.

Meg knew the helicopter extraction had been their only means of escape, and she also knew that her being angry with Harvath was just a way of ignoring the anger she felt with herself. It was her fault that they had gotten captured and that the mission had been botched, but what was done was done. They could only move forward.

"How'd the debriefing go?" she asked, trying to change the subject.

Harvath stared absentmindedly over the top of his coffee cup at her. Even after everything they had been through, she was still incredibly beautiful. Here they were sharing coffee, croissants, and the morning paper at this little breakfast table as they skirted an argument and Meg tried to steer the conversation in another direction. The whole scene was almost too surreal for Harvath.

"Not good," he replied as his mind slipped from fantasy back to reality.

"Not good how?"

"Morrell refuses to believe that a woman is running Abu Nidal's organization."

The indignation rose in Meg's voice as she slammed her

coffee cup down. "But we saw her. We talked to her! He has no idea. He wasn't there."

"And he doesn't seem to care."

"Why the hell couldn't a woman be manning the operation?"

Harvath smiled at her choice of words. "It's completely out of keeping with Islam and their male-dominated society. Muslim men, especially extremists, will not take orders from a woman."

"But they don't. They take them from the brother. He's the puppet and she pulls the strings."

"I told them all of that, and they wouldn't listen."

"What about the fact that you could connect her to all of those assassinations around the globe."

"A woman as an assassin, that they could accept, but it still doesn't make her their main focus. They see the brother as being in charge, and for the time being, that's where all their resources are going to be placed."

"So what's next?"

"I've given them detailed descriptions of both Hashim and his sister. The CIA is gathering all the materials they can from Oxford, and you and I are going to review every last scrap of it to see if maybe she slipped up and allowed herself to be photographed at some point during her time there."

"If she was ever there," said Meg.

"She could have been lying, but I don't think so."

"Is Morrell going to send another team back into the camp to try and take them out?"

"From what we can tell, the camp has been abandoned."

"*Abandoned?* Why?"

"I don't think there's a terrorist on this planet that isn't familiar with what we did to the Al Qaeda training camps in Afghanistan. Our satellites picked up a lot of vehicles leaving, followed by several very large explosions."

"From Avigliano?"

"No. These were explosions Adara's people set off afterward to cover their tracks. I'm guessing that whatever sensitive equipment or information they couldn't move out of there right away, they destroyed."

"So what happened to the two of them?"

"Now that we're on to them, Gadhafi won't be much help anymore. I've got to imagine we're already ramping up to teach him a lesson for harboring them. Adara and Hashim Nidal are probably going to be hotfooting it out of Libya real soon. For all we know, they're already gone. Which begs the question, *where* are they going?"

"With the list of places we know Adara has already been, the answer is *anywhere*."

"I know, and that's our biggest problem. I have a source that's been watching an old friend of the Nidal family and thinks Adara might have made contact with him. Shortly thereafter his yacht was seen leaving port."

"Which port?"

"Puerto Banus. It's on the Costa del Sol."

"Near Marbella, I know it. Where was it headed?"

"That's where it starts to get like a needle in a giant haystack. According to my source, the yacht was headed for an island somewhere off the southern coast of Italy."

"*Italy?* Maybe your haystack's not as big as you think," said Meg as she set down her coffee cup. She walked into the living room, retrieved an atlas from the bookshelf, and brought it back to the table.

Harvath watched her flip pages until she found the one she wanted and spun the book around so he could see it. "There," she said.

Her finger was resting on a small island west of Naples named Capri. "Why do you think this is our island?" asked Harvath.

"It's a hunch, but so many signs point to it, it's got to mean something."

"What signs?"

"When Adara made us have dinner with her, she said something about being so close to you in Jerusalem that you could have smelled her perfume."

"So?"

"Well, each time she leaned in my direction, I could smell her perfume, and I recognized it."

"You did?"

"Not only that, but remember when you guys came into my room and I mistakenly hit Avigliano with the vase?"

"Yeah. My room was totally bare. Never in a million years would they have left something behind that I could have used as a weapon."

"My room was bare too, but Adara brought me the flowers herself."

"Why'd she do that?"

"I think she was trying to put me further at ease, but that's not important. When the vase broke on Avigliano's rifle, we were both splashed. It took a few minutes, but that's what reminded me. I could smell the flowers on me from the water."

Harvath reached for a croissant, and said, "I'm not following."

"When I studied in Rome, we spent spring break on the island of Capri. There's a story about how the prior of a local monastery created a perfume out of water from a vase filled with the island's most beautiful flowers. When I was there, I bought some. It's manufactured exclusively on the island from twenty-five different types of Capri flowers."

"And that's what Adara Nidal was wearing?"

"Yes. It's called *Caprissimo*."

"Maybe she knows someone who gets it for her. Maybe she bought it in a duty-free shop at the airport in Milan while changing planes."

"There was also a picture of Capri in her study," said Meg, impatient with Harvath for not following her train of thought.

"What picture?" answered Harvath, his mind racing back to one of the pictures that was still sticking with him, but for what reason, he didn't know.

"There was a very provocative picture of her in a bathing suit on a yacht. I'm actually surprised you missed it."

"Another picture had caught my attention. What did you see?"

"The one I saw showed Adara sunning herself on the back of a boat with the *Faraglioni* in the background."

"What is the *Faraglioni*?"

"They're three huge rocks jutting out of the ocean on the southern coast of the island."

"Do you remember anything else about the picture?" asked Harvath. "Were there other people in it? Could you see the name of the boat, or anything else in the background?"

Meg was silent as she tried to remember the details of the photo.

"You saw Adara and you saw the *Faraglioni*," said Harvath, trying to coax her memory. "How do you know she was on a yacht?"

"She was sitting on a long white leather banquette, and the picture was taken from out on the ocean looking back at the island."

"What else did you notice? C'mon, Meg, think." There had to be more. Something that could validate Schoen's information and tell them that they were on the right track.

"I think the boat was either moving or it was windy."

"Why?"

"There was a big red flag billowing off the back."

"Were there other colors in it besides red?" asked Harvath.

"I don't know. It was all red . . . except for a small green star."

"Bingo. Morocco."

"What is it? Do you know the boat?"

"I do now."

54

The embassy's CIA station chief found Meg Cassidy's insights only somewhat interesting and said as much to Harvath. He reiterated that the CIA's primary efforts were focused, exactly as they were before, on stopping Hashim Nidal, period.

When it became obvious that the station chief wasn't going to be of any help, Harvath asked where he could find Morrell.

"He and his team left three hours ago."

Harvath got a sinking feeling in his stomach. "Where did they go? Back to the Point?"

"Actually, we received reliable intelligence that Nidal may be headed for Syria."

"Where'd that intelligence come from?"

"That's classified," replied the station chief.

"I'm part of this operation as well, so you can go ahead and fill me right in."

"Not anymore you're not."

"What are you talking about?"

"You and Miss Cassidy have been officially retired from Operation Phantom."

"By whom?"

"It came down from D.C. You're done. You're to stay here and review the Oxford material to try and ID Hashim Nidal's female accomplice—"

"You mean his sister."

"That has yet to be proven."

"And proof is exactly why Miss Cassidy in particular was brought onboard this operation. How are Morrell and his team going to be one hundred percent sure they've got Hashim, even if they do find him in Syria?"

"We have a photograph."

"From where?" said Harvath with a certain degree of amazement.

"Morrell's team got a few still frames of video from the Robofly during the meeting at the Hijrah Oasis."

"I didn't hear anything about that in the debriefing."

"It came up after you left."

"Was asked to leave," corrected Harvath.

"Nevertheless, based on the video stills and what the CIA has been able to gather, Mr. Morrell is confident that his team will be able to take care of Nidal. So, as you can see, they are no longer in need of your assistance."

"You guys have no idea of the mistake you're making."

"Be that as it may, you're to stay and review the Oxford material in an attempt to identify the woman in question, and then you'll be flown back to the States via military transport."

"First class all the way. That's great. Fine. You guys do it your way. I need to use the bubble."

"Again? What for this time?"

"I'm sorry," said Harvath. "That's classified."

By the time Harvath was finally able to get through to Lawlor in the situation room at the White House, he had a lot to tell him. Their conversation took over half an hour, during which time Lawlor put Harvath on hold six times while he quickly placed other calls.

Within forty-five minutes of hanging up, an embassy staffer was driving Harvath and Meg to the port at La Goulette. Because of an Italian aviation strike, they had been booked on the *Linee Lauro* overnight ferry to Naples. That was something that never ceased to amaze Harvath about Europe. France, Italy, Greece—they all chose to strike at the busiest times of year, thereby inconveniencing the largest number of people. *But at least the ferries were running*, reasoned Harvath.

Buying a ferry ticket in Tunis on short notice, especially in the summer, was normally an impossibility, but the embassy was able to slice through the red tape. A local Tunisian official met the party at the port and sped Harvath and Meg, along with their new passports, right through passport control and customs.

Onboard, they were shown to a sizable first-class suite, with two double beds, overlooking the bow of the ship. By the time the vessel left port at nine P.M. and sailed out of the Gulf of Tunis, Harvath and Meg were already in the main dining room having dinner.

They made small talk as they ate. Harvath was a million miles away. She knew that in his mind he had already landed in Naples and was trying to plot their next move. Wanting to be respectful of his need for space, when dinner was finished, Meg excused herself and returned to their cabin.

Harvath downed a strong espresso and then found his way onto the deserted deck outside. The warm night air was still and smelled of the sea. Far below the railing, where Harvath rested his arms, the ship's hull displaced a phosphorescent wake of foam. It was the only indication that they were moving. No lights ahead or astern of the ferry were visible. There was nothing but the empty blackness of the wide Mediterranean Sea.

Harvath closed his eyes and listened to the steady rush of water as the vessel plowed through the night toward Italy. He tried to fit together the pieces of everything that had happened. He was looking for a common theme, a thread of some sort. While they had learned a lot, they were still no closer to discovering what Adara Nidal and her brother had planned.

Scot Harvath and Meg Cassidy were still running far behind, playing a losing game of catch-up.

55

At three o'clock the next afternoon, the *Linee Lauro* ferry sailed into Naples's harbor and docked at the Stazione Marittima opposite the Piazza Municipo. Harvath and Meg were among the first passengers to disembark.

Outside the terminal they quickly hailed a taxi. Harvath gave the driver the name of the Hotel Santa Lucia, and the cab swung out of the port and headed southwest beneath the shadow of the enormous Castel Nuovo.

Like many international port cities, Naples had more than its fair share of crime. Tourists found themselves preyed upon by everyone from strung-out drug addicts who reached into car windows at stoplights to steal watches and purses, to unscrupulous restaurateurs who mercilessly padded dinner bills. Most of the city's neighborhoods were shabby and run-down, with laundry hanging from every balcony, window, and dingy alleyway. Pollution, poverty, and chaos held sway over the entire city.

One of Naples's few redeeming areas was the neighborhood fronting the small fisherman's marina of Santa Lucia. When the taxi stopped at 46 Via Partenope, Harvath paid the driver with the few remaining Euros he had been given at the embassy in Tunisia, and he and Meg pushed through the revolving door into the lobby of the grand hotel.

Harvath steered Meg toward the lobby bar and told her to order sandwiches while he picked up something from the front desk. He gave the concierge his name, and she disappeared into the office, returning moments later with a large, padded manila envelope. Taped to the envelope was a confirmation form for a private water taxi to the island of Capri with a company called Taxi Del Mare. Harvath thanked the concierge and silently said a thank-you to Gary Lawlor. Lawlor had dispatched an agent from the FBI's legal attaché office at the U.S. Embassy in Rome with exactly what he needed. Judging by the heft of the envelope, it was all there.

Harvath made his way to the men's room and, once he was sure he was alone, entered the last stall and locked the door. He tore open the top of the envelope and removed a smaller envelope filled with European currency. He broke the stack of bills into small piles and slid them into various pockets. Then he removed a blue black nine-millimeter Browning Hi-Power pistol with two extra clips of ammunition and a small holster. He clipped the Browning to the inside of his waistband at the small of his back, covered it with his shirt and left the men's room.

The Bay of Naples was known for its often roiling seas, and today was no exception. The sleek, sunburst yellow Taxi Del Mare yacht pounded over the crest of each wave, slamming down into the troughs on the other side. Sea spray covered the boat, along with its crew and two passengers. Though it was a perfectly sunny late afternoon, the captain kept the windshield wipers at full speed as sheets of warm water blasted over the bow and splashed down the wide expanse of deck.

Harvath was in his element. He had always loved the water. He watched the city of Naples recede into the distance and then looked off to the east, where he watched Mount Vesuvius, towering high above Pompeii, grow smaller and smaller. Off the port bow was Sorrento and dead ahead, the island of Capri.

The six-mile trip from Naples had taken nearly forty-five minutes. As the boat pulled into Capri's Marina Grande, the first mate hopped onto the pier with a long white line in each hand. Once the lines were secure, he ran off in search of a taxicab for his passengers.

Harvath helped Meg onto the pier and then stood next to her, to experience his first glimpse of Capri. The water of the harbor was a deep azure blue, punctuated by rows of brightly colored fishing boats. Short green trees clung tightly to the island's rocky limestone cliffs, which rose in two distinct peaks marking the tiny towns of Capri and Anacapri.

The first mate quickly returned with one of Capri's signature taxis—a convertible minivan. It drove up a long and winding switchback along which throngs of tourists slowly made their way downhill to the marina to catch the last ferry of the evening.

When they arrived at the four-star Hotel Capri, Meg went up to the room to freshen up while Harvath convinced the manager to allow him a few minutes on the hotel's computer to check his e-mail. Alone in the manager's office, Harvath logged on to the seemingly innocuous web site of an Israeli drywall manufacturer. Having been instructed by Schoen on how to navigate the site, he quickly found what he was looking for. Buried several layers down and accessible only by clicking on sections of seemingly random web images, Harvath found the surveillance photos taken by

Schoen's associates in Marbella of Marcel Hamdi and his two-hundred-fifty-foot Feadship yacht, the *Belle Étoile*. It was just as Schoen had described it. Something that big would not be hard to spot, even off Capri.

But there had been no sign of any yacht as large as the *Belle Étoile* in the Marina Grande. From what the captain of the Taxi Del Mare said, the big boats preferred the privacy and exclusivity of the Marina Piccola, on the other side of the island. Harvath had shared Schoen's description of the *Belle Étoile* with the captain, who had picked up passengers from the Marina Piccola earlier that afternoon, but he replied he had not seen a vessel of that size anywhere around Capri that day. *Maybe*, thought Harvath, *they had finally arrived somewhere first. Or maybe they were on a wild-goose chase.*

He logged off the manager's computer and went upstairs to the room. Large French windows gave onto an incredible view of the sea, with Sorrento off in the distance. A light breeze stirred the curtains and cooled the room. The sun was starting to set, and Harvath was anxious to get moving. He was about to knock on the bathroom door when Meg stepped out. She was still wearing the same clothes she had had on since boarding the ferry in Tunisia, but even wrinkled and two days old, they couldn't diminish how beautiful she was.

"We've got a lot of work to do," he said as he squeezed past her into the bathroom to examine his tired face in the mirror. He splashed cold water on his face and ran his fingers through his short brown hair.

"Where do you want to start?" asked Meg as she crossed to the minibar and retrieved a bottle of mineral water.

"Even though the captain said he hadn't seen Hamdi's yacht on the Marina Piccola side of the island, I want to give it a shot, especially since that's where the picture you saw of Adara was taken," said Harvath as he came out of the bathroom. "There are some brochures and tourist maps in the lobby. We'll get somebody behind the desk to help mark all the spots that sell Caprissimo perfume."

"And then?"

"And then we'll go to each one and inquire as to whether or not they are familiar with our little friend."

"We'll also need a pair of binoculars if we're going looking for that yacht, but there'll be a shop with them every fifteen feet. What we really need is some new clothes. I'm not wearing these another day," said Meg as she pulled her shirt away from her body. "If we're going to go around asking questions about the well-heeled Adara Nidal, we'd better look like we belong here. The last thing we want is for her to see us coming."

Meg Cassidy had no idea how right she really was.

56

Going to the marina first was the right decision. By the time the hotel manager had marked a map with all of the shops they were interested in visiting and they had bought a pair of binoculars, the sun was almost gone. The low light sparkling on the water cast every boat in shadow. Even so, there was nothing even remotely the size of the *Belle Étoile* at anchor.

As they returned to Capri Town, tourists, honeymooners, and young Italian couples strolled slowly past walled villas spilling over with bougainvillea and other fragrant flowers. A large part of the island's charm was that most of it was pedestrianized, but every once and a while a little motorized cart drove by with a porter, carrying luggage for one of the island's many hotels.

When they arrived back in the heart of Capri Town, Harvath didn't need to enter any of the boutiques. Just seeing the names Fendi, Gucci, Ferragamo and Hermès were enough to give any man, even one with pockets stuffed full of cash, sticker shock. To her credit, Meg was an incredible bargain hunter. She knew exactly where to look and what to ask for. It wasn't the labels she wanted, it was the look. She shopped faster than anyone Harvath had ever known. When it was all said and done, they looked like a handsome jet-set couple with lots of money to spend as they carried several bags from Capri's more upscale shops. Better yet, they now were able to completely blend in.

The first place on their list was the Carthusia perfume showroom at number 10 Via Camerelle. Harvath had agreed with Meg that it would seem less suspicious if she asked the questions and he looked like the bored husband being dragged around on a day of shopping.

Meg approached the counter, where an attractive, very tastefully dressed blond woman in her late forties was patiently waiting as a salesgirl made a phone call to one of the other shops on her behalf.

"May I help you?" said a second salesgirl who came around behind the counter from the showroom floor. Her English had a heavy Italian accent, and "help" sounded more like "elp."

"Yes," said Meg, who pretended to be looking over the merchandise. "I am looking for a certain type of perfume."

"Of course. We have many lovely perfumes. What are you looking for?"

"We had dinner with a woman who was wearing it. I think she said it was called Caprissimo?"

"Yes. This is a very nice perfume, but unfortunately we do not have it in this shop."

"Do you ususally sell it here?" asked Meg.

"Yes, but right now we are out of it."

"But they might be able to find it for you," offered the blond lady standing next to Meg. "They're calling the other shops for me right now. If you pay for it here, they'll deliver it to your hotel."

"Certainly," returned the salesgirl. "You pay now and we will have it brought to the hotel. Are you staying at the Quisisana?"

Harvath shot Meg a look, but it was unnecessary. She

would not needlessly divulge what hotel they were staying at. "Actually, we're not. The woman who wore the perfume was very kind, and without our knowing it, paid for our dinner last night. I was hoping you might know who she is or possibly where she is staying so we could repay the favor."

"Are you on your honeymoon?" interrupted the blond woman with a wide smile.

Meg looked at Harvath and he grinned. "Yes, we are," she replied as she slid her left hand behind her back, hiding her naked ring finger.

"I knew it! I just knew it," proclaimed the woman. "You two are just too adorable."

"Thank you for the compliment," said Meg, who turned her attention back to the salesgirl. "I'm sure you would know this woman if I described her. She is very beautiful, with long black hair."

"Signora, you have just described over half the women in Italy," replied the salesgirl.

"She is tall and has the most beautiful eyes. They look like silver. I'm sure very few women in Italy have eyes like that."

"I do not know this woman. Maybe she has been here to buy perfume and she was wearing sunglasses. Maybe another girl in the shop was helping her. I'm sorry."

Meg was disappointed. She sensed that this was going to be a losing battle, but she didn't want to give up. It was one of the only leads they had. "Perhaps one of your colleagues assisted her. It would mean so much for us to repay her kindness. Would you ask your associates for us? We would be happy to wait."

"Signora, tonight it is only two of us. Me and Francesca. During the day we have three different girls, sometimes others to help on the weekends. I cannot ask all of them. It would be too difficult. I am sorry. You understand I am sure, yes?"

Yes, Meg understood, but she didn't like it. The blond woman could see the disappointment written on her face and said, "Why don't you find a nice table at one of the cafés on the square and see if she walks by when everybody's doing the *passeggiata*—the evening stroll? Anybody who is anybody on Capri eventually walks through the Piazzetta."

The idea that Adara Nidal might just casually parade by them was about as far-fetched as tracking her down based on where she bought her perfume. Harvath and Meg thanked the woman and the salesgirl, and then left the shop.

They visited all of the other locations on their list only to find that no one they spoke to remembered ever having waited on a woman matching Adara's description. The salespeople were always very apologetic and said that many of their customers wore sunglasses, even in the evening. This could account for their not remembering the stranger who had supposedly picked up Meg and Scot's dinner check. They were repeatedly told that this was not unusual on Capri and that they should enjoy the mystery of it. One older gentleman went so far as to say the angels above had blessed their marriage with a complimentary meal. When pressed, they all returned to the same suggestion the blond woman at their first stop had made—to park themselves at a table on the Piazzetta and wait.

When they returned to Capri Town from Anacapri, Harvath was not in the best of moods. His feet were sore from his new shoes, and he hadn't eaten since Naples. Meg suggested that they drop their shopping bags in the hotel and give the Piazzetta a shot. Harvath reluctantly agreed.

They found an outdoor table, several rows in, against the wall of one of the busy cafés, partially obscured from view by a row of potted trees.

After several hours of people watching and several tiny cups of high-octane Italian coffee, Harvath decided a new approach was in order. They drifted from disco to disco and high-end hotel lobby to high-end hotel lobby, hoping to get lucky. The sun was coming up when Harvath and Meg made one more fruitless trip to the marina, then finally headed back to the hotel to get some sleep.

57

When Meg awoke, Harvath was already gone. She had only slept a couple of hours, so her guess was that Harvath hadn't slept at all. Knowing him, she concluded he had waited until she had fallen asleep and had gone back out on his own. Meg knew exactly where she would find him, though.

She took a shower and put on a fresh change of clothes. The complimentary buffet breakfast was already underway when Meg entered the hotel's main dining room. She selected some food from the buffet and then took a table near the window, where she asked the waiter for coffee. Her mind was turning over and over, trying to figure out how they could track down Adara Nidal and what might happen if they didn't.

After Meg had finished her breakfast, she asked the waiter if she could have one of the plastic pitchers full of coffee to take upstairs to her husband, who wasn't feeling well. The waiter was more than happy to oblige. Meg fixed a tray with some extra food, and when the coffee arrived, took everything up to the room.

Back in the room, she wrapped the food in paper napkins and placed it, along with the plastic jug of coffee and a cup, into one of their fancy shopping bags with silk cords that could be drawn shut at the top. Carefully slinging the bag over her shoulder, she put on a pair of sunglasses, walked downstairs, and exited the hotel.

She turned right and headed past the bus terminal and taxi stand into the main square. Having learned from her training with the Delta operatives the importance of varying your routine, she decided to take another route to the marina. Instead of heading straight through the Piazzetta and back past all the high-profile boutiques, Meg turned left and went a different direction. She passed under an archway and onto a tiny thoroughfare. From the map she carried, it looked to be an easy yet roundabout way to get down to the water. She now remembered how difficult Capri's windy little streets were to navigate, even with a map.

About fifty meters in from the Piazzetta, Meg stopped next to a restaurant called, Al Grottino, to once again check her map. As she was unfolding it, one of the little motorized luggage carts came careening down the narrow alley, and Meg had to jump to the other side to get out of the driver's way. It was then that something on the door of the restaurant caught her eye.

It was a small sticker proclaiming that the restaurant was a member of Italy's prestigious Unione Ristoranti Del Buon Ricordo. Meg's heart began to race. She crossed back over and read the menu posted outside, and when she found what she was looking for, her heart pounded even faster. Trying not to draw any attention to herself, Meg made her way as quickly as possible to the Marina Piccola.

58

When Meg got to the marina, she spotted Harvath sitting in a blue-and-white-striped canvas beach chair beside the water.

"I hope you brought some coffee," said Harvath, who was surveying the coastline with his binoculars as Meg approached from behind. "The restaurant here doesn't open for another hour."

"I've got coffee and something even better," she said as she unslung her shopping bag and took the empty beach chair next to him.

"Coffee first," he said as he pulled the binoculars away from his face. His eyes were red and bloodshot.

"I'll talk while you drink," said Meg as she handed him a cup of coffee and then pulled the food she had brought for him out of her bag.

Harvath took a sip of hot black coffee and then opened up a croissant and placed some of the prosciutto inside. As he took a bite of the sandwich, he said, "I'm thinking about renting a boat. I'm not convinced Hamdi is going to moor the *Belle Étoile* on this side of the island. All of the bigger yachts are definitely here, but if he wants his privacy, he might choose a more secluded spot."

"I think I have something else we should run down first."

"Meg, the clock is ticking. For all we know, Hamdi and the *Belle Étoile* are already here and we've been wasting our time looking in the wrong spot."

"What if I told you," said Meg, opening a small container of yogurt, "that I think I found one of Adara's haunts on Capri?"

"I'd be all ears," said Harvath as he raised the binoculars back to his eyes and once again scanned the water for any sign of the two-hundred-fifty-foot *Belle Étoile*.

"And eyes. Listen to me," she said as she pulled the binoculars away from him, gaining his undivided attention. "Remember the plates she served dinner to us on?"

"Kind of. They were odd little hand-painted jobs with some kind of cartoon and Italian writing."

"Exactly. Do you know what the writing said?"

"Mine said something about Pollo alla Romana, Frascati, and something else with the picture of a chicken in a toga. They looked like kids' plates to me."

"They were far from kids' plates. Mine was Bavette ai Gracchi, from the Dante Taberna De Gracchi—a very good restaurant in Rome near Vatican City. Do you know what Adara's had?"

"I didn't get a good look from where I was sitting."

"Well, I did. It had a lobster outfitted like a gladiator, but that's not the most important thing. Across the top it read, '*Risotto con aragosta e l'olio di tartufo*'—'lobster risotto with truffle oil.'"

"The same meal she served us?"

"Yes. The Italian writing on your plate was the name of the restaurant in Frascati that served the Pollo alla Romana."

"Meg, back up. I don't get this."

"It's the plates. Each one represents the specialty of the house for a different restaurant in the Buon Ricordo organization."

"What's 'Buon Ricordo'?"

"It's an exclusive club of restaurants that celebrate Italian cuisine."

"So what does this have to do with Adara?"

"I didn't see where her plate came from, but on my way down here I figured it out."

"Don't tell me. Capri?"

"You got it. There's a Buon Ricordo restaurant called Al Grottino right off the Piazzetta."

"And the specialty of the house?"

"Lobster risotto with truffle oil," answered Meg.

59

Al Grottino was still not open when Harvath and Meg arrived, so they killed time in a local bookstore, where Harvath bought a detailed topographical and coastal map of the island. If they came up empty at the restaurant, then the next move was renting a boat.

Meg was confident that Al Grottino would turn up something. A restaurant was much different than a perfume shop. People didn't wear sunglasses at dinner, even on Capri, and what's more, patrons were in a restaurant a lot longer than a shop, so chances were that someone in the restaurant would remember Adara Nidal. As a matter of fact, there was a very good chance that she had made a big impression.

Meg was even more certain when the restaurant was finally opened for lunch. The outgoing owner greeted them at the door, guided them deftly down several steps, and sat them at a table in full view of any passersby who might be considering his restaurant for lunch. There was nothing like a nice-looking young couple to draw in other customers.

The tiny restaurant had a beautiful arched ceiling and walls dotted with several small alcoves filled with different colored bottles of Capri wine, all artistically lit from behind. Harvath noticed the walls were also covered with photographs of the owner and what appeared to be numerous Italian celebrities. It was obvious that he was proud of his restaurant and took an active role in its operation.

On top of everything else, the man was very friendly and loved to speak English. It was not hard to draw him into gossipy conversation, especially about the famous people who came to eat in his restaurant.

The owner insisted on starting Harvath and Meg with a Caprese salad while they talked. When the dish arrived and Harvath took his first bite, it was easily the best mozzarella he had ever tasted. The owner could see the look on his face and was very pleased. He bragged about how he had a special source on the island for all of his cheese. Meg, clever woman that she was, brought the owner back around to talking about his clients. She shared with him that a woman they had met while out to drinks one night had recommend his restaurant. The minute she described Adara the man's eyes lit up.

"Che bella donna!" he exclaimed. "She has the eyes of silver, just like you say. The most beautiful woman who has ever come to eat at Al Grottino, after you of course, Signora."

"So you know her?" took up Harvath, acting casual and only mildly interested.

"She has been here many times."

"The lady must enjoy your cooking very much."

"Oh, very much," replied the owner. "Many times she asks me for my recipes and how can I say no to such a beautiful woman?" He shot Meg a quick, flirtatious glance. "The only thing I ask is that she not begin her own restaurant here on Capri. No one would come to see my face anymore."

Now Meg got back into the conversation. "She is such an elegant woman. Don't you think?"

"Very elegant and very beautiful," said the owner.

"Does she own a villa here? I would imagine it is quite impressive."

"No. No villa. She comes to visit and stays in the hotel."

"Of course. The Quisisana," said Meg with a smile.

"No, the Capri Palace in Anacapri. Last night she was here for dinner with a very handsome American man—"

"We'll have to keep our eyes out for them. We're staying at the Capri Palace also. I might know the man she was with," said Harvath as he described Marcel Hamdi from Schoen's surveillance photos.

"No. This man, he's tall like the woman, *bello*, but blond hair. We say in Italian, *con un pizzo*," said the owner, rubbing his chin.

"Ah, with a goatee," said Meg.

"*Ecco*. It's your first time to Capri?" asked the owner, changing the subject.

"My first. She has been here before," said Harvath as he nodded to Meg.

"*Bella donna*. You have not eaten in my restaurant before?"

"No," responded Meg. "This is my first time."

"Then I will make for you something special. I have a nice *gnocchi* for your husband, and for you I make a *linguine ai gamberetti*. A special shrimps with tomato sauce, good?"

"Sounds delicious," said Meg.

"Maybe also a nice wine. Something dry, but not too expensive. Okay?"

"*Bene.*"

"*Lei parla l'italiano!*"

"Yes, but my . . ." said Meg as she hestitated, "my husband does not."

"*Perfetto.* We can make our plans and he will never know," said the owner with a conspiratorial wink as he went to place their orders in the kitchen.

Soon after, the lunch crowd picked up and the owner was quite busy. When he stopped by their table to check on how they had enjoyed their meals, Harvath took the opportunity to ask one more question. "The food was wonderful. We will have to buy the lady who told us about your restaurant a cocktail." If the owner wasn't suspicious already, he would be soon, but Harvath felt he had to push just a little bit further. "I wish we knew her name. Do you by any chance?"

"I'm sorry, no. *Allora, il caffè?*" said the owner, indicating that the subject was closed for good.

Meg ordered her customary cappuccino, and Harvath, a double espresso, which they finished quickly. As soon as they paid their check and left the restaurant, they walked as fast as they could to the cabstand just off the Piazzetta.

60

The open-air taxi brought them to the small yet bustling heart of Anacapri. Perched on a low hill above the town square was the five-star Capri Palace. It was accessible via a series of steps followed by a short walkway winding past the lower half of the hotel swimming pool. Glass windows along the walk, much like a large-scale aquarium, allowed people to peer through the water and watch the guests as they swam above.

Stores around the piazza sold everything from sandals, sunscreen, and beach towels, to local ceramics, film, and postcards. Harvath and Meg secreted themselves just inside one of the shops that had a good view of the hotel's imposing white façade. Meg pretended to look for postcards while Harvath studied the tanned faces of the throngs of tourists milling around the piazza. They were everywhere—like ants crawling over an enormous hill of sugar. Harvath thought about using his binoculars to try and catch a glimpse of the guests around the pool, but being downhill from the hotel made it impossible. They needed to get closer.

He got Meg's attention, and they stepped out into the street. The sun was extremely strong. The whitewashed buildings surrounding the piazza seemed to bounce the sunlight back with twice its brilliance. Walking past the cabstand, Harvath noticed a narrow side street that wound up the hill and ended right next to the hotel's designer-clothing boutique. A taxi idled in the makeshift cul-de-sac.

As Harvath studied the sea of people once more, one in particular caught his eye. She was tall and thin, yet very toned. Her skin was a rich copper color, and though she wore a large straw hat and sunglasses, Harvath knew her right off by the way she moved. She was not one of the many casual tourists out strolling. This was a woman with a purpose and destination.

He grabbed Meg's left arm and flicked his eyes in the direction of Adara Nidal. It took Meg a moment, but then she spotted her too. Neither of them dared utter a word as they proceeded up the stone steps toward the Capri Palace. Harvath reflexively reached beneath his shirt at the small of his back. He grabbed the butt of the Browning nine-millimeter and prepared to draw, and that was when everything fell apart.

The element of surprise was ruined when the blond woman from the perfume shop the previous evening appeared out of nowhere and squealed, "If it isn't Capri's most adorable newlyweds! How are you kids? Are you having a fabulous time here, or what?"

The woman moved right in front of Harvath and placed both of her hands upon his shoulders. He tried to avoid her, but it was no good. Her wrists were weighted down with gold bracelets and designer shopping bags and as she reached one of her hands out for Meg, she continued, "Isn't this a small world? Or should I say *island?* What am I talking about? It is a small island. Don't you just love Anacapri? This is where I always stay when I come. I mean I might go over to Capri Town, but this is where anybody who is anybody stays."

Unfortunately, the woman had one of those voices that

really seemed to carry. The commotion had been enough to turn Adara Nidal's head and now she was staring right into Harvath's eyes.

"Sorry, we've gotta run," said Scot as he and Meg untangled themselves from the American woman and picked up their pace.

"Where's the fire?" asked the woman as Harvath and Meg took off after Adara, who was already way ahead of them and closing in on the idling taxi.

Harvath half pulled his gun, but knew that the flood of tourists would make it impossible to get off a clean shot. He slid the Browning back into the holster, grabbed Meg by the wrist, and spun her back in the direction they had come. There was no way they could beat Adara to the waiting taxi. Their only chance was to catch it when it came onto the main road at the bottom of the hill.

They ran back to the stone steps and down into the piazza. Crossing the tiny square, Harvath steered Meg to the front of the cabstand and, in a move that would have made even the most seasoned New Yorker jealous, elbowed out a crowd of drunk Germans and hopped into their cab. The driver started protesting immediately, and it wasn't until Harvath fished out a large Euro note that the man agreed to forget about their jumping the line. By that time, Adara Nidal's cab had already come down the hill and had swung onto the main road heading south.

Meg instructed their driver in Italian to follow the other cab.

"What's going on?" asked the old man, who was at least seventy if he was a day, as he pulled away from the piazza.

"Don't worry about it. Keep driving," responded Meg.

Despite his age, the old islander did a good job of keeping up, but not good enough. Adara Nidal's cab made a hard right and their driver missed it. He continued south and had to swing an even harder right up what looked like a one-way street to get back behind her.

They were now headed toward the very western edge of the island, with two buses and several cars separating them. Harvath had to hand the old man another large banknote to convince him to risk passing the other vehicles. The roads of Capri had not been designed with high-speed chases in mind.

The driver made several attempts to move out from behind the bus in front of them, only to have to jerk the wheel back hard to the right because of an oncoming vehicle in the opposite lane. Slowly, he began to make some progress as he threaded his way forward.

Meg asked the driver what was at this end of the island that caused so much traffic. After passing another car, the man responded, "Grotta Azzura." *The Blue Grotto.*

Harvath kept peeling off notes, crumpling them into balls, and throwing them into the front seat as he urged the driver to go faster. Though they had passed both buses and several of the cars, Adara Nidal's cab was far ahead and disappeared every time it took one of the many curves in the winding road.

Holding on to the seat in front of him, Harvath stood in the open-air convertible and tried to keep track of her cab. He wondered why she would be racing toward the Blue Grotto. It had to be Hamdi. Maybe he had anchored the *Belle Étoile* off the grotto and was sending a launch to pick her up. Then the road forked and their driver veered to the right, away from the heavy stream of traffic. Harvath almost lost his balance. He couldn't see the other cab anywhere, only a high cloud of dust hovering over the road in front of them, which hadn't escaped their clever driver.

There was also a road sign. Harvath now knew where Adara Nidal was headed. Eliporto di Capri—Capri Heliport.

Before the taxi had even come to a complete stop at the gate of the heliport, Harvath was already out and running. The roar of the powerful Eurocopter AS365 Dauphin was deafening as it quickly lifted off. Through the Plexiglas window of its plush nine-passenger-capacity cabin, Harvath thought he could see Adara smiling at him, but he couldn't be sure. The navy blue bird with its gold logos was flying directly west, into the sun.

The one thing Harvath did know was that he had seen that helicopter before. He had seen it in Ari Schoen's surveillance photos sitting on the helipad of Marcel Hamdi's megayacht, the *Belle Étoile*.

61

When Harvath and Meg returned to Anacapri, they headed right for the Capri Palace. Past a cascading fountain surrounded by votive candles, they entered the luxuriously appointed, snow-white lobby and headed left toward the bar.

Heavy columns throughout the room supported a multi-arched ceiling and created a multitude of private sitting areas. A short mahogany bar with four stools stood alone in a far corner, while a brace of dark wooden ceiling fans quietly stirred the air overhead. White couches and loveseats were scattered throughout, fronted by thick, low-slung mahogany tables. Lamps, their shades festooned with delicate gold tassels, added to the air of elegance.

Harvath and Meg proceeded past a large grand piano and out onto the flower-filled terrace. After they found a table, a waiter quickly appeared to take their drink orders. An evening cocktail at one's hotel was a tradition on Capri, and as Scot and Meg settled in to wait for the man who had been seen dining with Adara Nidal, their only hope was that he would actually show up.

The sun began its slow descent into the ocean, casting a glow of burnt orange over the Capri Palace's terrace. Large white candles, nestled in sand and set in large glass hurricane lamps, were lit and placed strategically around the terrace. The waiters began setting up a buffet table, and when Meg asked them what they were preparing for, one of the waiters explained that it was the manager's weekly cocktail party for hotel guests. Harvath began to think that their luck might be changing.

As the slow parade of guests began to file out onto the terrace, their man appeared. He was wearing a white linen suit with a pink-and-white-checked shirt. His hair was perfectly coifed, his goatee neatly trimmed, and it was obvious from the way he carried himself that he had no self-esteem issues.

"Is that him?" asked Meg quietly.

"He certainly fits the description," said Harvath as he discreetly eyeballed the man. "You know what to do."

Meg slinked across the terrace and got into line right behind the man at the buffet. As he picked up a complimentary glass of champagne and a few canapés, he noticed the attractive blond behind him, and that's when Meg began to make small talk. "What a beautiful sunset this evening. Don't you think?"

"Very lovely," he answered. As Meg reached for a canapé, the man noticed she wasn't wearing a wedding ring. "Are you staying at the hotel? I don't think we've met. I'm Neal Harris."

"It's a pleasure to meet you, Mr. Harris. Where's your lady friend this evening?" asked Meg, offering neither her name nor her hand.

"My lady friend?"

"Oh, don't play coy with me," said Meg flirtatiously. "We've all seen you and that goddess with those incredible eyes."

"Yes, that goddess," said Harris, glad that people had noticed him and the woman. "She does have the most beautiful eyes. Actually, I was hoping she'd already be here. I haven't seen her since this afternoon."

"Well, so much the better. You can join me for a drink while you wait for her."

"I'd be honored," replied Harris. "But I didn't catch your—"

"Outstanding. I have a delightful friend that you absolutely have to meet," said Meg as she latched on to Harris's elbow and steered him over to where Scot Harvath was sitting.

"Neal Harris," said Meg, "I'd like you to meet my friend, Scot. Scot, meet Neal Harris."

Harris offered his hand to Harvath and waited for him to rise. Harvath stayed seated.

"Oh, you'll have to excuse Scot," said Meg. "He has a bit of a problem."

"Oh, really?" said Harris, waiting for Meg to sit and then taking the empty chair next to Harvath. "And what might that be?"

Harvath had secreted his Browning beneath a linen napkin on his lap and now raised it just enough for Harris to see. "I have developed a real dislike for terrorist collaborators, Mr. Harris."

"Terrorist collaborators?" cried Harris, seeing the gun.

"Keep your voice down," whispered Harvath in order to heighten the intimidation factor, "or I swear I'll kill you right here."

"What the hell is going on?" said Harris, careful to keep his voice down.

"What's going on," replied Harvath, "is that you are in a lot of trouble, my friend."

"First, I am not your friend. And second, I have no idea what you're talking about."

"Well, let's start with a very leggy, attractive brunette with rather strange eyes that you've been seen about the island with over the last couple of days."

"Who? Penny? I hardly know her."

"She told you her name was, Penny?"

"Short for Penelope. She's British. From England."

Meg shot Harvath a look.

"What was her last name?" demanded Harvath, jerking the Browning for added effect.

"Stratton. Her name was Penelope Stratton. Now what is this all about?"

"Your girlfriend is one very serious character," said Harvath.

"She's not my girlfriend. I just met her a couple of days ago. Is she somebody's wife? Is that it? I had no idea. Honestly. She came on to *me*."

"Please. You expect us to believe that?" said Meg.

"Yes! It's the truth," pleaded Harris.

"Why would she come on to a guy like you?" asked Harvath.

"It's not my fault women like me."

"Meg?" asked Harvath. "You like this guy? You find him attractive?"

"I have no idea what she saw in him," answered Meg.

"Listen, Harris," continued Harvath, "I'm going to give you one chance to get yourself out of this mess."

"*Mess?* What mess? I have *no* idea what's going on."

"Whether you do, or you don't, I don't really care. Either way, if I don't feel I'm getting complete and total cooperation from you, I'm going to shoot you in the head and drop your body in a shallow grave. Are you going to cooperate?"

"Of course, I will. She was great in bed, but—" said Harris, pausing as both Harvath's and Meg's eyebrows went up. "I mean she was a lovely diversion for the couple of days we were together, but I don't owe her anything. As a matter of fact, screw her! I'm with you two. Especially this gentleman with the gun."

"Spoken like a true romantic," said Harvath, lowering the Browning.

62

Harvath knew that there wasn't a chance in hell Adara Nidal was going to return to the Capri Palace. She knew they were on to her and most likely she wouldn't even return to Capri. What they did have going for them was that, for once, they had surprised her. According to Harris, Adara—or Penny, as he continually referred to her—was planning to check out soon. She had said that she was about to change the world, but Harris said he thought she had some business deal cooking and was speaking metaphorically. Not only did he have no idea where she was going, he had absolutely no idea how literally she had been speaking.

Harvath cracked the fire-stair door and looked out into the hall once more. The coast was clear. While Harvath held the Browning on Harris, Meg slipped into the hall and walked toward the elevators. She picked up a house phone and dialed housekeeping.

"Housekeeping. May I help you?" said the voice on the other end of the line.

"Well, someone better," said Meg, adopting a haughty tone. "I want fresh towels placed in my room, three-twelve, before I return from dinner." Then she hung up before housekeeping could ask her name. While Adara Nidal might have told Harris her name was Penny Stratton, there was no telling what name she had used to register at the Capri Palace. The housekeeping operator was probably offended at having been hung up upon, but doubtless it wasn't the first time it had happened, nor would it be the last. The Capri Palace was all about impeccable service, no matter how rude the guests. Harvath was sure that the towels would be sent right up.

Right up, was an understatement. Meg had had just enough time to hide herself in another stairway before the maid appeared. The woman knocked once at the door and announced herself before using her passkey to unlock it. She placed a wedge beneath the door to keep it open and walked back into the bathroom. Meg quietly exited the stairwell and made her way down to room 312 as quickly as possible. The maid was startled to see Meg standing in the room when she came out of the bathroom.

"Did you put my extra towels in the bathroom?" asked Meg.

"Yes, Signora."

"Good."

"Shall I turn down the bed for you?"

"No. I'll do it myself when I am ready."

"Yes, Signora," said the maid as she gave Meg a wide berth and backed out of the room. Obviously, somebody in housekeeping had passed the word that the woman in 312 was not very nice. "*Buona notte.*"

The maid closed the door behind her, and several moments later there was a knock from Harvath. Meg opened the door, and Harvath shoved Harris into the room with the muzzle of the Browning. He sat him down in a chair against the wall as he began to tear apart the room. He was looking for anything Adara might have left behind indicating where she was going or what her plans were.

New clothes, many with tags still on them, hung in the closet. All of her cosmetics were new as well. Harvath found a bottle of Caprissimo perfume in the bathroom and popped his head out for a moment to show Meg. He continued his search under the bathroom sink, behind the dresser, inside and underneath drawers, all throughout the closets, under the mattresses, and behind the headboard. He even looked for loose pieces of carpeting. There was nothing.

Going back through the room a second time, Harvath noticed several foreign newspapers stacked on the desk, all folded over to the same story. *Le Monde*, *Der Spiegel*, *The Times* of London, and *The International Herald Tribune* each carried a piece with more or less the same headline, "Israeli and Palestinian Leaders to Meet on Peace." In light of the failed U.S. attempts at brokering a lasting peace, the European Union had organized a meeting in Italy to try and calm the tensions in the region before they erupted into war. Just like the Americans, they had chosen a serene, bucolic setting similar to Camp David—a sixteenth-century villa called the Villa Aldobrandini, in the hilltop town of Frascati, just outside Rome. Attending would be the Israeli prime minister and, of course, chief Palestinian negotiator Ali Hasan. *That was it!*

Harvath now knew *what* Adara Nidal had planned and could pretty much figure out *why*; all he needed now was *how*.

After tearing apart the room for a third time, Harvath sat on the edge of the bed and turned on the TV. He handed Meg the newspaper articles, and she immediately came to the same conclusion.

Harvath used the remote to select the automated-checkout feature. He clicked on *charges* and noticed that the room had not been billed for any faxes or phone calls.

"Did your girlfriend have a cell phone?" asked Harvath without looking at Harris.

"Not that I know of," he replied.

"Did you see her send or receive any faxes? Did she have a laptop at all that she might have used?"

"No."

"Did you ever see her talking to anyone else? Maybe someone you didn't recognize?"

"I never saw anything like that, but I did hear something."

Harvath turned around to face Harris. "You *heard* something? What did you hear?"

"We spent a lot of time in my room, you know. Even though she had her own room, I kind of gave her one of my keycards, so she could—"

"You said you overheard something. What was it?"

"I came back to the room one time from the pool, and she was finishing up a phone call."

"She was using the phone in your room?"

"Yeah. Why not?"

"That's it," said Harvath, jumping off the bed. He pointed the Browning at Harris. "Let's go."

"Where are we going?" asked Harris.

"Your place."

Harvath called down to the front desk from Harris's room, and they automatically assumed it was Neal Harris calling. Within ten minutes, a large white envelope was slid under the door, detailing Mr. Harris's room charges to date. Meg quickly scanned the list while Harvath bound and gagged Harris. She came up with three calls, all to the same phone number. She recognized the city code right away—Rome.

Harvath spent most of the night talking to Gary Lawlor from their hotel room in Capri Town. In addition to everything they discussed, Lawlor agreed to arrange for the Italian authorities to hold on to Neal Harris for a little while, just to make sure his story checked out. When morning came, Scot and Meg were the first ones aboard the hydrofoil for Naples. Thankfully, the waters of the bay were, for once, perfectly calm.

They caught the morning Eurostar train for Rome and arrived an hour and forty-five minutes later. A cab took them northwest across the city to one of Rome's quieter and less known areas called the Prati district. The phone number dialed from Neal Harris's room on Capri belonged to a tiny fabric shop called Dolce Silvestri. Adara Nidal had placed three calls to the shop, each one lasting for several minutes. Harvath doubted that she was planning to do any redecorating.

As they turned the corner and looked for a place to have the driver drop them off, Meg said, "Scot, look! Dante Taberna De Gracchi! When Adara served us dinner, my plate was from this restaurant."

Harvath signaled the cabdriver to keep going. Once he felt they were a safe distance away, he paid the driver and he and Meg got out of the cab. They walked back toward the fabric shop, found a secluded spot halfway up the block, and waited.

If this was a typical day of business, Harvath had no idea how the shop could stay open. No one entered and no one left.

The Eternal City of Rome, with its dark cobbled streets, baked like an oven. The temperature was almost unbearable. Late afternoon began to turn to early evening, and just when Harvath thought nothing was going to happen, a large black Mercedes crept around the corner and came to a quick stop outside the shop. When he saw the Middle Eastern driver, his antennae shot straight up. Three more Middle Eastern men, dressed in business suits, got out and entered the shop, while the car sped away.

Minutes passed and then the shop lights were extinguished. A balding, heavyset man of undistinguishable origin, exited the shop, pulled a ring of keys from beneath his blazer, locked the door, and headed down the street away from Harvath and Meg.

"That's a little strange," said Meg.

"More than a little. He just locked his three buddies inside."

"What do you want to do?"

"For now we'll wait and see if they come back out."

"And if they don't?"

"Then you and I are going to have to figure out a way in."

64

They had waited almost an hour when Harvath finally said, "Okay, now I really want to know what's going on in there."

"Do you have a plan?"

"Kinda, sorta."

"That doesn't sound good."

"Believe me. You're going to love it. We're going to put your acting skills to the test."

"I can't wait."

Harvath explained the plan as they walked. When they reached a nearby doorway, Harvath stepped inside while Meg covered the remaining couple of feet to the shop alone. She knocked on the door politely at first, and when no one answered, her knocking grew in insistency. There was no way anyone inside the small shop could have ignored it. The plan was to get one of the men to come and unlock the door. Meg had prepared a song and dance about how she was a decorator with a client who swore she had seen the perfect fabric in their shop. She would implore the man to allow her inside to make her purchase because she was returning to the States that night. As soon as Meg got one foot in the door, Harvath would spring from his hiding spot and force his way inside. The Middle Easterners might be innocent, but with the shop having received three phone calls from Adara and all of the additional suspicious activity of the past hour, Harvath doubted it.

Meg knocked her knuckles raw with no luck. No one even peeked out from within the shop to see what was going on. She walked back to Harvath and filled him in.

"Time for plans B and E," he said as he stepped out of the doorway, removed the Browning from the holster at the small of his back, and walked toward the shop front.

"What's B and E?"

"'*What's B and E?*' So much for being the daughter of a Chicago cop. Breaking and entering. What else?" said Harvath as he took one last look up and down the street and then drew back the butt of the Browning.

"Wait!" said Meg.

"What is it?"

"What if there's an alarm system?"

"First of all, I can tell from looking in the windows right here that there are no sensors anywhere in there, and secondly, we saw three people get locked in. You don't turn on an alarm system when you're locking people inside. Now stand back."

Harvath swung the butt of the pistol and shattered a large pane of glass on the front door. He waited to see if anyone would come running from the back of the shop, but no one did. He reached inside, unlocked the dead bolt, and opened the door.

The shop smelled old and musty. Harvath and Meg made their way to the back and found a doorway to a small office covered by an old tapestry. The musty smell was replaced by the heavy odor of cigarette smoke, but there was no sign of another living soul. Boxes and bolts of fabric lined one wall of the office, while file cabinets and a large armoire took up another. A square table stacked with catalogs and surrounded by folding chairs sat in the middle of the room.

The natural light reaching this far back into the shop was quite dim. Harvath was about to flick on a nearby light switch when he saw a box of flashlights sitting on the very last file cabinet.

"That's interesting," he said as he grabbed a flashlight and flicked it on. "I never would have guessed the interior design crowd to be a big market for flashlights."

"Rome does have its power outages."

"Well, either these people are extremely prepared, or the flashlights serve another purpose. My guess is they serve another purpose. What do you say we find out?"

"I've come this far. There's no way you're getting rid of me now," said Meg as she picked up a flashlight and helped Harvath search the room.

It didn't take long for them to discover a loose panel in the back of the armoire. When Harvath put pressure on it and tried to slide it to the left, it moved. A chill rush of damp air swept up from the passage on the other side. He shined his light into the darkness and discovered a series of worn stone steps that looked as if they had been carved thousands of years ago. Warning Meg to be careful of the lip of the armoire, he climbed through the opening and down the steps.

There was the faint sound of water dripping somewhere in the distance, but other than that, the passage was completely still. The cool, dark space was a welcome relief from the heat they had endured outside all day.

One by one, they took the old stone steps slowly and quietly. When they reached the bottom, the passageway gave onto a low, rough tunnel that seemed to slope down toward the center of the earth itself. Harvath kept the flashlight pointed toward the ground with his thumb on the switch, poised to turn it off at a moment's notice if he had to. His other hand was wrapped tightly around the Browning. Meg Cassidy followed right behind, with one hand holding on to the back of Harvath's shirt to help guide her steps in the darkness.

By the time the slope leveled out, Harvath figured they had walked at least half a mile. He turned off his flashlight when he could see light coming from up ahead. They covered the last fifteen yards and emerged within an enormous cavern. Rows and rows of wide alcoves were carved one upon another all the way to the ceiling. It was obvious to Harvath and Meg that this was a giant mausoleum, once part of the ancient catacomb system of Rome. Its present-day occupation was exponentially more sinister.

The room had been set up as a mini armory and supply depot. Ammunition, C4, and grenades, were stacked side by side with several assault rifles, pistols, and submachine guns. In addition there was a neat pile of antitank weapons, and surface-to-air missiles. Someone was planning one serious party.

There were boxes of food, bottled water, medical supplies, clothing, blankets, and even copies of the Koran, which made Harvath suspect that the place had also been set up to act as some sort of a safe house.

They picked their way further back into the cavern, where they found a large table covered with neat stacks of paper. As Meg examined the papers, Harvath saw something that stopped his heart cold.

65

Stacked against one wall of the mausoleum were about a dozen small canisters. Harvath didn't need to open them to know what they contained. In fact, opening them would have been a deadly mistake. He could tell from the emblems on the outside that they contained radioactive material. Totaling that with all of the plastique and various other high-grade explosives housed within the large depot, Harvath didn't even want to think about the potential devastation Adara Nidal could cause.

Meg was still looking at the papers when Harvath ran over with a very worried expression on his face and said, "We're getting out of here now."

"What's going on?" asked Meg.

"I've got to get to a phone and call Washington."

"Give me a few more seconds on these. There are FedEx and UPS airbills here made out to addresses in different cities across the United States. They appear to be for ten- and fifteen-pound boxes, but what would they be shipping to the U.S.?"

Harvath didn't have a chance to respond. He heard a sound and spun, just in time to see the three men in business suits enter from a tunnel at the back of the cavern and point their Italian-made Spectre M-4 submachine guns right at them. Harvath didn't waste any time. He knocked Meg to the ground and fired off two shots from the Browning. He saw one of the men go down, but couldn't tell where he had hit him.

The man's colleagues opened up with a storm of automatic-weapons fire, splintering the long wooden table to pieces and sending papers flying everywhere.

Harvath and Meg dove behind a nearby crate.

"There's only two of them now, so it's not even a fair—" Harvath was saying until he heard something roll toward them across the smooth stone floor. "Grenade!" he yelled as he covered Meg, and rolled as fast as he could with her away from where they had been hiding.

The man who had pitched the flash bang had miscalculated the slope of the floor. The small canister came to a stop and actually began rolling backward before it detonated. The concussion was still strong enough to set everyone's ears ringing.

Harvath grabbed Meg, who was busy stuffing the paperwork she had found into her shirt, and helped her up into a crouch. Mouthing the words and counting to three with his fingers, they ran out from behind a series of pallets and dodged a hail of bullets as they charged to the other side of the mausoleum.

Water everywhere and not a drop to drink, thought Harvath as he tried a crate of ammunition only to find it was nailed shut. "My kingdom for a crowbar," he muttered to himself. Then it hit him. He did have one. After handing Meg the Browning and a fresh clip, he reached into his pocket and pulled out his knife. He depressed the button, and the blade swung up and locked into place. Harvath slid the knife under the lid of the wooden crates and, with two hands, began working it up and down until the lid was loose enough to get his fingers under.

Meg exchanged fire several times with the men, who were maneuvering in closer for the kill.

"Whatever you're working on," said Meg as she ejected the Browning's spent magazine and replaced it with the fresh one, "I suggest you hurry it up, because they're going to be on top of us any minute."

"I've almost got it," said Harvath as he grabbed a can of 5.56 ammunition as fast as he could. He ripped it open and rammed three speed-loader clips of ten rounds into the magazine of each of the two Steyr AUG assault rifles he had pulled from where they leaned against the wall. The magazines in place, he handed one of the Steyrs to Meg and took back the Browning.

"Ready?" he asked.

"And then some."

"Short bursts. Just like we trained."

"Let's do it."

Harvath left Meg where she was and crept back behind several boxes. The idea was for him to move far enough away to trap their attackers in a deadly alley of crossfire from both sides. Harvath heard the firing of the nine-millimeter Spectres and ran across the aisle to another set of boxes, before making his way back down toward Meg.

When the men were almost on top of her, she opened fire with her Steyr as Harvath popped up and started shooting in rapid, controlled bursts from the other side. Until this point, the Middle Easterners had pursued their quarry thinking they only had one handgun between them. The machine-gun fire, coming from both directions, completely altered the equation, and the two men retreated toward the tunnel at the far end of the cavern.

Harvath chased them with every round he had loaded in his Steyr and when Meg caught up with him, he took hers and fired until there was nothing left. He had no idea if they would regroup or not, but he reloaded before he and Meg proceeded down the tunnel.

They had gone only twenty feet when they came upon the body of the first man Harvath had shot. With a hit to his chest and one to his forehead, he lay on the ground with the submachine gun still clasped in his dead hand. Harvath fished through his pockets, but only came up with several hundred Euros. Whoever he was, he was professional enough not to be caught with any ID. Harvath shouldered his Steyr and picked up the dead man's Spectre. He checked the fifty-round magazine and saw that it hadn't even been fired.

Meg covered Harvath as he ran down the tunnel to see what had happened to their two remaining attackers.

At the end of the passageway was an old freight elevator, which was on its way down. When the large wooden door was rolled open, the first man to step out was Hashim Nidal.

Harvath didn't wait to be noticed. He turned and ran back into the tunnel, where Meg was waiting.

"It's Hashim Nidal. Don't let him out of your sights," said Harvath as he ran past her.

"What if he moves?" asked Meg.

"Then shoot him," he said over his shoulder as he ran back into the mausoleum.

Harvath kept running until he got to the group of

Stinger missile cases he had seen earlier. He grabbed one and pulled it off the stack. When he opened it, it was empty, so he cast it aside and reached for the next one. This one was much heavier. He opened the case and pulled out the launcher. Just adjacent to it was a pyramid of machined aluminum tubes. He grabbed a tube, emptied the missile, and loaded the launcher. Next, he primed and readied the system. There would be no need to acquire a target as he had done in the Libyan desert.

Harvath ran back to where Meg was staring down the optical sight of her Steyr at the elevator emptying its load of terrorists. Harvath could clearly make them out from where he had lowered himself to one knee. Their two attackers were cautiously making their way toward the tunnel with several other men, including the man who had been driving the Mercedes that afternoon.

Harvath forwent his usual safety check before firing the Stinger. He depressed the launch switch, the missile uncaged and flew straight toward the first target it could acquire.

The minute the missile was loosed, Harvath dropped the launcher, grabbed Meg Cassidy's hand, and the two ran like hell for the mausoleum.

66

Harvath's first instinct was to make for the embassy as soon as they were free of the underground system of tunnels, but he knew it would take too long. He needed to get to a phone and brief Gary Lawlor on everything they had learned.

After coming back up the passageway and through the armoire of the fabric shop, Harvath decided they would just walk straight out the front door. When they hit the street, they immediately set out for the nearby piazza, which they hoped would be crowded with tourists. It had seemed like a good choice. No one was in the shop, nobody suspicious was on the street, and when they got to the square, it was relatively busy.

It had been easy. Too easy.

Suddenly, two rather large-looking Middle Eastern men appeared from one of the small side streets. One of them stuck a hand beneath his sport coat, but Harvath was faster, drawing the Browning and pointing it directly at the man's forehead.

People began screaming, and instantly, it became a mad rush as everyone ran for cover. Scot and Meg pushed their way into the swelling mob, which knocked over café tables and chairs as it surged forward. As soon as they found an open space, Harvath and Meg took off for the far side of the piazza.

They ran as fast as they could, constantly looking over

their shoulders for several blocks. When they finally slowed down to catch their breath, police and security checkpoints seemed to be everywhere. Harvath didn't understand why until he realized that they were nearing Rome's Palace of Justice. He quietly hoped the heavy police presence would dissuade the two men from pursuing them any further.

Harvath steered Meg into the first hotel he saw, and they slowly walked through the flower-filled lobby, with its brocaded sofas and European antiques, toward the pay phones. As he punched in the numbers, said his name, and then added "unsecure line" for the call, Meg began going through the papers she had taken from the mausoleum. In addition to the airbills, she had also found a map of Rome and its outskirts. The Roman hill town of Frascati had been highlighted in red pen with concentric circles that radiated outward. There was also a long blue line, which began in Rome and ended in Frascati's main square. In the upper-left-hand corner were the letters CDR, followed by a short series of numbers.

Meg picked up only snippets of Harvath's half of the conversation. He was speaking as quietly as possible so no one passing the pay phones would hear him.

"High-grade explosives . . . assault rifles . . . RPGs . . . and radioactive material . . . already sent via FedEx and UPS to operatives in the United States. . . . Hold a second."

It took Meg a moment to realize Harvath was talking to her.

". . . map. Meg? Hello? Are you listening to me?" whispered Harvath.

"What? I didn't know you were talking to me."

"I am. What's that map?" he said as he took it from her hands and stared at it.

"I took it with the rest of the papers."

Harvath turned back to the pay phone and said, "I'm positive about the attack. Yes, the peace summit in Frascati. I have the map right here. They've circled ground zero, with concentric rings based on the success of the device. . . . Make it fast. I don't think we have much time."

While Lawlor had Harvath on hold, Meg whispered, "Where did they get all that stuff?"

Harvath looked around before replying. "Iraq. Iran. North Korea. For all we know it could have come out of Russia."

"That's terrifying. How can it just be out there floating around?"

"Unfortunately almost anything is available if you can afford it."

"Do you think Adara plans to use a radiological bomb at the peace summit?"

"It sure looks like it. Even if she just uses a small percentage of what she has in that arsenal, the result will be devastating. I don't think she and her people know how powerful the attack will be. That's why your map has all those circles on it. It's got to be either a blast radius or a fallout radius."

Meg was about to say something else when Lawlor came back on the line and Harvath's attention was drawn once again to his call with Washington. The next words she heard from Harvath, coupled with the stress in his voice, chilled her to the bone.

"This *is* a legitimate threat. . . . They have no choice but to postpone. . . . It's not giving in to terrorism. . . . If they don't believe us, tell them to look in those catacombs themselves."

67

The Italian Rapid Reaction Force Augusta A 109A helicopter that touched down in the wide piazza to pick up Harvath and Meg flew south southeast at over one hundred eighty miles per hour and was able to cover the distance between Rome and the hilltop town of Frascati in less than ten minutes. The sleek chopper circled in over the sixteenth-century Villa Aldobrandini and landed in the ornate gardens before a large statue of Atlas holding up the world.

Heavily armed Carabinieri met Harvath, Meg, and the six Italian Special Forces soldiers when they landed. The soldiers carried a wide array of sensors, which they hoped would help them locate any radioactive or explosive device inside the villa. With more of the property dedicated to the expansive gardens than to the actual buildings themselves, the helicopter lifted off again to conduct a coordinated search of the grounds.

While the soldiers swept the buildings, Harvath had Meg translate his questions to the staff, including questions about deliveries, probing for anything that might be out of the ordinary. What came back was that the level of security in place for this summit was unprecedented. No one could remember security ever being so high. The Rapid Reaction Force soldiers were not finding anything either. In fact, as they talked with the Carabinieri, they were convinced that every conceivable measure had been taken to protect the summit members.

Harvath was quickly running out of answers. As the soldiers moved outside the villa to sweep the nearby shops, parked cars, restaurants, and other buildings, Harvath had a moment to talk with the summit's chief of security, who had been guiding the soldiers through the different rooms inside. When Harvath showed him the map, the man's eyes instantly widened.

"Where did you get this?" he demanded.

"Why? What do you see?"

"Those three letters followed by the numbers," he replied, jabbing his finger at the upper-left-hand corner of the map. "And this blue line."

"What is it?" asked Harvath as he stared at the map.

"That is a frequency designator for the helicopter transporting guests from the airport in Rome."

"And the blue line is the flight pattern, correct?"

The man nodded his head and said, "You hold in your hand one of the most closely guarded secrets of this summit."

"So if the helicopter is the target, it could be anybody they're after."

"No. Only the Palestinians are using the helicopter. The Israeli prime minister arrived in Rome with his people yesterday and is staying with the Israeli ambassador. As today is the Sabbath, he is not traveling. He arrives tomorrow by car. There is only one guest arriving in the helicopter and he arrives this evening—Ali Hasan, the chief Palestinian negotiator. We must change the flight pattern immediately."

"Maybe not," said Harvath.

"What are you saying?" asked the security chief. "We are trying to prevent a war here, not start one. The security of the summit participants is our highest priority."

"How much time do we have until Ali Hasan is expected to arrive?"

The security chief looked at his watch and said, "Two hours."

"Do you have a more detailed map of the area we can compare this one to?" asked Harvath as he pointed at the map Meg had taken from the catacombs.

The security chief shouted to one of his men, who quickly brought over a detailed map and laid it on the table in front of them. Harvath took a pencil and, using the straight edge of a clipboard, drew an identical line from Rome to Frascati, reproducing the flight pattern. "Just because we haven't been able to find any explosive device at the villa or in the surrounding area doesn't mean that the summit itself still isn't the target. Your men need to keep looking. At the same time, I think we need to consider the very likely possibility that there is going to be an attack on the helicopter which will happen somewhere along this line." Harvath retraced it with his pencil. "The question is, though, where?"

"It could happen anywhere during the flight," replied the security chief.

"True, but there is a lot of air traffic around Rome. With only the frequency designator to go on, it would be hard to get a visual lock on the target. If I was doing it, I would wait for the helicopter to get out here into the countryside, where it's an easy mark."

"Of course," replied the man as he pointed to a section of the flight path. "This corridor along here has been set aside as restricted airspace."

"So the only aircraft coming through there—"

"Is going to be the summit helicopter," answered the security chief, finishing Harvath's sentence.

"That narrows things down, but where along this line am I going to get the cleanest shot?" wondered Harvath aloud. "I would have spent a lot of time studying the area. I need a big open space, not a lot of trees. Something easy. I want to give myself plenty of time to be able to identify the helicopter and launch my attack. Where can I do that?"

The man surveyed the map for several moments and then, pulling out a red pen, circled the location he felt would be the most likely. "Here."

"What's that?" asked Harvath.

"The perfect place. They would be able to see the helicopter coming from almost two kilometers and would have plenty of time to prepare. The Fontana Candida vineyard.

68

The fact that there was a Buon Ricordo restaurant within driving distance of the vineyard was simply icing on the cake for Harvath. When Adara Nidal had tried to impress Scot and Meg with her worldliness and lull them into cooperating, little had she known that the dinner would come back to haunt her.

The crew of the Rapid Reaction Force helicopter had gotten in as close as they dared, dropping off their passengers on a small access road five miles away. The Frascati vineyards of the Fontana Candida estate were shrouded in an ever-deepening mist, and the night air had an unnerving chill as Harvath and Meg crept slowly over the rich volcanic soil and down perfectly manicured rows of vines. Once they had penetrated far enough into the vineyard and had covered the appropriate distance, they stopped. Harvath pulled up his sleeve and looked at his watch. It had taken almost the entire two hours to coordinate his plan and put it into effect. Now it was all just a waiting game.

Scot picked up the sound of the approaching helicopter and pulled the slide back on his Browning to double-check that he had a round chambered. Meg did the same with the nine-millimeter Beretta she had been given by one of the Italian Special Forces soldiers. She was still amazed at how the men had simply seemed to vanish as they entered the first row of vines.

As the sound of the helicopter grew louder, Harvath's body tensed. He knew it would happen at any moment. The large helicopter appeared over a far hill and banked to make its pass over the vineyard. Harvath held his breath and counted the seconds.

As he reached five, a bright flash, two hundred yards to their left, lit up the night sky. A streak of fire raced toward the helicopter. Immediately, the pilots of the Rapid Reaction Force Augusta took dramatic evasive action and deployed their countermeasures. The Stinger missile took the bait and veered dramatically off course. Arriving in advance and posing as the Palestinian leader's helicopter by emitting the same radio frequency had worked.

Harvath's victory was cut short by an off-pitch whine from the Rapid Reaction Force Augusta. It was losing altitude fast. The pilot had banked too hard to avoid the Stinger and had lost control. It was going down. As the helicopter disappeared over a nearby hill, Harvath heard the sound of heavy machine-gun fire erupt from within the vineyard.

Because the Italian Special Forces soldiers had only a rudimentary grasp of English, Harvath had decided that Meg should carry the headset and radio they had offered. Reports, and not good ones, starting coming in the minute the shooting started.

"Man down," translated Meg as they hurried in the direction of the area from which they had seen the Stinger launched.

A minute later, Meg again announced, "Man down. That's two men down. And the pilots are not responding."

Bursts of weapons fire echoed throughout the vineyard and seemed to be coming from all directions. Meg reported two more men getting hit and that the soldiers couldn't get a fix on their target. Whoever was shooting at them kept changing position.

"Ask them if there's a pattern. Does the shooter seem to be moving in any one direction?"

Meg asked, and once she had her answer, replied, "They thought it was toward the southwestern edge of the estate, but now it looks like the main buildings."

"Tell them we're going along the outside and will try to get there first."

Meg relayed their plans and then ran with Harvath toward the main Fontana Candida buildings. There was a fierce barrage of fire as they reached the bottling plant followed by total silence. Harvath and Meg crouched against a wall and tried to catch their breath. Moments passed. The night was quiet, too quiet.

"Ask them for a sit rep," whispered Harvath.

Meg tried to raise the soldiers, but not a single one responded. Meg tried again, but still there was nothing. It was as if no one was there.

Harvath peered into the misty night and thought he saw movement at the edge of the vineyard. As he squinted his eyes to get a better look, a form completely wrapped in shadow raced out from behind the last row of vines and began running across the driveway. Having not heard from any of the Italian Special Forces members and assuming the worst, Harvath decided to open fire. He took three quick shots, aiming low. The figure stumbled and then pitched forward behind a short rock wall. Harvath heard what sounded like a weapon clatter onto the driveway.

Carefully, Harvath and Meg made their way forward to where the figure had fallen. Meg covered his back as Harvath swung around the wall and pointed the Browning, ready to fire. There was no one there. He bent down to examine the path of crushed gravel behind the wall. There were splatters of blood leading toward the villa, which served as the estate's main offices. Several feet away, on the edge of the driveway, Harvath discovered an Israeli Galil assault rifle. *What the hell is that doing here?* he wondered.

They followed the gravel path, but soon lost track of the blood. Harvath tried the main office doors, as well as several of the windows, but everything was locked up tight, and there was no sign of any forced entry. Whoever he had shot was not inside the villa. That meant they had to be somewhere on the grounds outside.

Harvath and Meg hugged the building's stone walls as they slowly worked their way around to the back. They kept trying every door and every window they came across, but just as in front, they were all securely locked.

Suddenly, as they neared the rear of the villa, they heard a shot, followed quickly by a muffled scream. It almost didn't sound human. It was wild and fierce, like a trapped animal.

Harvath instructed Meg to try and raise the Italian Special Forces soldiers again. There was still no answer from them or the pilots.

They peered around the corner of the villa toward where the scream had come from. An enormous terra-cotta urn stood next to a short flight of flagstone steps. As they approached they could see the steps led down to a huge, half-open wooden door with its lock blown off.

"Wonderful," whispered Harvath. "Another catacomb."

He was half right. The door marked the entrance to the vineyard's ancient cellar, where vintners used to store their wine until the maturation process was complete.

The lightbulbs, which hung over the steep stone steps leading to the cellar floor, had all been broken. Harvath used his free hand to feel along the wall as they descended, their shoes crunching on the shards of broken glass. At the bottom of the steps, the cellar branched out into two long, parallel corridors, one to the right and one to the left. Orderly rows of old wooden casks lined both sides. A faint light glowed from the end of the corridor on the right, where sounds of a scuffle could be heard. As quietly as they could, Harvath and Meg made their way in that direction.

They tried to stay within the shadows and protective cover of the casks for as long as possible. When they came to the end of the corridor, the tunnel widened briefly, and Harvath and Meg were met with an unbelievable sight.

Adara Nidal was on her hands and knees on the rough stone floor with a gun to the back of her head. The man holding the pistol was the most hideous thing Meg Cassidy had ever seen. His face was so deformed it seemed scarcely human. Harvath had no difficulty gazing on the man. It wasn't the first time he had seen the face of Ari Schoen.

"Agent Harvath," said Schoen as Harvath and Meg stepped out of the shadows and walked closer. "Israel owes you a great debt."

"Last time I saw you, Ari, you were in a wheelchair. Helluva quick recovery, wouldn't you say?"

"I have found that with my deformities, using the wheelchair makes me pitiable, as opposed to just being unbearable to look upon," he replied.

"Your appearance and ambulatory abilities aside, I can't help but feel I've been played here," said Harvath, the Browning still grasped tightly in his hand.

"I don't like to use the word *play*, Agent Harvath. It sounds so manipulative. I'd rather say that we have had a successful collaboration."

"Collaboration?" said Harvath. "You *used* me to get to Adara."

"If that's the word you want to use, then we used each other."

Harvath was nearing his limit. "What the hell you are doing here?"

"I'm here for the same reason you are. I followed a string of clues—"

"Bullshit. I don't know how, but somehow you followed us."

"I will admit, Agent Harvath, that when you logged on to the web site I gave you for the surveillance photos of Marcel Hamdi from your hotel on Capri, it made it easier for us to locate the island he was traveling to and of course to listen in on your conversations. That being said, I can't give you all the credit. I have had a team very hard at work, tracking down every lead."

Something was pounding at the back of Harvath's mind. There was something about seeing Adara and Schoen together. There was a link somehow between them. Something about the photograph he had seen in Adara's study in Libya and a photograph he had seen somewhere else flashed in Harvath's mind. Could the other have been in Schoen's office? *That was it!* Both Schoen and Adara had the same photograph. But why? What was the significance? What was the connection between these two?

"Most of the details of this woman's life are inconsequential and reprehensible at best, but we all know where they lead. The records of her birth and her twin brother's in an East German hospital were conveniently destroyed. As she showed the greatest promise of the two monster children, her private education in the West was secured and funded by her father—"

"You are not fit to speak of my father," spat Adara.

Schoen ignored her and continued. "Are you aware, Agent Harvath," he asked, "of this woman's other recent accomplishments?"

"What are you talking about?"

"She has been quite busy. In addition to reviving her father's ailing organization, she has started another of her own. Why don't you tell our American friends what you have been up to?"

"Go to hell," she said.

"I will, don't worry. And you are coming with me, but if you don't feel like talking, maybe I should tell them." Schoen pushed the pistol harder into the back of Adara's head for emphasis as he said, "I'd like you to meet the mastermind, as well as the sole member of, the Hand of God organization."

Harvath was floored, and Schoen saw it written across his face.

"Yes," said Schoen, "she wasn't above killing multitudes of her own people, as long as it united the Arab world against the Jews."

"And killing Ali Hasan?"

"Would have all but assured the unity of the Arab states in a war against Israel. It was all very ingenious. Incredibly well thought out. It is a shame a woman this talented wasn't working for us."

"So, that explains the Galil I found outside," said Harvath. "It would have been left behind for the Italian police as an added piece of evidence that an Israeli terrorist organization was behind the attack."

"As well as this letter she was carrying," said Schoen, removing it from his pocket and holding it up with his free hand for Harvath to see. "In it, the Hand of God organization takes full credit for killing Hasan. The world would have had no choice but to blame Israel for the assassination, and war would have been all but guaranteed." Schoen placed the letter back in his pocket and cocked his pistol.

"Take it easy, Ari," said Harvath.

"You think garbage like this deserves mercy?" asked Schoen.

There was no question that Schoen's life had been ruined by the injuries he had suffered in operation Rapid Return, but there was something else happening here. There was something deeper about Adara Nidal that had unhinged him. Finally, it all made sense to Harvath.

"I want you to explain something to me."

"First you explain something to me, Agent Harvath. Why do you pity her? How many of your people are dead because of what this animal and her brother have done?"

"Too many. Too many people who were important to me. How many people who were important to you?" said Harvath.

"Every Israeli who has died because of her is important to me," replied Schoen, his body beginning to tremble with rage.

"But there is no one in particular. Your son went to Oxford, didn't he? What was his name?"

"I don't want to talk about my son."

"What was his name?" repeated Harvath.

"No!" screamed Schoen.

"Daniel," rasped Adara, so quietly at first no one could hear her. Then she spoke louder until there was no mistaking what she had said, "He was named Daniel!"

"How dare you speak his name!" yelled Schoen as he jerked his pistol back and struck her across the jaw.

"That's enough," said Harvath, raising his Browning and pointing it at Schoen's head.

"I don't think so, Agent Harvath," answered Schoen as several heavily armed men sprung from behind the casks.

"What the hell is this?" demanded Harvath as one of Schoen's operatives took his Browning, as well as the Beretta from Meg.

"We were also hoping to take the brother," said Schoen. "But for the time being, one out of two will have to do."

"The brother is dead. I saw to it myself," replied Harvath.

"We have also been to the catacombs beneath the fabric shop and while, yes, there were several bodies, there was not one that could be identified as the brother," said Schoen.

"Impossible. The Italian authorities sealed it off."

"After we had been there. There were still several men alive. Some, weren't even wounded. I can only assume they were trying to regroup. You have to learn to finish what you start, Agent Harvath."

Schoen had been shadowing him the entire time. Harvath had no choice but to believe him. "What's this all about, Ari? Revenge?"

"Look at me," said Schoen. "Wouldn't you want revenge for this?"

"But this isn't about you. It is about your son, Daniel. Isn't it? Tell me why you and Adara Nidal have the same rowing club picture."

"It's not true."

"One of the men in that picture was your son, wasn't it? This woman, the daughter of Abu Nidal, and your son were somehow connected. Were they friends? Was it more? Were they lovers?"

Schoen swung the pistol back again, but stopped in midair. Adara, on her hands and knees, was sobbing. Blood trickled from her mouth as well as her thigh, where one of Harvath's shots had caught her and knocked her down outside.

"I had no idea my son had become involved with an Arab. I sent him to Oxford to propel him forward in life, and he made a decision that could only drag him down. What's worse, it could have dragged me down along with him. Can you imagine? A top-ranking member of the Mossad with an Arab for a daughter-in-law? I had no idea at the time who her father was or what he had planned for her. But in hindsight, I can see that my intuition and actions were one hundred percent justified."

"*Justified?*" said Harvath. "What did you do?"

"I did the only thing I could do. I tried to reason with

my son, but he wouldn't listen. He actually wanted to marry the girl. Can you believe it?"

"What *did* you do?" repeated Harvath.

"I withdrew my son from Oxford and forced him to come home to Israel. His mother was sick, and I used that to get him back. When the letters from the girl came, I intercepted them. I had one of our forgers at the Mossad draft a new letter—a Dear John, as you call it. I did the same thing in reverse to the girl at Oxford and included a doctored photo of Daniel with a young Israeli girl. It worked, Daniel never heard from her again."

"You bastard," sobbed Adara. "All of you Jews are fucking bastards! Every one of you deserves to die."

"It is not the Jews who deserve to die. It is your people who must be eradicated," said Schoen as he grabbed a handful of her thick black hair and jerked her head back. "You know," he said as he looked at Harvath, "my Daniel never got over her. I tried to encourage him to find another love. I introduced him to nice Israeli girls, but until the day he volunteered for that terrible mission and never came home, he pined over this Arab whore."

"Whore?" said Adara. "If I am a whore, what does that make your son? He wanted me to bear his children—your grandchildren."

"Liar!" screamed Schoen as he repeatedly brought the butt of the pistol down into her face. "Liar! Liar! Liar!"

"Schoen, stop it! You're killing her," yelled Harvath

"This is war and Israel will triumph!" he screamed.

It was obvious, even to Schoen's men, that Schoen was so consumed with rage he couldn't even think straight anymore. One of the men finally intervened and took Schoen's pistol from him. Another pulled him down the corridor toward the exit of the cellar. Two others lifted Adara and started marching her in the same direction.

"Where are you taking her?" demanded Harvath as he took a step toward of one of the remaining men.

The man's response was simple and straight to the point. As a matter of fact, he needed no words at all to convey his meaning. He simply raised his submachine gun and pointed it first at Harvath's chest and then Meg's, as he backed down the corridor and finally disappeared from sight.

Meg looked at Scot, who had been mumbling to himself and whose voice was now getting louder, ". . . eight Mississippi, nine Mississippi, ten!"

He grabbed Meg's arm and started running for the stone steps that led out of the cellar.

"What are we doing?" she yelled as they ran.

"We're going after them. Adara is going to pay for what she did, but not at the hands of Ari Schoen."

"They'll kill us. We don't even have a weapon."

"We don't need one."

"Are you crazy?"

"They probably have a car or a van stashed somewhere up there. We need to ID it so we can get the Italian police on their tail right away."

The door to the cellar was barricaded from the outside. Harvath figured it was probably the large terra-cotta urn he had seen when they came in. He rammed the door several times with his shoulder, but the object wouldn't move. It wasn't until Meg threw her weight in as well that it began to budge.

When the door finally opened, they ran up the short flight of flagstone steps toward the villa and the sound of an engine growling to life. Clearing the parking lot, they could see Adara and Schoen being loaded into a windowless, black Fiat van. They hid behind one of the vineyard's tractors parked off on the grass. Harvath tried his best to make out the van's license plate number and soon detected another sound over the noise of the engine. It was faint, but growing—*sirens!*

"I don't believe it. The cops! Thank God," said Harvath.

"No, thank Cassidy," replied Meg.

" 'Thank, Cassidy'? What are you talking about?"

Meg held up the Italian Special Forces radio she had been given. "I heard one of the pilots come back on the radio while we were in the cellar. I kept the transmit button depressed so long I thought my finger was going to fall off. We were live the entire time."

Harvath was about to give Meg a huge kiss, when his blood froze in his veins. Appearing like a wraith out of the vineyard was Hashim Nidal. He was running right at them with several hand grenades in each hand. He also had a headset and radio, which he must have taken from one of the dead Italian soldiers. Harvath prepared himself for the attack, but Hashim ran right past them.

The torture and ignoble death that he knew Adara would face at the hands of the Israelis was more than Hashim could bear. Without her, his life and their cause meant nothing. There was no other choice. The Jew who had caused his sister and their people so much pain would finally be put to death.

Screaming at the top of his lungs, Hashim Nidal took the Israelis completely by surprise. He jumped into the van just as the door began to close.

Harvath threw himself on top of Meg. The grenades detonated and the van exploded into a billowing fireball.

69

It was a picture perfect day in Washington as Harvath cleared White House security and made his way down to the situation room. A week had passed since he and Meg had left Italy, and the time off had provided him with ample opportunity to decide what his next moves, both personal and professional, would be. On the personal front, he knew Meg was going to be a very important person in his life. In terms of his career, he knew the president was not going to like what he had to say, but his mind was made up.

There was the familiar click of the situation room door lock releasing, followed by the hiss of air as it swung open. *The things I'll miss*, Harvath thought to himself.

Seated around the long cherry-wood table were all the faces he had expected to see and one that he didn't.

Rick Morrell rose from his chair and walked across the room to meet him halfway. "I never got a chance to tell you what a hell of a job I thought you did," said Morrell, offering his hand. "You didn't get near the cooperation from us that you should have, and I apologize. We should have listened to you."

Harvath couldn't believe his ears. Rick Morrell, *apologizing*? He shook the man's hand and said, "It's the final outcome that matters the most."

"Precisely what we're here to talk about," said President Jack Rutledge, who had entered the situation room behind Harvath. "If everyone would please take their seats."

As Morrell turned to walk back to his chair, he said, "After this, the team is meeting at the Old Ebbitt Grill for a couple of beers. Why don't you join us?" Harvath nodded his head and said he'd be there, then took the empty seat next to Gary Lawlor.

"First of all," began the president, "I want to congratulate everyone involved in Operation Phantom. We were able to stop the Nidals and, in so doing, avert a war. I cannot overstate what an all-out war in the Middle East would have meant. Despite our direct support, if pushed hard enough, this administration does not doubt that the Israelis would have exercised their nuclear capabilities against the Arabs. But, as I've said, that was all successfully avoided. And now that the truth about the Hand of God organization is out in the open, the Arab world has so much egg on its face, I think it'll be a long time before they dare point any fingers at Israel, about anything.

"That being said, I think it's important for you all to know that with some subtle pressure from the United States, the Israelis were willing to make some notable concessions in the Italian peace summit. We should all be hearing about significant breakthroughs later today."

A round of applause broke out around the table and the president waited for it to die down before continuing. "There are a couple of loose ends I would like to address before we adjourn this meeting. As to the radiological material found in Rome, the Department of Energy is still trying to find out who sold it to the Nidal family. The source of the money for its purchase, a Mr.—" the president paused to refer to his notes, "Marcel Hamdi, is less of a mystery. Mr. Hamdi was briefly detained by Moroccan authorities upon his return to Casablanca and during questioning, with no less than a dozen lawyers present, admitted to knowing Abu Nidal's daughter, but emphatically denied any knowledge that she was involved in terrorism. When asked about his substantial cash withdrawal from the Palma de Mallorca branch of Deutsche Bank, his attorneys argued that as one of Morocco's most prominent businessmen, Hamdi was constantly moving large sums of money and that he had broken no laws in doing so.

"Moroccan authorities bought it, but the United States didn't. After reviewing our extensive file on Hamdi and his funding of various terrorist organizations hostile to the United States, I have made a decision. Suffice it to say that very soon, Mr. Hamdi will cease being a problem for this country, or any other, for that matter."

Another, more subdued round of applause swept the situation room and when it had died down, the president continued. "The FBI believes it has succeeded in tracking down almost all of the cells here in the U.S. to whom the Nidal organization had sent the components for fabricating dirty bombs. In conjunction with several NEST teams, the remaining shipments are being investigated. We have also launched a major investigation into the international shipping practices of both FedEx and UPS. Homeland Security director Driehaus has assured me that this is a hole in our national security that he intends to plug immediately."

The president addressed a handful of additional items and then adjourned the meeting. As the attendees filed out of the situation room, he asked Harvath and Lawlor to stay behind. Once the door had clicked shut, the president looked at Harvath and said, "I want to talk with you about your promotion to director of White House Secret Service Operations."

Here it was—the moment Harvath had known he was going to have to face eventually. "I'm glad you brought that up, Mr. President, because I would like to talk about that as well."

"Listen to what I have to say first. As much as I hate to do it, I'm going to have to rescind my offer," replied the president. "I don't think your qualifications are right for the position."

Harvath couldn't believe his ears. "I'm *not qualified?*" he said. "This has got to be a joke."

"It's no joke," replied the president. "This is very serious."

"I must be missing something, because this doesn't make any sense."

"Scot, you're the best agent the Secret Service has ever seen," continued the president, "but the Secret Service isn't the right place for you."

"Mr. President," interjected Harvath, "if there's a particular issue you have with my work, I'd like to know what it is."

The mind was a funny thing. Harvath had arrived that morning fully prepared to tell the president he wouldn't accept the position of director of White House Secret Operations, but the minute it became obvious the job was being taken away from him, he wanted to fight for it.

"Actually there's several," said the president.

"*Several?*"

"Maybe '*not qualified*' isn't the best way of characterizing this," offered Gary Lawlor.

"Very true," answered the president. "Scot, the fact of the matter is that you are *over*qualified for the position. You've done great work for the Secret Service, but your talents are being wasted. You've proven that."

"Wow, fired before I've even started. That's got to be a world record, even by Washington standards."

Both President Rutledge and Gary Lawlor smiled.

"We want to offer you something else," said Lawlor, "a way to serve your country and utilize your training and abilities to their fullest."

"I'm listening," replied Harvath.

"Scot, the world has changed and so must we," said the president. "I know it sounds cliché, but the best defense the United States can mount is an exceptionally superb offense. And I want you to lead that offensive."

"How so?"

"From here on out, America is going to be operating on a well-defined 'strike first' policy. We will never again wait for terror to come to us."

"Whom would I be working for?"

"Me," said Lawlor, drawing Harvath's attention. "The president is creating a special international branch of the Homeland Security Department. It's being called the Office of International Investigative Assistance, or OIIA, for short. The OIIA will represent the collective intelligence capability and full muscle of the United States government to help neutralize and prevent terrorist actions against America and American interests on a global level. As I've been asked to head the division, you would be reporting directly to me."

"And what would my job be?"

"Exactly what you have been doing since the president was kidnapped—hunting down terrorists."

"When would you want me to start?"

"Immediately," said the president.

"Then I accept," answered Harvath.

"Excellent," replied the president as he nodded to Gary Lawlor.

Lawlor withdrew a folder, slid it across the table to Harvath, and said, "Marcel Hamdi will be in Havana tomorrow night for a meeting. We do not want him to leave that meeting alive."

Harvath smiled to himself. He could already tell he was going to love this new job.

Acknowledgments

I realized when writing my first novel, that no book is created in a vacuum. An author relies heavily upon the advice, input, and feedback of many other people. Now, if an author can find people who are actually interesting, fun to be around, and prefer to share their wisdom and hard-won experience over a good bottle of wine—then so much the better. To the following, I am deeply indebted.

Chad Norberg, who was there with excellent advice and intriguing ideas for this book from day one. Though hearing, "How many pages did you write today?" gets to be a pain in the ass after a while, it's a small price to pay for his friendship and the fact that I can call him several times a day with questions about his former profession and what happens when Americans are sent "away from the flagpole" to carry out some of this country's most serious business.

Chuck Fretwell, whose "adventures" in his former profession are the stuff legends are made of. Not only was Chuck extremely helpful during the writing and editing phase of the manuscript, but going into the Special Operations community as his friend opened amazing doors for me, a fact for which I will always be exceedingly grateful.

Brad Thor, Sr., whose impeccable taste and wide knowledge of the finer things in life came in handy on more than one occasion while writing this book. I can't help but cringe when I think about what it is going to take to keep this man happy in his retirement. Dad, you were only kidding when you said you expected me to fund your "Platinum Years," right? Thanks for all of the exceptional help with the writing and promoting of my novels.

Gary Penrith, FBI (retired), a great friend of our family, who continues to be my guide through local, federal, and international law-enforcement agencies. I have come to believe that there is not a single door that Gary can't open. His ongoing help in my writing career has been invaluable. Trish and I look forward every year to our "law enforcement" trip to Sun Valley and getting to spend quality time with Gary and his lovely wife, Lynne.

Scott Hill, Ph.D., who helped me right into the hospital! The terrible lunch he took me to (which I know pushed me over the edge into emergency surgery during the writing of this book) notwithstanding, his help in developing the psychological aspects of the book, exploring character motivation, providing insightful commentary on the manuscript, and his friendship are all greatly appreciated.

Ancil Sparks, FBI, who I am convinced has had so many wonderful things said about him that it is impossible to come up with something new. Ancil opened the FBI Academy at Quantico to me, and as his charge, I had access to literally anything I wanted to learn more about. Being the kind of guy I am, I chose to spend half the time shooting Glocks and MP5s with the very knowledgeable **Wade Jackson,** Chief of the Firearms Training Unit, and the other half with the very accommodating **Hostage Rescue Team,**

who brought me along on some intense helicopter fast-roping exercises. After spending time with these guys, it's easy to see how people become "addicted" to the lifestyle. Many, many thanks.

Thomas J. Baker, FBI (retired), another great friend and part of the Sun Valley team. Tom's experience and contacts as an FBI Legal Attaché were very helpful with the Italian aspects of the book. He is yet another gentleman I am fortunate enough to be able to call on for real-world answers on a regular basis. Despite my "colorful" language at times, Tom has graciously taken me in and continues to share much.

Frank Gallagher, FBI (retired), who gave me the cook's tour of FBI Headquarters and provided access to some incredible people and places. On top of all that, Frank insisted that he pay for lunch. Frank, you are a gentleman of the highest order, and now that you have changed careers, you'll be able to read the books I send you without having them irradiated.

Will Cragun and the Ogden Metro SWAT Team, who strapped the body armor on me and let me shadow their Hell Week participants. Live-fire CQB runs and the armored Suburban were two of many great experiences. Thanks for sharing your tactical wisdom with me.

Willie Brauner, Glock—Asia, who has been a close friend of mine since childhood and who hosted Trish and me when we visited Hong Kong and Macau. Despite the great distance between us, we still manage to stay in close contact. His help in rounding out some of the Asia details in the manuscript was very much appreciated.

Richard Levy, American Airlines, who is invaluable when it comes to airline information, airplane information, and any information relating to sushi. Sorry we missed the wedding of the century. Congratulations to you and Anne, and thanks for your continued friendship and assistance with my novels.

Robbie Barrkman, The Robar Companies, a true warrior-artist and an all around great guy who invited me out to Arizona to shoot the Robar RC 50. What a rush. I don't think there's anything I could have asked Robbie for that he wouldn't have gladly provided—short of being given my own RC 50 for free. Business is business after all, right? Thanks for an unforgettable experience, Robbie.

John Meyer, Heckler & Koch, who also was kind enough to invite me out to play with some incredible toys. I'm looking forward to hitting the H&K classes, and as soon as the baby comes, we're going to get Trish in the Tac Med course. Thanks for everything.

Joan Harvath, what can I say? Thanks for all of your continued support and the great dinners when I'm in D.C.

Tom Hunter, www.SpecialOperations.com, a fellow USC Trojan with a great Special Operations and terrorist database. Thanks for your help with the book early on.

Doreen Martin-Ross, Department of Anthropology—Chicago Field Museum, who explained to me how antiquities are packaged, as well as transported, and was also willing to discuss some "what if" scenarios.

Chuck Thomas, one of those rare individuals who knows a little bit about everything and then knows exactly where to locate more information. If I can't track something down, I call Chuck, and he can always help me find what I'm looking for. Thanks, Chuck.

Bob Boettcher, who actually put his hands on a schematic of the 747's APU for me. Well done, Bob.

Joe Ellis, who helped me narrow down a biblical passage appropriate to the Hand of God organization. Thanks, Joe, and as you suggested, I'll remember to call you if I ever need any Appalachian snake-handling information.

Kyle Mills and Dan Brown, who both shared with me their thoughts about writing book number two. Thanks for the input and sage counsel.

In addition to those mentioned above, there are the people who "ride herd" on my writing career and are immeasurably involved in both the business and creative ends of the spectrum.

The Atria/Pocket Books Sales Force—you really make it happen. You have my deepest gratitude.

The Atria/Pocket Books Art Department—Paolo and team, there is no way to measure the impact of your incredible creativity. Thanks for the fabulous art work.

Cathy Lee Gruhn, Atria/Pocket Books, who is my publicist. Having done my own PR in the past, I thoroughly appreciate what Cathy and her office do for me. A million *thanks-you's* would still not be enough.

Heide Lange, Sanford J. Greenburger Associates, who is my fantastic agent. When an excellent business relationship develops into an even better friendship, one is doubly blessed. A few simple lines hardly seem appropriate for everything you do for me, Heide.

Emily Bestler, Atria Books, who is my editor extraordinaire. Thank you for your friendship and for helping to take my work to the next level. Though I tell so many people how fabulous you are, I don't think anyone can truly understand until they have had the privilege of working with you. I grow as a writer because of you.

Scott Schwimer and Angela Cheng-Caplan, who are the equal halves of my L.A. Dream Team and who still know the appropriate weapon to bring to a gunfight. Thank you for your vision, friendship, and unwavering support.

Esther Sung and Sarah Branham, who both will never know how much I appreicate everything they do for me.

Cecilia Hunt, who is my copy editor. To say Ceci has a keen eye for detail would be an amazing understatement. Though we don't always see eye to eye, I wouldn't dream of going to press without her. Thank you for keeping my bacon out of the fire.

If I had to choose one person to dedicate every book I write to, it would easily be my beautiful wife, Trish. No one is more involved in the day-to-day aspects of my writing than she is. She is my single greatest source of inspiration, and I thank her for everything she does for me and everything she puts up with before, during, and after I write a new book. I love you, sweetheart.

Cindy Jackson, Simon & Schuster, has gone from being a stranger on a European train, to being one of my dearest friends. I have learned more about the book business and the writing process from her than I ever thought possible. As I continue to grow as an author, I have no doubt it will be due in large part to her unfailing friendship and tireless efforts on my behalf. Cindy, I owe you a deep debt.

Finally, I want to thank you, the readers, and all of the wonderful booksellers around the world. It is because of your encouragement and support that I am able to enjoy such a fulfilling and rewarding career.

Many thanks,
Brad Thor

ATRIA BOOKS
PROUDLY PRESENTS

THE FIRST COMMANDMENT

The next thrilling novel
by Brad Thor

Turn the page for a preview
of *The First Commandment.* . . .

De inimico non loquaris sed cogites—
Do not wish ill for your enemy . . .
plan it

hen hot and humid, Cuba hovered somewhere between absolute misery and "the bath is ready, does anyone have any razor blades?" But when it was cold and raining, Cuba was downright unbearable. Tonight was one of those nights.

When the guards arrived at X-ray block they

were in a bad mood—worse than usual. And it wasn't because of the weather. Something was wrong. It was written all over their faces as they pulled five of the camp's most dangerous prisoners from their isolation cells and ordered them at gunpoint to strip.

Philipe Roussard hadn't been at Guantanamo the longest, but he had definitely been interrogated the hardest. A European of Arab descent, he was a sniper of extraordinary ability whose exploits were legendary. Videos of his kills played on continuous loops on jihadist websites across the Internet. To his Muslim brothers he was nothing short of a superhero in the radical Islamist pantheon. To the United States, he was a horrific killing machine responsible for the deaths of over one hundred U.S. soldiers.

As Roussard looked into the eyes of his jailers he saw more than the pure hatred they normally viewed him and his fellow captives with. Tonight it was coupled with absolute disgust. Whatever middle-of-the-night interrogation tactic the Task Force Guantanamo soldiers had in store for Roussard and his four colleagues, something told him it wasn't going to be like anything they had seen before. The guards appeared on the verge of losing control.

Had an attack been successfully executed against the United States? What else could have put the soldiers in such a state?

If so, Roussard felt certain that the Americans would make the prisoners pay. That was how life was at Guantanamo. The guards were petty and never missed an opportunity to lord their power over them. Undoubtedly, they had devised yet another humiliating exercise designed to insult their Muslim sensibilities. Privately, Roussard hoped it involved the attractive blond soldier who would disrobe down to her underwear and rub herself against him. Unlike the other prisoners, Philipe was not exactly a devout Muslim. His sensibilities were more along the lines of his captors, and his fantasies of what he wanted to do to that woman more than kept him occupied through many of the long, lonely hours of isolation he withstood on a daily basis.

He was still speculating about their fate when he heard the door at the far end of the cell block shut. Roussard looked up, hoping it was the blond, but it wasn't. Another soldier had entered carrying five paper shopping bags. As he passed, he threw each of the prisoners a bag.

"Get dressed!" he ordered in awkward Arabic.

Confused, all of the prisoners, including Philipe, removed the civilian clothing from their bags and began to get dressed. Not accustomed to seeing anyone other than their guards, the prisoners looked at each other as they tried to figure out what was happening. Roussard was reminded of stories he'd heard about Jewish Concentration Camp prisoners who were told they were being taken for showers when they were actually on their way to the gas chambers.

He doubted the Americans were dressing them in new clothes only to take execute them, but nevertheless the uncertainty of what they were about to face filled him with more than a little trepidation.

"Why don't they try to make a run for it," one of the guards whispered to his comrade as he stroked the trigger guard of his M16. "I just want one of these fuckers to rabbit on us."

"This isn't right," replied the other. "What the hell are we doing?"

"You two, shut up!" barked their commander who then called in a series of commands over his radio.

Something definitely wasn't right.

Once they were completely clothed, shackles

were placed around their wrists and ankles and they were lined up against the far wall.

This is it, thought Roussard as he held the stare of the soldier who was hoping for one of the prisoners to rabbit.

The soldier's finger went from his weapon's trigger guard to its actual trigger, and he seemed about to say something when a series of vehicles ground to a halt just outside.

"That's us," shouted the Task Force commander. "Let's mount up."

As the prisoners were shoved toward the door and maybe when they got outside and he could see where they were going things would make more sense.

That plan was dashed as one-by-one, hoods were placed over each man's head before they were taken outside to a waiting column of tan Humvees.

Ten minutes later, the convoy came to a stop. Before Roussard's heavy hood was removed, he could make out the distinct, high-pitched whine of idling jet engines.

On the rain-soaked tarmac, the prisoners stared up at an enormous Boeing 737 as their shackles were removed. A metal staircase had been rolled up against the side of the aircraft, and its door stood wide open.

No one said a word, but based on the demeanor of the soldiers, Roussard came to a stunning conclusion. Without being directed to do so, he took a step forward. When none of the soldiers tried to stop him, he took another, and another until his feet touched the first metal step, and he began climbing upwards two at a time. His salvation was at hand. Just as he had known it eventually would be.

With the sound of the other prisoner's pounding up the gangway behind him, Roussard burst into the cabin. Five rows of seats had been completely removed and replaced with five surgical beds. Bolted to the floor next to each were large medical contraptions which looked like dialysis machines and next to those coolers marked *Human Blood*.

Roussard raced past the medical personnel toward the back of the plane searching each of the faces he saw for the one that would convince him this all wasn't just some dream born of prolonged and tortuous isolation. That face never materialized.

Instead, Philipe Roussard felt a heavy hand on his shoulder. When he turned the plane's first officer addressed him in Arabic. "We were told to give you this," he said as he handed him a heavy black envelope.

Without even opening it, Roussard knew who it was from.

"If you wouldn't mind taking a seat," continued the first officer. "The captain is eager to be underway."

Roussard found an empty place near the window and buckled himself in.

He then opened the envelope and read its contents. A slow smile began to spread across his face. Not only was he free, but it looked as if he would have his revenge—and much sooner than even he would have thought.

Opening his window shade, Roussard could see the soldiers climbing back into their Humvees and driving away from the airstrip, several with their hands out the windows, their middle fingers raised in mock salute.

As the aircraft's engines roared to life and the heavy beast began to roll forward, cheers of "Allah Akbar," *God is great*, erupted from the front of the plane.

Allah was indeed great, but Roussard knew it wasn't Allah who had arranged for their release. As he caressed the black envelope, he knew their gratitude was owed to someone much more powerful.

Turning his attention back to the window and with the soldiers quickly disappearing from view, Roussard cocked his thumb and forefinger took aim, and pulled his imaginary trigger.

Now that he was free, he knew it was only a matter of time before his handler turned him loose inside America to enact their revenge.

UNFORGETTABLE BESTSELLERS FROM POCKET BOOKS

Blue Valor
Illona Haus
To solve a crime that defies the imagination,
a Baltimore cop must take a twisted journey into
the dark recesses of a killer's mind.

Saving Cascadia
John J. Nance
Washington state's Cascadia Island is a tranquil
Northwest paradise—until a disaster only one
man can predict threatens the lives of thousands.

The Pandora Key
Lynne Heitman
She's a tough, sexy private investigator—and
she's unlocking explosive secrets form the past.

Live Wire
Jay MacLarty
A high-stakes delivery and a high-risk courier
make for an explosive combination.

The Greater Good
Casey Moreton
Even in the top-secret world of Washington
politics, some crimes can't be justified.

POCKET BOOKS
A Division of Simon & Schuster
A CBS COMPANY

POCKET STAR BOOKS
A Division of Simon & Schuster
A CBS COMPANY

Available wherever books are
sold or at www.simonsays.com.
14181

Not sure
what to
read next?

Visit Pocket Books online at
www.simonsays.com

Reading suggestions for
you and your reading group
New release news
Author appearances
Online chats with your favorite writers
Special offers
Order books online
And much, much more!

POCKET BOOKS
A Division of Simon & Schuster
A CBS COMPANY

**POCKET
STAR BOOKS**
A Division of Simon & Schuster
A CBS COMPANY

13456